ALL THINGS TOGETHER

ALSO BY REBECCA HARTT

The Acts of Valor Series

Returning to Eden

Every Secret Thing

Cry in the Wilderness

Rising From Ashes

Braving the Valley

All Things Together

The Lost Are Found

Fear No Evil

ALL THINGS TOGETHER

ACTS OF VALOR
BOOK SIX

REBECCA HARTT

RISE UP
PUBLICATIONS

Book and cover design by eBook Prep
www.ebookprep.com

April 2024
ISBN: 978-1-64457-644-1

Rise UP Publications
644 Shrewsbury Commons Ave
Ste 249
Shrewsbury PA 17361
United States of America
www.epublishingworks.com
Phone: 866-846-5123

This book is dedicated to single mothers everywhere. Being a single mom is the toughest job out there—I would know. Keep putting your children first, and God will bless you for it.

"Or what woman, having ten silver coins, if she loses one coin, does not light a lamp and sweep the house and seek diligently until she finds it?"

— LUKE 15:8

PROLOGUE

*S*tanding at the height of the floodwall overlooking the dark, ballast-paved street of Savannah's historic waterfront, two impeccably dressed men stood unobserved as they watched Carl Moulton hand over the purse he'd just retrieved from a young thief.

The glum manner in which Carl thrust the purse at its grateful owner suggested he was tempted to keep it for himself; only the woman had been joined by a gaggle of friends who'd witnessed Carl's heroic act.

As the original thief crested the steps of the floodwall stairs holding his bloody nose, the taller of the two men passed him a hundred-dollar bill for his trouble.

"Well, Carl did the right thing," the shorter man observed as the boy hurried off.

"I thought he might." Actually, the taller man had been holding his breath until Carl actually surrendered the prize. How reassuring to discover his biological son had a noble bone in his body.

"He didn't need to bludgeon that boy half to death, though."

"True, but the boy's been compensated. All that matters is Carl made the right choice. He has the heart of a Centurion."

His lawyer made a scoffing sound. "That's not what the foreman on the jobsite says."

"He's all I've got, Lynwood. You know the rule. Only a son can step into my shoes."

"Then I advise a trial period, Jared. Don't tell Carl who he is. Give him a job in your home and watch him."

Jared Jones nodded thoughtfully. "Very well. I'll hire him as a gardener. Come with me, Lyn." He didn't fully trust Carl Moulton not to rob him if he approached him alone.

CHAPTER 1

*W*ith the rain coming down in sheets outside her minuscule rancher and with her two older sons chasing each other wildly through the rooms, Emma Stuart fought to not pull her hair out.

"Boys!" Looking up from the textbook in her lap, she glowered at them as they barreled into the living room. "I've had enough. Go to your room this instant and find a game to play or a book to read!"

"I've read all of my library books," protested ten-year-old Christopher, whose brown hair distinguished him from his younger, blond brothers.

"And I hate readin'!" Eight-year-old Colton never minced his words.

Emma blew a long strand of golden-brown hair from her eyes, set her book aside, and rose ominously from the couch. "Then we'll just have to practice math."

Skirting fifteen-month-old Carter, who toddled into her path, she crossed the room to snatch up a pack of study cards from the dining room table she used as a desk. Her middle child's performance in second-grade math was a matter of concern to his teacher and, of course, to Emma, who struggled to find the time to help him.

Delaying her own studies, she carried the Walmart-purchased flash cards to the sofa while ordering Colton to sit upon it. The towheaded boy threw himself onto the furniture with a rubber ball in hand, knocking her textbook to the floor.

"Careful!" Hearing her voice fray, Emma reined in her frustration. Being a single mother was the toughest job a woman could have, short of living in a dingy trailer by a swamp in Mississippi with a lazy, cheating husband named Carl.

"Chris." She appealed to her responsible eldest. "Could you take Carter to your bedroom, please, so Colton isn't distracted?"

Chris grimaced. "Yes, Mama."

As her other two sons vanished, Emma went to stand over Colton, cards in hand. "What's six plus six?"

"Eleven."

"Twelve. We just did that one this morning, remember?" It was hard to tell if Colton had a problem remembering or if he was being deliberately obtuse. Either way, her middle son was going to give her a nervous breakdown.

The vision of an old white Chevy truck pulling into her driveway startled an exclamation out of her. Well, look who was back from God-knew-where.

Colton jumped to his knees to see what she was looking at. "Yay!" he bellowed. "Mr. Ben's back!"

"Stay put!" Emma pointed a finger at him as he made to jump off the sofa.

Seeing Ben dart from his truck to her front stoop with a plastic sack in one hand, Emma opened the door for him, her heart racing.

Chief Petty Officer Ben Harmony was her landlord. The day she'd met him ten months earlier, she realized he was dangerous—not because he was a SEAL and a sniper but because he was charming. With a bald head and muscular body, he resembled Mr. Clean, minus the earring. His twinkling blue eyes and killer smile made it apparent her landlord was a ladies' man, with no more staying power than a butterfly on a lilac bush.

When Emma and her boys were new to Virginia Beach, keeping clear of Ben hadn't been easy, as he'd come by every day to put the finishing touches on the little rancher he'd just renovated. He'd also built a sandbox in the backyard for the baby and brought bicycles for the older boys. But then, for the last six months, he'd been away on a mission somewhere, and life had settled down into a grinding but stable routine.

She'd forgotten how unsettling his presence could be.

"Hi." With a smile that carved dimples into his cheeks and rainwater clinging to his eyelashes, his appeal rolled over her like hot oil, completely visceral and utterly undesired. "Are the boys here?" His eyes seemed bluer than ever, set against a sun-kissed face.

Emma swallowed hard. "Of course. Come on in."

Her fifteen-hundred-square-foot rental always seemed smaller when Ben was here, just as the scent of citrus always seemed to cling to him. Emma caught herself breathing it in as he brushed past her only, to be tackled by Colton, who threw his arms around Ben's waist.

"You're back!"

With a mock roar, Ben swept up Colton in his arms, then staggered toward the couch, where they collapsed.

Christopher came out of the hallway, grinning and holding the baby.

Ben's eyes rounded as he caught sight of Carter. "Holy smokes!" He rolled to his feet and took the toddler from Chris, hefting him on one powerful forearm. "Whatcha been eatin', big fella?"

The fifteen-month-old grinned as if they shared an inside joke.

"You got teeth now!"

"He can also walk—and run," Emma pointed out.

"Let me see." Ben put Carter on his feet, pointed at Chris, and said, "Go!"

The baby took several steps toward Chris, changed his mind, and ran back to Ben, throwing chubby arms around Ben's bare thighs. With a laugh, he swooped Carter so high he nearly hit the ceiling, then flew him around like he was an airplane.

Colton jumped up and down. "Do that to me! Do that to me!"

"Enough!" Addressing Ben as much as she was Colton, Emma held up the cards she was clutching. "Colton is practicing his math facts." Her tone let Ben know he had intruded on Colton's tutorial.

"Oh, sorry." He didn't sound the least bit contrite. "I brought you guys presents." He put the baby down and opened the plastic bag dangling from his arm.

The older boys crowded closer.

"What is it?" Colton's face glowed with excitement.

Emma nearly rolled her eyes. *Santa Claus is back.* She picked up the baby before he could tackle Ben again.

After delving into the bag, Ben pulled out a tin cylinder and gave it to Christopher. "This is for the two of you to share."

Chris and Colton dropped to their knees as Chris tore off the wrapping. "It's a magnet set. Cool!"

Ben reached back into the bag. "And this is for the little guy." He pulled out a sock monkey and handed it to Carter, who grasped it around the neck, staring in amazement at the monkey's painted eyes.

Emma thanked Ben for his thoughtfulness. "You don't need to bring them gifts, you know. They're just happy to have you back."

"Hmm." He considered her a moment. "What about you?"

"Me?" She pretended not to understand.

His blue eyes crinkled at the corners. "You happy to have me back?"

Did he have to flirt with her? It made her knees weak. "I wouldn't have a home without you." She kept her words terse, loath to let him see his effect on her.

As his gaze rested warmly on her face, she acknowledged she was the antithesis of the perfectly made-up women she'd seen dangling on his arm from time to time. And that was fine by her. She didn't want him to find her attractive. Men were trouble, in general. Plus, her friends had warned her about Ben—first Amos in his no-nonsense way and then his wife, Grace, who suggested she ignore Ben if he ever flirted with her. Even her neighbor, Belinda, had made some comments about Ben being a love-'em-and-leave-'em type if ever there was one. Having been bitten by one man, Emma had the sense to be twice shy.

"So, listen." Ben scratched his clean-shaven chin as if uncertain of himself. "You think I could take the bigger boys right now to Fun Zone?"

Colton lifted his face from the magnet set. "Fun Zone!"

Chris's dark-blue eyes swiveled up at her. "Can we go, Mama? Please?"

Emma heaved an exasperated sigh. "Colton has to practice his math facts." She showed him the cards still in her hand.

"No problem." Ben angled his head to see what kind of math they were doing. "Addition is our mission. By the time I bring 'em home, Colton will know how to add anything up to…?"

"A hundred," Colton said.

Emma frowned at him, surprised he knew, before looking back at Ben. "How are you going to teach addition in Fun Zone?" Picturing Ben and the boys clambering through tubes and coasting down slides, she almost wished she could go, too.

"Now, Miz Emma." Ben sent her a long-suffering look while laying on a thick southern drawl that was nothing like how he normally spoke, hailing from Illinois. "Not all boys learn math like you girly girls with books and cards and all. We learn by doing, ain't that right?" He glanced at Colton for corroboration.

"Yep."

"They got those colorful little balls in the pen," Ben continued.

"At least a hundred of 'em. We'll stockpile 'em, we'll count 'em up, and we'll have a war with 'em."

"Yes!" Colton lit up like a Christmas tree.

She had to admit her son would probably learn better that way.

Chris came to his feet with a worried look. "But I can learn by reading."

Ben laid a hand on his shoulder. "That's 'cause you're book smart, like your mama."

Colton raised a taunting finger at his brother. "Chris is a girly boy. Chris is a—"

Ben's sharp frown cut him off.

He sure has a way with them. Emma prayed he wouldn't let them down like their daddy had.

"So, can we go?" Ben eyed her expectantly.

The man brimmed with energy—something she could only envy. "I don't have any money." She angled her chin higher as she admitted to her biggest challenge these days.

"No problem. I've got free tickets." He patted the wallet in his back pocket. "MWR was giving them away."

MWR had to be some kind of perk for the military. Emma threw her hands up. "Go ahead. It's not like I can tell them no now." Besides, she could use the reprieve to study for her final exams while Carter took his nap.

Ben gestured to the older boys. "Come on, fellas. Put your shoes on."

With a whoop and a holler, they scattered.

Left alone with Ben, Emma pretended absorption in playing with Carter and his monkey. She could sense Ben's regard as he watched her.

"I should have gotten you something, too."

His softly spoken apology brought her gaze to his. "No, you should *not* have."

"Why not? You deserve something. When's the last time

someone gave you something?" His eyes glinted in a challenging manner.

"'Bout nine months ago when you gave me this house to rent."

"Emma—" His broad chest expanded as he caught himself and drew a deep breath. "You have no idea—"

"Mama, where are my new shoes?" Colton's cry from the back of the house cut him off. As Emma hurried toward the bedrooms to help him, her heart skittered. *What had Ben been about to say?*

"They're right here, honey." With the baby still in her arms, she kicked his new red-striped sneakers out from under his and Christopher's bunk bed.

Colton jammed his feet into them, not bothering with the laces. "Okay, I'm ready!"

Emma followed him as he ran for the door. Chris was already there.

"I'll have them home by suppertime," Ben promised as he shepherded them out the door. "Run! The truck's unlocked." He swung back around.

Aware she was essentially alone with him, Emma clutched Carter like a talisman, both worried and excited by what might come out of Ben's mouth.

"I hope you get some studying done." His gaze jumped to her textbooks still lying on the floor. "What subject?"

"Biology."

"You should be proud of yourself, you know, going back to school and all."

She'd received so few scraps of encouragement in her life that his words seemed to lift her right off the hardwood. Was that all he'd been about to say earlier? "Bein' a nurse is all I ever wanted to do ever since my granny got sick. I liked taking care of her."

Ben stared at her. "I bet you were good at it."

The warmth of his gaze made her cheeks grow hot.

Ben sucked in a breath. "Well. See you." With a wink and a smile, he vanished out the door.

She watched him jog through the rain to his truck, which he usually drove when he dropped in on them, instead of his yellow Mustang. The boys tussled in the cab, fogging up the windows.

Minutes later, his truck shot out of her driveway in reverse, and silence closed around Emma. Carter rested his blond head on her shoulder as if feeling depleted. Ben's presence was like a sunbeam on a cloudy day. She wished she'd been invited to go along with them.

You fool, scolded a voice in her head that sounded like Granny Annie's. *Not every itch needs scratching.* Her attraction to Ben would only distract her from the goal she'd set for herself—becoming a licensed practical nurse. Mooning over a man would get her nowhere. Hadn't she learned that lesson from marrying Carl?

Kissing Carter's plump cheek, Emma willed away the neediness clawing at her. *You're not a naïve sixteen-year-old.* She'd been stupid enough back then to think the all-star high school quarterback would save her from foster care. What a mistake that was! No way would she entertain feelings for a Navy SEAL whose code name was "Harm." That had to be the stupidest thing any woman could do, especially her.

❀

"Daddy, you wanted to see me?" Twenty-three-year-old McKenzie Jones slipped through her father's office door and shut it quietly behind her, even as she watched him put away the key to his file cabinet. She'd discovered years ago what the small key went to—not that she'd ever wanted to use it.

Jared Jones sent her a fond smile as he shut his desk drawer. "How's my favorite daughter doing?" His dark eyes, as usual, were impossible to read.

She smiled wryly. "I'm your only daughter, Daddy."

"True." He put his large hands on his desk and stood up slowly. At six-feet-four inches, with a head of dark hair and always impeccably dressed, McKenzie's father never failed to intimidate her for some reason. She scarcely breathed as he rounded his desk to approach her. "Thank you for coming. I have a matter to discuss before you leave for the shelter today."

His gentle southern drawl was part of his charisma. Men flocked to him for guidance and support. McKenzie not only admired him, but she owed him everything. She'd inherited his dark hair but her mother's petite stature and light-green eyes.

Stopping before her, her father put his hands out, palms up, indicating she should lay her hands over his.

As always, their personal salutation left her feeling powerless and insignificant, at least compared to him. Then, again, she'd yet to make her own way in the world since her degree in art had left her with few job prospects.

"As the daughter of a Centurion, I'm sure you understand your obligations."

McKenzie tried to guess where this talk was going. Only males could be Centurions, and only their male heirs could inherit, which ran counter to Georgia law, but who was she to point that out? "Of course."

"You've known for years I've intended for you to marry Ashton Ravenel. He and I have decided to move up the wedding date."

Her heart suspended its beat before matching the ticking of the grandfather clock standing against the wall. "Up to when?"

"This June." Her father's dark-brown stare dared her to defy him. "We'll have a small wedding, thus averting publicity."

"But why? I have Mama to look after."

His grip tightened. "For your benefit, McKenzie. You are not a son. If something should happen to me, you'd be left with nothing."

She cocked her head. "But you don't have a son, Daddy, so wouldn't I inherit anyway?"

"No, darling." His tone became patronizing. "As leader of the Centurions, I must uphold the standard. I will name a male heir. But don't you worry. Ashton will look after you."

After pulling her hands from his, McKenzie spun toward the rear window to hide her dismay. Below her, Carl, their gardener for the past few months, snipped back the shriveled stalks of dead lilies, his lanky hair falling over his eyes. She clutched the velvet drape for the courage to speak her mind. "What if I don't want your wealth?"

Her father made a scoffing sound. "Honey, you have no idea what it means to go without."

She pivoted with affront. "What do you mean? I work at a homeless shelter!"

"Right." He sent her a tolerant smile. "And then you come home to a mansion with servants."

"But Ashton is more than fifty years old!"

"Ah. So, that's the issue, is it?" He stepped closer. "Think of it this way. You'll only be married for twenty years or so before he dies, leaving you a wealthy widow."

The calculated thought appalled her. Digging her fingernails into her palms for courage, she forced herself to articulate her protest. "I am a grown woman, Daddy. I get to choose who I will and will not marry."

The flash of anger in her father's dark eyes struck fear into her heart.

"Tonight, Ashton is giving you a ring." He spoke barely above a whisper. "If you even think of refusing him, I will revoke my protection and make certain your little accident five years ago becomes public knowledge."

McKenzie gaped at her father, scarcely able to reconcile that the man who'd saved her from certain imprisonment was now using her disgrace to blackmail her.

"Now." He patted her cheek with a light hand. "I've kept you long enough. I'm sure the men at the shelter are missing their guardian angel, so go. Just keep my words in mind."

With the feeling that he'd ripped the rug right out from under her, McKenzie fled to the door and slipped through it, careful not to slam it in her wake. Jared Jones, high consul of the Centurion Cohort, abhorred unseemly displays.

~

At just past midnight, Ben swung into Emma's driveway in his Mustang GT, wary of the message that had summoned him here. Sure enough, every light in the house was out, just as her voice mail, left an hour earlier, had advised him.

Nothing's working—not the switches or the outlets. There must be a problem with the main breaker in the electrical box, but I can't get it open.

He'd listened to the message twice, loving her Mississippi drawl and the way she stretched short little words into long, molasses-smooth ones. But was she telling the truth—or was her call just a ploy to get him to drop by, late at night when the boys were sleeping? It wouldn't be the first time a woman had lured him over with some excuse.

But he hadn't pegged proper Emma—a woman who'd made no secret about her faith—as the type. But if she *did* have ulterior motives, would he find the strength to turn her down? Probably not.

Candlelight flickered faintly behind her drawn blinds, stirring Ben's imagination even as it stirred his doubts. He had a long-held policy of avoiding romantic entanglements with women who had children. Why? Because he fell in love with the kids, and leaving them behind left a bad taste in his mouth. Maybe he shouldn't have come here tonight. He got out of his Mustang anyway.

The snapping of a twig in her side yard stopped him on his way to the door. *What was that?* Had somebody been lurking around the house? Or was it just a wild animal? After all, there were plenty of deer and raccoons in this suburban neighborhood.

Emma's front door popped open, vaporizing Ben's thoughts as he absorbed the vision of her in a well-worn cotton nightie, holding up a candle. The flame cast a warm glow on her young face and accentuated her curves under the lace-edged gown. His suspicions rose sharply. Was there really an issue with the breaker?

He mounted the stoop, helplessly drawn to her. "Sorry, it took me so long to come over. I had duty tonight."

"Honestly, it's fine. I'd given up on you coming at all." She seemed nervous about his timing. "This can wait till morning. It's awful late."

"Then why are you still up?" He thought he'd call her bluff.

"I was studyin'. I've got finals this week."

A closer examination of her red-rimmed eyes supported her story. She must have been working at the car dealership earlier because her hair was still in the French braid she wore to work. Golden-brown curls had escaped it to frame her face like a halo. He'd never known a woman with so much hair.

"So there really is a problem with the fuse box?"

Her gaze jumped up from his sidearm holstered to his webbed belt. "'Course, there's a problem. You think I'd text you in the middle of the night if there wasn't?"

He had to smile at the affront that made her eyes flash. "Wouldn't be the first time I got a text like that. Don't mind me, Emma. Might as well check it out while I'm here, okay?"

A small frown betrayed her misgivings. "All right." She pushed the door open and stepped back.

As Ben eased past her, he inhaled the scent of fresh cotton and magnolia. *Don't you so much as look at her.* Weird that his conscience spoke in Senior Chief McLeod's voice. But then it was McLeod who'd first introduced Ben to Emma, so that made sense.

Emma's candle cast a wavering light on the walls as Ben led the way into the kitchen, to the breaker panel above the washer and dryer—two used appliances bought at a garage sale and tucked into the laundry closet.

"Why do you lock it?" Emma asked as he parted the closet doors.

"What, the electrical panel? I don't lock it."

"Well, it's locked now, or I'd have thrown the switch myself."

Reaching for the metal door, he tugged it and found it stuck. "Huh." It did have a little lock on it, but he didn't know where the key was. He gave it a hard jerk, popping it open and flinging a paper clip onto the dryer.

Ben picked up the paper clip. Had one of the boys put it there, or had Emma herself done it for an excuse to have him over? He glanced at her sidelong.

She gasped indignantly. "Don't look at *me!*" Reaching past him for the fuse box, she threw the main switch, causing light to beam down on them from the recessed fixture overhead. "Colton must have done it."

Ben, realizing the material of her nightgown was translucent, snatched his gaze up.

Emma snapped up the paper clip and held it before her like a tiny sword. "You'd better go."

Her firm tone seemed to bely the hungry look in her eyes. Did she really want him to stay? Reminding himself of who might ultimately get hurt—the three little boys who looked up to him—Ben backed away, then headed for the door, aware that Emma trailed him at a distance.

The hallway light was now on. He allowed himself a backward glance, branding the vision of her bosom, barely concealed by thin cotton, onto his retinas.

Go! his conscience ordered. But he couldn't stop himself from saying something as he reached for the doorknob. "You know, if things were different, you'd have trouble getting rid of me right now."

Her eyes flared. "Different, how?"

Great, now he'd offended her. Releasing the doorknob, he swung around and approached her, causing her to back up against the wall. "You have no idea how amazing you are, do you?"

The desire to show her how she affected him burned in him. By the thinnest thread of self-control, he held himself in check. "Look, I just really like your boys, and I don't want to hurt them."

~

Heat surged into Emma's face as she interpreted Ben's meaning. Did he seriously think she'd lured him over by inventing an issue with the fuse box?

She pushed off the wall and took a menacing step toward him. "Now, what makes you think I would let that happen, Mr. Harmony? You may be good with my boys, but I don't need or want a man in my life, especially not a man like you." *Oh no. Why did I just say that?*

Ben's tawny eyebrow rose. "Is that right?"

She curled her fingers toward her palms. "Is that so hard to believe? Women just throw themselves at you, so you assume the same is true of me? Well, it's not."

Just shut up! Instead, she poked him in the chest.

"What's a man good for when all he does is take up room in the bed and snore? Carl couldn't even watch his own kids without calling it babysittin'. And forget about changing diapers! You think I want a man who'll just run off with another woman when the going gets tough—or off to war?"

Ben let loose a disbelieving laugh, infuriating her further. The sudden wail of the baby told her she had awakened Carter with her tirade. "Now look what you've done!" Throwing up both hands, she whirled toward the bedrooms, growling, "Kindly see yourself out."

To her consternation, he followed right on her heels as she stalked down the hall to the baby's diminutive bedroom. The smallest room in the house was lit by a nightlight that bathed it in a soft, reddish light. Heaving Carter from his crib, Emma determined his diaper was soaked and turned toward the changing table next to which Ben stood, making the room feel even smaller.

Conscious of his brooding silence, Emma laid Carter down—he barely fit on the narrow shelf—and popped the snaps on his pajama bottoms. An apology trembled on the tip of her tongue.

All at once, Ben edged her aside with a challenging look and wrested the wet wipes from her hands. "I got this."

With brisk and certain movements, he peeled back the Velcro on the wet diaper and eased it out from under Carter's bottom while rolling it partway up. Then he grabbed a wet wipe and efficiently swabbed the baby's loins before he dropped the wipe onto the old diaper and sealed it into a little ball. Emma passed him a fresh diaper, and within three seconds, Ben had taped it into place.

By the time Carter's pajama bottoms were snapped back onto his shirt, the baby was grinning at him in full approval, and Emma was stewing in humiliation. "How'd you learn to do that?"

"I'm the oldest of seven. You got him?" Ben left the room, crossing the hall to wash his hands in the home's only bathroom.

With dread now pooling inside her, Emma picked up Carter, kissed his cheek, and swung him back inside his crib. "Go to sleep, sweetie." Ignoring his whimper of protest, she left the room and shut his door behind her.

Now she'd done it. All her life, from her earliest memories of living with her alcoholic father and a string of stepmothers to the day Granny Annie died and Emma had been handed over to Social Services, her life had been a series of uprootings. Not even Carl had thought twice about selling that shabby old trailer out from under her and the boys. How could she be so stupid as to offend her landlord just when things were settling down for them?

Ben was waiting for her by the front door. Coming out of the hallway, she quickly attempted damage control. "Look, I'm sorry. I lost my temper. I shouldn't have said all that."

His mouth gave a rueful quirk, relieving her. "Well, I'm glad you did. Now I know where I stand." His blue eyes slid over her as if memorizing every detail of how she looked. "And now *you* know never to challenge a SEAL, darlin'. There ain't anything we can't do well." With a wink that took the edge off his boast, he pulled the front door open and let himself out.

A second later, she heard his car start up and pull away.

Emma sagged against the door as she locked it. Was that it? He wasn't going to evict her for going off on him? Was he really that magnanimous, letting her compare him to Carl and then proving her wrong instead of getting angry? She'd had no idea a man could be like that.

Grateful for his forbearance, she closed her eyes and breathed, "Thank You, Lord."

At least one good thing had come from her outburst: Ben wouldn't be sniffing around her skirts anymore. For some reason, disappointment sat heavy in her stomach.

CHAPTER 2

*M*iles Ellis regarded the simple yet nutritious meal on his tray with disappointment. *Why did I volunteer for this job again?* He would do anything for some Chinese food right about now—or, better yet, Thai. But it was chicken, peas, and carrots again tonight.

Being an undercover special agent for the FBI was anything but glamorous. From the moment he'd skulked into this homeless shelter in Savannah, Georgia, his dignity had been stripped from him, and every day just seemed like the last.

He was four months into his assignment, yet all he'd discovered about the Centurion Cohort and its leader, Jared Jones, could be written on one side of a Post-It note. Time to attempt a new tactic—to befriend Jones's daughter, McKenzie.

Tray in hand, he made his way across the large front room through Romanesque arches to the dining area. The original cherrywood table seating thirty-eight men had once belonged to a wealthy Savannah family, but now it hosted only derelicts and the dejected.

McKenzie Jones, with her head of dark ringlets and light-green eyes, resembled an angel of mercy seated amidst the bedraggled and unwashed poor. But looks could be deceiving, as Miles knew well. For years, his slight build and baby face had allowed him to pass for a teenager, first in high schools around the D.C. area, where he'd ferreted out gang members who trafficked drugs and guns. Now he was here, under the guise of a runaway teen.

As innocent as McKenzie appeared, she had to know *something* of her father's dealings. Jared Jones, leader of the quasi-religious Centurion Cohort and the longtime object of FBI scrutiny, used charities like this one to launder money, only the FBI hadn't managed to convict him yet. Some at Quantico put the number of his flock into the thousands. Having infiltrated every level of state and national law enforcement, they worked to protect their own.

Miles, who'd observed the man's daughter for some time, could tell she was sincere in her charity toward others. She welcomed the pathetic men who ambled in, searching for a warm meal and a place to lay their heads. He'd overheard them murmur that the girl was a saint. But could such be true when her father was unquestionably a sinner?

"Mind if I sit here?" Miles drew a startled look from her as he slid his tray onto the spot next to hers.

"Not at all." She sent him a quick smile and turned back to the Iraq War veteran, regaling her with tales of his heroism.

Miles nibbled on his mixed vegetables while pretending to listen. All he knew about McKenzie was that she'd graduated from the Savannah School for the Arts but still lived with her father. Her mother, once heralded the "Jewel of Savannah," now lay bedridden with Alzheimer's at Savannah Hospice, and McKenzie divided her time between caring for her mother and rehabilitating homeless men. But if she had even a clue of her father's illicit dealings, and if he could persuade her to tell him, Miles would know more than he did now. It was certainly worth a try.

When the veteran picked up his tray and finally left, Miles set out to win her over. "Hi." He grinned at her like the eighteen-year-old he pretended to be.

"How are you?" Her smile carved a dimple into both cheeks, but it failed to reach her lovely eyes. "Miles, is it?" She held his gaze.

"Yes, very good." He chased down the bland food with a swig of his milk. "You doin' okay?"

The personal question caused her to blink. "Of course. I'm surprised you're still here. It's almost summer now. You do landscaping, don't you?"

Bravo. She'd turned the focus right back on him. "I want to." He shrugged. "I've applied everywhere, but no one's hired me."

"Not even Bushwhackers? I thought they always needed help."

"Oh, yeah, but they—uh, they heard about my former habit."

"Oh." She assessed his worn T-shirt gravely. "Are you still attending the group sessions?" The shelter offered free drug counseling every other afternoon.

"Oh yeah." He nodded several times. "I've been clean for weeks, but, you know, it's hard to shake a reputation." In retrospect, he regretted adding a drug addiction to his cover story.

"Don't let that dissuade you. You're young and strong." Her gaze flickered to his muscular biceps, then back to his face.

Could she see the tiny lines fanning from the corners of his eyes, betraying that he was older than she was? "So, I noticed you're wearing an engagement ring."

For a second time, he startled her into silence. Her gaze dropped to the immense diamond on her left hand, and she swiftly hid it in her lap. "It's really too gaudy to wear here."

He noted the self-conscious reaction. "Who's the lucky guy?"

She tried to smile—and failed. "His name is Ashton Ravenel. He's a friend of my father's."

Seconds ticked by as Miles read between the lines. "Wait a

minute. You mean, like, he's your father's choice? Not that it's any of my business."

She looked away, out of the arched windows with a view to the small walled garden. "I've known Ashton all my life."

That didn't really answer his question. "What does your mother think?" He felt mean even asking since he knew the answer.

McKenzie's hand rose to clasp the pendant dangling from the chain around her neck. "My mother has Alzheimer's. She doesn't even know me."

Miles suffered an urge put his arm around the young woman. Man, was she really this vulnerable, or was her behavior just a front? "I'm so sorry." His gaze dropped to the pendant she was fingering. "Did she give you that?" It looked like a key.

"When I was younger." The corners of her bow-like lips drooped. "It's the key to her heart."

Miles could tell she was repeating words her mother had told her when she'd given it to her. "So...do you love him, this Ashton guy?"

Her downcast gaze and sudden silence supplied an answer. This time, he wanted to throw her over his shoulder and run for the door. "You know, I have a dad who used to run my life."

She nodded but didn't look up or say anything.

"He's the reason I ran away from home." That part wasn't true, but his father was the Public Corruption section chief within the Criminal Investigative Division, which made him Miles's boss's boss, so he did pretty much control his life.

A sheen of moisture had slipped over McKenzie's eyes. "If you'll excuse me." She started to push her chair back. "I have to go. My mother's waiting."

"Oh, sure." He jumped up and pulled the chair out for her.

She rose with a curious but grateful look.

"Be careful," he added. "It's raining out there."

As she headed through the arches and across the shelter's main room to the little office where the residents were screened, he caught himself admiring her graceful walk. Armed with her purse and keys, she opened the heavy front door, hesitating just long enough to send him a backward glance.

Warmth flowed through Miles as their eyes locked. *Looks like I found an informant.*

"If you sissies can't complete this course in less than four minutes," Ben bellowed at the dozen or so junior SEALs scrambling up the wall of the obstacle course, "you'll be here all freakin' morning!"

His subordinates glanced at him quizzically but picked up the pace.

"What in heaven's name has gotten into you?"

Ben glanced over at the man standing next to him, Senior Chief Amos McLeod, code-named Mako because of the silver streak that ran like a fin through his black hair. Ten months ago, Amos would have framed his question with more colorful language, but marriage and fatherhood had reformed him.

He and Ben stood with their backs to the Team building on Dam Neck Naval Annex in Virginia Beach. A brisk spring breeze blew in over the sand dunes while the sun, rising over the Atlantic, shone into their eyes. Amos, who hailed from Maine, wore just his PT shorts and T-shirt, while Ben shivered in his sweat suit.

He met Amos's narrowed gaze and shrugged. "Nothing."

"You're lying. You've been surly ever since you got back from Syria."

Ben shot him a quelling glare. "Whatever."

"And normally, you're a pushover on Mondays." The senior chief smirked, his thick black mustache lifting. "What's the matter? Haven't you met up with any of your usuals yet?"

"Mind your own business, Mako." The man loved to tease him about how many women he juggled at one time.

But Amos persisted, pushing off the building to face him.

"What happened to that blonde at the NCO club last Saturday, the one with the pierced nose?"

"Claudia."

"Aye, her. I thought you got her phone number."

Ben shrugged again. "Not interested." Only one woman was of interest to him, and Amos wouldn't like to hear who it was. Moreover, ever since Emma had gone off on Ben the other night, stating all the reasons why she didn't want or need a man in her life, he'd been obsessed with thoughts of proving her wrong about men—which was stupid, as his track record suggested he would end up hurting both her and her boys, should he persuade her to give him a chance.

Amos stared hard at him. "Who *does* interest you?"

Clearly, the man wouldn't cease interrogating him until he got an answer. So why not tell him? Amos's response might be just the wake-up call he needed.

"All right." Ben folded his arms across his chest and met his senior chief's steely gaze. "It's Emma. I thought about her the whole time I was in Syria. And now that I'm back, I'm thinking about her more. You happy?"

Amos's thunderous expression might have been funny under different circumstances. He took a step toward Ben, going nose-to-nose with him. "You leave Emma alone."

If Ben didn't know better, he'd say Amos was jealous. But Amos's world revolved around his lovely bride, Grace, and their small family. No, Emma was more like a little sister to Amos, having raised his son Simon for the past few years after his late wife ran off with the baby, only to drop him off with her one-time stepsister in Nowhere, Mississippi. Emma's financial straits had eventually prompted her to reunite little Simon with his father. Since then, Amos had done everything in his power to make Emma's life a little easier. He admired her grit as much as Ben did.

"You wanted to know," Ben pointed out. Looking over Amos's

shoulder, he scowled at the SEALs' progress on the obstacle course. "Gibbons, go back and help your partner! This isn't the *Survivor* series. You're a team!"

Amos hadn't stopped glowering at him. "What are you going to *do* about it?"

"I don't know." Ben quelled a shiver as a chilly breeze licked over him. The coffee in Amos's hand caught his eye. He could really use a caffeine fix.

"What about that golf pro?" Amos suggested. "The one you said you never get tired of."

"Oh yeah, Tiffany." Ben pictured the feisty little brunette with the faintest stirring of interest. "I wonder if she's around."

"Call her." Amos quaffed down the rest of his coffee before pointing a finger at him. "And stay well away from Emma." With that order, he stuffed his cup into the recycling bin and stalked toward the entrance of the Team building.

Ben glanced at his watch. "Time's up!"

The men on the course ceased their struggles with groans of defeat.

"My little sisters can run faster than you, pansies. Now, start over!"

Boy, was he irascible this morning? A little caffeine probably wouldn't help. Maybe he should take Amos's advice and give Tiffany a call.

A shadow fell over Carl as he wormed a finger into the soft soil, intending to uproot a dandelion weed. The crooked smile on his face died, and a cool sweat beaded his brow as he recognized the silhouette folding over him.

Mr. Jones must have been watching through the window. Since being offered a gardening job and a place to live five months earlier, Carl had been conscious of his employer assessing and monitoring his every move. He must have overheard him whistle at Miss McKenzie when she hastened from the garage to the rear entrance of the house, hiding under her umbrella.

Scrambling to his feet, Carl prepared to answer for his crime. "Sir?"

"I'd like a word with you." Jared Jones studied him through eyes as dark and still as the swamp by Carl's old mobile home in Mississippi.

"Sure." He managed a careless shrug, and his cheek twitched.

Jones gestured with a manicured hand. "Let's take a stroll."

Together, they passed along the crushed-shell path leading to the fountain at the center of the garden. It was here in this historic walled garden that Carl had labored this past spring, pruning branches, raking up debris, and coaxing exotic shrubs to bloom as the weather warmed. The griffin statue spouting water seemed to stare at Carl as he waited for the ax to fall.

Jones faced him, slipping his hands into the pockets of his golfing trousers. "I've located your sons, Carl. The ones you claimed your wife ran off with?"

The announcement was so unexpected that Carl could only gape at his employer. "My sons?"

"Christopher, Colton, and Carter?"

Those names, on very rare occasions, had gnawed on Carl's conscience. He'd sooner just forget about them.

"The Cohort wouldn't approve of the way you've washed your hands of your obligations, Carl." Jones's voice dripped with disapproval. "Any man who fosters children is responsible for their welfare."

"But Emma took 'em from me. I...I wanted to pay child support, honest." Tears of fear sprang to his eyes, lending credence to his assertions. "I've looked everywhere for those boys. Wh-where'd you find 'em?"

"It doesn't matter where." Jones glanced up at the windows of his Federal-period home, apparently owned by generations of Joneses before him. "What matters is that you've sworn, as a member of the Cohort, to protect your progeny. And while our daughters are a blessing, it is our sons who are our greatest treasure and legacy."

Carl nodded in agreement.

"Soon, your boys will be returned to you."

The unexpected words turned Carl hot, then cold. To him? How was he going to look after them? He barely made enough to support himself.

"They'll remain at The Centurion Academy for Boys just outside the city until you have the means to look after them yourself. Once I find a gardener to replace you, I'll employ you as my chauffeur. The pay is more, which should afford you a higher standard of living so you can support your sons."

Carl nearly wilted with relief. He was off the hook for a while longer, thank goodness. "Wh-what about Emma, my ex-wife?" He couldn't envision Emma relinquishing her boys.

Jones laid a large hand on his shoulder. "Don't concern yourself with her." His dark eyes glinted. "She'll get what she deserves for keeping them from you."

A chill rippled down Carl's spine. Was there nothing this man couldn't do?

"Doing right by your sons is the only way to advance your position in the Cohort." Jones's stare compelled him to do what was necessary. "I need you to trust me implicitly in all things, Carl."

He swallowed against a dry mouth. "Oh, I do, sir. I do."

"Good." Jones released him. "Well then, carry on." He sent Carl a dismissive nod and turned away.

Mouth agape, Carl watched the Centurion high consul stride confidently back into his mansion.

Ben was proud of himself, darned if he wasn't. Thanks to Amos's suggestion, he was thinking less about Emma and more about his upcoming four-day weekend with Tiffany.

The lady golfer had invited him to join her in traveling to Williamsburg, where she was about to participate in the annual LPGA tournament. To Ben's surprise, his commanding officer, James Monteague, hadn't batted an eye when he'd asked to take off both Thursday and Friday. By the time he returned, Ben was sure he would have forgotten his obsession for Emma.

And yet, as he approached Tiffany's condo on Thursday morning, reluctance to leave the area made his feet drag. What if one of Emma's boys got hurt while playing, and she needed his help? *She'll call Amos, of course.* He forced himself to climb Tiffany's stoop and ring her doorbell. Wasn't Emma taking her exams this week? She could use somebody to play with the boys so she could study.

The door opened, and there stood Tiffany in a halter top with her midriff bare, showing off her belly button piercing. Yet, it was all Ben could do to dredge up a smile for her.

"You're late," she scolded with just a hint of annoyance. "We need to hop in your car and go."

"My car?"

"Yes, mine's in the shop. Come on in. I need you to carry my golf bag for me."

The suspicion that Tiffany was using him as a caddy and a chauffeur cooled Ben's tepid attraction even further. All this to keep Amos happy.

"Colton, quit." Emma reached over the back of her seat to put a calming hand on Colton's knee. "Leave the baby alone!"

The blare of a horn jerked her gaze forward, giving her just enough time to slam on the brakes as a white delivery van pulled out of the cross street right in front of her fast-moving car. Great day in the morning! Had she just run a stop sign?

Extremities tingling, she checked her rearview mirror. No, she hadn't, thank God. It was the van's fault for pulling out while she was driving along at forty-five miles an hour. Then again, she had a lot on her mind, not the least of which was getting the best possible grade on this last exam so she could keep her academic scholarship.

What a day this was! Following her eight-hour shift at the Chevy dealership, she'd fetched the boys from her neighbor Belinda, who watched Carter all day, and the older boys when they got off the school bus. Emma had fed them all dinner, then piled them into her car to head to Tidewater Community College. The childcare facility there made it possible for single mothers like her to better themselves. Christopher and Colton enjoyed playing with the older children. It was Carter who clung to her, wanting his mother, who'd been away from him all day, just to hold him. And who could blame him?

Guilt tugged at Emma. She would be a better mother to all of them once she became a licensed practical nurse.

"We're almost there, guys." This shortcut to her community college was a long, straight road lined with ditches and trees. Yet the white van frustrated her desire to drive at just over the speed limit. She peered around it, hoping to pass, which the double-yellow line suggested was a bad idea. Besides, the gathering dusk made it hard to see any approaching cars that hadn't turned on their headlights.

"Come on." She glanced at the time on her dashboard, dreading the possibility of arriving late for her exam.

Luckily, the professor for this class had told her students that if they were ever running late, they could just text her.

Emma pulled her cell phone from her purse. Dividing her attention between the screen and the road, she brought up Professor Stein's contact information before handing her phone to Christopher. "Honey, please type a text to my professor telling her I might be a few minutes late."

"Okay." Chris loved to practice texting. According to him, every kid in the fifth grade had a cell phone but him.

The brake lights on the van flared suddenly, forcing Emma to slow down and then come to a full stop right there in the middle of a straightaway. Luckily, there was no one behind them.

"There isn't even a stop sign here!" She threw both hands up. "What is going on?"

The van's rear doors popped open. Emma stared in confusion as two strangers leaped out, both dressed in dark clothing. One of them shut the van's rear doors while the other approached Christopher's side of the car.

It wasn't until the man's hand came through Chris's window, unlocking his door and yanking it open, that Emma realized this was bad. Shock pegged her to the seat as he stuck his head inside the car and thrust a gun against Chris's chest. "Unlock your door, or this kid dies."

"What?"

The second man was tugging on her door handle. "Unlock your door!"

With Chris's horror apparent under her dome light, Emma hastily unlocked her door. The second man hauled it open and reached across her to release her seat belt. He then grabbed her arms and started pulling her from the driver's seat.

Emma clung to the steering wheel, refusing to budge. Her senses expanded to take in everything at once: the pocked face of the stranger menacing her son, the nauseating odor of the man tugging on her, Chris's breathless expression of horror, Colton's stunned silence in the back seat, and Carter's soft, sleepy snores.

"No!"

Her assailant was prying her fingers off the steering wheel. The instant they slipped, he dragged her upper body out of the car, grunting at the force required.

Realizing her Impala was still in gear and her foot was on the brake, Emma shot out a knee and knocked the car into reverse. With her head now out of the car, she jackknifed her hips, straining to reach the accelerator, but the man covering Chris lunged toward the key in her ignition and cut the engine.

"Hurry up!" He shot a look out the back window. "We gotta go."

The last thing Emma saw as she was thrown onto the street was Chris crawling into the back seat as his assailant took his place. Her car doors slammed. Her motor kicked back on. Climbing to her knees, she gaped with disbelief as the heavier man reopened her door and threw her purse down beside her.

Emma ignored it, jumping to her feet to rush at the car. "No!" With bloodied palms, she reached for the handle and beat the window.

Chris and Colton cried out for her. "Mama!"

As she grasped the driver's door handle, the locks engaged. To her horror, the van started forward, followed by her car.

Emma clung to the handle while hammering the window. "Open the door!" In the twilight, it was hard to see the driver's face.

Her car accelerated, forcing her to jog and then sprint as she hung on. Her gaze locked on the man's fat pinkie finger and the thick ring glinting there.

As the car sped up, her legs began to wheel beneath her, her feet scarcely touching the ground. With a spurt of acceleration, the car shot forward, tearing the handle from Emma's grasp and sending her into a bone-jarring roll onto the quiet road.

Paralyzed by the impact, the breath knocked clean out of her, she lay there a moment until she heard another car approaching. With all four limbs abraded and bleeding, the material of her clothing shredded, she rolled over painfully and rose to her feet to get out of the way.

Stepping off the road, she stared after the taillights of her Impala as they grew smaller and dimmer, then disappeared altogether.

CHAPTER 3

*C*arter was crying again, making the bad men angry. It was completely dark outside, and they'd been driving for a long time.

"Shut that baby up!" The gun in Ugly Man's hands glinted as he swung it over the seat and pointed it at Colton.

Chris, who'd been staring down at his lap on the other side of Carter's baby seat, looked up at the threat. "I can make him stop. He just wants his sippy cup from his bag."

Ugly man swung his gun at Chris. "Well, get it out and give it to him, then."

Colton watched as Chris reached for the diaper bag at their feet. Too bad it didn't have a weapon in it, like that big ol' knife Mr. Ben kept hidden in his truck.

"Here you go, Carter. Shh." Chris stuck the sippy cup in the baby's mouth, and Carter grabbed it with both hands, keeping it there.

His silence prompted Ugly Man to face forward, taking his gun with him.

Colton returned his attention to the highway. Given the signs he could read, they were heading south. Mr. Ben always said, *"Pay attention to your surroundings, and you'll never get lost."*

Ugly Man said a word Mama did not like. "Why'd we nab the baby, anyway? He's gonna cry again when his drink's gone."

Chris spoke calmly. "He won't cry unless his diaper's wet. I could change it for you."

"We'll be there in forty minutes," Sweaty Man interrupted. "We'll put 'em all in the back of the van, and then older brother can change his diaper if he needs to."

Almost where? Colton's stomach lurched as he remembered how Mama had run beside the car, yelling and beating on the window. Was she coming after them?

A while later, they passed a sign that read **Medoc Mountain State Park**, and then they took the exit, zipping off the highway onto a smaller road. Carter started fussing again. Chis hushed him and distracted him. They drove a little farther, into woods that were pitch black and scary. Colton had to pee all of a sudden. These men weren't gonna kill them, were they?

Sweaty Man drove past a dark playground with a jungle gym that looked like a giant spider. He stopped the car behind the same white van the men had jumped out of earlier, parked between a picnic shelter and a little river twinkling with starlight.

Ugly Man pointed his gun over the back seat. "Don't move."

As the two men got out, Chis whispered, "Colton, I've got Mama's cell phone."

"What?"

"Shh. Mama's phone locked on me, and I can't remember the password. Do you know how to call 911 without it?"

"Yeah, I remember." Mr. Ben had shown them just the other day.

"Good!" Chris thrust the phone at him, then started unbuckling the baby. "We're going out your side and making a run for it. You dial 911 while I carry Carter. Stay close to me. Ready?"

"Yes." Colton had already shaken off his seat belt and was reaching for the door handle.

Chris hauled Carter into his arms. The baby was too big for Colton to carry. Meeting the glimmer of his brother's eyes, Colton waited for his nod, then quietly opened his door. Since the car was off, no light came on.

"Go."

They eased out of the back seat, one after the other. Leaving the door open, they tore past the picnic shelter away from the men, who immediately heard them. They cursed up a storm and yelled for them to stop.

"Run faster, Chris!" The men were chasing them. Glancing back, Colton saw Sweaty Man closing in on his brothers. Carter was too heavy for Chris to run fast.

"Now, Colton!" Chris shouted at him as Sweaty Man grabbed him.

Diving blindly into the woods, Colton adjusted his grip, feeling for the lower button on his mother's Android. He had to push it three times. One. Two—

The screen lit up, shining on a holly bush just as he crashed into its prickly leaves. Throwing his hands up to protect himself, he dropped the phone. In the same instant, Ugly Man seized him by his thick, blond hair.

"No!" Colton swung around and kicked him. He had to get to the phone and finish the call. Ugly Man shoved him, and he ended up lying on the leafy ground. He patted it down, feeling for the phone. A glance showed it lying too far away to reach.

Ugly Man dropped to his knees and pinned him with a heavy hand. Colton thrashed to free himself, losing a shoe in the process. *Crack!* The slap across his face stunned him.

Ugly Man snatched up the phone, turned it off, and stuffed it into his pocket. Then he hauled Colton to his feet and marched him back to the picnic shelter, wearing just one shoe.

Chris was sitting under a dome light on a folded blanket,

holding Carter. He burst into tears when Ugly Man pushed Colton into the van and slammed the door shut. The dome light went out, and the doors locked with a *clunk*.

Colton scooted closer to his brothers. "Don't cry, Chris'fer. It ain't gonna help nothin'."

"Did you call?"

"I tried. I lost my shoe, and Ugly Man took the phone."

Chris drew a shaky breath and nodded. "That's okay. The police can trace where our phone went. They'll find your other shoe."

Just then they heard their car start up and pull away. Colton shot to his knees to look out the filthy rear window. In disbelief, he watched the shadow of their car roll down the bank straight into the little river, hitting the water with a mighty splash.

"They're drownin' Mama's car." Seeing the men return, Colton scuttled back to Christopher.

Sweaty Man got into the back with them. With a mean glare, he pulled a folded blanket under his butt and sat on it. Then he pointed a sausage-like finger at them. "'Cause any more trouble and I'll kill you myself."

Ugly Man shut the back door from the outside, and the dome light went out. Then, Colton heard both doors up front open and close. He could hear voices through the thin metal door separating the back from the front.

So much for escaping on their first attempt. But Mr. Ben always said, *"If you don't get it right the first time, you just try, try again."*

～

Ben intentionally ignored his phone while on leave. He avoided the television and radio, too—anything to keep from hearing that the world was falling apart without him holding the line. But even

Mr. Fix-it needed a break from time to time. How else was he going to put Emma Stuart out of his mind?

As early as Friday morning, he had no idea what manner of chaos was happening where, and he was still thinking of Emma every other minute. His break from her seemed to be making his obsession worse, not better. And for reasons he could not name, he felt guilty for sleeping in Tiffany's bed, even though nothing had happened. Lucky for him, she'd been so drunk on their first night together that she passed out the instant she lay down.

"Hey, Tiff," he said as they breakfasted at an outdoor table over-looking the James River. "I think I'm gonna head back today."

She looked up with dawning outrage. "What? Who's going to caddy for me this weekend?"

The selfish question made her even less appealing to him. "I'm sure you'll find a guy willing to caddy for you." He laid a fifty-dollar bill on the table to cover their check.

She blinked her wide brown eyes. "You drove us here. How am I supposed to get home?"

Ben shrugged, feeling a little mean when he said, "Uber?"

Her hurt expression had him leaning over and pecking her cheek. "Sorry. Take care of yourself." He strode back to their unit to pack his stuff.

Maybe it was just Tiffany's pampered lifestyle that made him walk away. Sure, it was fun to escape to a resort, complete with a massage and an open bar, but real life was filled with hardship, duty, and honor. Meals-Ready-to-Eat didn't come with room service, and a life of indolence didn't suit a guy who needed to *fix* stuff.

It wasn't that he preferred to be with Emma and her boys. Nah. He just had the habit of checking up on things, was all.

After slipping into his sun-warmed Mustang, Ben took his cell phone out of his bag and, for the first time in days, powered it up. The little apple icon appeared, then immediately vanished. His phone was dead. He went to charge it with the cable he kept in his car, only to realize he'd left that in his truck when he used it to haul mulch last week.

With no way to update himself on what he might have missed, Ben left Kingsmill Resort listening to country music on his XM radio station. As he approached the Hampton Roads Bridge Tunnel headed toward Virginia Beach, he switched over to classic rock. The need to touch base with Emma battled with his determination to forget about her. But when her exit popped up on the highway, he took it.

I'll just stop by for a moment. The grass probably needs its first cut of the year.

Three minutes later, he pulled into her driveway only to see her car gone. No one was home.

Ben braked to a halt, his spirits sinking. He was about to push his gearshift into Reverse when he realized the blinds in her windows were all drawn. Emma only closed her blinds at night. So, what was this about?

An uneasy feeling skittered through him, prompting him to park his car and get out to investigate.

His knock at the door resulted in nothing but silence. *What to do?* Normally, he wouldn't dream of marching right in, but his gut urged him to put his concerns to rest. He found his landlord's copy of the key and stuck it in the lock.

The scent of stale milk hit him as he crossed the threshold. The scene that greeted him stopped him in his tracks. The sofa's cushions had been upended; toys were strewn across the carpet; Emma's schoolwork lay scattered on the floor. His scalp tightened. Something awful had happened here.

He hurried to her bedroom, terrified he might come across a body or several bodies. At her door, he drew up short to find her mattress ripped from its frame, drawers yanked from her dresser, their contents thrown helter-skelter about the room. Even her worn nightgown lay in a mangled heap.

"What the...?" Reeling, he returned to the living room, where he raised her blinds. Bright spring sunshine flooded in. His gaze went straight to Belinda's car, parked next door.

The neighbor would have answers. He left Emma's house, jumping the chain-link fence between the properties to get to Belinda's. Breathing hard, he rapped on her front door.

Her stricken countenance as she opened it confirmed his worst fears.

"What happened?"

Belinda's double chin wobbled. "Emma's at the jail."

"What?"

Belinda hitched her two-year-old daughter more securely on her hip. "Emma's boys were snatched from her yesterday on her way to school. It's all over the news. She says two men pulled her from her car and took off with the boys, but now the media's sayin' that maybe she killed them. Of course, she didn't. You and I know that."

Ben's internal temperature dropped, turning his skin cold. He could only pivot on Belinda's front stoop and stare over at Emma's house and the empty driveway. How could all this have happened while he was away?

He had to talk to Amos. "Can I borrow your cell phone? Mine's dead."

"Sure." Belinda produced her cell from her back pocket, unlocked it with facial recognition, and handed it to him.

It took Ben a full ten seconds to remember Amos's number. What an idiot he was to leave his charger in his truck! Amos was going to give him hell.

"Hello."

"Mako, it's me." Ben braced himself, wincing at the furious stream coming out of Amos's mouth. To his credit, he called him a son of a monkey and demanded to know why he hadn't answered his flipping phone. Ben cut him off. "Where is Emma now, and how can I help?"

"I don't know. I'm at work. Call Grace. She stayed at home today with Emma, who slept on our houseboat last night."

"What's her number?"

As Amos rattled off the number, Ben typed it into Belinda's phone and then hung up on him. Grace's phone started ringing. Just when he despaired of her picking up, she answered breathlessly, "Hello?"

"Hi, it's Ben Harmony. Where's Emma?"

"Oh, Ben. Thank goodness. The police came here a couple hours ago to collect her. They went to her house to look for evidence and said I couldn't come."

"I'm at her house now. She's not here."

"Well…they must have taken her back to the station then—the one on LeRoy Drive. That's where they questioned her last night after taking her from the hospital."

"Is she hurt?"

"She's banged up pretty badly, but nothing serious. If you want, I'll meet you there."

The phone beeped in his ear. Distracted, Ben looked at it and recognized Mako's number. "Hey, Amos is calling me back. Gotta go." With a tap of his finger, he took Amos's call. "How could this happen?" he demanded in lieu of a greeting.

"It's been all over the local news, Harm. I told you to stay away from Emma, not disappear off the ducking planet!"

Ben didn't bother pointing out that his spending time with Tiffany had been Amos's idea. "I'm heading to the station to be with her right now. Why is Emma even a suspect?"

Amos made a scoffing sound. "Who the heck knows? She was thrown out of her car on Harper's Road by two guys who drove off with the boys. Heads up if you're going to the station: The police will want to question you, too."

"Me?" Stunned, Ben raised a hand to his forehead.

"They'll want to know where you were last evening."

He'd been dining with Tiffany at the Kingsmill Restaurant.

"If I were you, I'd get a hold of your lawyer friend before walking into the station. Emma's going to need one, too."

Ben pinched the bridge of his nose. "This is insane!"

The urge to rush to Emma's side was overpowering, but if the police honestly thought she or he had anything to do with her boys' abduction, they were better off armed with legal counsel. "Have you seen what they did to her house?"

"No, is it bad?"

"The place is a wreck. I'm going to swing by my lawyer's office on my way to the station. I'll pay for him to represent Emma, too."

"Thank you."

Heaving a sigh, Ben hung up and returned Belinda's phone to her. How he wished he could relive the last two days. Taking off with Tiffany Hughes might be the worst mistake he'd ever made.

Emma's stomach roiled. She'd kept nothing down since her boys had been snatched from her eighteen hours ago. Nor had she slept. The need to go after them clawed at her, but her car was gone, and the police were holding her hostage in this room with the two-way mirror, asking her the same stupid questions as they had asked her late last night. Why couldn't they remember her answers?

At first, they'd seemed helpful. When she was still at the hospital being treated for shock and multiple abrasions, they'd put out a preliminary BOLO for her Chevy Impala and taken steps to trace her cell phone, which she recalled giving to Chris right before the incident.

They'd dispatched an officer to her house to pick up photos of her boys and disseminated the photos to the media. At midnight, Amos McLeod had collected her from the police station and taken her to stay the night with him and Grace on *Camelot*. He'd tried calling Ben, whom he said was on leave and not answering his cell phone.

Down in the berthing area of Amos's boat, where Emma had stayed for a week the previous summer, she had struggled to pray while sleeping in a bunk across from Simon and Mateo, their younger, adopted son from Venezuela.

God, help me. She'd searched desperately for the faith that had sustained her through dozens of hardships.

There it was, a feeble, wavering flame burning at the center of her heart. She leaned immediately into it. *Give me the strength to endure this, Father. But, more than anything, be with my boys. Protect them from harm. Let them be okay.*

The next morning, the police picked her up soon after Amos went to work. Grace, who'd called a substitute to cover her first-grade class, had bristled as Sergeant Peyton explained that they needed to search Emma's home for clues.

Grace had propped her hands on her hips. "Where is Emma's cell phone? You should have traced it by now."

Sergeant Peyton had frowned at her. "Phone company's working on it."

"You're notifying the FBI today, right? They get involved after twenty-four hours."

Grace would know since her nephew had been kidnapped back in January, luckily to be found within days.

Peyton curled a beefy hand around Emma's elbow. "We have ten more hours before the Feds get involved. Come with me, Miss Stuart."

On the way to her home, Emma had signed a Consent to Search document, allowing them to swab the boys' toothbrushes for DNA samples. Once they arrived, however, she'd watched in disbelief as they'd overturned every box of toys, every drawer and mattress, in total disregard for her feelings.

"Why are you doing this?" Their destructiveness had appalled her.

They assured her they were looking for clues, something to

explain why her boys had been snatched from her. Only, they hadn't found any.

They returned her to the station, where they'd proceeded to quiz her more insistently than they had the night before. Where was she from? What had brought her from Mississippi to Virginia in the first place?

Emma answered candidly, hoping her replies would point to the kidnapper. But with no sleep the night before, her recollections grew less distinct. Like an impressionist painting, the details of the abduction seemed undefined when viewed in isolation.

Peyton's chair creaked under his weight. "Why would anyone want to steal a 2002 Chevy Impala?"

"I don't know."

"Why didn't they take your purse?"

"I don't know! I told you this already. They threw it at me." She had pawed through it on the side of the road only to realize she'd left Christopher holding her cell phone. If a passing car hadn't slowed down to ask if she was okay, she might still be standing there in shock.

"Call my cellular provider," she demanded. "They *have* to know something by now."

Peyton ignored her. Emma's gaze dropped to the signet ring on his right hand as he wove his thick fingers together, resting them on the tabletop. The ring kept drawing her attention, prodding something in her memory, but she didn't know what.

"Tell me about your ex-husband."

The question had her raising both her eyes and her eyebrows. "Why do I have to repeat myself? Carl never wanted a thing to do with his boys. He didn't take them."

Peyton sent her a hooded look. "Tell me more about your landlord, then. He's sure been layin' low."

Amos had told her, with a frown, that Ben had taken leave and had a habit of turning off his cell phone so he could relax.

"He's been overseas." Emma had to quash the resentment rising in her that Ben had yet to come to her defense. "He needed some time off."

"According to your neighbor, Belinda Cartwright, he's more than just your landlord."

Emma's eyes flew wide. "I don't know where she got that notion! It's most certainly not true."

Peyton glanced down at the notepad in front of him. "Says right here his car was parked at your house last Sunday, 'long about midnight."

Emma's jaw dropped. "He came by to fix the lights! Our electricity went out."

"At midnight?" Peyton's voice dripped with skepticism.

"Yes, I was studying by candlelight. Ben had duty on base and couldn't come any earlier. He's just my landlord. It could never be more than that."

"Oh. And why is that?"

With a feeling that she'd said too much, Emma drew a steadying breath. "Ben Harmony's a Navy SEAL and a ladies' man. He's not the kind of man who settles down and has a family. Besides, I don't need or want a man in my life."

Peyton sent her a patronizing smile. "With three boys, I imagine it's tough to have any kind of social life. I know how it is. I've got two of my own, you know."

The design on his ring, she realized, was a dragon or some kind of violent creature just like him. "Then, you should count yourself lucky." Emma pushed the words through clenched teeth and hugged herself to quell her shudders.

"Oh, I don't know. I'd like to strangle 'em both sometimes."

His cell phone buzzed loudly, startling Emma. Noting her shot nerves, Peyton kept his eyes on her as he took the call.

The realization that she was not in this room to be helped crept into her awareness. Peyton's lips took on a cynical twist as he listened to the voice on the other end. "Understood." He hung up, meeting her gaze. "Sorry 'bout that. You were saying you don't need or want a man in your life? Now, we both know that's not true."

They were trying to frame her.

Something in Emma snapped, bringing her to the edge of her seat. "Why are you here talking to me? You and I should both be out there"—she jabbed a finger at the door—"looking for my boys!"

He cocked his large head. "Let me ask you this. Don't those boys keep you from getting a man?"

A red haze filmed Emma's vision. She rose to her feet, looming over him like an Amazon queen. "I love my sons!" Tears gushed into her eyes. "No man in the world could *ever* be more important to me than them. Don't you dare imply that I did something to hurt them? They're my life. My whole life!" She slammed her hands on the table to get her point across.

A brisk knock at the door curtailed her outburst.

Annoyance clouded Peyton's fleshy face as he rose to answer the summons.

Emma dragged air into her tight lungs. She clenched her battered hands to keep from howling in frustration. How could the police believe, for one second, that she'd done something to her own boys? She had heard of mothers like that—women who did unspeakable things to their children. How dare they put her in that category?

She had to find a way out of here. Whatever it took, she would find her boys and prove Peyton *wrong*.

He cracked the door open. "What is it?"

"Sir, Miss Stuart's lawyer is here to pick her up."

Peyton looked back at her. "She has a lawyer?"

Emma blinked in confusion as a friendly-looking, middle-aged man dressed in jeans, paired with a suit jacket, stepped into the room.

"Reno Silverman." After thrusting his card at Peyton, he came straight for Emma and gently took her elbow. "Hello, Emma. Is my client under arrest? No?" He started to lead her out the door.

Peyton hooked his thumbs over his belt and blocked their path. "We were just making progress."

Silverman sent him a steely smile while guiding Emma around him. "We'll be in touch."

Just like that, she was free of the horrible Peyton.

"I can just leave?" she asked as Mr. Silverman ushered her down a hall to the exit.

"I'm sure they didn't tell you that." He pushed open one of the large double doors and led her out into the bright sunshine.

The angle of the sun suggested it was midafternoon. The flawless blue sky was filled with winging seagulls. How could the sun even shine with her boys stolen and gone?

Suddenly, a swarm of reporters, toting microphones and cameras, rushed at them from the front lawn.

"Miss Stuart! Miss Stuart!" They clamored for her attention.

A tall male reporter thrust a microphone at her. "Any idea who took your children?" The rest leaned in, hoping to catch Emma's reply.

"No comment," Reno said before she could speak. "My client is distraught and exhausted. Now, if you'll respect her privacy."

With a firm tug, he drew Emma through the crowd to a well-used Ford Explorer. As he opened the passenger door, Emma hesitated. "Why are you helping me?" He had to be a gift from God.

"This isn't the place for an attorney-client conversation, Miss Stuart." He glanced toward the reporters who were hovering and listening in. "Please, get in, and I'll explain once we're on our way."

Emma didn't move. "I can't afford a lawyer. I mean, I will pay you, but it might take a long time." She clung to the open door as the world seemed to spin.

"Your bill's being covered, Miss Stuart. Up you go."

Covered? She allowed him to trundle her into his car, then watched as he rounded the front and got in next to her. She'd never been in trouble with the law before. Was this how things worked?

"Are you a court-appointed lawyer? Are they arresting me?"

"No, and not yet." He backed out of his parking space. "Let's get you safely to Ben's house, and then we'll talk."

"Ben!" Relief left her light-headed. "Is he back?"

"Yes. He would have come to the station himself to get you, but I advised against it."

So *Ben* had sent Mr. Silverman to rescue her. Relief vied with resentment that it had taken him so long to show up. Where could he have been that even Amos couldn't get a hold of him?

CHAPTER 4

*E*mma kept her face averted as Ben stepped out of his house to greet his visitors. As he opened Reno's passenger door to help her out, she could only imagine how she looked, all battered and skinned, wearing a sundress of Grace's that was a size too small, her hair tangled and unrestrained.

"I'm so sorry, Emma."

As Ben wrapped his powerful arms around her, she wanted to melt into the wall of his body and vanish.

"I should've been here sooner. I turn off my phone whenever I take leave."

His earnest distress made her forgive him instantly. "Amos told me." And now that Ben was present, every ache and pain that came from striking the pavement so hard hit her. She pushed her face into his neck and moaned.

"Reno." Emma felt Ben shake Reno's hand. "Thanks, man. Come on in so we can talk."

As Ben escorted Emma into his driftwood gray contemporary, she caught him assessing the abrasions on her hands and forearms. Once within his foyer, he turned her to face him, examining her from head to toe. Her ravaged knees, peeking out from the hem of Grace's dress, caused his jaw to flex and his ears to turn red.

Emma had never seen Ben get mad before. The air in the foyer seemed to crackle. "It's my fault. I wouldn't let go of the car."

Her words only seemed to make him angrier. "No, Emma." His blue eyes flashed. "This is definitely not your fault!"

The memory of the handle slipping from her grasp brought a fresh flood of tears to her eyes.

Ben pulled her into his arms again, squeezing her gently but firmly. "We'll find them, Em. Don't you worry. We're going to find them. Come sit down."

He ushered her toward a pair of immense cream-colored couches, set at a ninety-degree angle from one another and facing a stone hearth. The wide-screen TV mounted over his mantel made her picture him with his teammates watching football.

"What can I get you both to drink?" He helped her to sit at one end of a couch. "Iced tea? Beer?"

"I'll have an iced tea." Mr. Silverman sat catty-corner to her while loosening his necktie.

"Emma?"

"Water, please." She watched Ben move into the kitchen, which flowed seamlessly from the living area. All smooth gray granite and stainless-steel appliances, it could have come straight from a magazine.

"The police think I killed them," she relayed as Ben came back, holding a water bottle and a glass of iced tea. "Belinda saw your car over at my house the other night. She told the police we might be lovers. They think I killed my boys so I could be with you."

Ben froze. The stupefied look on his face made her regret ever calling him over that night. He'd just been doing what landlords did when their tenants had problems. "It's not your fault," she added when he said nothing.

He put the water bottle in her hands, passed Reno his glass, and then seated himself on the coffee table right in front of her. Their knees touched, sending warmth up her legs into her chilled heart. "I need to know what happened." Both his voice and his expression conveyed his apologies for making her relive the event—yet again.

After a sip of cold water, she told him, in spurts and starts, she described the worst moment of her life. Ben smoothed his hands up and down her forearms.

Mr. Silverman spoke up. "Did anyone make composite sketches of the perps?"

"Yes. On the night of the incident." The energy it had taken to describe the kidnappers' features had sapped her last ounce of strength. "One of the sketches looks just like the man who opened Christopher's door. The other sketch is wrong. I didn't get a good look at the big man's face."

"Who are these guys?" Ben wondered out loud.

"I don't know." Emma's throat closed. She wanted to keel over on the couch and die, except in her head, she could still hear her boys calling for her.

"Obviously, they planned this in order to pull it off." Ben pushed off the coffee table to pace to the kitchen and back. "This is not like some random kidnapping. You haven't had any calls for ransom money, have you?"

Emma took another sip of water while shaking her head. "My cell phone's gone, in any case. Christopher had it last. I asked him to text my professor because I thought I might be late."

Ben shared a startled look with Silverman. "Well, the police should have found your phone by now."

"They said they were waiting for my provider to tell them where it is."

"That's ridiculous."

His lawyer cut him off. "The FBI will be all over that phone, and they'll be taking over the investigation shortly. After twenty-four hours, it's assumed the boys have been taken across state lines."

The thought of them in another state flattened Emma.

"What about your ex-husband?" Ben asked. "Could he have taken them?"

"No." She set her bottle on the coffee table before hugging herself. "Carl never wanted the boys. Why would he take them from me now?"

Seeing her shiver, Ben grabbed up a small burgundy throw and tossed it over her shoulders. The warmth dispelled her chill, but despair drove her to drop her head against the cushions and close her eyes.

Why is this happening, Father? How can anything good come from this?

With his heart in his throat, Ben watched Emma quietly fold. It amazed him that she'd kept it together this long. Shooting Reno a silent message to stay put, he bent over and scooped her into his arms, ignoring her feeble protests.

"You need to sleep, Em." He used his SEAL-chief voice to elicit her cooperation. As she went limp with acceptance, her head resting on his shoulder, he carried her up his floating staircase to the second story. The owner's suite at the top of the stairs was comprised of a California king, which took up much of the space. Given his room-darkening shades, Emma could sleep for as long as she was able under his chocolate-brown comforter.

He set her on her feet while pulling down the blankets. An impression of her willowy figure branded itself on his tactile senses as she swayed against him. He didn't dare undress her or give her something else to wear. He lowered a semi-conscious Emma gently onto the mattress, then bent to pull off her Skechers and tiny socks. As she slid her bare feet under the covers, he pulled the comforter to her shoulders, crossed to the windows, and lowered the blinds.

In the subsequent darkness, all Ben could make out of Emma as he moved to the door was the curve of her body as she rolled onto her side. "Try to sleep. I'll be right downstairs with Reno."

Silence answered him as he pulled his door shut behind him. How bittersweet that the only woman he considered off-limits was now asleep in his bed.

Reno had found the remote control. As Ben came down the stairs, his lawyer waved him over.

"Check this out. They just found her car."

Eyes on the screen, Ben braced himself for the news that the boys' bodies had been found. A familiar copper-haired reporter stood before a narrow, fast-moving river, gesturing.

"The pings of Emma Stuart's cell phone drew state police to Medoc Mountain State Park in North Carolina, where minutes ago, her 2002 Chevy Impala was pulled out of the river behind me—empty. So far, Stuart's three sons, ten-year-old Christopher Moulton, eight-year-old Colton, and fifteen-month-old Carter, remain at large."

Relief uncoiled the knots in Ben's stomach that the boys had not been drowned in the car.

As the attractive newscaster turned and approached the camera, Ben realized he knew her.

"In addition to the car, the FBI retrieved a boy's red-striped shoe that is believed to belong to Stuart's middle son. While the pings on her cell phone brought investigators to the area, the phone itself has vanished." Perfectly groomed eyebrows rose to suggest foul play. "Virginia Beach police have released these composites of the suspected kidnappers."

The screen flashed to computer-generated composites of two men. Ben studied them intently, one with broad, indistinct features, the other with pocked cheeks and a beaked nose.

"Virginia Beach police were quite clear in stating that Emma Stuart, herself, remains a person of interest. This is Ruby Bonheur for Channel Ten news."

At the familiar name, Ben threw his hands up. "I knew she

looked familiar." He swung around to face his lawyer. "That's my teammate Tony's fiancée. She'd better not side with the police."

"Don't worry about the media." Reno's calm advice soothed Ben's agitation. "The law won't charge Emma without probable cause."

Ben frowned. "What would that look like? Give me an example."

"Bodies," said Reno with an apologetic shrug. "If they find the boys dead and it looks like their mother killed them, then they'll arrest her. If they find a murder weapon with her prints on it or if a witness steps forward claiming to have seen something, again, they'll arrest her. But the clock starts ticking if that happens, and they have a set amount of time to find the proof to convict her. For now, she's just a person of interest."

"Yeah, and so am I." Ben scrubbed a hand over his bald head. "The neighbor told the cops we're lovers."

Reno stared at him. "Are you?"

Ben frowned. "No." *Not that I don't want to be.*

Reno's mouth quirked. "Well, that's a first." He hid a smile behind a swig of tea.

"Emma deserves better than me." Ben marched to the kitchen to pull an energy drink from the fridge. "Her boys are great." He pictured Chris's earnest face while tossing back a swig. "No one loves her boys the way Emma does. She doesn't deserve this!"

Reno regarded him with an odd light in his eyes.

"What?"

The lawyer waved a hand. "Nothing. So, assuming she's innocent—because I've never known you to be wrong about people's motivations—who would have abducted Emma's boys? You mentioned an ex-husband."

"His name's Carl." Ben had nothing but contempt for the man, given that it was *his* fault Emma had driven all the way from Mississippi, looking for help from Amos. "Emma says Carl left her for a cocktail waitress over a year ago. Then, he sold the mobile home they'd been living in, forcing her to find somewhere else to live."

"Where was this?"

"Mantachie, Mississippi."

Reno touched his steepled fingers to his chin. "Fastest route to Mississippi wouldn't take you through North Carolina."

"She says Carl wouldn't take them." Ben screwed the lid on his bottle before thumping it down on the counter. "We can't just sit on our tails and let the media create a feeding frenzy—which they will, as soon as they hear that a Navy SEAL is Emma's *lover*."

Reno sat back, crossing his legs at the ankle. "What do you want to do?"

Ben considered his options. "I need to talk to my commander. In person." He looked back at Reno. "Who's watching your kids?" Reno's wife had died of cancer, leaving him with no less than six children under the age of fifteen, poor man.

"My oldest." Reno sat forward and scooped up the remote. "Go ahead. I'll fend off the cops when they show up to question you."

Ben stared. "You think they'll show up today?"

"Yep."

Shoot. He really didn't want to explain where he'd been when Emma's boys had been kidnapped—especially not in front of Emma. "I'll be back soon."

Twenty minutes later, Ben had secured an extra week of leave. More than that, the CO promised to put Ben into contact with the XO, Lieutenant Strong's wife, who was an FBI special agent. He thought Charlotte might have some good advice for Ben.

Thankful for his SEAL family, Ben left the CO's office with a lighter step. But then he spotted Tony Caruso in the supply closet and remembered how his fiancée had said Emma was a person of interest in a voice that insinuated guilt.

With a frown, Ben headed straight for Bambino. If anyone needed to paint a more sympathetic picture of Emma, it was the journalist Ruby Bonheur.

~

Hearing footfalls, Tony swiveled to see his chief and close friend Ben bearing down on him. "Harm, you're back."

"Not really. We need to talk." Ben's tone made it clear he wasn't going to kiss Tony on both cheeks today, a habit he'd acquired lately to harass him.

Tony tossed a box of bandages back on the shelf. "What's up?"

"Do you know where your fiancée is?"

"Er—sure." Tony thought back to their phone conversation this morning. "She's following a news story down in North Carolina. Some kids went missing, and the car they disappeared in was found in a river." He was disconcerted to see Ben's face harden. "Why?" What had Ruby done now?

"Those kids are the sons of Emma Stuart, who rents my old house. You met her at Mako's Labor Day party last year when her name was still Moulton."

Moulton. That nugget of information made Tony's stomach drop. "She's the one whose kids were taken?"

"Correct. And I just overheard your fiancée on the news describing Emma as a person of interest." Ben poked Tony in the chest with a firm finger. "I need you to call your woman and tell her never to say those words again. Got it?"

Tony felt his swarthy face blanch even as Ben's fairer complexion turned ruddy.

This was not the time to tell Ben that Tony never got involved in Ruby's business. She was the one with a nose for hunting down corruption, and he admired her doggedness when it came to cornering her quarry. "Sure."

"And while you're at it, you'd better explain to her that I am *not* Emma Stuart's lover, and if she tries to take that angle, I'll sue Channel Ten News for slander."

"Okay. Yeah, sure, I'll talk to her." Tony fell back on his more comfortable role of confidant. "Are you okay, Harm? You seem pretty stressed over this."

Ben just shot him an impatient glare. "You have no idea." Pivoting on his tennis shoes, he stalked away.

"Hey, where are you going?" Tony called as Ben headed for the exit.

"To find the thugs who took those boys."

Tony expelled a breath. Harm resembled a Tasmanian devil when he was worked up. He almost felt sorry for the bad guys.

CHAPTER 5

"*N*o!" Jerking awake, Emma found herself in an unfamiliar bed in a darkened room. Her heart hammered in the wake of her nightmare.

But then, it wasn't just a nightmare, was it? In her dream, her boys had been locked in a car that was sinking into a body of water. A vision of their three faces plastered to the rear window, crying for her help, had her kicking off the damp sheets in a panic. She couldn't afford to sleep. But where was she?

She glanced around. Oh yes, in Ben's room, in a bed with citrus-scented sheets that smelled like him.

Hearing voices, she slipped on her socks and wriggled her feet back into her Skechers. Ben was talking to someone at the door. She left his room and started down the floating staircase, her ears pricked to the discussion underway. Ben's living space was filled with golden sunlight that streamed through the west-facing windows as well as the open door where Ben stood, barring someone's entry.

Emma recognized the voice outside and froze. Sergeant Peyton! Was he here to arrest her?

"After what you did to Emma's house?" Ben's tone was incredulous. "You're gonna have to come up with a warrant for that, Sergeant."

"I'd be more worried 'bout how it looks *not* to let us look around."

"We've chatted long enough. Take yourself off my property and do something more productive, like finding Emma's boys."

"That's exactly what I'm doing, Mr. Harmony."

"*Chief* Harmony." Ben's hand tightened around the doorknob. "And from what I understand, the FBI has taken over the investigation."

"The FBI can't keep us local boys from doing our job. By the way, you can tell Miss Stuart that her car turned up, but her cell phone's gone."

Something had happened that Emma didn't know about. Her knees folded, causing her to sit abruptly near the top of the stairs.

Ben shut the door in Peyton's face, saying nothing. For a tense moment, he gripped the doorknob, his shoulders rising and falling as if deliberating whether to go after Peyton and thrash him soundly. In the sudden quiet, he spun around, his blue gaze rising to the top of the stairs. "How long have you been there?"

"Long enough. Where'd they find my car?" She tried to rise, but her legs were shaking so badly she could only stand with the help of the banister.

Ben shot up the stairs to help her. "I got you." He kept an arm around her while guiding her down the rest of the steps.

Mr. Silverman was gone. "Where was the car?" Ben's silence only fed her fear.

"Sit." He brought her to the same spot she'd occupied earlier and gently pushed her down before sitting once more on the coffee table, facing her. "They found the car in North Carolina in a state park. Someone drove it into the river."

Just like her dream. The room began to whirl. "The boys!" They were dead. She knew it.

"The boys weren't in it."

"They were in it?" The blood was roaring in her ears too loudly for her to hear.

"No! They were *not* in the car, Emma." He shook her gently to get her attention. "No one's found your boys yet."

At last, his words penetrated her despair, and Ben's handsome, worried face came abruptly into focus. *Alive! Not dead.* Emma burst into sobs of relief.

With a sound between a groan and a mutter, Ben moved to sit beside her, putting an arm around her and pulling her head to his shoulder. "It's okay, sweetheart."

But it wasn't okay to cry because her boys still needed her. Emma dragged in a breath and drew away from his embrace. Ben probably called all his women *sweetheart*.

"Let's go find them." With shaky fingers, she dashed the wetness from her face. "Let's go right now."

Ben seemed as eager to take off as she was, but then his lips firmed. "Might not look good for us to leave the area."

Frustration made Emma's chest hurt. "I don't care. I *have* to search for them, or I'll go crazy!"

"I get that, Emma. And that's exactly what we're going to do. But we don't even know where to start."

"We can start at that park where they found my car!"

"The FBI will have taken all evidence by the time we get there. What about Carl? Are you *sure* he didn't take them?"

She groaned with frustration. "I'm positive."

"How do you know that? He's the only one with a motive. Can you get a hold of him?"

"The police called his number already. They said it was disconnected. They even called the place where he used to drink every night. The owner said Carl's mama died of cancer this past winter. He got a job in Savannah, Georgia, and left but didn't leave a forwarding address."

"Don't you think that's odd?"

"Typical, if you ask me."

Ben's bright eyes narrowed. "What about the woman he ran off with, the cocktail waitress. Did she go with him?"

Emma shrugged elaborately. "I don't know." Nor did she care.

"Well, who would know?"

"Marty, I guess. He was her boss."

"Call him, then. Need me to look up the number?"

"Nope. I know it. I'll need to borrow your phone, though."

One second later, Emma was tapping out a number that brought to mind her miserable previous life. At least, back then, she'd had her sons with her. As the call went through, she put Ben's phone on speaker so he could hear.

Intrigued by this glimpse into Emma's past, Ben listened intently. Emma rarely talked about what she'd been through, dropping only crumbs of information from time to time. All he'd gleaned so far was she had been orphaned at twelve, lived with her granny for a while, and then wound up in foster care.

"Steamboat," said a male voice.

"Marty, it's Emma Moulton." Using her married name so as not to confuse the man, she said briskly, "I really need to find Carl. Did Tammy go with him when he went to Savannah?"

"Heck, I don't know. I don't keep track of all the waitresses."

"Well, does Faye know?"

"Hold on. Hey, Faye!" Marty's voice grew muffled as he relayed the question.

Marty finally spoke up. "Yeah, Faye says she left with Carl, and she's got a forwarding address. You got somethin' to write with?"

"Um..."

Ben took the phone from Emma's grasp, opened the map application, and sent her a nod.

"Go ahead."

As Marty supplied the address, Ben typed it in with dexterous thumb work before hitting the Directions button, which high-lighted the route to Savannah, Georgia.

"Thanks, Marty."

Hanging up for her, Ben showed Emma the map. "The way to Savannah takes you straight through North Carolina, where the car was dumped."

Uncertainty clouded her blue-gray eyes. "But why would Carl want the responsibility of three boys now when he never wanted it before? It makes no sense."

Ben thought a moment. "Maybe it was Tammy's idea."

Emma scoffed. "Why would she want someone else's kids?"

"Some do. I've heard of women kidnapping babies." He winced, immediately regretting his choice of words.

The heartbreak on her face as she pictured Carter was hard to witness.

"Sorry." Ben was about to embrace her again when his cell phone rang. The number was unknown to him but local, so he answered anyway. "Chief Harmony."

"Hi, Ben, this is Charlotte, Lucas's wife. Monty just called me and explained your situation."

"Yes, ma'am." He sent Emma a reassuring nod. "Thank you for calling."

"Is Emma's there with you?"

"Yes, ma'am. I'll put you on speaker so she can hear." He thumbed the button.

"Hi, Emma."

"Hi."

"I'm Charlotte. We met at Amos and Grace's surprise wedding last September. I'm the tall redhead with the even taller husband."

"I remember."

"So, I work for the FBI at the Norfolk Field Office, and I reached out to my colleague who's covering your case. Butler says he's been having trouble reaching you. Currently, he's at Medoc

Mountain State Park, where the car was found. He'll be back in Virginia Beach tomorrow and wants to talk to you then. Is this a number where you can be reached?"

Emma glanced at Ben, who nodded. "Yes."

Ben interrupted. "What if Emma and I went to Butler? We can't just sit here doing nothing. Plus, the law dogs here seem intent on pinning this on us."

Charlotte hesitated. "Well, tell you what. I'll ask Butler and get right back to you. Or I'll have him call you directly if you don't mind me passing on your number."

"No, that's fine. Thanks for calling, ma'am."

"Charlotte. I hate being called ma'am."

"Yes, ma'am—I mean, Charlotte. Thanks again." Ben hung up and set his phone aside.

Emma started to rise. "I need to go to my house and pack some clothes."

Ben pictured the mess awaiting her and tugged her back down. "No, you don't need to go there." He made a note to ask Amos if he and Grace might be willing to put the place back to rights. "I'll buy you something else to wear."

Emma's chin rose. "*I will.*"

"Listen." He smoothed a hand up and down her spine. "Just let me do something nice for you, just this once." Pity roughened his voice. "You deserve a little kindness, Emma. Just let me take care of you. It's no big deal."

Given her uncertain glance, she'd never been told she deserved a little kindness. Ben was about to kiss her smooth cheek when his cell phone rang a second time.

"Harmony."

"It's Charlotte again. I spoke to Greg Butler, and he says he's fine with you driving down to talk to him, as that would expedite matters. He told me to give you his number, as he wants you to call him on your way down."

"Go ahead." Ben added Greg Butler to his contacts, thanked

Charlotte, and then hung up before adding Charlotte to his contacts, too.

Emma had slipped off the couch and moved away to collect her purse—the only possession she still had with her besides her own socks and shoes. The need to alleviate her suffering rode Ben hard. If someone dared to suggest she had disposed of her sons, he might hurt that person.

Emma Stuart had been through enough, for heaven's sake.

Emma studied the Best Western motel near Medoc Mountain State Park while Ben circled the lot, searching for somewhere to park his car. FBI Special Agent Butler was expecting them this evening in his room at the only hotel adjacent to the park.

Ben cut the engine and looked over at her, his eyes reflecting the hotel's lit sign. "You ready?"

Emma pushed her door open by way of an answer and climbed out. Butler, she hoped, would help her find her boys, not waste time quizzing her like the local police had.

She was grateful for Ben's light hold on her elbow as he escorted her into the hotel, pausing to explain to the clerk where they were headed, then proceeding down the hall to Butler's room.

At Ben's brisk knock, the door popped open. Emma's hopes took a dive. The fortysomething agent with thinning brown hair and unremarkable features looked nothing like the superhero she was hoping he would be.

"Thanks for coming." Butler stepped back, inviting them in.

Sitting tensely on the end of the queen-sized bed, Emma was conscious of Ben's stalwart presence as he stood next to her.

"How was the drive?" The agent resumed his seat at the desk, where his laptop stood open, reading glasses placed to one side.

Ben shrugged. "Uneventful."

Butler flicked him an uneasy look as if wary of his muscular frame and grim expression. "So, I've spoken to Sergeant Peyton of the Virginia Beach police. He described your recollection of the abduction, Ms. Stuart. And let me first say that I'm very sorry you had to experience that."

Emma swallowed the lump in her throat. "What have you found here?" She didn't want his sympathy. She wanted answers.

Butler drew a breath, then admitted on a note of apology, "We only have a few leads. The river water, unfortunately, erased any fingerprints or DNA that might have been helpful in identifying the abductors. While drawing us to the right location, your phone vanished—probably tossed into the water, as well. A boy's shoe was found in the woods. Perhaps you could identify it for us?" He slipped on his glasses, opened a file on his laptop, and showed Emma a picture of Colton's red-striped tennis shoe, bagged and marked.

Ben put a hand on her shoulder as nausea roiled up, pushing tears into her eyes. "It's Colton's. We just bought those shoes at Payless. He liked the red stripe. Why—why do you think it fell off?"

Ben squeezed her shoulder reassuringly. "Knowing Colton, he was making a run for it."

Over the rim of his glasses, Butler met her panicked gaze. "The area was trampled, suggesting a tussle. Still, it's a good sign that the boys are alive."

Right. A good sign. Emma swallowed hard and nodded.

Butler sat back, taking off his glasses. "We also found a second set of tire tracks close to where the car went in. Of course, we've taken a cast of them to see what kind of vehicle we're talking about."

"It was a white van, with a double door in the back, inset with windows."

The agent grimaced. "Yes, I believe Sergeant Peyton gave me that description."

"Listen." Ben pulled out his cell phone and showed him Carl's address. "We managed to track down Emma's ex. I think you should pay him a visit."

Butler frowned at the address. "Sure. Why don't you forward that to me?" He waited for the information to arrive on his cell phone before dividing a curious look between them. "How long have you two known each other?"

As Emma stiffened at the renewed suggestion that she and Ben were lovers, Ben abruptly removed his hand from her shoulder.

"I've known Chief Harmony since last summer when I came out east from Mississippi. He leases a rental house to me."

"Then you're his tenant." Butler's eyebrows flexed. "And you're a Navy SEAL." His gaze flickered over Ben a second time.

"Yes, sir."

"And where were you the night the boys were kidnapped?" he asked Ben.

Emma took immediate offense. "Mr. Harmony had nothing to do with my boys' being taken!"

The agent regarded her mildly. "Perhaps Mr. Harmony would like to answer the question."

As Emma blushed at the reprimand, Ben stated tersely, "I was out of town with a friend."

Butler put his glasses back on, faced his laptop, and poised his fingers over the keys. "I'll need a name and a contact number."

With a set jaw and a frown, Ben lifted his phone again, accessed his contacts, and forwarded it to Butler, whose phone buzzed a second time.

Butler regarded the information, then glanced up at Ben. An unspoken message seemed to pass between them, rousing Emma's curiosity. Was Ben's friend a SEAL like himself? SEALs were private people. They did secretive things. That had to be why Ben couldn't say the name out loud.

As Butler typed himself a note on his laptop, Ben demanded, "When are you planning to question Emma's ex?"

"Soon." The agent tapped one more key, then lowered his hands to his lap. "Why don't you two get a room here for the night? We may have more questions for you in the morning."

"We'll think about it," Ben said before Emma could answer. He patted his flat stomach. "Right now, I think we'll catch a bite to eat. Thanks for talking to us." He thrust out a hand, forcing Butler to shake it.

The agent grimaced. "Good night, Ms. Stuart. We'll have information on those tire tracks by morning."

Emma frowned at him. What good would that do? She already knew what kind of vehicle the kidnappers drove. Dismayed by the lack of progress, Emma followed Ben mutely out the door. They'd driven all this way just to identify Colton's shoe. Shouldn't the FBI have found more clues than that?

As they crossed the parking lot, she was scarcely conscious of the fresh night air or the peeping of tree frogs. Ben opened her door, and she dropped into the passenger seat, grappling with conflicting urges to scream, weep, and throw something. Ben slipped behind the wheel and sat for a moment brooding.

"Something's not right," he stated.

She choked out a sound that was half sob, half hysteria. Without her boys, nothing would ever be right again.

"Butler isn't the least bit suspicious of Carl. I don't understand that." Ben shook his head.

"That's because I convinced Peyton that Carl didn't do it." Emma rubbed her burning eyes.

"You don't know that for sure. We have to, at least, check him out."

The trembling that had abated during their drive returned suddenly, putting a tremor in Emma's hands. She gritted her jaw against the cold tide enveloping her.

Ben was still reflecting on their meeting. "Butler sounded more suspicious of *me* than of Carl."

Emma dropped her hands. "He's paid to think of everything, Ben, that's all. You have an alibi, right?"

"Right." He turned his face away from her.

She almost asked him who he'd been with, but it was none of her business.

When Ben looked back at her, his jaw had hardened with resolve. "I think we should go to Savannah and find Carl ourselves."

The suggestion caught her off guard. "Do what?"

"Savannah's only five hours and fifteen minutes south of here."

"But Butler wanted us to stay here."

"More reason to leave." Ben reached for the ignition button, only to pause, waiting for her permission.

Emma gripped herself harder. It was so hard to *think* clearly, let alone listen for the still, small voice of God prompting her. "I can't decide."

Ben punched his ignition, making the decision for her. "We're going. We can grab some food along the way. If we find Carl and question him, would you know if he was lying?" He shot them backward before pulling away from the hotel.

Emma's upper lip curled. "Oh yes. He gets a tick in his cheek whenever he lies."

"Okay, then. We're going to find him and have a chat."

"But won't we get into trouble for going so far away?"

"Nah. We'll be back in Virginia by midday tomorrow. I'm sorry, Emma. But I can't just sit around while the authorities try to frame me—or the both of us."

Recalling Peyton's words to Ben earlier, she could see why he would feel uneasy. Besides, if the law was expending all its energy trying to frame Emma and Ben, then who was searching for her boys?

As they neared the interstate, Ben's hands tightened on the wheel of his car. "I'd like your permission before I take you farther south."

Emma drew a shaky breath. "I agree." The instant she made up her mind, the weight pressuring her chest eased, making room for hope.

"That's the spirit." Ben swerved, turning them sharply onto the southbound ramp.

Emma cast him a discreet glance. Ben had a way of making her feel special. She had better keep her guard up, or she'd fall under his spell.

An hour down the road, the country music on XM radio began to get to Emma. Song after song of heartbreak and loss kept her in a state of despair. "Can we please change the station?"

"'Course, sweetheart. What do you want to listen to?"

Sweetheart again. "I need Christian music. Contemporary Christian."

"All right." He toggled a button on his steering wheel, allowing him to scroll through dozens of options, all named on his display, according to genre. "Here we go. This one's called The Message. This okay?"

Emma heaved a sigh at the familiar words sung by Kari Jobe. She wasn't alone. God would go before her; He would never forsake her.

Eyes sinking shut, Emma lost herself in the lyrics. Bit by bit, the certainty that she was loved and protected grew stronger. Had God ever failed her in the past? He had not. Nor would He desert her now. Even in this terrible circumstance, she could rely on Him to comfort and strengthen her.

Thank You, Lord, for Your abiding presence.

Three hundred and sixty miles away, in his office at CyWatch, located outside of Washington, D.C., the executive assistant director of the Criminal, Cyber, Response and Services Branch, Steven Sauers, pulled up the report by Special Agent Butler and frowned. The plot hatched by Jared Jones, high consul of the Centurion Cohort, left a bad taste in his mouth.

Steven had been a follower of Jones's father in the 1970s and a mere legionnaire in The Cohort when he'd gone off to the FBI Academy. Thanks to the lessons of diligence taught to him by Henry Jones, Steven had steadily climbed the ranks in the Bureau. Now, as executive assistant director of the CCRSB, he protected the younger Jones from on high.

Steven's own passage through the Cohort had come long before the advent of computers. Thus, while Steven knew all about Jared's illicit dealings, the Centurion leader knew Steven only by his moniker, The Architect. In return for substantial deposits in his Swiss bank account, Steven kept Jones's money laundering, extortions, and embezzling from coming to light.

Abducting three young boys from Virginia was a deviation for Jones, who stuck strictly to white-collar crimes. He wanted Steven to make it look like the mother's boyfriend had killed off her boys.

If the man were something other than a Navy SEAL, Steven wouldn't think twice about crafting the evidence needed to frame him. But this man wasn't just a SEAL; he was a sniper with the elite SEAL Team Six. God help Steven should Ben Harmony ever uncover his role in ruining his life.

Then again, how would he ever find out? Not even Jared Jones knew who The Architect was.

With that pep talk, Steven Sauers squelched his doubts and pondered the steps necessary to implicate the fall guy.

CHAPTER 6

The songs on XM radio's The Message were a balm to Emma's soul. What a relief to lean on God's protection. Not only was He perfectly aware of the evil that had happened to her sons, but He was going *before* her, clearing the path to find them. This wouldn't end up as some senseless tragedy. If anything, God would use this awful circumstance to bring about something good. She was *sure* of it!

The music cut off abruptly. Emma lurched from her meditations, her eyes flying open. "What'd you do that for?"

The light from Ben's dashboard showed him frowning. "The music's upsetting you."

She hastily wiped her cheeks, only then aware that she'd been crying. "No, it's helping me. Please, don't turn it off."

Ben went from handing her a napkin to turning the radio back on, though he kept the volume down.

Emma searched for the clock on his display. It was after midnight. "Are we close?"

"Just ten more minutes."

She drew a centered breath. "We're going to find them, Ben. I just know it."

His blue eyes darted curiously in her direction.

Did Ben ever rely on faith to get through? "Are you familiar with Romans 8:28?" She quoted the New Revised Standard version for him. "'We know that all things work together for good for those who love God, who are called according to His purpose.'"

Ben's silence spoke for him.

"You don't think that's true?" Disappointment tugged at her.

He shrugged. "I've seen a lot of evil, Em, and from what I can tell," his tone darkened, "God needs a little help to make things 'work together for good.' Know what I mean?"

She searched herself. "God's never needed my help, but I've sure needed His. Like when you showed up after my car broke down on the side of the highway. That was a God-thing."

"Hmm. Well, you deserve help. You're a good woman, Em."

"Bein' good has nothing to do with it."

He sent her a quizzical smile. "You seem a lot better. I'm glad about that."

"I *am* better." She embraced the feeling now sustaining her. "We're going to find them." She nodded several times. "This was the right thing to do."

"I'm glad you agree."

"Not that I think Carl took them, but maybe he knows something," she clarified.

"Guess we'll find out. Here comes the bridge that takes us over to Savannah."

Lit by a full moon peeking through luminous clouds, the Talmage Memorial Bridge rose like a four-masted sailing vessel spanning the Savannah River. As they crested its height, Emma spotted a dozen old cotton warehouses lining the waterfront below. She could tell from the glimmering lights and gleaming paving stones that the buildings had been converted into upscale boutiques and restaurants.

Coming down off the bridge into Savannah, they drove under the boughs of centuries-old live oak trees, all dripping with Spanish moss. Intermittent gas lamps cast a romantic glow on the Colonial and Victorian structures vying for preeminence around grassy squares. Quaint and mismatched, the buildings had just one thing in common: They'd all been built high above the ground to avoid being flooded. The word that came to Emma's mind was decadent.

"This place is lovely." Emma couldn't begin to picture Carl here.

Ben was busy following the prompts on his car's navigation pane. He turned right down a street called East York and traveled several more blocks. The buildings around them grew less lavish and more run-down. At last, he slowed before a sprawling clap-board Victorian dwelling.

"This is it."

The only light in the house's darkened windows was a neon sign blinking in a first-floor window near a side entrance.

"Vacancy," Emma read. Apparently, Carl and Tammy rented a room.

Ben cut the motor. "Let's talk about this." Leaning over Emma's knees, he popped open the glove compartment.

Her mouth went dry as he drew both a holster and a wicked-looking handgun.

He pulled back the slide, checking for rounds. "How about I talk to Carl first?"

"No, I should do it."

Ben frowned at her decision but shrugged. "Stay put for a sec." He pushed out of the car to strap the holster around his lean waist. With his T-shirt untucked, she couldn't even tell he was armed as he walked around the front bumper to pull her door open.

Joining Ben on the curb, Emma caught him scanning the dark urban block before taking her arm. At one o'clock in the morning, they were the only ones on the streets, their footfalls inordinately loud as they coursed a crumbling cement walkway toward the entrance.

Emma wouldn't have dreamed of waking people up if it weren't for her sons' kidnapping. She gave the old door with glass panes a tentative knock. When no one answered, Ben reached past her and rapped his knuckles firmly enough to make the panes shudder.

Almost immediately, a light blinked on in the upstairs windows. Someone thumped down the stairs, calling loudly, "That better not be you, Carl."

Recognizing Tammy's high-pitched voice, Emma steeled herself to face the woman who'd stolen her ex.

The curtain covering the windowpanes parted. Tammy, with her hair still dyed bloodred, peeked out of it, then blinked in surprise. She immediately unlocked the door and cracked it just a few inches. "Emma, what're you doin' here?" Her eyes widened as she took in Ben, hovering protectively close.

"I need to find Carl. Shouldn't he be here with you?"

Tammy made a face. "That bum had better not show up here again. I kicked him out five months ago for not helping with the rent. He used to come by looking for some affection," she rolled her eyes, "but hasn't been by lately." Leaning toward Emma, she pitched her voice lower. "Who's your friend?"

Emma ignored the question. "Listen, I really need to talk to him. Does he have a phone number?"

Tammy shrugged like she could care less. "Well, if he does, I don't know it. Couldn't tell you where he is—probably living on the streets since he can't seem to keep a job." Curiosity sharpened her gaze. "Is he in trouble for something?"

Despair tugged at Emma as she weighed whether to tell Tammy. "Someone kidnapped my boys. All three of them." She still couldn't believe the words she was saying.

The woman's mouth fell open. "Oh, my Lord, you poor thing!" Opening the door wide, she stepped across the threshold and threw her arms around her.

Emma's opinion of the woman shifted as she accepted her heartfelt hug.

But then Tammy pulled back, her expression incredulous. "You think *Carl* had something to do with it?" She cackled at the mere idea, only to sober at the recollection of Emma's plight. "Oh, you must be sick to death, hon. What can I do?"

Unable to think of anything, Emma glanced back at Ben, who stepped closer, causing the wooden stoop to wobble. "Would you happen to have a picture of Carl lying around, ma'am?"

Tammy scoffed, but then she caught herself. "Now, wait just a minute. I do have a box of personal stuff, which he left behind. It's full of old pictures. Why don't y'all come up?" With a decisive nod, she stepped back to admit them.

Tammy had let them take the box.

Though it was 2:00 A.M., Emma pawed through it while sitting cross-legged on the floor of their hotel room at the Holiday Inn Express, right in the historic district. Carl's I-LOVE-ME box was all too familiar. Filled with memorabilia from his glory days as the all-star high school quarterback, everything in it brought back Emma's painful past.

There were plaques, certificates, newspaper clippings, and letters from potential colleges. And there were photos of Carl from elementary school through high school. What was *not* in the box was a single suggestion of Carl's romance with a high school sophomore, a girl who'd naively worshiped him.

"I guess he was pretty good at football." Ben emerged from the bathroom smelling of fresh lemons and dressed in a T-shirt and sleep shorts. Lowering himself next to her, he inspected the trophies she had set aside to get to the photos underneath.

"Guess he was." Ben's clean scent was a fresh contrast to the essence of the stale cologne Carl used to douse himself in before going out to drink. She held up a picture of Carl looking young and athletic, his hair sun-bleached, a big cocky smile on his face. "He got a full-ride scholarship to Mississippi State."

"Really? Why didn't he take it?"

"He had to marry me instead." Allegedly, she had ruined his life because she'd let him seduce her. Carl's grandparents, who'd helped his single mother raise him, had insisted Carl do right by her or else face being cut out of their family business—one that had folded anyway. Every day of Emma's eleven-year marriage, Carl had reminded her that she'd robbed him of his future.

Why would a man that resentful of the past want to be stuck with three little reminders?

"There aren't even pictures of my boys in here." In disgust, Emma tossed Carl's birth certificate back into the box. The dust rising from it made her nose itch. "He didn't take them." Despair hit her hard. They'd reached a dead end already when, just an hour earlier, she'd been sure God was pointing them in the right direction.

Ben stifled a yawn. "We don't know that, Em. But Tammy thinks he's pretty hard up right now, which means he might do anything for money."

Compared to Ben, who looked squeaky clean, Emma was suddenly conscious of how bedraggled she had to look, still wearing Grace's red sundress, her hair a mess, her skin scabbed and grubby.

"How would his boys bring him any money?" Rising painstakingly to her feet, she discovered she was so exhausted that all she wanted to do was to fall into bed and seek oblivion. "I need to shower."

Ben sprang to his feet, catching her as she weaved on her feet. "Easy, there. You good?"

She would never be good again, not if her boys weren't found.

"Listen." Ben must have sensed her growing devastation. "Don't give up on Carl yet. I still think we're on to something. His circumstances have changed, right? We don't know what they are, but they could have prompted him to steal his kids."

The confidence in Ben's eyes was like a life-giving elixir.

"We've got pictures now." He glanced at the box. "And after we sleep some, we'll hit up every homeless shelter in Savannah and ask who might have seen Carl. Sound like a plan?"

"Sure." She managed a weak smile for him.

"That's my girl."

My girl. Emma stood there a moment, warmed by his words but knowing he hadn't meant to say them. His idea of inquiring at homeless shelters was a shot in the dark.

Carl didn't have her boys. Someone else did. Helpless tears filled her eyes.

Ben noted them with a grimace. "Now, what would Colton say if he saw you crying? He'd say, 'Mama, stop that wastin' water and get busy findin' us.'"

Ben's imitation of Colton's Mississippi drawl pulled a reluctant laugh from her.

He chucked her chin. "That's better. Now go and take your shower. Turn out the lights when you come out. I'll sleep in this bed." He nudged her toward the bathroom door.

As Emma locked herself in the bathroom and flipped on the fan, Ben's cell phone vibrated. Butler was calling him. He walked across the room before answering. "Chief Harmony."

"Butler here. May I ask where you are?"

Given that the FBI special agent was calling him at two thirty in the morning, he had to know exactly where they were. "We drove down to Savannah."

"Trying to do my job, Mr. Harmony?"

"Figured we'd save you the trouble."

"Have you found Mr. Moulton yet?"

"We just got here."

"It doesn't look good for the two of you to take off together."

Ben responded to the agent's insinuation with stark silence, followed by a cold question. "Have you checked out my alibi yet?"

"We're working on that. Miss Hughes isn't answering her phone. I'm sure she'll call us back when she checks her voice mail."

"So, until then, I'm considered a suspect?"

"Person of interest, Mr. Harmony." Butler's light tone gave nothing away. "Look, I'll give you forty-eight hours down there. After that, you need to return to Virginia or risk being slapped with a grand jury subpoena and an obstruction warrant."

The man couldn't be too suspicious, or he would order them home right now. "Forty-eight hours," Ben agreed. Battles had been won and lost in less time.

"If you find Mr. Moulton, make sure you contact me before approaching him. Let us do our job."

"Gladly. You should've been down here days ago."

"We have procedures, Mr. Harmony."

Annoyed with the man's excuses, Ben ended the call with a jab of his finger. He checked his texts. He'd missed an update from Reno.

I have news: One of Emma's neighbors told the police a van was parked in front of his property two nights in a row prior to the kidnapping. He didn't get plates, but the description of the van matches the one Emma gave. That ought to take some suspicion off her.

Ben frowned. The news wasn't all good. A white van being sighted days in advance of the kidnapping suggested a well-planned abduction. And, according to Emma, Carl couldn't have tied his own shoelaces without making knots. That meant there was a larger entity at work. If they didn't discover what it was—and soon—Emma might never see her boys again.

Dale Robbins, a graduate of The Centurion Academy for Boys in Savannah and special agent with the Cybercrimes Division of the FBI, answered a call at his cubicle at nine the following morning.

"Dale Robbins."

"What song does the mockingbird sing?"

Dale's heart pumped faster. It was the question he'd been told to expect at any time over the course of his life without ever knowing the day or the hour. For a terrible second, he couldn't remember the answer, but then it came to him. "Whatever song he wants."

"The high consul has need of your services."

An image of the high consul sprang to mind. Stern and imposing, with dark eyes that demanded loyalty, the man's portrait hung in Dale's meeting hall in a suburb of Washington D.C.

"Of course." At last, he had a chance to repay the Cohort for giving him a leg up all those years ago. "What can I do?"

"You'll need secure administrative access to a college email account."

That sounded simple enough. "Um, sure. Which college, and what's the name of the student?" With trembling fingers, Dale scribbled the reply on the back of a gum wrapper.

"You have twenty-four hours before you'll hear from me again."

As the line went dead, Dale glanced surreptitiously at his colleagues while lowering his phone into the receiver. Everyone was busy in their cubicles. No one was watching him. With a secretive smile, he went straight to work, carrying out the caller's wishes. What a privilege it was to be a Centurion, doing good things for people without them ever knowing!

CHAPTER 7

*E*mma dropped into the passenger seat of Ben's car, despondent by their lack of progress. Why was finding Carl so hard? It was late afternoon already. They had visited two of the city's three homeless shelters, canvassing dozens of individuals and dispersing photos of Carl they'd photocopied in the hotel office. Not one single person claimed to have recognized him.

As Ben started the engine and pulled away from the curb, the sun-warmed interior lulled Emma into closing her heavy eyes.

The apathy they'd encountered at the homeless shelters, the smell of unwashed bodies, and the repeated negative responses were like spikes driven deep into her heart. Why had God encouraged her to come here if there was nothing to see?

With the sun still high in the sky and with plenty of time to visit the third and last shelter, Emma yielded to the weight of her eyelids. She would nap on the way to the last shelter in the hopes of refueling her energy. The throb of Ben's engine lulled her into dozing.

"Hey." Ben shook her awake several minutes later. "We're at the hotel. You want to walk, or should I carry you in?"

"What?" Rousing but still sluggish, Emma recognized the dim interior of the hotel's parking garage. "Why are we here?"

"You need to rest, Em. We can visit the third shelter later or even tomorrow."

"No." But even she could hear the exhaustion making her voice scratchy.

"Come on." Ben took off his seat belt. "We'll get there. Trust me, right now, you need to sleep." He rounded the car, collected her on the other side, and led her, nearly catatonic, to their fourth-floor hotel room.

Trust me, he'd said. For the first time since Carl had shattered her trust, Emma was tempted. But why Ben? If anyone was going to repeat the lesson Carl had taught her, it was the playboy SEAL.

When he opened their door, she crossed straight to the bed, wearing the same dress she'd worn for two days. With just enough strength to kick off her Skechers, she crawled wordlessly under the covers and went still.

"I'll wake you in a couple of hours." The lights went out, the door clicked shut, and Emma succumbed immediately to sleep.

Ben didn't have the heart to wake her two hours later. He'd driven to the closest Target, where he'd picked out some clothing for her: a lavender-colored sleep shirt, two pairs of shorts, two short-sleeved blouses, a pack of practical cotton ladies' underwear since he couldn't picture Emma wearing anything less than sensible, and a pack of bootie socks like the pair she wore with her Skechers.

Shopping for women wasn't new to him. He could tell Emma's size, more or less, by how she'd felt in his arms on the few occasions he'd held her.

By the time he returned to their hotel room, the sun was setting, filling the room with gentle shadows. Emma didn't so much as stir as he let himself inside and laid his purchases on the other half of her bed.

Settling into the armchair, he stuck an earbud in one ear and found a recording on his cell phone of the Virginia Beach local news. He fast-forwarded through WAVY TV 10's recorded program, halting when he recognized Ruby Bonheur standing in front of the police station in a jade-green dress with golden hoop earrings. Not again.

"...DNA testing on a single boy's sneaker confirms it belonged to eight-year-old Colton Moulton. According to Virginia Beach police, his mother, Emma Stuart, has left the state with Navy SEAL Ben Harmony, allegedly to look for her sons, though police were quick to point out that the couple are considered persons of interest in the boys' disappearance. This is Ruby—"

Stifling a curse, Ben shot to his feet and paced the length of the room. Had Tony not spoken to his fiancée about her pejorative language? Ruby had used the word *couple* to describe Emma and him like they were lovers, which merely fed into Peyton's conspiracy theory.

Ben firmed his lips as he texted Tony. *Tell your woman to stop playing into the hands of the police, or I'll tell her myself!*

Simmering, he put his phone away. Thank goodness Emma had no way of looking up the news stories from back home.

Ben's stomach growled in the quiet room. The last time he'd eaten was at a drive-through five hours earlier. Moving to stand over Emma, he started to wake her up, only to stare in appreciation at her shadowed face.

With her features relaxed, she looked as young as she really was, only twenty-seven, four years his junior. Her eyelashes, as thick as her mane of golden-brown hair, feathered her cheeks. The peaceful rise and fall of her shoulders told him her sleep was undisturbed by dreams, which was exactly what she needed.

He swiveled toward the desk, turned up a notepad and a pen,

and scribbled, *Gone to catch a bite. I'll bring back some grub for you. STAY PUT.* He underlined the last sentence three times, then added his phone number just in case she wanted to call him using the room phone.

Pausing at the dresser, he took his sidearm from the drawer and pushed it back into his holster. Georgia had a reciprocal concealed-carry agreement with Virginia, so he had every right to carry it.

The flyers they'd distributed at the shelters were still in the car, so he helped himself to the original photo and slipped it into his wallet. Then, he grabbed his card key and quietly left the room.

Their hotel was just two blocks from the Savannah Riverfront. Following his nose toward the aromas wafting from the waterside restaurants, Ben soon found himself on River Street. Blues music floated out of a pub called Isaac's, along with a pungent bouquet of grilled grouper, steak, and fries.

Entering the dimly lit pub, Ben noted the exits while helping himself to the only empty stool at the bar. Next, he studied the clientele, classifying them as either yuppies fresh from the office, laborers in their work wear, or tourists.

"What can I get you?" The middle-aged bartender—or maybe he was Isaac himself—eyed Ben suspiciously.

"I'll take a Bud Light, an order of the grouper special, and a second order to go."

"You got it."

Twelve minutes later, Ben was demolishing his dinner while Emma's food sat in a brown bag by his plate. Ignoring the come-hither looks of the pretty blonde strumming her guitar on the stage by the front window, he concentrated on cleaning his plate. Then he paid his tab, picked up the to-go bag for Emma, and went to show his picture of Carl to the other patrons.

"Excuse me. I'm looking for this man." He held out the photo at one booth, then the next. Patrons eyed him with varying degrees of wariness. "Any chance you've seen him?"

One older man came right out and asked, "You a cop?"

"Nope, just looking for an old friend."

"Sorry, haven't seen him."

Ben moved on. Making his way toward the rear of the pub, he arrived at a booth occupied by two middle-aged men, both of whom struck him as prison rough. Their navy-blue coveralls suggested they worked together. One was small and wiry with a thick black mustache reminiscent of Charlie Chaplin's. The other was corpulent and unwashed, with a thick gold ring glinting on his pinkie.

Ben knew trouble when he saw it. He even knew when the words *escape* and *evade* were apropos. He just couldn't resist dipping in a toe to test the waters. "Hi."

The men lifted incredulous expressions at him.

"I'm looking for a friend." Ben laid the photo between them so they could both see it. "You seen him anywhere?"

"Nope." Charlie Chaplin didn't even look at Carl's picture.

But his partner's curiosity got the better of him. Ben caught the flicker of recognition as Ring Man angled his thick head, though he quickly concealed it.

An awkward silence fell over the table.

"Maybe you need more time." Ben gestured toward the restrooms. "I'll go use the head." He left the photo on the table as he moved away, ducking into the two-stall restroom with his blood thrumming. Wouldn't it beat all if these guys could point him in Carl's direction?

Of course, they might need a little persuasion first. He checked his gun and returned it to his holster. With a breath of resolve, he left the restroom.

Only the men were gone.

As Amos would say, dag nab it! They'd even taken the photo with them.

Clasping Emma's to-go bag in his left hand, Ben headed briskly for the exit.

"Where you goin', big guy?" purred the singer on his way out.

He pretended not to hear her. The thugs couldn't have gotten that far, plus the street was a better place to question them.

Pausing on the curb, Ben looked around. Night had fallen, and plenty of young people were enjoying the mild weather, strolling alongside the street paved with ballast stones from the colonial-era ships that used to dock here.

Deciding his targets would have wanted to disappear quickly, Ben turned inland onto a street so narrow it was basically an alley, wide enough for a wagon or a small car to cut between two warehouses. Hadn't taken ten steps before a silhouette sprang out of the shadows, swinging a two-by-four.

As it made stunning contact with Ben's head, he staggered but refused to fall. Two pairs of rough hands grabbed hold of him and dragged him farther up the alley, where they flung him against the wall of a warehouse. Emma's to-go bag slipped from Ben's hand as the fat man plowed a fist into his stomach, driving the air from his lungs.

"Who are you?" The smaller man stood back, watching as Ben doubled over.

He sucked in a painful breath. "Friend of Carl's. We went to high school together."

"Oh, yeah? Hit him again, Grimes."

Ben spun, and the fat man's fist hit the wall. Howling, he whirled away to shake his bruised knuckles. By the time he looked up again, Ben had whipped out his Glock and pointed it at Charlie Chaplin, then at Grimes, whose name Chaplin had stupidly let slip. "Your turn." He made a show of releasing the safety. "Tell me where Carl is."

With genuine bravado—or was it stupidity?—the littler man told him to burn for eternity in the netherworld.

"That's not the way it works." Ben lunged at Chaplin, grasped him by his coveralls, and whipped him back to front against his chest. With an arm locked around his neck, he pressed his Glock to the man's temple. "This is how it works." He addressed the fat man. "Tell me where to find Carl, Grimes, or I shoot your buddy's brains out and drop his body in the gutter." Man, he was glad Emma wasn't here to hear him.

Grimes gaped, looking to his companion for direction. But then he focused on something over Ben's shoulder, and a smile of relief split his broad face. "Cops are comin'."

A siren chirped on the heels of Grimes's observation. Blue light strafed the wall in front of Ben, who cursed his luck. How'd the cops get here so fast? "Tell me where Carl is." He gouged Chaplin's temple harder.

"Don't tell him anything!" the little man said with bravado. "He ain't gonna shoot me. Not with the cops this close."

He was right, of course.

With a mutter of annoyance, Ben peered farther up the alley, happy to see that it led to a space between the back of the warehouses and the floodwall. Thrusting Charlie Chaplin at his fat companion, he bolted toward it, spotting a run of concrete steps that led to the top of the wall. As he darted up them, he remembered that he'd dropped Emma's dinner against the wall.

Shoot! Emma would wake up hungry, and that grouper was delicious.

I'll just go back for it. Arriving on a walkway, which his phone informed him was called East Factors Walk, Ben joined a knot of pedestrians in trooping toward the access stairs he'd descended earlier that evening before he knew about the shortcut he'd just taken.

As he neared Isaac's Pub, his gaze locked on the squad car with its front end stuck inside the alleyway. There stood Grimes and Chaplin, chatting up two policemen. Ben ducked into the doorway of a closed store and watched them.

For several minutes, all they did was converse, exchanging pleasantries like they knew each other. Grimes laughed, clearly at ease with the lawmen. *Huh.* Ben would have sworn both men would be the type to avoid policemen.

Finally, the officers got back into their car, and Carl's two acquaintances walked off toward the far east end of River. Ben was tempted to follow them, but Emma had to be awake and hungry by now.

Ducking back into the alley, he recovered the bag he'd dropped and continued toward the floodwall, climbing the handy steps back up to East Factors Walk.

As he covered the two blocks back to their hotel, Ben mulled over the encounter. The good news was the thugs knew Carl, which meant the man was somewhere in Savannah. Bad news was the police were now on the lookout for Ben, probably having received a detailed description of him. Time to start wearing his baseball cap.

When he let himself into the hotel room, he found it steeped in darkness. The light spilling in from the hallway showed Emma wide awake, sitting up in bed with her back to the headboard, cradling a pillow in her arms.

The desolation on her face hit Ben like a punch in the gut. "Hey, you're up." He flicked on the lights, then felt bad for it when she flinched and covered her eyes.

"Sorry. I thought you would call me." He wished he could crawl onto the bed and comfort her.

She dropped her hands from her red-rimmed eyes and blinked at him. "What happened to your head?"

He touched the tender spot above his eyebrow. "I came across some guys who recognized Carl's photo."

His words transformed her expression, bringing hope to her dull eyes. "What did they say?" She set aside the pillow and threw back her covers.

Putting her to-go bag on the dresser, Ben took his time choosing how to answer while divesting himself of his holster and sidearm.

"And why did they hit you?"

With a grimace, he faced her. "They didn't confess to knowing Carl. I just saw it in their faces. So I followed them out of the bar, and they lured me into an alley, thinking they could beat me up."

She gasped. "They beat you up?"

At least she sounded incredulous. He folded his arms across his chest. "No. But then the cops showed up, so I decided to leave. Later, I circled back, and they were talking all chummy-like with the police." He shook his head. "Something's not right about that."

He could see her drawing her own conclusions, ones that would send her plunging toward despair again. To keep that from happening, he added, "The good news is, those men know Carl. We'll probably find him at the third shelter tomorrow."

"What did those men look like?"

Only Grimes bore some resemblance to the composite sketches he'd seen on TV, but it was too much to assume that just because he was fat, he was one of them. "One was big and beefy and went by the name Grimes. The other was small with a thick, dark mustache."

"Oh." She looked down at the end of the bed.

He could feel her sorrow from across the room. "I brought you some dinner—grilled grouper with a side of coleslaw and fries. You might want to warm it up first. There's a microwave right here."

"Thank you." Given her flat tone, she still had no appetite. Belatedly, she stretched a hand toward the clothing she'd taken out of the Target bags. "And thank you for these clothes. They're perfect. I'll pay you back—"

"They're a gift." Her pride really irked him at times. "You should eat while the food's still fresh. I'm going to take a shower."

He spent ten minutes in the bathroom, scrubbing the day's grime away with a washcloth and a bar of his own soap—for sensitive skin. As he toweled himself dry, he eyed himself sternly in the mirror.

Emma's vulnerability made him want to hold her. *Just behave yourself,* he ordered his reflection.

When he emerged in his sleep shirt and shorts, he was glad to see her seated at the desk, scraping the last bite of food into her mouth. "How was it?"

"Good."

She tried so hard to sound enthusiastic, but he could tell she'd only eaten it to keep from wasting his money.

He crossed to the bed he'd slept in the previous night, giving in to an enormous yawn. "You're probably not tired after napping, but I'm bushed. We'll get up early tomorrow and find Carl."

Keeping her face averted, she bagged the empty to-go cartons, tying off the bag to contain any odors. Even running on autopilot, she was tidy and thoughtful. Honestly, Ben couldn't think of anything about Emma—apart from her stubbornness—that he didn't like, though her faith in God was over-the-top at times. Believing everything would work out for the best was just naïve. Not that he would tell her that. He wanted her clinging to hope for as long as possible. But in the end, the truth was going to break her.

As Emma disappeared into the bathroom, Ben slipped under the covers and switched off the lamp at the base. As he lay back against the pillows, closing his eyes, he pictured Shawn, his Irish twin. There wasn't a day that went by that he didn't think of him or miss him. That was how Emma felt—times three.

An ache filled his chest. He wasn't big on trusting God, but this current crisis was more than he could fix by himself, giving rise to a prayer. *You there, God? You know, Emma is relying on You to come through. So maybe You could keep Your promise and work all things together for her good. That's what I would do if I were You. Just saying. Amen.*

～

Awakened by the jangling of his desk phone in his adjoining office, Jared Jones shot to an elbow and glanced at his bedside clock. Just past midnight. He got out of bed and waded through moonlight into the adjacent room to snatch up the receiver. "What is it?"

"What song does the mockingbird sing?"

Picturing the small Charlie Chaplin look-alike whose voice he recognized, Jared gave the expected reply, adding, "You'd better have good reason for waking me up at this hour, Bates."

"Yes, sir. To get right to it, there's a stranger in town looking for your man, Carl."

Carl? Jared stiffened. "Did he say what he wants?"

"Wants to talk to him, I guess. He said he went to school with Carl, but I'm not buying it. They don't talk the same."

"I don't pay you to speculate, Bates. What's this stranger look like?"

"Like a mercenary or a wrestler. He's bald and built like a line-backer but quick on his feet."

Jared searched his memory. The only player in this intricate scheme who fit Bates's description was the fall guy. "Await my orders. Let me find out who the man is."

"Yes, sir." Bates hung up, sounding disappointed.

Drawing upon his faultless memory, Jared tapped out The Architect's number. It irked him to no end that he couldn't identify the man by his given name.

The Architect answered groggily, sounding a decade older than Jared. "Hello."

He bypassed the cipher phrase to demand, "Are you aware that the boyfriend is making inquiries down here?"

"Why? Has he caused some kind of trouble?"

So he *was* aware. "Not exactly. He's asking questions of my employees. I fail to understand why he's down here."

"I promise you, Consul, a warrant for his arrest is impending."

Mollified by the man's efficiency, Jones muttered, "If the SEAL becomes a problem, I'll take care of him myself."

"Oh, he won't." The Architect sounded utterly certain. "He'll be out of the picture completely within a week."

"Good." Those were exactly the words Jared wanted to hear. After hanging up, he exhaled deeply. The Architect was entirely loyal to him, and together, they were unstoppable.

CHAPTER 8

$\mathcal{M}$iles Ellis carried his backpack wherever he went since it concealed his work phone, ID, and listening devices. As he hustled toward the shelter for brunch, the hot May sun summoned a layer of sweat beneath his shirt and his jiggling backpack.

He could see the Centurion Men's Shelter on the corner straight ahead of him, a nineteenth-century, fortress-like structure built in the Romanesque style with a rough brick façade, steeply pitched roof, and heavy, half-rounded arches over every window. Two stone griffins guarded the gate that led into the walled enclosure and to the shelter's front door.

Since seven o'clock that morning, Miles had sat under the shade trees in Troup Square, two blocks from the shelter, listening to a man in the Civil War cap play his saxophone while mulling over his options. There weren't many left.

Yes, living at the shelter had gotten him one foot in the world of the Centurion Cohort, but for him to find evidence incriminating to its leader, he would have to slog his way through the ranks, and that took time—lots and lots of time—which the Criminal Investigative Division, or CID, was unwilling to invest.

They urged him to find informants, instead, to befriend men close to Jones, like his shifty-eyed gardener, Carl Moulton, who attended every one of Jared Jones's meetings and was already a princeps prior. He'd become an apparent favorite of High Consul Jones, and, for the life of him, Miles could not see why.

Maybe Carl Moulton would make a good informant. But Miles would much rather cozy up to McKenzie, whose sleek creamy-colored Acura was parked outside the shelter in its reserved spot along the curb. Problem was, McKenzie had avoided him since their talk the week before. He could only assume his supposed drug addiction and immaturity had dissuaded her from getting to know him better. Then again, her soul-numbing obligations to both her father and her ailing mother were enough to keep anyone preoccupied.

Regardless, Miles had been warned by the section chief—namely, his father, who reported directly to the CID's assistant director—that time was running out. Unless he made substantive progress within a week's time, he'd be pulled from this assignment and given another one, the setting of which would likely be another urban high school. The opportunity to expose corruption within the Centurion Cohort would be lost, at least to him.

The rumble of what sounded like a 5-liter V8 motor pulled Miles from his introspection. He looked over to see a canary-yellow Mustang GT glide into a parking space not far behind McKenzie's car. The engine died, and an impressive man, about six feet tall and wearing a Chicago Bears ball cap, got out and rounded the car to help his companion out.

Miles slowed his step. This was no ordinary man. Every defined muscle in his body and the way he carried himself screamed special operator. Did Soldier Boy here work for Jared Jones?

The woman was nothing unusual, as far as Miles could tell.

Young and sweet-faced, both her head of disheveled light-brown hair and her pained expression signaled a personal hardship. But why would she be coming to a men's-only shelter? Perhaps to volunteer?

Wanting to know more, he picked up his pace so he would overtake the pair. "Dude, nice car."

Blue eyes flickered over Miles as he took the woman's arm. "Thanks."

"You, uh, you lookin' for someone?" Miles jerked his head at the shelter.

Soldier Boy inspected him more closely. "What makes you say that?"

"Well, this parking space is for deliveries to the shelter. I assume that's where you're headed."

Rather than answering him, the stranger took a flyer from the few that the woman was holding and passed it to him. "Have you seen this man?"

Startled to recognize Carl Moulton, Miles kept his expression neutral. "I'm not sure." Until he knew what the game was, he would play his cards close to the vest.

"You're not sure."

"Nope." Miles handed back the flyer with a shrug. "I've seen a lot of guys come and go."

"Uh-huh." The stranger wasn't buying it.

"You might want to talk to Miss Jones, though." Miles nodded at the open gate. "She kind of runs the place."

"Thanks." Drawing his companion with him, Soldier Boy headed that way.

Miles pretended to admire the car a minute longer, though not so long that he would miss McKenzie's response to the couple's inquiry. Would she admit to knowing Carl Moulton, or would she protect her father's privacy?

〜

From her vantage at the head of the buffet line, McKenzie took immediate note of the couple's entrance. So did the homeless men who'd convened for brunch. Grizzled heads turned to size up the newcomers, especially the woman since women were sent to the Magdalene Project—not that this clean, young woman in khaki shorts and a pink print blouse looked homeless, though she could use a hairbrush. Neither did the man, who carried himself with the kind of self-assurance the men at the shelter lacked.

"Mary, would you take over?" Handing her ladle to the nearest volunteer, McKenzie skirted the table to assuage her curiosity.

"Welcome to the Centurion Men's Shelter." She greeted them with her usual warmth. "How can I help you?"

"Are you Miss Jones?" Though he was rude not to take off his ball cap, his friendly countenance put her at ease.

"Yes."

"Ben Harmony. And this is Emma Stuart." He handed her a sheet of paper with a picture on it. "We're looking for a man named Carl Moulton. Any chance you've seen him here?"

McKenzie's breath caught as she recognized her father's pet project. "He sure doesn't look like this anymore." Surprise pulled the words right out of her.

The woman gasped, her dark-blue eyes flying wide. "You know him?" She speared a hopeful look at her companion.

McKenzie couldn't lie, though it occurred to her belatedly that her father might object to her telling the couple. "Carl works for my father."

Ben raked the area with eyes that noticed everything, especially the attention they were getting from the men eating their food. "Is there somewhere we could talk in private?"

His request heightened McKenzie's worry that she might be poking her nose into her father's business. Even so, Emma Stuart's expectant gaze proved impossible to disappoint. "Um, sure. There's a meeting room on the second floor. You can follow me."

Leading them up the broad creaking staircase of the historic building, she imagined what the couple had to be thinking of the Romanesque revival architecture. The ponderous, blocky building with its thick columns and arched, narrow windows was among McKenzie's least favorite architectural styles.

Arriving on the second floor, she led them straight across the hall into what was once a ballroom. When the Centurion Cohort had chosen it for their meeting room, they enclosed the space in paneled walls, covering all the existing windows. They were, after all, a secret society.

"Would you like to sit down?" She gestured to the dozens of brocade chairs facing the raised dais where her father gave his sermons.

The couple declined while looking around at the curious space, no doubt taking note of the jewel-encrusted scepter her father held when he entered or exited, the podium draped in red cloth, the tapestry of a griffin hanging behind it.

Her visitors could have no idea that the paneled walls contained secret compartments, each one filled with relics and curiosities—enticements for society members to remain in the brotherhood if only to discover the next great secret. McKenzie herself only knew about the secrets from overhearing snippets throughout her childhood.

The woman named Emma faced her abruptly. "Is Carl one of the homeless here?" Her husky voice carried a note of urgency that roused McKenzie's curiosity. Given that she spoke in a deep-south dialect just like Carl's, she and Carl were likely well acquainted.

McKenzie spared a thought to the consequences of answering honestly. "No, I don't believe he was ever homeless. My father hired him five months ago to tend our garden, though I've heard he's going to be my father's chauffeur now."

This information drew an incredulous laugh out of Emma.

McKenzie glanced quizzically at Ben.

"Carl is Emma's ex-husband. Her boys were recently kidnapped. We need to know if Carl had anything to do with it."

The wholesome-looking woman didn't seem like Carl's type at all. Her sons were kidnapped? "Oh, you poor thing." Touching the woman's arm, McKenzie could feel her trembling.

"When's the last time you saw Carl?" Ben asked her.

McKenzie thought back. "Why, just this morning when he was spraying pesticide on the roses."

"Has he left the area? Have you seen him with three little boys?"

She reviewed the last few days and shook her head. "No, I don't believe he's left town. And I certainly haven't seen him with any children."

Emma seemed to shrink in stature. As the hope dimmed in her eyes, she lowered them to the worn Persian rug under their feet.

"I'm so sorry." McKenzie knew an urge to hug her. "Is there anything I can do to help?"

Ben answered. "Could you arrange for Emma to ask Carl in person?"

Emma's gaze came up.

McKenzie should have seen the request coming. The prospect of sneaking behind her father's back gave her pause. "Oh, I don't know. My father's a very private man."

"Please."

Glimpsing tears in the woman's deep blue, compassion over-rode McKenzie's wariness. "Well, maybe." She pondered the best means to put the two together. "Carl lives in our carriage home. Perhaps you could meet him in the garden on the side of the house. I could unlock the gate so you could get in." The deception made her heart race. "You would have to be very discreet, though. If my father were to catch you trespassing, he'd have you arrested."

Ben didn't appear terribly intimidated. "Can we do it tonight? We have to go back to Virginia tomorrow."

McKenzie bit her bottom lip while considering her father's schedule. For the past few evenings, he had been leaving the house right after supper and not coming home until ten or so.

"What about nine o'clock tonight, after the sun sets?" The

garden would be dark. "The house is just off Whitaker on East Jones Street, number twelve."

Below the bill of his cap, Ben's eyebrows rose. "He has a street named after him?"

"Oh, Jones is an old family name here. You'll see a brick wall on the left side of the home, with a gate leading to the garden. If the gate's unlocked, that means it's safe to enter. Only, keep to the shadows and out of sight of the windows. Carl should come out within fifteen minutes."

Ben stared hard at her. "You sure he'll come?"

McKenzie squelched her distaste. "Yes."

"Tonight at nine, then." Ben extended a hand. "Thank you."

"Of course." As his hand swallowed hers, McKenzie experienced a spurt of panic. "Please, if you're caught, don't tell anyone I helped you."

"No worries. Emma, you ready?"

The woman kept her hands, covered in scrapes and scabs, tucked against her sides.

"Thank you," she said in a choked voice.

"Of course." McKenzie couldn't begin to fathom what she'd been through. Turning toward the door, she found Ben already there, pulling it open. He stiffened as he watched someone dash down the stairs.

McKenzie glimpsed Miles's dark head, turning on the landing.

Ben cast her a frown. "Who is that kid?"

"Oh, he's just one of our younger residents, a runaway teen."

"Hmm." With a thoughtful look, Ben reached for Emma's elbow, considerate of her battered hands.

McKenzie trailed after them. Were the two lovers or just friends? They seemed comfortable together. Either way, she wanted to help connect them with Carl, even as her stomach soured at the prospect of luring him to the garden. There was only one sure way to get him there. At least she could be sure he wouldn't complain to her father when Emma showed up instead of McKenzie.

By the time she reached the bottom of the stairs, the couple was halfway to the door.

"Everything okay?"

The voice in her ear made her jump. "Miles!" Where had he come from?

"Sorry." The teenager grimaced his apology even as his alert hazel eyes rested on her face. As always, his proximity sharpened her senses, heightening her awareness of his compact yet muscular frame. Both the curve of his lower lip and his clean scent appealed to her. Her father encouraged all the men at the shelter to shower daily and to launder their clothing in the free facility at the back of the house. Miles most certainly did both.

"Can we talk?"

The unexpected request made her blink at him.

"In private?" He gestured with his chin to the room upstairs, making her think he might have been eavesdropping earlier, but how could anyone hear through a door hewn from chestnut?

"Oh, I don't know if that's a good idea." The mere thought of being alone with him made her blood flow faster.

He pitched his voice lower. "Look, I couldn't help overhearing you in here with that couple."

She widened her eyes at him. "You *were* eavesdropping."

"I was keeping an eye on you." His gaze flicked toward the door. "That guy looked dangerous."

Flattered by his protectiveness yet concerned he might now reveal their plans to Carl, McKenzie firmed her lips and marched resolutely back upstairs, where she planned to chastise him. Perhaps in deference to her reputation, Miles waited a full three minutes before joining her in the meeting hall and shutting the door behind him.

Her heart fluttered as he approached her. "Listen." She propped her hands on her trim waist to remind him who was in charge. "You can't tell Carl what we're up to."

Miles didn't look at all cowed by her lecture. "How are you going to get Carl into the garden at nine?"

Was he jealous? Her pulse doubled. "That's none of your concern." But the blush heating her face betrayed her, causing his lip to curl into a cynical smile that made him look much older.

"Yeah, that's what I thought. How about this," he added before she could defend herself. "You help me get Carl's job once he becomes the chauffeur, and I'll forget what I heard here."

His ultimatum confounded her. He wasn't the easygoing wanderer she thought he was.

"Your father's going to need a gardener, right?"

"Right." Was Miles just ambitious and looking for a landscaping job that paid well, or was he also interested in working where she lived? Or was that just wishful thinking on her part?

At her continued silence, he added, "Look, I need a job. I don't want to be here forever."

Yes, but the thought of him living and sleeping on the third floor right above her own room was so appealing she had to glance at her left hand to remind herself she was about to be married. Even if the opportunity arose to get to know Miles better, what would a deeper relationship accomplish? He was just a kid, and she was a puppet for her father.

"I'll see what I can do." To her own ears, her voice held a tremor of excitement. "Just—please—stay out of this business with Carl."

"Sure, if you'll promise me one thing." His voice had deepened. He stepped suddenly closer. "Don't ever let that creep kiss you."

Without warning, he inclined his head and dropped the sweetest, most reverent kiss on her lips before stalking away and letting himself through the door without looking back.

McKenzie stood stock-still in his wake, rocked by the beat of her heart, shocked at having been kissed by a mere boy. Yet her lips still tingled pleasurably.

She would give anything for the kiss to have lasted longer. Obviously, she was losing her mind. Miles was just a homeless teen. And she had a useless degree in art and no experience whatsoever at making her own way in the world. She'd been born to be a wallflower and a breeder. Once she married Ashton, this crazy desire to break free of her gilded cage would wither and die.

But she would never forget how it had felt to be kissed by a boy who cared about her.

Cybercrimes Special Agent Dale Robbins nailed the passphrase this time. Of course, he'd been expecting the call.

"Did you succeed in the task I gave you?"

The dry, uninflected voice sounded like nobody he knew. "Yes. Yes, I have administrative access to the email account at Tidewater Community College." Dale cast a glance over both shoulders, but all his colleagues were engrossed in their own work. Even so, he pitched his voice lower. "She began using it on September 3rd of last year."

"Excellent," said the stranger. "You will shortly receive an email containing further instructions. Open it when you receive it."

Dale's computer chimed as a new email arrived in his inbox. With a tremor in his fingers, he went to see who'd sent it, but the return address was unfamiliar. "I got it."

The body of the email contained instructions to create an exchange between Emma Stuart and a government employee named Benjamin F. Harmony. The attachment contained the contents of those emails. Was the exchange even real, or had it been fabricated?

"I want this correspondence to appear authentic. Can you make the dates work?"

Dale broke into a light sweat. "Um, I can alter the sent date at the client server, but the stamp on the receiving server would reflect the actual time received. Maybe no one would notice?"

For a tense moment, the voice remained silent. "That'll have to do. Make sure the exchange shows up in the woman's Sent folder. Print out a hard copy and drop it in the in-house mailbox addressed to Special Agent Greg Butler, Criminal Investigation Division, without a return address. He needs to get it by tomorrow."

Greg Butler, CID. Dale scribbled down the name. Given his title, Butler was a criminal investigator with limited powers—he couldn't be the owner of the voice.

"Yes, sir." It was both flattering and terrifying to be part of a society so well-networked yet still so secretive. "He'll have the hard copies by morning."

Without a word of thanks, the caller hung up.

"Good luck." With those whispered words, Ben swung wide the wrought-iron gate leading to Jones's walled garden, and Emma eased inside.

The scent of gardenias and honeysuckle permeated the humid enclosure. She immediately hid herself, per Ben's suggestion, between the high brick wall and a mature hydrangea bush, lush with purple blooms. Peering over the bush's broad leaves, Emma kept an eye on the lit fountain at the garden's center. Footpaths, made from crushed oyster shells, led to every corner of the garden. What a lovely bit of paradise—the last place she would expect Carl to work.

Over the fountain's gurgling and the hum of insect wings, Emma heard a faint click as if a door from the big house next to her had just closed. She wet her dry lips, waiting.

The sound of a stem breaking under someone's heel made her freeze. That had to be Ben. He'd promised he would watch from the top of the wall, close enough to rescue her if need be. Although she couldn't see him, his presence was a comfort.

"Oh, Miss Jones?" Carl's singsongy voice cut across the garden, silencing the insects. "Are you here?"

Emma's skin crawled at the familiar tenor of Carl's voice. How she'd ever thought him attractive was beyond her comprehension. Through a screen of thick leaves, she watched him approach the fountain, where the light it gave off revealed that he'd put on weight, especially around his midsection. Life had to be treating him well, but well enough to raise three boys?

"Show yourself, pretty bumblebee." He hovered by the fountain, turning full circle to peer into the shadows.

Emma emerged from her hiding place. Repugnance edged aside her nervousness as she closed the distance between them. "Hello, Carl."

His smile of anticipation gave way to stupefaction. "Emma! Wh-what're you doin' here?" He glanced around guiltily as if still expecting McKenzie.

"What do you think, Carl?" She advanced on him, causing him to back away. Maternal fury made her want to attack him physically. "I'm here for my boys. Tell me where they are—*now*."

His bobbing head resembled that of a nervous chicken. "Your boys? How would I know where they are? They're with you, aren't they?"

His confusion stripped away her fury in an instant, leaving nothing but despair. "You didn't take them?" She'd always known it to be true, so why was she so sharply disappointed?

He scoffed at the mere idea while flicking the hair from his eyes. "I can't believe you bothered to even look for me down here. Would've thought you knew me better'n that."

"Wait." Something struck her as peculiar. "Why aren't you more surprised to hear that they were kidnapped?"

He blinked at her. "I am surprised. I thought you'd watch 'em better'n that."

His words made her face burn. "How dare you! You have no idea how hard I fought for them."

Carl just shrugged. "You're right. 'Cause I wasn't there. I had nothing to do with it."

She glared at him, waiting for the muscle in his cheek to twitch, only it didn't. Not once.

"Well, then." Emma's voice went hoarse with the need to weep. "Guess I'm wasting my time here."

He spread his hands. "Guess you are."

Devastated, Emma turned and walked blindly back to the gate, only vaguely aware that Carl was muttering to himself as he stalked back into the big house.

She pushed out of the garden, waiting quietly on the sidewalk for Ben to join her. Jones's tree-shaded neighborhood, occupied by stately, historic homes, held itself aloof from the rest of the teeming city. Emma hugged herself hard as tremors seized her anew.

This wasn't supposed to happen. God had pointed her toward Savannah by filling her ravaged heart with reassurance. How could she go back to Virginia knowing nothing more than when she got here? It made no sense.

A shadow loomed over her, and Emma startled away only to recognize Ben as he leaped lightly off the top of the wall. In the next instant, he pulled her into his embrace.

"You did good, Em," he murmured in her ear. "Listen, I need you to keep yourself together." He led her across the street to his parked car, where he brought her to the driver's side. "Here, get in."

Emma roused from self-absorption as he opened the driver's door. "What's going on?"

Again, he put his mouth to her ear, his rich voice teasing a pleasant shiver up her spine. "There was a fourth person in the garden. I want you to drive my car around the block—slowly." He thrust his keys into her palm. "Come back and pick me up in three minutes."

With the weight of his hand pushing her down into the driver's seat, Emma cooperated. Apparently, she couldn't fall apart just yet. Ben needed her to drive around the block. A fourth person in the garden? Ben shut her in, then opened and shut her door a second time—to make it sound like they'd both gotten in.

As he vanished into the darkness, she set the key fob into the cup holder the way she'd seen him do and pushed the button to start the ignition. It took all her attention to remain in the here and now. She could fall apart later.

Emma eased the Mustang away from the curb and started slowly around the block. Who else had been in the garden? It was probably McKenzie. Honestly, Emma was too heartsick to care.

Miles waited for the rumble of Ben Harmony's Mustang to fade before daring to relax. Trying to fool a Navy SEAL—for that's what the stranger turned out to be when Miles had researched him—was daunting, to say the least. Since accidentally stepping on a stem that had snapped under his shoe, Miles had been sweating bullets, thinking Chief Harmony, who was no less than a freaking sniper, was going to realize he was in the garden with them and sniff him out.

But now that the couple had left, Miles could leave his hiding place, a narrow aperture behind a trellis of dark-purple clematis. It was the kind of space a large man wouldn't think to hide behind, which was why he'd chosen it four months ago when he'd started watching Jones's mansion.

Jones wasn't even at home tonight. Miles was only there to make sure McKenzie didn't get caught up in a drama that didn't concern her—the kidnapping of Carl Moulton's sons. How curious that an event attracting media attention farther north had washed up on Jared Jones's doorstep.

Carl's insistence that he knew nothing about the boys had raised an interesting possibility: Could Jared Jones, a man with dozens of connections, have masterminded the kidnappings on his gardener's behalf? Why would he do something like that for his gardener?

Emerging with a few new scratches to show for his skulking, Miles crossed the short distance to the gate. At least he didn't have to climb the wall tonight. The gate's well-oiled hinges scarcely made a sound as he peeked out onto the empty sidewalk, slipped out, and closed the gate behind him.

Whistling casually, he began the twelve-block walk back to the shelter, passing thick-trunked trees. When the air shifted and a pistol gouged him in the back, he realized he'd been outsmarted.

"We meet again."

Alarm spurted through Miles as he found his arm seized in an unbreakable grip.

"How 'bout we go for a drive?" the SEAL suggested softly.

As if on cue, the yellow Mustang cruised around the corner with Emma's pale face at the wheel. *Idiot!* He should've known better than to test the instincts of a sniper. Now, he either admitted to being an undercover investigator, which could blow the lid off his entire investigation, or he kept his mouth shut and dealt with whatever punishment a Navy SEAL could dish out.

The first option sounded so much more appealing.

CHAPTER 9

*A*t the light tap on his door, Christopher jerked his face out of the book he was reading and noted his visitor with mixed feelings. Mr. Jones, President of the Centurion Academy for Boys, had started dropping by each evening, right at bedtime, shortly after Colton fell asleep.

The three brothers had met the dark-haired gentleman the same day they were ushered from the van into this building of marble and stone.

"Your mother is dead." He'd spoken in a gentle voice, his hands heavy on their shoulders. "Carter will be cared for by this nice lady who lives nearby. And you two will remain at this school until your father can be found. I know that change is hard. But the sooner you accept your new circumstances, the happier you'll be."

He'd gone to shake their hands, and Colton had bitten him.

That had only been a few days ago, but it felt like a month. For Colton, who'd been fed only bread and water as punishment, it had to feel like an eternity.

Shutting the door behind himself, Mr. Jones checked first whether Colton was asleep on the bottom bunk before approaching them. The upper bunk put Chris at eye level with his visitor. Mr. Jones smiled with approval as he noted the book Chris was reading.

As much as Chris tried to dislike Mr. Jones the way Colton did, the man's kindness toward him made that difficult. With every visit, he brought him amazing gifts: a bronze spearhead that once belonged to Julius Caesar and the shrunken head of a Nigerian captive. He talked about far-off places and powerful leaders in history, carrying Chris's imagination beyond the locked doors and their strange, new circumstances. Best of all, he'd brought him the book he was reading, which helped him, at times, to forget how much he missed his mother.

"Good evening, Mr. Moulton." Mr. Jones smiled warmly at him.

Disconcertingly, the man's dark-brown eyes were the exact same hue as Colton's.

"Hello." Chris set his book politely aside.

"How do you like it?" Mr. Jones hitched the sleeve of his light-weight, handsome blue blazer and rested an elbow on Chris's mattress. "I see you're halfway finished already. Well done."

Being a slow, thorough reader, Chris drank in the compliment. "It's good. Um, I like how the grandfather goes searching for his grandson."

The president's dark eyes narrowed. "Family is important, don't you think?"

A wave of sorrow crested in Chris at the reminder of his mother. His throat tightened. "I want to go home."

Impatience tightened Mr. Jones's face before he masked it with a tolerant expression. "I've told you, Christopher, your home is here now."

Chris flinched with surprise to feel the man's hand on top of his head. "I have good news tonight." He sent Chris an encouraging smile. "Your father has been found."

An image of a weak-willed, unpredictable man came to Chris's mind.

"Aren't you pleased?" Mr. Jones's smile turned quizzical.

Chris didn't want to say the wrong thing. He could guess what Colton would say, though: *"He ain't my daddy."* Mr. Ben was more of a father to them than their own dad.

"I'll bring him here shortly." Mr. Jones removed his hand. "Then you may see him for yourself."

Chris gave a tiny nod of acknowledgment.

"Now, let's see here." The gentleman reached into the pocket of his blazer. "What have I got for you tonight?" With a sphinxlike smile, he withdrew his gift and placed it in Chris's palm.

Chris drew a breath of appreciation as he gripped the stem. "It's a magnifying glass!"

"You'll need it to examine some very old documents I'll be bringing with me in the future."

Colton gave a loud snore on the bunk below them.

Mr. Jones stepped back to frown at him. "Keep it from your brother."

"Thank you." Not even at Christmastime had Chris ever received so many spectacular gifts, back-to-back.

"I will leave you to your reading now." Mr. Jones patted the edge of his bed. "Until tomorrow." He started for the door, where he looked back. "Colton will also be allowed to visit his father if he behaves. Good night, my boy."

I am not your boy. "Good night."

As soon as the door closed behind his guest, Chris peered over the edge of his bed to look down at his brother. "I know you're awake."

Colton stopped snoring. His brown eyes snapped open, and he shot to his elbow. "He's lyin' again. He didn't find our dad."

Colton believed Mr. Jones was lying about their mother, too.

"I don't know." Chris examined the magnifying glass still in his hand. "I keep thinkin' he knows something he's not telling us."

Colton rolled out of the bed and clambered up the ladder to join Chris up top. "Lemme see that magnifier."

Chris passed it to his brother. "I read a book once where the boy used a magnifying glass to send a distress signal."

Colton wrenched his gaze up. "Yeah? Maybe we could use it to escape."

Chris considered the possibility before shaking his head. "Haven't you noticed? There's nothing around this school but woods. Who would see the signal?"

"Then we should just run away. I hate it here."

"Shh." Chris cut a worried glance at the door. "Somebody could hear you. Besides." A chill raced up his spine. "Escaping is pointless. Mr. Jones would find us, no matter what." Just like the grandfather in the book he was reading.

"Not if we made it back to Ben. He could protect us."

Chris pictured their hero and nodded. "Yeah, he could. If we could make it back to him." From what he'd gleaned, they were all the way down in Georgia. They'd have to find a way back to Virginia without Mr. Jones catching up to them.

The man wanted them for something. Chris swallowed hard. He especially wanted *him*.

Ben shoved the Peeping Tom facedown onto the hood of his car, frisked him, and found a switchblade inside of his right sock but no other weapons.

All the while, Emma watched through the window, clearly bewildered. Grabbing the kid by the back of his shirt, Ben yanked him upright, then steered him around the car to the passenger door. He flipped the seat forward and shoved him into the back. Keeping his Glock trained on him, he dropped into the front seat and shut the door. "Keep driving, Emma."

"Where did he come from?" Her husky voice was breathier than ever. "Why are you pointing your gun at him?"

"Calm down, sweetheart. I'm just going to ask Miles here some questions while you drive around town, nice and slow-like."

"I suggest you head for a different street. Jones will be home any minute."

The kid's bravado impressed Ben—he sounded more grim than fearful. Ben stared at him hard, then gave voice to his suspicions. "You're not a homeless kid, are you?"

The young man sighed. For a second, it wasn't clear whether Miles would answer. "I'm an undercover special agent with the FBI."

The quietly spoken words stunned Ben. He met Emma's astounded glance. *FBI?* The kid didn't look old enough to be out of high school, let alone to be working for the Bureau. "You got any proof of that?"

"In my backpack, which isn't with me tonight."

"Then why would I believe you?"

"Well, for starters, I can tell you who *you* are."

Ben's scalp tightened. He didn't like being at a disadvantage. "Go ahead."

"You're Navy SEAL Chief Petty Officer Benjamin F. Harmony, code name Harm, a sniper for SEAL Team Six, location Dam Neck, Virginia, and a person of interest in the abduction of Emma Stuart's three sons."

Emma made a sound between a whimper and a laugh. Anger flared in Ben. "I didn't kidnap Emma's boys."

"Obviously. You wouldn't be here looking for them if you did."

The man's reply snatched the wind from Ben's sails. "Then, explain why you're following us. Did Butler send you?"

"I don't know who Butler is. And I wasn't following you today, per se. I'm investigating Jared Jones, McKenzie's father, high consul of the Centurion Cohort."

Ben laughed. "The what?"

"The Centurion Cohort runs the shelter, plus all kinds of civic charities in and around town. They're a quasi-religious group made up entirely of men, kind of like the Masons, only more local-ized, with a shorter history. The group got started at the end of the Civil War when ten plantation owners banded together to recoup their losses. The Bureau has reason to believe the Cohort launders money and hides their racketeering behind their charities."

Ben lowered his Glock. This man wasn't a threat to them. "Okay. What's all that got to do with Emma's boys?" He leaned forward and slipped his gun back in its holster.

"Well, I have no evidence to back what I'm about to say, but Jared Jones certainly has the resources to carry out a kidnapping." He said the last words on a note of apology.

But Emma was shaking her head. "Why would a man that powerful want to do anything for Carl? Carl can't care for the boys. He said so himself."

"Look, I'm not saying Jones did it. But I will say Jones has taken a shine to Carl that I can't explain. The man's been a member of the Cohort only a month longer than I have, and he's a princeps prior already, which usually takes four years. Jones gave him a ring already. And here's something else: The Centurions have this idea that only their sons can carry on their legacy. So, without his sons, Carl's status is meaningless."

Emma gave a bitter laugh as she drove them around a lamp-lit square. "So now Carl's boys are his legacy?" She wrung the steering wheel as if picturing Carl's neck.

"Easy, Em." Ben assessed their location with a quick sweep of his eyes. "There's a cop right there. Watch your speed, hon." He glanced back at Miles. "You're saying Jones might have helped Carl secure his legacy?"

"Maybe." The agent shrugged.

"Why would he break the law for his gardener?"

"I'm not sure. But Carl is more than his gardener. He accompa-nies Jones to every Wednesday meeting and even sits on his right side, at the front of the room. I heard he's about to be Jones's chauffeur."

Curiosity tickled Ben's imagination. Emma was still shaking her head. He looked back at Miles. "Think you could dig deeper for us? Emma and I are returning to Virginia Beach tomorrow. There's not much more we can do here, but maybe you could make some inquiries?"

Miles considered for a moment. "Tell you what. If you two keep quiet about my investigation, I'll keep my ears open. That means telling nobody who I am—not McKenzie, not Carl, not even this Butler guy you mentioned, whom I assume is FBI. If I overhear anything that points to a possible kidnapping, I'll alert the right authorities."

Content with their arrangement and believing in the man's integrity, Ben retrieved the cell phone he'd left in his glove box. "Let me give you my contact information. I'd rather you reached out to me directly."

"I don't have my phone with me, but text me, and I'll reply at the first opportunity."

As Miles spieled off his number, Ben typed it into a new text, added his name in the body of the text, and tapped the Send arrow. He stretched a hand into the back seat. "Sorry for the mix-up."

Miles grasped his hand firmly. "No big deal."

Facing forward, Ben was impressed to discover that Emma had found her way across town. They were just blocks from the Centurion Men's Shelter.

Miles sat forward. "Uh, could you drop me off right here? Don't want anyone from the shelter seeing me in this car."

Without further instruction, Emma pulled alongside the curb next to a fire hydrant. Ben got out and flipped the seat forward. As Miles stepped out, Ben caught him by the sleeve. "You catch the guy."

Miles sent him a hard smile. "Planning on it."

Ben released him and then watched him walk away. With every step, Miles took on a slouch and down-and-out air. Admiration put a smile on Ben's face.

Getting back into the car, he found Emma staring vacantly at the car parked in front of them. "You want me to drive, hon?"

They were five blocks from the hotel, where they could catch just a few hours of sleep before heading home.

Emma's hand moved automatically to the shifter. Without answering, she pulled the car onto the quiet street and then made her way into the left turn lane. Her sense of direction impressed him, but what was going on in her head?

"What do you think of Miles's theory that Jones is involved?"

Emma took a stiff left turn. "I don't know what to think anymore."

Sensitive to her distress and the real reason for it—tomorrow they were heading home without her sons—Ben decided to act on their latest clue. Consulting his address book, he looked up Special Agent Butler's number and then put a call through.

Emma glanced over at him but said nothing.

"Mr. Harmony." The man greeted him on an agitated note. "It's about time for you to head back to Virginia."

Curious how the agent always seemed to know where they were. "You told me to call if I found Carl Stuart."

A subtle pause ensued. "Why do I get the feeling you approached him when I told you not to?"

Ben ignored the question. "He's the gardener for a man named Jared Jones; maybe you've heard of him."

"Can't say that I have." A pencil drawer opened and closed. Butler was evidently working late tonight.

"He's the leader of the Centurion Cohort."

"I have heard of that," the man conceded.

"Are you familiar with the importance they place on having male heirs?"

"No. What are you saying?"

"If Carl's a Centurion, then he has a motive for wanting his sons. Moreover, his employer has the means to pull off a successful kidnapping."

"And why would Mr. Jones commit a crime to help his gardener?"

Ben hesitated. "I don't know, but Jones has advanced Carl's ranking in the Cohort and is about to make him his chauffeur. Clearly, Jones is invested in him."

"Well." Butler sounded bemused at best. "That's an interesting theory, Mr. Harmony. Tell you what, I'll run it by my superiors and call you back. If you don't hear from me, remember I expect you in Virginia Beach by morning."

"We'll be there." Ben brought the call to a close and checked his watch. If they left at dawn, they could make it back by 11:00 A.M. That was early enough.

Emma swung them into the hotel's parking garage and nosed the Mustang into a spot close to the elevator.

"Nice driving."

She said nothing, not even acknowledging Ben's compliment.

Coming around the car to collect her, Ben drew her toward the entrance, then up the elevator to their room. Disappointment overtook his conviction that they were on to something. The last thing Emma wanted to do was to go home to an empty house—even if Amos and Grace had managed to put it back to rights as he'd requested. Conscious of her despair, Ben said in his gentlest voice, "We need to pack up before we sleep, sweetheart. I'll set an alarm for 4:00."

Emma nodded, crossed to her bed, and carefully folded her clothing before placing them into the plastic sack. Helpless to comfort her, Ben watched her carry the sleep shirt he'd bought her into the bathroom and shut the door behind her.

He filled his own backpack less methodically. Then he crossed to the window, where their fourth-story room looked down on East Bay Street, providing easy access to nearby River Street. Gas lamps lit the city with intermittent golden light, but still, it had plenty of dark shadows.

Miles's input about Carl replayed in Ben's mind. If Jared Jones was somehow responsible for the boys' disappearance, then the thugs at Isaac's Pub might have been employed by Mr. Jones, which meant that man had likely heard about the bald man looking for Carl. Were Grimes and Chaplin also Centurions? What about the cops they'd been so chummy with?

The sound of stifled sobs coming from the bathroom pegged Ben in the chest. He pivoted to stare at the door. Poor Emma. After all she'd been through in her short life, she was the last person who should have to suffer this way. Anger flared in him, making him want to throttle whoever was responsible for her suffering.

When the sobs gave way to the sound of running water, Ben dropped onto the carpet in a plank position and cranked out a hundred push-ups.

Five minutes later, the doorknob turned, and Emma emerged with red-rimmed eyes, her hair hanging in damp ringlets, and wearing the lavender sleep shirt he'd bought her with the words *I need coffee* emblazoned across her chest.

Keeping her gaze averted, she crossed to her bed and slipped stiffly under the covers. Still breathing hard, Ben clambered to his feet just as she rolled away from him. He watched her press her clasped hands to her forehead and close her eyes.

Did she honestly think praying was going to help at this point? Ben marched around the end of the bed, planting himself in front of her, startling her eyes open.

"Come on, Emma." He stood over her, hating the devastation written on her face. "Don't quit on me now. It's not like we didn't find out something tonight. We know Carl's a Centurion, and his employer has the resources to help him. That's something, right?"

She regarded him through lackluster eyes. "Why would a man like that help Carl get his legacy back?"

Her scratchy, pain-filled voice only frustrated Ben more. "I don't know. Maybe he wants Carl to feel indebted to him."

She jerked to her elbow, suddenly testy. "Carl doesn't even *want* the boys. He told me straight to my face, and I *know* he wasn't lying. Besides, a rich man like Jones doesn't need loyalty. He can pay people to like him!"

She had a point there. "True, but you have to admit, there's something strange about this place." He gestured to the dark window. "What about those guys who wanted to jump me last night? Who were they protecting? Just Carl? I don't think so."

Instead of taking heart from his words, Emma sank back onto her pillow, looking like a wounded soldier. Frustration tapped at Ben's temples. He would rather see her glowing with faith than giving up. "So, that's it for you? You're just going to let the bad guys win?"

She shook her head, her face crumpling. "This wasn't supposed to happen." A gasp convulsed her lungs. "God spoke to my heart. He wanted us to come here, but we haven't found *anything!*"

The sight of her falling apart nearly did him in. To keep himself from sprawling onto the bed to hold her, he clung to his anger. "Let me get this straight. You really think, in this crazy world full of angry, selfish people, God can fix things for you?"

Her eyes flared as if he'd just plunged a knife into her heart. "Yes!"

"Well, I hate to tell you this, sweetheart," Ben smoothed the gravel from his voice as he reached into his pocket, "but bad things happen to good people all the time." Flipping his wallet open, he dropped onto the edge of her bed to show her the picture of his brother, which he looked at every time he opened his wallet.

She studied it a moment, her eyebrows knit together. "Is it you?"

He could see why she might think that, as all the Harmony kids resembled each other. At fourteen, Shawn had a head full of reddish-blond hair, peach fuzz on his upper lip, and a smile that was pure sunshine.

"No. This is Shawn. He was eleven months younger than me, my Irish twin, and my best friend growing up. Soon after this photo was taken, he was diagnosed with Chronic Myeloid Leukemia."

Emma made a sound of dismay.

"Back then, kids didn't have the kind of odds they have today. He fought as hard as he could, and my whole family prayed for him. We all shaved our heads so he wouldn't be the only bald one."

She glanced up at his bald head.

"Well, now I shave it 'cause I can't grow hair. This was thirteen years ago. Just after his seventeenth birthday, he died." Ben's throat closed up all at once, forcing him to swallow hard. "Like I said, bad things happen all the time, so you tell me how all things work together for good."

Tears welled in Emma's eyes. "I'm so sorry." When she stretched out a hand and threaded her fingers through his, Ben felt the connection clear to his toes.

She held his gaze, clearly intent on comforting him. "I know what that feels like. My Mama died when I was four, but I barely remember her. Then Daddy died when I was twelve—a car accident. He was drunk. But I still had my Granny Annie for a few years after that."

The enormity of her loss—first her parents, then her grandmother, and now her sons—kept Ben speechless. All he could do was lift their threaded fingers and kiss her knuckles. "Don't ever stop that."

Puzzlement knitted her brow. "Stop what?"

"Seeing the glass half full." Shame burned in him belatedly. Here, he'd been trying to make Emma angry, to tell her God *didn't* work all things together for the good of those who loved Him. How would he know? He'd gone to church with his family every Sunday, but had he ever loved God like Emma did?

To his dismay, her eyes puddled up. "It's hard to see anything good in this."

"I know, sweetheart. But we're not giving up yet." The urge to hold her overwhelmed his common sense. Tossing aside his wallet, he slid his hands beneath her and scooped her into a sitting position so he could wrap his arms around her. She gratified him by hugging him back, practically melting into him.

But then her lungs convulsed. Hiding her face against his collarbone, she burst into soul-deep sobs that dredged up memories of his own loss, making his vision swim.

Rocking her gently, he held Emma through the tempest. Moisture gathered on his T-shirt. He didn't care. The scent of her shampoo and the feel of her lush bosom pillowing his chest crept into his awareness. His body predictably stirred, for which he took himself to task. This wasn't just any woman in his arms. This was *Emma*, and her heart was literally disintegrating in his hands.

After many long minutes, she drew a shuddering breath and raised her head, mopping her face self-consciously. Her gaze connected with his and then dropped to his lips. He deduced by the longing in her eyes what she wanted from him. Treacherous heat streaked along his arteries.

Temptation nipped at him. How much could it hurt to find out whether her lips were as soft as they looked? He slowly lowered his head, then molded his mouth to hers, not at all surprised when pleasure licked over him.

Dear heaven. He'd always known kissing her would be this good.

Picturing Amos's outrage, Ben regretfully released her, untangled himself from her embrace, and clambered off the bed, putting several feet between them.

Hurt and rejection filled her eyes.

Ben stuffed his hands into his pockets. "So, that's not a good idea," he said gruffly.

"I'm sorry."

He shook his head. "Don't apologize. It's not you. Well, I mean, it is you, but I respect you too much, Emma, to…" He floundered as the right words evaded him.

"To use me," she finished for him, "like you use other women."

Dang. She didn't pull her punches, did she? He frowned at her. "Something like that."

To his surprise, she sent him a tiny smile of approval, amazing him that she could still find humor amidst the wreckage of her heart. "You're a good man, Ben Harmony."

He found himself basking in her praise before protesting. "Oh, I doubt that."

"No, you are."

The conviction in her tone humbled him.

She reached for the lamp between their beds. "Mind if I turn this off?"

"No, go ahead. I'll, uh," he backed toward the bathroom, "I'll be out to sleep in a moment. And I'll set an alarm for us. We gotta leave here by four thirty."

With a sigh, she snapped off the light, plunging the room into darkness. As Ben edged toward the bathroom, gathering his clothes for the morning, he listened to her snuggle into her pillow. Her whispered words gave him the impression she was praying again.

He closed the door of the bathroom before turning on the light.

Stripping off his T-shirt, he studied his reflection in the mirror. Emma's praise left him feeling different somehow—better.

He turned at the waist to regard the tattoo running from his left deltoid and over his tricep. *RIP Shawn* was inked in Celtic-style font in honor of their Irish ancestry. Twisting the other way, he examined the tattoo on his right deltoid. *Mr. Fix-it.*

Emma had called him Mr. Fix-it that morning he'd pulled onto the shoulder of the interstate to help a woman in a stranded vehicle. She turned out to be Emma, a single mother of three young boys, all of whom had slept in their car the night before.

Considering he'd been wearing his Naval Working Uniform, Emma couldn't have possibly seen his tattoo. The coincidence made Ben wonder if God hadn't chosen him—Ben Harmony—to make *sure* all things worked together for Emma's good.

He met his thoughtful gaze in the mirror. If they walked away from the leads they'd found in Savannah, could they really trust the FBI to dig deeper down here? He doubted it.

So, no. They shouldn't leave. They needed to stay here and find Emma's boys themselves until the FBI forced them to come back.

Making up his mind to stay, Ben felt immediately better. As he twisted the faucet in the shower, he murmured, "Help me to fix this, God." After all, he had to live up to his reputation.

CHAPTER 10

*E*mma awoke to the sun shining behind the curtains of their hotel window. Bolting upright, she glanced first at the clock—7:15 A.M.—then at Ben, who was sitting on the edge of his bed, tying off his tennis shoes. "I thought we had to be out of here by four thirty."

Freshly shaven, looking vibrantly awake and wearing a bright-yellow T-shirt, Ben double-knotted both sneakers with efficient tugs on his laces. "Change of plans, Em. I got to thinking about those thugs who recognized Carl's photo the other night. I'm certain they know something, and I'm not leaving Savannah until I find out what."

She let his ultimatum roll around in her head for a moment. "But Butler said we had to be back in Virginia Beach, so it didn't look like we ran off together."

As he stood up, brimming with energy, the memory of their kiss the night before wafted through her, shortening her breath. It was everything she had imagined and more.

"Look." He folded his arms across his broad chest, making himself appear as unstoppable as a Mac truck. "Something tells me we need to find out what's going on down here, and I don't trust Butler to do it."

"How do we find out?" She tossed back the covers, more than willing to help.

His gaze skimmed over her as she jumped out of bed. "I have a notion."

"Okay, give me five minutes." Snatching up her bag of clothing en route to the bathroom, she drew up short at Ben's sudden silence. "What?"

"Well, I thought you might like to relax here, order some room service, and watch TV till I get back."

Raising her eyebrows, Emma drew herself to her full height. "Whose boys were taken, Mr. Harmony, yours or mine?"

Ben firmed his lips. "Fine. Just promise me you'll do as I say if things go sideways."

"I promise." Hope sparked to life within her. If anyone could help her find her boys, it was Ben.

~

"Look, Mama." Bending over her mother's shoulder, McKenzie held out a journal and tried to wrest Genevieve Jones's attention from the roses climbing the trellis outside her hospice window.

Every morning, McKenzie was the first visitor to arrive at Savannah Hospice. Her mother was more prone to remembering her first thing in the morning.

"This is your garden journal. Do you remember writing all this?"

McKenzie riffled the pages, managing to capture her mother's attention with the noise she made. As Genevieve's light-green eyes lowered to her own dainty scrawl, a frown creased her brow. Did she recognize the drawing of irises made by her own hand ten years earlier?

"My garden."

The words brought McKenzie to her knees. "Yes, Mama!" For her mother to recognize anything from the past at this last stage of Alzheimer's was a miracle. "You wrote about every plant and shrub and tree. You loved your garden, didn't you, Mama?"

Genevieve, who in 1985 was described by *Southern Living* magazine as the Jewel of Savannah, lifted a delicate hand to the open page. "Where...where did you get this?"

"You gave it to me, Mama." She drew her mother's attention to the pendant hanging from her own neck. "Along with the key to your heart, remember?" She held her breath as her mother's seemingly lucid gaze fixed on the solid silver key.

Genevieve reached for it, rubbing it between her thumb and forefinger. "Not your heart, McKenzie. You've always had that."

At the sound of her name on her mother's lips, tears flooded McKenzie's eyes. "Oh, Mama, you remember me!" Even as she threw her arms around her, joy morphed into sorrow at knowing that, within seconds, Genevieve would soon forget her again.

Her mother pulled back as if struck by a thought. "It's the key to your future, darling. I gave it to you on your sixteenth birthday."

"Yes."

Alarm tightened Genevieve's still-beautiful face as she studied McKenzie's face. "How old are you now?"

"I'm twenty-three now, Mama."

"No." Genevieve reached for her left hand, only to stare in horror at the gaudy diamond solitaire. "Who are you going to marry?"

"It's Ashton Ravenel, Mama. You remember Daddy's friend, don't you?"

A pallor bleached Genevieve's lined face. She gripped her hand harder. "No, McKenzie. You *have* to save yourself. You *cannot* end up like me."

"It's okay." But her mother's distress filled her with alarm. "I'll be fine."

"Listen to me." Genevieve's firm voice contained a quaver that suggested her lucidity was beginning to fade. "Use the key."

The key was nothing but a pendant. It didn't go to anything. "I don't understand, Mama."

"Father Jacobs knows."

"Father Jacobs?" McKenzie envisioned the retired priest from the Cathedral of St. John the Baptist, which she and her mother used to attend when McKenzie was a girl. More recently, she'd gone to seek the priest's forgiveness following the incident in which she'd struck and killed the homeless man.

"Will he come visit you today?" The priest was a longtime friend of her mother's.

Seeing a cloud of vagueness steal over her mother's eyes, McKenzie swallowed her sorrow. At least they'd had this one unexpected moment. But did it mean anything?

Mama never answered her question. Lapsing into a long stare, she turned her face toward the window to gaze back at the roses.

A tap sounded on the privacy window. Carl, who guided the Bentley Flying Spur up the interstate toward a rendezvous point halfway between Savannah and Charleston, spent a flustered moment searching the dashboard display for the switch that lowered the partition between the front and rear seats.

Sweating in his new chauffeur's uniform, he braced himself for a negative comment on his less-than-solid driving skills. Who could blame him? He hadn't even owned, let alone driven, a car this past year, and certainly not a luxury vehicle like this one. By luck alone, his Mississippi driver's license was still valid.

Finding the right button, Carl lowered the partition while craning his neck to see Jones in the rearview mirror. "Sir?"

The man had just put away his cell phone. His dark eyes

snapped with anger as if he'd been in receipt of some bad news. "Have you been approached by anyone about your sons, Carl?"

Carl turned hot, then cold, swallowed against the sudden constriction in his throat. How could his employer have discovered so quickly what had happened last night? How much should he say? Or was there any point in hiding the truth when the old man seemed to know everything?

"Y-yes, sir." Sweat trickled between his shoulder blades. "My ex-wife tracked me down." He bit back the confession that McKenzie had tricked him into meeting Emma in the garden by penning him a little note with a heart on it. "She asked me if I had anything to do with her boys bein' taken."

Mr. Jones's dark eyes bored into his through the mirror. "How would your ex-wife know where you are?"

"I-I don't know, sir. Last time I saw her was near a year ago."

"The man Bates called about," Jones muttered to himself.

"What's that, sir?"

"Never mind. What did you tell her?"

"Nothing." Carl's denial came out with a squeak. "Honest, sir. I-I don't know a thing about them."

Jones's faint smile relieved him immensely. "You just keep singing that tune, Carl." He sent him a nod. "If you're approached again, by anyone, your answer remains the same. Are we clear?"

"Yes, sir." Carl breathed a silent sigh of relief. Was that it? Jones must not have realized McKenzie's involvement, nor was Carl stupid enough to betray her and implicate himself in the process.

He went to raise the partition again, freezing when Mr. Jones added, "Once the fuss dies down, you may visit your sons."

The words exploded like tiny bombs in Carl's mind, inspiring awe and fear. The man had snatched his boys from their mother just like that! Yet, he was smart enough not to tell Carl exactly where they were.

"Until then, I wouldn't want you to tell prevarications. The Cohort preaches honesty, after all."

"Yes, sir. Thank you, sir." Carl was in no hurry to see his boys, anyway. And for all of Mr. Jones's precautions, he could not envision Emma ever allowing the fuss to die down. She'd been a thorn in Carl's side for all eleven years of their marriage. "About my ex-wife, sir," he hedged, wondering how to warn Jones of her persistence.

"Let your ex-wife be my concern." Jones shook out his newspaper and blocked his face from view.

"Yes, sir." As Carl went to raise the partition, the signet ring on his right hand glinted.

Holy cow. It sounded like Jones planned to get rid of Emma—permanently. Regret mingled with a pinch of relief that he wouldn't have to face her anymore. So much for her prediction that bad things happened to bad people. The only person to whom bad things were happening was to Emma herself.

"Thanks." Ben carried two coffees and a bag of muffins to the table closest to the kiosk at the Riverfront Plaza, where Emma sat under the shade of an umbrella, gazing out at the Savannah River.

"Muffin?" He passed her a lemon-poppyseed muffin before sitting down across from her, in plain view of anyone walking down River Street, no hat today. He wanted to be recognized. How else would he entice Grimes and Charlie Chaplin to seek him out?

The sun's warmth, paired with the cool breeze blowing off the water, heightened Ben's awareness. The clanging of a bell drew his gaze to the tanker gliding past them on its way to the ocean. A thought occurred to him that had him searching upriver. Sure enough, he spotted a ship terminal north of the Talmage Bridge.

What were the odds that Grimes and Chaplin worked at the shipyard by day and wandered down to the bars every evening, still in their coveralls? They were probably at work there right now. All Ben had to do was get a message to them that some bald, buff guy was looking for them—and provide them with his phone number.

As his cell phone buzzed on the tabletop, Emma stopped picking at her muffin.

Ben glanced at it. "Guess who?" He answered, putting it to his ear. "Harm here."

"You were supposed to be back at the Beach by now."

Special Agent Butler's tone was rife with suspicion. Annoyance shot through Ben that the man monitored their whereabouts so closely. "Change of plans. We know the boys are down here, and we're not leaving until we find them. So you can either spin your wheels up at the Beach, or you can join us down here looking for them."

"You don't need to threaten me, Chief. I've been reading up on these Centurions, and I'm heading down there tomorrow."

The heartening news made Ben put his phone on speaker and set it back on the table for Emma to hear. "So, we can stay here in the meantime?"

"For now. I'll be there around noon tomorrow. I'll text you when I'm close."

"Cool." Finally, the FBI seemed to be taking them seriously. All they needed now was more proof that the Centurions were involved in the boys' abduction.

"How's Ms. Stuart holding up? I'm sure she's with you?"

The man's concern seemed genuine enough. "Yes, sir. She's right here, doing as well as can be expected."

"Good. Good. Well, I'll see you tomorrow. In the meantime, stay out of trouble."

"Yeah, sure. See you." He tapped the call to a close and raised his eyebrows at Emma. "Well, looks like Butler's going to listen to us now."

"Lord, I hope so," she said with feeling.

His gaze dropped to her half-eaten muffin. She'd barely touched her coffee. "You going to finish that?"

She slid the coffee wordlessly in his direction. As he drained a second cup, she managed to finish her muffin.

"All set? Let's walk."

Emma looked up at him sharply. "Where are we going?"

He swept their garbage into a nearby receptacle. "To find the goons who jumped me."

The idea clearly appalled her. "Why?"

"Because they know more than we do, and I might learn something that way, something I can tell Butler when he gets here." He pulled her chair back.

After rising, Emma fell into step alongside him as they followed the ballast-paved street past the converted warehouses to Isaac's Pub. This morning, the pub's windows sparkled. With a light hand on her arm, Ben steered her through the open doors. The tiled floor was freshly mopped, and the bar stood empty, save for a lone man drowning his miseries.

The same barkeeper who'd been working the other night glanced over and did a double take.

"What can I get you?" he inquired as Ben and Emma occupied two stools.

Ben ordered two iced teas and waited for the bartender to slide their glasses across the smooth counter at them. "Thanks. You remember me from the other night?"

Emma picked up her lemon wedge and squeezed it.

The hard-faced man stared at him, his expression inscrutable. "Yeah, sure."

"Remember the guys sitting at the table in the back?"

"Nope."

The denial came too quickly. "One was wiry with a black mustache; the other was a bigger guy with a pinkie ring, goes by the name Grimes."

Next to him, Emma drew a sharp breath, but Ben was too busy watching the barkeeper's reaction to pay her any heed.

"Sorry, don't remember." The man stuck a toothpick in his mouth and turned his back on them.

"Ben," Emma whispered, then tugged on his T-shirt.

"Hang on." He stretched out a hand, snatched a pen out of a cup near the cash register, and scribbled his cell phone number on his cocktail napkin. When the bartender glanced their way, he thrust the napkin at him. "Have them call me. Tell 'em I want to talk. Come on, sweetheart."

He grabbed Emma by the arm and drew her to the door, leaving their drinks untouched.

A backward glance showed the barkeeper scowling after them, napkin in hand. Oh, yeah, he knew Grimes and Chaplin, probably personally, which meant soon enough, those goons would call or text Ben and arrange a meet-up.

But what would he do with Emma when the time came?

"Ben." Emma tugged him to a halt—no easy feat as he stalked forward, lost in thought.

"What?" She finally had his full attention.

"You said something about a pinkie ring. The big man who pulled me out of the car had a pinkie ring. Was it thick and gold?"

Ben clapped a hand on his bald head. "Then Grimes *is* the kidnapper. I thought he looked like the composite of the big guy. But who's the Charlie Chaplin lookalike? He doesn't resemble the second sketch at all."

"He could have been driving the van."

Ben groaned. "I forgot all about the van." With a glance over his shoulder, he drew her into the nearest cobblestone alley. "This is where those two tried to jump me the other night. There's a set of stairs that'll take us to the top of the floodwall. We shouldn't hang out down here; too many windows."

As he drew her through the alleyway, Emma's mind made a

connection that had niggled when the police questioned her in the room with the two-way mirror. She stopped in her tracks. "There's someone else who wore a ring like Grimes's!"

Ben tore his attention off their surroundings. "Who?"

"The detective back in Virginia Beach, the one who's trying to frame us."

"You mean Peyton?"

"Yes." She'd obviously been trying to forget him. "Peyton had a ring like the one Grimes was wearing, a signet ring with a flat top, only he wore it on his right hand and not on his pinkie. Did Grimes have an engraving on his?"

"Possibly. I didn't get a good look at it."

"Peyton's ring had something like a dragon on it. I remember it had wings."

He cast another uneasy glance at the windows. "Come on. Let's find a place where we can lie low and do some research. It'll probably take a while for the perps to take the bait." Ben hustled her up the steep stone steps ahead of him.

"Are you sure that bartender knows them?"

"I'm sure. I'm also sure they'll want to talk to me again."

Recalling the red mark on Ben's head the other night, Emma balked at the idea of a second encounter. With every step up the face of the floodwall, her anxiety rose. At the top of the stairs, she turned, meeting Ben's gaze and, since he stood one step below her, their eyes level.

"I'm scared," she admitted. "It's like we're up against the mob or something."

His expression softened as it lingered on her face. "You don't have to be scared, Em. I deal with bad guys all the time."

"But, Ben, this is bigger than just two men. It's like a powerful network."

"Look." He surprised her by hiking up the sleeve on his right arm and showing her—not just his bulging biceps with a farmer's tan—but a tattoo written in a fancy font.

Emma read the words *Mr. Fix-it,* and her eyebrows rose. "Did you get that after you helped me start up my car?"

"Nope." A rueful smile kicked up the corners of his mouth. "I got it after three months of sniper school about six years ago."

Her gaze met his. "Seriously?"

"Cross my heart. Now, have a little faith in me. God's put me in your life for a reason, so let me do my thing."

She nodded, struck by wonder. God had known all along that her sons would be taken from her. Why else would He have brought Ben into her life but to help her get her boys back?

"Okay." She nodded her agreement. "I'll let you do your thing. Just don't get into any more trouble on my account."

His gaze dropped to her lips even as he cracked a smile. "Don't worry about me, sweetheart. If we can find your boys, any trouble I get into will be totally worth it."

His declaration melted her. Oh, dear. It was getting harder and harder to remember why she couldn't have feelings for Ben. Truth be told, she was half in love with him already.

CHAPTER 11

*M*iles Ellis trod the uneven sidewalk while brainstorming his next move. Time was running out on his investigation. As he chased his shadow past the Colonial Park Cemetery and the Cathedral of St. John the Baptist with its massive double spires, he asked himself where he was going.

McKenzie's absence at the food line today left him feeling restless. Aside from the Sundays she took off regularly, this was the first morning since his arrival at the shelter that she hadn't shown up to serve brunch to the shelter's residents.

She's probably planning her wedding. The explanation further soured his mood. Looking up, he realized he was making his way along a familiar route: Liberty to Whitaker to East Jones Street. To what purpose? He couldn't just knock on her father's door, looking for her.

The vision of a vanilla Acura turning toward him at the intersection ahead stopped his heart. Was that McKenzie's car? Yes, it was. His spirits winged upward.

He stood taller, willing her to see him. When her vehicle pulled along the curb next to him, he grinned with relief. Her passenger window came down, revealing her answering smile. "Hi, Miles."

"Hi." He stepped toward her window, taking note of her casual attire. She wore distressed jean shorts and a wheat-colored cropped top, making her look younger and more carefree than he'd ever seen her. He had to drag his attention from her bare midriff. "We missed you today."

"Sorry." An unrepentant smile deepened her dimples. "I went to see my mother. And my father's out of town, so I'm playing hooky."

So that was the reason for her brighter complexion.

"I'm glad I ran into you, though." She reached under her seat and pulled out a composition notebook, which she extended toward him. "I wanted to give you this."

"What is it?" He cracked the cover, intrigued to see a sketch of irises and delicately penned notes. Flipping through subsequent pages, he saw more flowers and more notes.

"It's my mother's garden journal. I figured you should brush up on your landscaping skills before your interview tomorrow."

He looked up sharply. "Interview?"

"My father agreed to consider you for the gardening position." Her smile turned smug.

At the last second, Miles remembered to react like a teenager. "Oh, sweet!"

"Don't get your hopes up, though. He doesn't know you very well." She glanced in her mirror as if worried her father might suddenly roll up behind her.

"This is awesome!" Miles took another look at the detailed notes. Every local shrub and flower had been named, both in English and in Latin, along with directions for its care and keeping. Wow, he actually had a shot at getting the job as Jones's new gardener. McKenzie might have just saved his investigation from being tanked. "Thank you, really. This book shows a lot of love. I'll make sure you get it back."

A shadow of sorrow crossed her face. "My mama practically lived in her garden. When she was first diagnosed with Alzheimer's, she wrote everything down so someone else could care for it the way she did."

"Well, if I get the job, I promise you I'll do my best to follow her instructions. So, what time is the interview?"

"Tomorrow at eleven. Do you know where we live?"

"Um. Yeah, I think so." He could probably walk there blindfolded.

"Just knock at the front door, and Jakes, the butler, will let you in."

He already knew they had a butler. "Will *you* be there?"

She averted her pained expression. "No. I've got a fitting in the morning."

For a wedding dress, he guessed, his stomach pitching. "Where are you headed now?" Hopefully not to spend time with her fiancé.

She bit her lower lip, then admitted. "To the beach."

She clearly felt guilty about it. "Good. You could use some time to yourself."

She sent him a small smile.

"You still going to marry that guy?" The tactless question just popped out of him, but it sounded like something an eighteen-year-old would say.

McKenzie gave a quick shrug. "I guess so."

According to FBI analysts, the Charleston millionaire, Ashton Ravenel, was fifty-two years old. "You could cancel." He tried to keep his tone light. "I mean, hey, this is the twenty-first century, and arranged marriages aren't really trending anymore."

She managed a weak laugh while glancing into her rearview mirror. "I have to go."

"Wait." He put his hand firmly on her car door, keeping her there.

As her widening eyes traveled from his knuckles to his mouth to his eyes, desire seemed to leap out and grab hold of his throat.

"Let me come with you," he heard himself beg. He waited, the air stripped from his lungs, for her answer.

"Miles." She shook her head, but her eyes conveyed longing.

"Your dad's out of town, right? He'll never find out." He couldn't believe he was pushing himself on her so blatantly. *For the sake of the investigation.*

She tore her gaze away to assess the area. Nobody seemed to be looking at them. "Okay. Get in, quick!"

Miles didn't hesitate. He ripped open her car door and jumped into the seat next to her. As McKenzie accelerated into her lane, driving them swiftly toward the Islands Expressway, he tamped down his guilt.

Yes, he was taking advantage of her misery, but he was desperate to get her to himself. She might know nothing of her father's crimes, but the only way to know for certain was to ask her.

Strolling beneath branches drenched in Spanish moss, Emma marveled that such a lovely town could disguise a criminal element. Upper Factors Walk, a bricked walkway built at the top of the floodwall, looked down onto Lower Factors Walk, the alley behind the old warehouses. From this height, shoppers crossed flyovers and catwalks to access boutiques and restaurants located on the warehouses' third floors.

Between the wooden placards naming each venue and the old-timey gas lamps, a romantic ambiance kept Emma distracted from thinking of the meeting Ben hoped to strike with the kidnappers.

As they strolled past the Savannah Cotton Exchange, a red brick building where cotton used to be priced before being exported globally, the statue of a winged lion out front made her think of the smaller statues guarding the gate at the men's shelters, only those had the heads of eagles.

Crossing a footbridge, they strolled over the cobblestone ramp they had taken down to River Street for coffee earlier that morning. On the other side of the Regency Hotel, East Factors Walk became West Factors Walk. Emma spotted a placard with the painted image of a cat standing on a stack of books.

"Look." She pointed it out to Ben. *Savannah Shelves. Vintage Books, Antiques and Collectibles.* "Maybe we could do some research while we're waiting."

"Let's check it out." He drew her over an elevated walkway railed in wrought iron to the store's entrance.

Bells jangled softly, announcing them. The scent of lavender, old parchment, and furniture polish filled a store that was deep and narrow and devoid of people. Bookshelves lined every wall save for the front, where stained-glass frames hung in the windows, casting warm colors on the worn Victorian carpet. A mishmash of antique furniture and curio cabinets filled the center of the space.

As Ben shut the door behind him, a dusky-skinned woman straightened from a display case. Her dark eyes went from Emma to Ben and widened. "Welcome to Savannah Shelves. Can I help you find something?"

Ben nudged Emma ahead of him, conveying that she should do the talking.

"Oh. We're just...looking around." Noting the kind expression on the shopkeeper's face, Emma decided she could be trusted. "Actually, we need to research the Centurion Cohort. Have you heard of them?"

The woman stiffened, then darted a worried glance at the door.

Noting the woman's discomfort, Emma pitched her voice lower. "I believe they kidnapped my three sons." Her raw words hung in the quiet store, reminding her of her devastation.

The middle-aged store owner studied her with rounded eyes, then bit her lower lip as if deciding whether to say anything.

Ben stepped closer. "Please, if you know anything, we could really use your help."

"Just a minute." Coming out from behind the cabinet, the store owner crossed to the door and locked it, causing Ben and Emma to share a look of concern. "You've come to the right place." She gestured for them to follow her toward the bookshelf on the back wall. "I've got a book you need to see."

Standing on tiptoe, she pulled a slim hardback volume from the crush of books and handed it to Emma.

Centurion Cohort Handbook, Emma read with a tingle of amazement. Talk about God leading them straight to the right place.

"This was my father's. Before he met my mother, he was a member of the Cohort. This was in the seventies, mind you, and since my mother is Black, the Cohort voted my father out. He wasn't supposed to keep this book. It's extremely rare."

Noting the hefty price on the faded red cover, Emma cracked it open and flipped through the pages while Ben joined her, looking over her shoulder.

"You're welcome to sit down and read through it." The store owner waved them toward a set of ladderback chairs. "I'll unlock the door because I need the business. But if someone else comes in, please don't say the word *Centurion* out loud."

Bemused, Emma led the way toward nearby chairs. Ben's chair creaked as he eased down next to her. Holding the book in such a way that they could both see its contents, she leafed through its yellowed pages. Chapter 1 was devoted to hierarchy. The name Henry Jones, high consul, jumped out at her.

She pointed it out. "Is this Jared Jones's father?"

He shrugged. "Hard to say with a name like Jones, but it could be. Maybe the position is inherited."

"We could ask his daughter."

On the next page, Emma slid a finger over the list of leadership positions from highest to lowest. "Where do these ranks come from: high consul, prefect, princeps, princeps prior, and legionnaire?"

"I think they're the ranks of the Roman Army. Princeps prior—that's what Carl is already. He was supposed to be a legionnaire for four years."

"Hmph." With much to ponder, Emma flipped to Chapter 2, which detailed the behavioral expectations for its members. "Well, they have high standards: 'No public drinking, brawling, or swearing.' And this one." She pointed to the line: *No consorting with individuals of a different race.*

He raised his eyebrows. "Maybe that's changed in the past fifty years. What else?"

Emma flipped to Chapter 3, titled *History of the Centurion Cohort*, which detailed how the Cohort was founded, just as Miles had told them, at the end of the Civil War.

Emma moved to Chapter 4, *Symbolism in the Cohort*. "Oh, this is interesting." She skimmed the text, flipped the page, and froze as she beheld sketches depicting various creatures.

Ben leaned closer, examining each small drawing the way she was. "Now we're onto something."

Emma named each animal in turn. "Badger, stag, wolf, bull, eagle—" She gasped, pointing to a sketch near the bottom. "This one was on Peyton's ring."

Ben scanned the text next to it. "It's a griffin, like the statues at the gate of the Centurion Men's Shelter."

"With the head and wings of an eagle and the body of a lion. There's also one on the fountain in Jones's garden."

Ben read the paragraph beside the sketch. "*'The griffin signet is awarded to loyal members with twenty or more consecutive years of service to the Cohort, who have also completed four acts of selfless service.'*" He met Emma's gaze. "No wonder Peyton was determined to pin this on us. He's a Centurion, too. He's part of the conspiracy!"

A chill skated up Emma's spine. "What do you think *selfless service* means?"

"I'm afraid to ask."

Fear prickled her scalp tight as the realization that her boys' abduction had been planned down to the minutest detail. "Ben," she whispered, glancing toward the proprietress who busied herself behind her display. "If they've penetrated law enforcement, how do we know they're not in the FBI? Butler might be one, too. He might be coming here to trap us!"

Ben expelled a breath. "We have to trust Butler. He's the only one who's taken us seriously so far."

Overwhelmed by their discovery, Emma thrust the book at him and folded her arms to hug herself. "This is a nightmare."

She wasn't so overwrought that she didn't notice Ben's hand come to rest at the base of her neck. He spent the next few seconds kneading the tense muscles there. Even in her misery, her stomach swiveled with awareness of his pleasant touch.

Catching himself, he patted her back platonically, then closed the book with a snap. "I'm going to buy this for Butler."

Emma watched him make his way toward the store owner and tell the woman he was going to buy the book. An awful feeling spread through Emma. Less than an hour ago, Ben's tattoo had reassured her that he was in her life to make this situation right. Now, she was afraid for Ben—even if Butler turned out to be their ally. They were up against an evil entity rooted in power and history.

Clasping her moist palms together, she prayed for their protection.

"We have a potential problem."

Coming on the heels of nine rounds of golf with his buddy, The Architect's greeting cast a shadow over Jared's sunny mood.

"What now?" With his cell phone pressed to one ear, Jared jammed his golf club into the bag on the back of his cart and stalked to a distance where his conversation could not be overheard. While Ashton was also a Centurion, he relied on Jones to keep their operations running smoothly.

"The Navy SEAL is putting the pieces together," continued the disembodied voice, ever disguised by some voice-changing software. "He's identified Grimes as one of the kidnappers and insists the Centurions are behind the boys' disappearance. As of yet, he's only mentioned this to the investigating agent, but if he takes his suspicions any further, it could spark an inquiry."

Jared voiced his annoyance with a curse. "Peyton should never have allowed the fall guy to come down here."

"Evidently. Then again, your men, Bates and Grimes, shouldn't be showing their faces in public."

"Enough," Jared cut him off. "I'll have the SEAL brought in. He won't get the chance to talk."

"That won't be necessary. The investigating agent is headed to Savannah to do the same thing."

"I said I'll handle it. Your people are taking too long."

"He's a SEAL. Are you certain your people can contain him?"

Jared turned his back on Ashton's curious scrutiny. "Don't deign to condescend to me," he hissed. "You forget to whom you pledged your service."

"And you forget," The Architect countered with a dark smile in his voice, "who protects you."

Frustration threatened Jared's self-control. "Then do your job! With the Navy SEAL out of the way, it shouldn't be all that difficult."

"Consider it done."

The phone clicked in Jared's ear, depriving him of the satisfaction of hanging up first. Drawing a deep breath, he willed his blood pressure to lower. He had paid The Architect phenomenal sums over the years to cover his trail. Why, this time, was he having to handle matters himself? The Architect was slipping.

Or did he secretly wish for Jared's downfall? Despite the bright sun, an icy finger of fear raked Jared's spine. Oh, hellfire. If anyone could ruin him, it was his nameless, faceless protector.

The sky was an impossible shade of blue, so pure it almost hurt to look at it. Miles and McKenzie had walked at least five kilometers in a southerly direction. In all that time, she'd talked nonstop, admitting—at first hesitantly—and then in a great gush of anxiety, her hopes and fears.

Humbled to be trusted with her deepest secrets, Miles remained quiet and just listened. The dainty imprints of her bare feet in the sand and the way her dark-brown ringlets danced in the breeze kept him spellbound. Given the quantity of personal information McKenzie was divulging, she had craved a listening ear for some time.

Her voice grew husky whenever she mentioned her mother. Listening to stories of her childhood, he was struck by their parallel upbringing. Both of their fathers were busy and aloof, while their mothers, friendly and concerned, had been their allies.

"I've only ever wanted to be like her." The wind blowing in off the ocean wicked away the moisture shining in McKenzie's light-green eyes. "She was as beautiful on the inside as she was on the outside."

"That's where you get it from."

His compliment earned him a self-conscious smile. "Oh, I'll never be as beautiful as she was. And I know she's still with me, but..." She cut herself off as a sob crept into her voice. "But I miss her so much."

Miles longed to ask whether Genevieve Jones had kept daily memoirs in addition to her garden journal, but this wasn't the time to ask. McKenzie required his comforting. Throwing caution to the wind, he reached for her hand.

The gesture earned him a startled glance, but her palm remained nestled against his, and their fingers folded harmoniously together. Miles's breath shortened. He would never forget this day.

If he wasn't careful, he might end up spilling his heart to her, the way she was spilling hers to him, and jeopardize everything. It took all his discipline not to comment on the parallels in their lives.

"Does your mother realize your father's marrying you off to Ashton Ravenel?"

She came to a startled stop. "How do you know Ashton's name?"

"You told me the day you showed me your ring. He's the luckiest guy on earth. How could I forget it?"

Her gaze shifted past him toward the grass-tufted dunes and the houses built a hundred yards from the water to protect them from flooding. "You really think he's lucky?"

The question blew him away. He stepped into her field of sight, forcing her to look at him. "I *know* he's lucky. McKenzie, you're incredible. You're beautiful, kind, intelligent."

"You don't know me." Without warning, she tugged her hand free and kept walking.

Her sudden vehemence startled him. He pursued her. "Yes, I do. I've seen how you are with the guys at the shelter. You're like a ministering angel."

"No." She shook her head and kept marching. "I'm not. You want to know why I'm marrying Ashton?" She rounded on him suddenly. The wind molded her clothing to her delicate, shapely body. Her eyes glimmered with anguish.

"Why?" He was dying to understand her.

"Because I killed someone."

The words ricocheted inside his head, making no sense. "You what?"

"It's true." Her voice frayed with shame. "When I was a freshman in college, I decided I would drink like everyone else was doing, only I wasn't used to it. And then I drove home. I was turning left onto Oglethorpe when a man appeared right in front of me, and I hit him. When I got out to help him, he was dead!"

The horror tightening her face was hard to look at. *Oh, honey.* "What did you do?" He could only imagine how her sensitive soul would have reacted.

"I called my father, who called the police. Only they never arrested me." She shrugged her tan shoulders. "They said the man was homeless, anyway; no one would miss him. Because of who my father is, no one filed any charges. I never even went to court. It was like the whole thing never happened." Tears now glimmered on her lashes. "For the rest of my life, I will owe my father for that."

Anger simmered in Miles at the suspicion that Jared Jones never let her forget it, either.

"You don't owe him anything."

She shook her head, dismissing his heated objection as irrelevant. "See, I'm not wonderful. And I won't blame you if you find me repulsive now." She began to turn away.

Miles caught her arm, pulling her back around. "Repulsive?" If anything, her humanity made her more appealing than ever. "I could never find you repulsive, McKenzie. But now, I understand why you spend all your time at the homeless shelter."

Tears spangled her eyes as she gazed back at him.

Miles couldn't stop himself. He embraced her. It came as no surprise to discover she smelled of honeysuckle, and they fit together like yin and yang. The desire to protect her, to whisk her away from her callous father, had him adding in her ear, "Your father uses your secret to make you do what he wants. Am I right?"

"Yes." She choked back a sob.

"Listen to me." He pulled back just far enough to see her expression. "You don't have to marry Ashton. There's got to be another way."

"What way? I'm not as brave as you, Miles. I can't just run away. Who would look after my mother?"

The need to tell her who he really was, to promise her shelter under witness protection, trembled on the tip of his tongue. Except he couldn't be sure whether McKenzie's fear of her father outweighed her desire to be free of him. "I don't know. But I'll find out."

She smiled at him with what was clearly gratitude. "You're so kind. I never knew a man could be so kind."

All at once, she stiffened, obviously recalling that he was just an eighteen-year-old runaway with a history of addiction. Pulling away, she shook her head as if to tell herself it wasn't right for her to have told him so much. "We'd better head back." She slipped her fingers in her pockets to keep him from taking her hand.

The desire to admit to everything burned in Miles. But now was not the time. "Yeah."

Retracing their footsteps, they began the long walk back to her car.

Perhaps, one day soon, he could tell her who he really was. Right now, his priority was to get the gardening position at Jones's mansion. A job like that would give him access to Jones's office so he could put a tracer on his car, bug his office landline, and eventually even rifle through his personal files.

He couldn't let this impulse to rescue McKenzie get in the way of his investigation.

Tiffany Hughes balanced her rolling suitcase on one hip as she stuck her key into the door of her condo and wriggled it, but the lock stuck. With a mutter of annoyance, she tried again, managing to release the lock this time. She reached inside and flipped on the light.

She'd been swinging golf sticks for five days straight, topping off the tournament by partying with the champions the night before. Every muscle in her body ached. Exhaustion tugged at her, making her long for a hot shower and a full night's rest.

After locking up behind herself, Tiffany dragged her suitcase down the hallway. She left her bag inside her door to unpack the next day and went straight into her bathroom, where she stripped and stepped into her shower, enjoying the glide of warm water over her aching muscles.

With the lyrics of a drinking song stuck in her head, she twisted off the faucet, reached for a towel, and stepped out of the shower. The open door showed a bedroom steeped in darkness. How about that? She'd been so tired that she hadn't even turned on the light!

With a shrug, she toweled off, tied the towel around her torso, then brushed her teeth. She was dragging a comb through her damp, dark hair, softly singing the ditty in her head, when a middle-aged man appeared in the mirror, emerging from her bedroom. Her song morphed into a yelp. Tiffany whirled, thrusting out her comb to ward him off.

The stranger hushed her with a finger to his mouth. Seeing the latex gloves on his hands, she dragged in a breath to scream. He lunged at her, clapping his gloved hands over her nose and mouth and closing off her airways. Then, he pulled her by the head into the darkened bedroom.

CHAPTER 12

*B*en waited with the patience of a sniper for Grimes and Chaplin to contact him. Amos called at 3:00 to tell him he, Grace, and their two boys had put Emma's house back to rights, but not before Amos took pictures of the mess and filed a complaint with the chief of police.

At 4:30, Reno checked in to ask when he could expect Ben's return. The local police had been hounding him since Ben and Emma disappeared. And at 5:00 P.M., Tony texted *Will do*, in response to Ben's irate text ordering him to tell his fiancée to sing a different tune.

But the communication Ben had been waiting for did not arrive until 1:30 A.M.

Ding!

The sound of its arrival awoke Ben from a light slumber. He noted the local area code from which it had been sent while reading the cryptic message CITY MARKET, 10:00 A.M. and tamping down a surge of adrenaline, which made it hard to fall back asleep.

At dawn, he gave up the pretext of sleeping and rolled out of bed. Moving across the room to keep from waking Emma, Ben googled *City Market* on his cell phone, discovering it to be a touristy area for shopping just a few blocks inland from River Street.

On both Google Maps and Google Earth, he studied the layout, pleased with what he saw. The two-block area with limited exit points and no adjacent structures tall enough to conceal a sniper offered an ideal venue for a face-to-face encounter. Hopefully, Ben would learn something today—anything—that would be helpful to Butler when he arrived.

But what would he do with Emma in the meantime?

"So, they texted me," he told her when she stretched and opened her eyes.

Emma jerked to a sitting position, her hair a golden-brown halo. "What did they say?"

"They gave me a meeting place and time. City Market, 10:00 A.M. today."

She eyed him tensely. "Where's that?"

"It's close, but I think I'll drive there. I want to get there early and recon the area." He'd located a parking deck online, just one block over.

Emma tossed back her covers and sprang out of bed. "I'm coming with you."

"Emma, you can't." He flinched at her look of affront. "Yesterday was one thing. But today, I'm going to talk to the perps, and I can't be worrying about you when that happens."

Her eyes flashed. "So don't. I can take care of myself." On her way to the bathroom, she spotted the fob to his car and snatched it up, taking it with her into the bathroom so he wouldn't leave while she showered. "I'll be ready in five minutes."

As he waited, Ben wondered how to get the fob from Emma without caving into the very real desire to kiss her again. He should never have kissed her in the first place because all he could think about was doing it again.

Minutes later, with her hair subdued into a French braid and wearing the blue patterned blouse and shorts he'd bought for her, Emma emerged. "Okay, let's go." She marched briskly toward the door, snatching up her purse along the way. "I'll drive."

Ben managed to reach the door before she did. Planting a hand on it, he stopped her from pulling it open.

She met his gaze with sparks in her dark-blue eyes. "Let me pass."

"Please, Em. I can't put you in harm's way. Give me the fob, or I'll take it from you."

To his surprise, she went on the offensive, fisting the material at the front of his green T-shirt and giving him a shake. "You didn't put me in this situation, Ben. I was dragged along the road because of those two men, not you. They took my boys from me! What can happen that's worse than that?"

He pictured something a lot worse. "You'd be surprised."

"I don't care! I'm going with you."

Staring her down, he was all too aware of the way her chest rose and fell, the heightened color in her cheeks that made her exceptionally beautiful. The thought of her coming to harm sickened him, but he didn't see how he was going to keep her here short of tying her up in this room, which he knew better than to try.

"Fine. But when we run across our guys, I will deal with them, not you. And when I put you somewhere safe, you are going to stay small and not move. No coming to my rescue. I'm good at what I do, and I don't need your help doing it."

She rolled her eyes at his confident assertion.

"And if something unexpected happens, you'll drive back to this hotel." He pulled out his wallet and handed her Reno's business card. "Call Reno from this room. He'll know how to help you." Next, he tried handing her his credit card.

"I don't need your money."

"It's for emergencies, Emma. If you want to buy something with it, I'll add the expense to your rent. Take it."

With a sigh of acceptance, she took it, then slid the two cards into her pocket right next to Ben's car fob. "Has it occurred to you that this is a trap?"

"Of course, it is. But I have a knack for self-preservation, and the only way to learn more about what's happened to the boys is to engage with the kidnappers. So let's go."

"Wait." She threw her free arm around his neck and planted a platonic kiss on his cheek. "Be careful."

Desire shot straight to Ben's toes. Turning his head, he caught her lips before she pulled entirely away. If something bad happened, he wanted the memory of kissing her properly.

And what a memory it was! He could have stayed there all morning, kissing her. But they weren't going to find her boys this way.

Digging deep, he set her at arm's length and opened the door. "Let's go."

They were crossing the hotel parking deck and headed for his car when his cell phone vibrated. It was Lucas's wife, Charlotte.

"Yes, ma'am." He put his phone on speaker so Emma could hear her.

"Hi, Ben. Butler just shared some disturbing facts with me. I'm calling to see if you're aware of them."

Ben stopped walking, forcing Emma to do the same. "Like what?"

"Well, for one, the casts made from the tracks at Medoc Mountain State Park match the tread on your truck tires."

Emma sucked in a startled breath. Ben shot her a frown. "It's probably a common brand of tire." Emma couldn't possibly suspect *him*.

"Possibly, but Butler was granted a warrant to search your vehicle, and that turned up a Gerber tactical blade with Colton's DNA on it."

Emma bit her bottom lip and stared at him.

Colton had found his *knife*? This was getting worse by the second. "I keep it hidden under my driver's seat. He must have found it when I left him in the truck for a short spell." Ben defended himself as much to Emma as to Charlotte.

An uncomfortable feeling lodged in the pit of his stomach—the feeling a sniper got when he was spotted. "Are you saying Butler suspects me? I have an airtight alibi."

"Someone can vouch for you the evening the boys were abducted?"

"Yes, I was up in Williamsburg. Do you want that information now, or—?" He dreaded having to mention it in front of Emma. In light of their deepening intimacy, it seemed disloyal to mention Tiffany.

"Just make sure Butler has it."

"I told him days ago. I don't know why I would still be considered a person of interest...unless." The unthinkable occurred to him. "Unless Butler's a Centurion."

"A what?"

Ben raked his gaze over the empty car garage for any possible eavesdroppers. "It's a secret society down here in Savannah. Emma's ex-husband is a Centurion now. And they only acknowledge male heirs, which gives him a motive for snatching his sons."

Emma pressed a fist to her stomach while staring at the concrete floor.

"Okay." Charlotte didn't sound at all convinced.

Ben didn't have the time or the patience to explain it to her. "Listen, I have to go. If something goes left after Butler gets here, remember what I told you. Look into the Centurions. They're way more influential than anyone realizes."

"I'll keep that in mind."

"Thank you. And thanks for the heads-up about the so-called evidence. Once my alibi is checked, I'm sure I'll be cleared."

"I hope so. Take care, Ben."

Ben put his phone away and dared to meet Emma's stare.

"You keep a *knife* in your car?"

He winced. At least she didn't sound suspicious. "It's for all sorts of things, not just protection. One time, I hit a deer with my truck, and I had to put it out of its misery."

She grimaced and looked away.

"I don't know how Colton found it. I keep it hidden in the springs under the seat. I'm sorry. I'll get rid of it." If they didn't find the boys and get them safely home, it wouldn't matter, anyway.

"What were you doing up in Williamsburg?"

So now, she wanted to hear his alibi. To avoid having to answer, he said, "Why? You think I would actually try to kidnap your boys?"

"Of course not."

The certainty in her tone reassured him. "Good. Now, let's stop wasting time on this nonsense and make some headway on finding them." He continued toward his vehicle.

At some point, he would have to tell her about Tiffany.

Why even hesitate? Because he didn't want her thinking less of him, that was why. And after all this time they were spending together—not to mention the two amazing kisses they'd shared— he didn't want her pulling away from him, not now, not ever.

It had taken him long enough to realize it, but Emma was his next mark—obviously not to kill but to keep forever. Man, no wonder he hadn't been able to get her out of his thoughts when he was in Syria. He'd fallen in love with her! The realization stunned him, keeping him both quiet and disquieted. He'd always hoped he would meet a woman one day who outshone every other woman in the world. Emma was the one.

But unless and until he found her three sons and brought them safely home, his future, he was sure, would never be with her.

Jared Jones reminded Miles of a raptor, complete with a beak-like nose, talons tucked out of sight, and eyes that saw everything. Having heard many a speech delivered by Jones on Wednesday evenings in the big, paneled meeting hall on the second floor of the Centurion Men's Shelter, Miles knew what the high consul respected: hardworking, closed-mouthed individuals determined to pull themselves up by their bootstraps—while looking out for their fellow Centurions. It all sounded so noble.

Miles portrayed himself as just that: a young man eager to climb the ranks of the Cohort, pledge allegiance to the Centurion agenda, and perform whatever ungrateful task he might be called upon to complete.

"I'm a philanthropic man." Jones studied Miles across the acre of polished cherrywood that was his desk. "I take pleasure in enriching the lives of those less fortunate, a fellow Centurion, such as yourself."

"Thank you, sir." It was hard not to sneer at the man's hypocrisy. He owned a sweatshop in Vietnam where children were forced to work twelve-hour days for paltry pay, and he had the audacity to call himself philanthropic? "Does this mean I have the job?"

"Not so fast." Jones held up a long, manicured finger. "Let us walk through the garden first. I'd like to get a feel for your experience."

Thanks to his photographic memory and McKenzie's generosity, Miles smiled with confidence. "Sure thing."

Thirty minutes later, Jones's handshake sealed the hiring process. Miles would show up at 6:00 A.M. sharp the very next morning to begin his gardening duties. He promised to keep off the streets, drug-free, and to remain in good standing with the Cohort. In exchange, he would receive one of the bedrooms reserved for staff on the third floor and paid a respectable weekly salary. The forcefulness of Jones's grip left his knuckles aching as Jakes escorted him out the front door.

Miles couldn't wait to update his supervisor. The investigation had just taken a huge step forward. Thanks to McKenzie, he'd gotten the big break he was hoping for.

~

"Oh, this is lovely." One block from the parking deck where they'd left the car, Emma paused to take in City Market.

Ben was glad to see the area looked exactly as it had online: a couple of city blocks with a pedestrian promenade down the center of it, paved with brick and dotted with flower-filled planters, even small shade trees. The buildings on either side were also made of brick, two stories tall, and standing shoulder-to-shoulder—no alleys to lure him down, like on River Street. Each shop distinguished itself from its neighbor with a painted façade or a colorful awning. With plenty of spectators and no tall, adjacent buildings handy for sniping, it was almost too good of a place for the perps to want to meet.

As Emma had pointed out, this had to be a trap. But Ben wasn't terribly concerned so long as they fell for the bait, which was him. Anything overtly aggressive on their part would be witnessed. All he wanted was the opportunity to rattle the kidnappers' cages and get them to say something useful, something he could share with Butler when the man showed up.

By the time Ben completed a circuit of the area, he desperately needed a caffeine fix. He steered Emma toward the only restaurant serving breakfast. In the outdoor seating area, they shared a bowl of shrimp and grits while Ben downed two cups of coffee while keeping his eyes peeled for the perps.

By 10:00 A.M., there was still no sign of them. They left the restaurant to stroll the promenade.

A beaded necklace shimmering in the display window of a jewelry store caught Emma's eye.

"Let me buy it for you," Ben offered. Maybe she would realize, then, that he was serious about her.

She cut him a startled glance, seemed to consider the offer, then said firmly, "No."

But her tone didn't match the longing in her eyes when she looked back at the necklace.

"Why not? I want to."

But all she did was firm her lips and tow him toward the next store over. Reflected in that store's bay window was a familiar figure crossing the promenade behind him. As Ben glanced casually over his shoulder, Charlie Chaplin ducked into a bar right across from them.

Ben's extremities tingled. Excellent, the perps were keeping their appointment. Sweat popped onto his brow as he considered where to stow Emma while he cornered the man.

A sign for Savannah's Candy Kitchen provided an immediate solution. "Let's check out the local candy." He tugged her toward the adjacent door.

Even though he'd kept his tone casual, Emma cut him a sharp glance before looking around. "Who did you see?"

"Just get inside." He ushered her into the candy store ahead of him, desperate to put her somewhere safe.

The scent of pralines, fudge, and saltwater taffy sweetened the shop's cool interior. Ben steered Emma toward the back of the store, out of sight of the store's front windows. In a separate room, where twenty flavors of custard created a palette of colors behind a glass partition, he caught her by the shoulders.

"Buy yourself some custard with my credit card and wait here for me." He pointed at a small table with their parlor-style chairs. "Stay small, and don't move until I come back."

She nodded nervously. "Please be careful."

He squeezed her arms. "Relax, sweetheart. Just sit here and enjoy your custard. If anyone approaches you, make a scene. I mean it, scream loud."

Brushing a kiss across her startled lips, he left her there and helped himself to the Candy Kitchen's rear exit, marked STORE PERSONNEL ONLY, which put him on the street behind the market.

By the time Ben rounded the end of the promenade, Charlie Chaplin was peering through the candy store's front window. Despite the summery heat, he wore a denim jacket and kept a hand in his pocket.

Delving his own hand under his T-shirt, Ben casually approached him. "Hey, Charlie. You want to sit in that gazebo right there and talk?"

The perp gave a visible start. To Ben's surprise, he smirked and bolted away from him, scattering the little birds pecking at crumbs as he fled.

Ben hesitated, wary of a trap. Chaplin didn't seem all that interested in talking. Alert for an ambush, Ben pursued the man, cutting a diagonal path across the promenade toward the trafficked street that bisected it.

Chaplin had disappeared around The Signature Gallery of Savannah. Through the art store's many windows, Ben kept him in sight. But then the man jumped into a car at the curb, and it took off. Frustrated, Ben rounded the corner, hoping at least to get a license plate, but the car was too far away.

The suspicion that he'd left Emma vulnerable to attack had him backtracking swiftly. He turned the corner, colliding with an old man walking his Chihuahua. The man yelped, Ben threw his arms out to keep the man from toppling over, and the dog bit Ben's ankle.

Ouch! Razor-sharp teeth dug into his Achilles tendon. Ben steadied the man on his feet while trying to shake loose the ankle-biter. "Sorry, sir. You okay?"

"You should watch where you're going!"

"Yes, sir." Ben managed to wrench his ankle out of the canine's tiny jaws. "You're okay, though, right?" A glance at his ankle showed blood oozing into his sock.

"Well, I'm not sure. I think I hurt my neck." The old man put a blue-veined hand to his neck.

Ben hadn't hit him all that hard. "Maybe you should sit down." He gestured to the closest planter while peering anxiously toward the candy shop, worried about Emma. In his peripheral vision, he spotted them: two uniformed policemen closing in fast.

Oh no. The suspicion that the Centurions had trapped him, after all, clamped down on him.

CHAPTER 13

"*E*verything okay over here?"

With a cold feeling in the pit of his stomach, Ben took stock of the approaching officers. One was pushing sixty with a beer gut that lopped over his belt. The other was young and anxious looking, clearly primed for a confrontation, given that his hand was already resting on the butt of his sidearm. People around them gawked, curious to know what was going on.

The old man answered before he could. "This large man bumped into me, and my dog bit him."

The older officer noted Ben's bloody sock. "Dog bite, huh?"

"It's no big deal. I'm fine. He's fine. No need to trouble yourselves." Ben tried to back away.

"Not so fast." The younger officer stepped closer, his manner intense. "Dog bites have to be reported. It's a city ordinance."

"That's true." The senior officer held out a hand and waggled his fingers. "I'll need some ID from the both of you."

Ben gave a thought to Emma as he took his military ID from his wallet. Handing it to the older cop, he prayed the man would take one look at it and let him off the hook. Instead, he passed it to his partner and pulled a notepad from his pocket.

As Ben heaved an inward sigh, the smug expression on the old man's face caught his notice. Not only had he not apologized for his dog's behavior, but he seemed content with all this attention. *Don't tell me this was all a setup.*

A glance toward the candy shop showed Emma hurrying toward him. Ben averted his gaze while shaking his head. To his relief, she interpreted his wishes correctly and went to hover behind the gazebo in the middle of the promenade. Still, her worried stare remained pinned on him.

The experienced officer made short work of copying the old man's address and getting the name of his dog. "Is Cisco up to date on his rabies vaccination?"

"Of course."

He returned the old man's ID. "Mr. Dulay, you're free to go."

Ben took heart. If the geriatric got to leave, then he would be next. But the younger cop who'd been studying his ID took a step closer.

"What branch of service are you in, Ben?"

"Navy." He kept his tone affable.

"Oh, yeah? And what brings you down to Savannah? I take it you're not from around here."

"Vacation." Good thing his concealed-carry permit was honored in Georgia. He had a feeling they were going to find it soon.

"Alone?" The young officer scanned the crowd now gathered around them.

Ben willed Emma to avert her gaze. "Yep."

"Huh." Instead of returning Ben's ID, he informed the older man, "I'm going to run his name, just in case." He walked a short distance away while talking into his radio.

The cold feeling in Ben's gut spread. He wanted to protest that the police were harassing him for nothing, but if he caused a scene, he was certain Emma would rush to his defense. A glance in her direction showed her done with her custard and wringing her hands anxiously. He shot her a warning glance. *Stay put.*

The older cop thrust a pen and a pad of paper at him. "Sir, I need you to sign your name right here."

Ben examined the write-up. It didn't look like anything more than a dog bite report.

"How's the ankle?" the officer inquired as Ben scribbled his name on the designated line.

"It's fine. No big deal."

"Hey, Phil." Excitement tinged the younger policeman's voice as he approached them again. Ben's anxiety rose as that man whispered into Phil's ear. When they both regarded him suspiciously, he knew he was in serious trouble. They drew their weapons simultaneously.

"Freeze! Put your hands behind your head. Now!"

They bore down on him, sidearms pointed at his head and his chest, respectively. Ben did exactly as they said while berating himself mentally. This whole thing *was* a setup. The old man with the dog was probably a Centurion, used by the brotherhood whenever the Cohort needed to waylay somebody. Ben ought to have realized that smirk on Charlie Chaplin's face meant something bad was about to happen.

Like Amos said a lot lately, *son of a monkey.*

"Turn around," barked the younger officer. "Put your hands on the wall now and spread your feet apart."

As Ben turned and splayed his hands on the brick exterior of The Signature Gallery of Savannah, onlookers speculated. His face burned with equal parts embarrassment and self-directed anger. "I have a concealed-carry permit," he stated as the officers simultaneously frisked him.

The younger officer discovered Ben's Glock and seized it. A steel manacle closed around his right wrist before his left hand was jerked off the wall and pulled behind his back. Disbelief kept

Ben tongue-tied for a second. "You can't arrest me. I haven't done anything wrong!"

"You're wanted by the FBI, Mr. Harmony. Resist arrest, and I'll put a bullet in your leg."

Wanted by the FBI? The words reverberated in his head. Charlotte had tried to warn him. The young officer set his handcuffs deliberately tight.

"Stop!" A woman's fraying voice broke into the bizarre scene.

Ben groaned and whipped his head around, letting his frustration show. "Emma, no."

But she was too overwrought to pay him any heed. "You're making a mistake! Ben is here helping me find my boys who were kidnapped. He has an alibi! And we're meeting with an FBI agent today at noon!"

"Let me guess." The younger officer narrowed his gaze at Emma, his tone hostile. "You must be Emma Stuart, mother of the three missing boys. You're wanted for questioning, too."

The older cop unlatched the cuffs from his belt. "You heard him, ma'am. Turn around now. If you don't want things getting unpleasant, you'd best remain docile."

"Ben!" Emma appealed to him with a cry that was part apology and part despair.

"Do as they say, Emma. Reno will fix this later."

The older officer was patting Emma down. He found Ben's credit card, Reno's business card, and Ben's car fob in her pocket but let her keep them all. "You have an ID on you, Emma?"

"No. It's in my purse in Ben's car."

The officer clearly wasn't worried that he was arresting the wrong woman. Ben reeled at what was happening. How could he and Emma be wanted by the FBI?—unless that was the real reason Butler was coming down to see them.

For the first time, Ben envisioned the unthinkable: facing judgment for a crime he hadn't committed.

"Walk. This way." The younger cop shoved him toward the curb of the trafficked street where a squad car that hadn't been there before was now parked behind the horse-drawn carriage offering tours of the historic district. They hadn't been there earlier.

He glanced over at Emma, finding her pale and shaken. This was his fault. He'd underestimated the enemy.

A woman in the crowd pitched her voice loud enough for the crowd to overhear her. "Hey, that's the mother of the boys missing from Virginia Beach! I bet you she got her boyfriend to kill them."

The words broke Emma's stride. She whipped around, all the color draining from her face, only to be shoved from behind by the older cop.

"Easy!" Ben snarled at the man, a follower of Jared Jones, no doubt. The Centurion Cohort was ruining Emma's life.

And how Ben loathed himself for underestimating them. He was supposed to be Emma's Mr. Fix-it, yet there was nothing he could do for her—not right now, at least. But as soon as Reno sprang him out of custody, he would move heaven and earth to prove that both he and Emma were innocent. Then, he was going to find her boys.

But first, he had to tell her about Tiffany before someone else told her, sowing seeds of doubt into her already-disillusioned heart.

It occurred to Emma there was something worse than losing her boys—being blamed for their disappearance. Her stomach roiled. Her heart pounded. Wedged in a cage of Lexan glass in the rear of a squad car next to Ben, she tried to get comfortable on the slippery plastic seat, but with her hands cuffed behind her, that was impossible.

"I'm scared." The words came out of her tight throat as the officers got in up front, slamming their doors shut. They pulled into traffic while spectators gawped after them.

Ben slid closer until their knees touched. "It's going to be okay, Em. Just remember, we've got as many good people on our side as they have bad people."

She swallowed down the tears that clogged her throat. "How could anyone think I killed my own sons? I love them more than anything!" The thoughtless accusation wrung her heart.

"Who cares what they think?" Ben's tone was both harsh and comforting. "What they think doesn't matter."

His sudden silence prompted her to look over at his frowning face. She could tell he had something to tell her. "What?"

His eyes conveyed remorse. "I want to tell you where I was the night the boys were taken."

Finally. Emma held her breath, having wondered more than once.

"I took a couple days of leave so I could accompany a friend to the LPGA tournament up in Williamsburg. She's a professional golfer. I've known her for years."

It took Emma a moment to digest what Ben was telling her. As the truth hit, she shifted away so their knees no longer touched. In other words, while she'd been fighting with every ounce of strength to keep two strangers from abducting her sons, Ben had been enjoying the company of a *woman?*

"But I didn't sleep with her, Emma. I haven't been with anyone in over six months. In fact, I left her there in Williamsburg after the first night because I wanted to be with you."

Was that supposed to make her feel better? His alibi was a woman. Well, of course, it was. She'd been warned by Amos, Grace, and Belinda alike that Ben had lots of girlfriends. Shame on her for forgetting that, even for a second!

Averting her face, she stared out the window on her side of the car, seeing nothing but a blur of buildings as the cruiser carried them...where? To central booking?

"I'm sorry, Emma. I should have told you before. I just wanted you to know in case they try to convince you that I'm responsible for the boys'—"

"Just be quiet! I know you didn't do it."

He fell instantly silent.

Emma shook her head. The sense of betrayal cutting deep into her heart was entirely her own fault. She'd known Ben was a ladies' man, and she'd still fallen for him. Worse, she had let herself *rely* on him after promising herself that she would never, ever, rely on *any* man for *anything*.

Self-loathing turned her face hot.

Yet, in the grand scheme of things, Ben's playboy nature meant very little compared to her fears that her boys might never come home—or that she might find herself in jail for a crime she hadn't committed.

The squad car, which had been speeding them out of the downtown area, merged onto a larger road bearing them to the outskirts of Savannah. Shocked into silence, Emma couldn't say a word. She could scarcely even *feel*. Ben, for his part, kept grimly alert as he paid attention to where they were being taken.

Minutes later, they arrived at a sprawling complex, much of it surrounded by a high chain-linked fence topped with barbed wire. Patrol cars filled the parking lot. The flags fluttering on flagpoles gave it an official air, and large lettering on the side of two adjacent buildings made it apparent where they were: **Chatham County Sheriff's Office** was emblazoned on one building, **Detention Center** on another.

As they pulled up close to a set of double glass doors, two hulking officers emerged and approached their car. The arresting officers got out, and the advancing officers exchanged words with them. The rear locks popped open.

Emma was taken out one door, Ben out the other. With each of her elbows in the grip of the arresting officers, Emma cast a harried glance back at Ben and gasped to see him being wrestled toward a different squad car by the second set of officers.

She ground to a halt, only to be yanked forward again. "Ben! Wait? Where are they taking him?"

Rather than answer, the officers drew her inexorably toward the double glass doors.

"Ben!" Emma dug her heels in, to no avail.

Her last glimpse showed him resisting the two men trying to stuff him into the back of a second cruiser. Her escorts thrust her through the entrance to the sheriff's office and marched her down a sterile hallway lined with doors. The older officer knocked on the last one on the left before pushing it open and shoving her inside.

Emma stumbled into a carpeted office with a large window and a single desk. A slim man in a navy-blue suit stood at her entrance.

Emma gasped. "Special Agent Butler!" He was supposed to be meeting with them at noon to hear their suspicion about the Centurions. "What are you doing *here?*"

"Ms. Stuart." He remained on his feet behind his desk, a peculiar look on his face as if he didn't know what to make of her. "You can uncut her," he said to the officers lingering behind her.

"But she's a susp—"

"Just do it."

With her wrists freed, Emma massaged the blood back into her hands. "They're taking Ben somewhere else. Where are they taking him?"

Butler approached her. Cupping her elbow, he drew her toward a sturdy chair. "You can leave her with me," he said to the officers in lieu of answering. "I'll reach out when we're done here."

Done here. The words sounded so final. "Where are they taking Ben?" she repeated as the officers disappeared. "You said you were coming here to meet us!"

Butler regarded her like she was a creature he had never seen before. "Chief Harmony's being taken right around the corner to the regional detention center where they have the means to contain him. He's too dangerous to keep here. I'll visit him next. Please, have a seat." He tried pushing her down into the chair.

Emma locked her knees, refusing to sit. Suspicion swirled in her. "You *said* you would look into the Centurions yourself, and you were coming down here to hear our theories. You lied to us—why? Are you one of them?"

His forehead furrowed as if her question puzzled him. Leaving her standing there, he returned to his chair, sinking onto it and pressing his head and shoulders against the high seat back.

He heaved a sigh. "The jig is up, Ms. Stuart. Perhaps I should make you aware of the evidence that implicates the both of you."

"Evidence? Of what?" The strength drained abruptly from her legs, compelling her to sit down after all.

"Well, for starters, the tire tracks of the second vehicle at Medoc Mountain State Park match the tread on Mr. Harmony's truck tires."

"Yes, I know that."

His gaze sharpened. "How could you know that?"

"What's it matter? It's probably a common brand of tire." She gave him the same excuse Ben had given Charlotte.

Butler's eyes narrowed. "Do you also know about the knife?"

"Yes. Ben keeps it under his seat in his truck. Colton must have found it and touched it at some point, so what? He didn't kill my sons, Agent Butler. He's been like a...like a father to them." Her throat tightened at the realization that Ben, regardless of the limited time he could spend with her boys, had made a huge impact on them—especially Colton.

"Hmm." The agent dropped his gaze to a manilla envelope sitting on one corner of his desk. He opened it, slid out the two pages inside, and handed them across his desk for her to peruse. "I'd like to hear your explanation for the emails you wrote to Ben Harmony a few months ago while he was overseas."

Baffled, Emma glanced down at the papers she was holding—

obviously printouts of emails. "I never wrote Ben any emails. I don't even own a laptop."

Butler sent her a tight smile. "But you leased one from the IT resource center on campus."

"Well, yes, I had to have a laptop for my classes, but I never sent any emails to Ben on it."

Butler's smile disappeared. "Maybe you've forgotten. Please read what you wrote, starting on the second page and moving up. Perhaps the words will jog your memory." His tone turned harder, colder.

Swallowing down the nausea that made her want to retch, Emma went to the second page and read the final message.

Dearest Ben,
There are just weeks left now until your return, and not a day has passed that I haven't dreamed of our future together.

"This is forgery! I never wrote these words." She jerked to the edge of her chair, trying to thrust the papers back at him.

Butler refused to take them. He studied her through weak blue eyes and sparse eyelashes. "Perhaps you've just forgotten. Please continue reading. You'll see Ben's response right above that."

With great reluctance, Emma read the message that was supposedly Ben's response. The words leaping off the page sounded nothing like him.

Only three weeks left here, baby. When I come home, I'm going to rock your world.

Too appalled to comment, she viewed the email above that—written on the first page, allegedly by her, and sent from her school email address.

If only I didn't have three mouths to feed. I work all night and day, and I never have time to myself. Sometimes, I don't want to be a mother anymore. It's just too hard to do it alone. Life would be so good if it were just the two of us.

Rage rose in Emma like magma, lifting her out of her seat. She loomed over the desk, slamming the papers down on its surface and pointing at them.

"*These* are forgeries. I never wrote such disgusting words. Never! We're being framed, can't you see it? It's the Centurion Cohort. Jared Jones and his father before him have brainwashed hundreds of men over the years to work for them. He's got thugs and even policemen doing his bidding everywhere. People are afraid of him down here. For all I know, you're one of them!"

"Calm down, Ms. Stuart." Butler's voice came out on a firm note. "I am certainly not one of them."

The hope that he might actually believe her had her pulling herself together. She dragged in a shaky breath.

"Please, sit. We're just talking here."

With her heart still pounding, Emma lowered herself back into the chair. Without Ben around to defend her, she felt as vulnerable as when she was fourteen and headed into foster care. *God, help me get through this.* She gripped the arms of her chair with both hands.

Butler had raised a hand and was rubbing his eyes as if thinking about her words. But then he shook his head and dropped his hand. A look of resolve hardened his bland features.

"Look, we can clear any suspicion regarding your participation in this crime with a simple test, a polygraph. If you pass it, you'll be stricken as a suspect, barring any new evidence. Then, I can focus all my attention on who really made your boys disappear."

"It wasn't Ben," she told him through gritted teeth. "He has an alibi. Why haven't you checked on that?" Hurt skewered her anew as she pictured him with another woman.

"I did check on that, Ms. Stuart. Unfortunately, his alibi can't testify on his behalf. She's in a coma. She might have had an aneurysm in her own bed. In any event, she was found unconscious and remains unresponsive."

Shock silenced Emma momentarily. But then a thought occurred to her. "Don't you think that's a remarkable coincidence, Mr. Butler? Isn't it obvious somebody got to her before you did?"

His expression might have seemed skeptical if it weren't for the speculative glint in his eyes.

"If I were you," he pitched his voice to a persuasive murmur, "I would take the polygraph. If you pass it, you'll be free to go."

The promise of freedom clinched it for Emma. Ben had instructed her, if anything went wrong, to get back to the hotel and call Reno Silverman. Something had definitely gone horribly, terribly wrong.

Confident that the polygraph would exonerate her, Emma lifted her chin in the air. "I'll take it."

Ben struggled to shake off the effects of being Tasered. Fifty thousand volts of electricity had walloped his kidneys and seared his spine. It had forked into every extremity and rendered his muscles uncontrollable.

Even incapacitated and barely conscious, it had taken both officers to trundle him into the back of the second cruiser and lock him in. He'd felt the car moving.

After several minutes of near paralysis, Ben managed to pull himself into a sitting position and peer out the window of the speeding patrol car. Through a splitting headache, he noted that the compound where Emma had been dropped off was long gone. They were flying down a double-lane expressway, with low-lying marshes on either side and the occasional housing area. With the sun beating down on the hood of the car, he couldn't tell if they were headed east or west.

"Hey! Where are you taking me?" Ben raised his voice to be heard through the Lexan.

The cops glanced back at him, then exchanged dark looks—not a good sign.

Ben focused back outside. The expressway spanned a bridge, leading him to guess they were headed east toward the ocean. They passed more marshy areas and fewer houses. Minutes later, the cruiser drove by a sign called Whitemarsh Island and exited the highway. It couldn't be more obvious these officers were taking him to some remote area to kill him.

Closing his eyes, Ben drew several calming breaths. Through the pounding in his head, he marshaled his thoughts and planned his escape. Their proximity to water was a good thing.

Rocks pinged the cruiser's undercarriage as it turned off the asphalt road onto a gravel drive, headed toward an estuary. Ben's arteries flooded with adrenaline, which helped to ease his headache. At the end of the drive stood a ramshackle marina consisting of a rusting boathouse and a long, listing pier. An old-timey fishing vessel, maybe forty feet long, bobbed at the end of the pier, manned by two fishermen who stood in wait for them.

Ben swallowed hard. The plan was obvious. They were going to kill him, put his body on the boat, and discard him out at sea. His mouth went dry. *Not if I have any say-so.*

As the cruiser parked near the head of the pier, he readied himself. All he had to do was make it to the water before they shot him. Once he dived beneath the surface, he could conceal himself—a little challenging with his hands trapped behind his back—but not impossible.

The officers got out. The locks on the back door released. As the door swung open, Ben exploded out of it, knocking over one officer and brushing past the other.

"Halt!"

He sprinted, zigzagging to avoid the bullets he anticipated. A glance toward the pier showed the fishermen on the boat gaping at his antics.

Thoop! Thoop! Thoop!

Bullets pelted the sandy soil as he flew over it. His quads and hamstrings strained to make him faster. A fourth bullet whizzed by his shoulder, prompting him to break left.

Almost there. He was just a couple yards from the bulkhead, praying the water on the other side was deep enough for him to dive into headfirst, when—*Bam!*—he got tagged on the side of the skull, hard enough to hurl him to the ground.

He was still conscious when he sprawled face-first into sun-warmed sand.

CHAPTER 14

*J*ared reached eagerly for the landline ringing on his desk. He'd been waiting for a call from Bates advising him that the SEAL was dead and no longer a threat.

"What song does the mockingbird sing?"

The Architect was calling and not Bates. "What do you want?" Jared demanded in lieu of answering.

"Just checking to see how you're doing with the Navy SEAL."

The man seemed to be mocking him. "He's been dealt with, just as I said he would be."

"Good. Good. And you'll inform the press that he eluded officers on his way to jail?"

"I will."

"Clever of you, I must say."

The Architect's praise restored a portion of Jared's goodwill. Perhaps the man recognized his superiority after all. Not only would the SEAL's so-called escape make the man look guilty, but it eliminated the necessity of going to trial and risking outside scrutiny.

"What about the woman?" Jared queried. "How are your people handling her?"

The Architect hesitated. "The media will be told her polygraph results were inconclusive."

"But that's not enough to keep her behind bars."

"No, it's not. We'll need more evidence if we decide to convict her."

Jared frowned, suddenly concerned. "But you can do that. You've done so in the past."

"I could." The Architect paused thoughtfully. "However, I don't believe there's any pressing need."

"How so?" Jared glanced toward his study window, where his new gardener had gotten right to work pruning the climbing roses.

"Only in a courtroom does she pose a threat to us."

"Explain," Jared growled.

"She's a white-trash girl from Mississippi." The Architect's tone became contemptuous. "What's she going to do without her boyfriend's help? She has no money. She'll get nowhere appealing to state or federal law enforcement, who, having seen the news, will already consider her guilty. On the other hand, if she's brought to trial and given a court-appointed attorney, she might persuade some curious soul of Centurion's involvement. We're better off releasing her. Who's to say some accident won't befall her later?"

"I see." Jared had to admit The Architect had a point. Why tempt fate in a trial when the woman could be quietly killed at a later date? "Perhaps inconclusive results will be enough to convict her in the public eye."

"Indeed." The Architect's tone turned condescending again.

With a shudder of dislike, Jared dropped the receiver into its cradle, severing the call. Rising from his leather-covered chair, he left his office to prepare for an evening function at city hall. Now that the threat posed by the Navy SEAL and the boys' mother had been eliminated, Jared could concentrate on other matters, like his daughter's upcoming wedding, for instance.

"Thank you for your cooperation, Ms. Stuart. You are free to go."

The sweat at the base of Emma's spine abruptly dried. "I'm sorry?" Was Butler now toying with her? Just a minute ago, he'd been shaking his head at the report sent to him by the polygraph technician, leaving her to think she had failed the test miserably.

"The results were inconclusive." He sent her a rather baffled shrug. "As such, you are not being arrested at this time. So, there's no need to call that lawyer you mentioned." He helped Emma to rise from her chair, then escorted her to the door, not to lead her to another room for testing but to let her go, apparently.

Cautious relief washed through Emma. "What about Ben?"

Butler reached for the doorknob. With a grim look, he turned to face her. "I'm afraid there's been an incident with Mr. Harmony." He must have learned about it while she was being quizzed by the polygraph technician.

Emma searched his unremarkable features. "Incident?"

Butler avoided eye contact. "En route to the detention center, Mr. Harmony escaped his police escorts. Now, there's a manhunt underway to recapture him."

Emma stared at the agent, unable to digest his words. "Why would Ben have done that?" True, he'd been frustrated when they'd separated him from Emma, but his advice to her earlier had been to cooperate. "That makes no sense. He has no reason to resist arrest."

Butler set his jaw, not answering. Taking a card from his shirt pocket, he thrust it at her. "His so-called alibi is nonresponsive, and the evidence against him is overwhelming, Ms. Stuart. I cannot stress this enough: If he tries to get in touch with you, you must contact me right away. I would hate to see you drawn into this any more than you already have been."

Emma refused to accept what he was saying. Keeping her thoughts to herself, she slid his card into her pocket next to Reno's card and Ben's VISA.

Butler pulled the door open. "Good luck, Ms. Stuart." His tone conveyed concern for her, but apparently not enough to take her Centurion conspiracy seriously.

Stalking away from him, Emma left the building the same way she'd come in.

How could Butler be so convinced of Ben's guilt? He had no more killed her sons than she had written those awful emails. He'd been framed—they both had. Yet, for some reason, the law was letting her go while blaming everything on Ben. Or was it the Centurions who were letting her go? Why—because she posed no real threat to them?

Stepping into the humid outdoors, she could tell by the angle of the sun that it was midafternoon already. A mockingbird twittered with incongruous joy in the branches of a pink crape myrtle tree.

Now what? Without Ben around, Emma's vulnerability chilled her to the core. At least, he'd told her what to do if they got separated: Get back to the hotel and call Reno. Only, where would she find a ride back to the parking deck near City Market?

The apparition of a yellow taxicab provided an answer as it pulled right up to the door she had just exited. Out of the back seat popped a young man with a dejected look on his face. As he plodded into the police station, Emma stepped forward, catching the eye of the dark-skinned driver through the cracked window.

"Excuse me. Do you take credit cards?"

He sent her a friendly smile. "Of course, miss."

"Can I get a ride to City Market?"

He checked his screen. "You're in luck, miss. I'm heading that way."

"Thank you!" Sitting rigidly in the back of the taxi, Emma

succumbed to frightful thoughts. No way had Ben escaped from his police escorts. So, what had happened to him, really. Was he okay?

Her attention was caught by the rosary swinging from the taxi's rearview mirror. *For I am with you, wherever you go.* The reassuring verse from Joshua sounded in her head, giving her the courage to unfurl her fisted hands and draw a steadying breath.

Noticing her anxious silence, the driver's gaze made contact with hers through the rearview mirror. "Can I say a prayer for you, miss?"

Her heart swelled with gratitude. "Say a prayer for Ben, please."

"You got it. Lord God, please watch over Ben wherever he may be. Keep him from all evil and bring him safely back to where he belongs."

He belongs with me and my boys.

With a spasm of sorrow, Emma acknowledged her deepest desire. However long she'd resisted it, the truth was, she wanted Ben to be part of her and her boys' lives from here on out. Yet, her sons were still missing, and now, Ben was on the run. Only God could fix this mess.

She spotted his name on the ID clipped to his visor. "Thank you, Travis."

"My pleasure, miss. Just remember, you are never alone."

Travis had been put here by God, not just to give her a ride but to keep her strong in her faith. But having just witnessed the Centurions' far-reaching powers, Emma couldn't quell the churning suspicion that Ben had been murdered rather than taken to a secure detention center. And without his help, she didn't have the first clue what to do next. She could only hope that Reno did.

"No way." Tony Caruso stared in disbelief at his fiancée, who'd just relayed startling news: Ben Harmony, now wanted by the FBI for abducting Emma Stuart's three boys, had evaded police escorts on his way to a high-security facility.

"It's true." Ruby stood in the kitchen of Tony's beachfront rental, having let herself in with the key he'd given her a while back. She gestured toward his muted television. "I just watched the story on the national news."

"No." Tony shook his head emphatically. "That's wrong. That's crazy. Ben loves those boys. He talks about them all the time. He would never hurt them." Grasping hold of his dark hair, he tugged until his scalp burned.

"Honey, don't do that." Ruby stepped up to him, her turquoise gaze full of concern. "You'll go bald like Ben if you pull all your hair out."

He allowed her to pull his hands to his sides, but her touch merely angered him. "This is your fault," he blurted without meaning to.

Her lovely eyes widened, and her lips parted. "What?"

"If you hadn't kept calling them a couple and persons of interest, nobody would've suspected Ben in the first place."

Ruby's back stiffened. "I was only repeating what the police said!"

"Forget the police!" Tony's Italian temper hijacked him. "Ben is my friend, my *brother*." He jabbed a hand at the muted television. "He's obviously been framed by someone 'cause he would never, *ever*, kill three kids. Instead of standing here telling me he's missing, why don't you be a real journalist and go find out who's framing him!"

Ruby took a sharp step back, astonishment and affront stamped into every line of her face. "A real journalist?"

His words came back and bit him. "No, that's not what I meant. You're already a real journalist. I'm just—I'm speechless that my closest friend is wanted by the cops and running from the law. None of this makes sense!"

Ruby wouldn't look at him.

"Hey." Tony reached for her, embracing her stiff figure. "I'm sorry. I didn't mean to take it out on you."

"Actually, you're right." She twisted from his embrace and crossed to the wall of windows overlooking the Atlantic Ocean. At this time of the evening, the water was already a charcoal gray with the pink-hued sky stretched out over it. "I should be down in Savannah, digging into this further."

Her words caused him to freeze. She was taking off on him *again*? Between his work with the Team and her job as a journalist, their time together was already sporadic. He had just gotten back from Syria a short while ago, and already she was leaving?

"Maybe I can go with you," he proposed.

She arched her eyebrows at him. "Asking for leave takes time, Tony. I have to go tonight while this story is hot and while Emma Stuart is down there in Savannah. I need to talk to her."

Tony watched her spin toward the couch to collect her purse. "How're you gonna find her?"

She flicked a hard look at him. "A *real* journalist can find anybody."

Trailing her to the door, Tony contemplated using force to prevent her departure. But he wanted answers even worse than she did.

"I'll try to get leave so I can join you," he told her as she wrenched the door open.

She sent him a cool shrug and a guarded glance. "Suit yourself."

He wished he could take his thoughtless words back. But, instead of groveling, he attempted damage control. "If anyone can figure out what's going on down there, it's you, Ruby."

She wouldn't even look at him as she stepped outside. "Guess we'll find out."

He gave her bottom a friendly swat before she got away. "Go get 'em, tiger."

She leaped away from his touch, then marched down the

wooden run of steps to her car with her chin up and her shoulders back.

Unsettled by her prickly aloofness, Tony watched her slip into her brand-new, cherry-red Range Rover and back out of his driveway. Remembering Ben's plight, he grubbed in the pocket of his NWUs for his cell phone. Senior Chief wasn't going to believe what Tony was about to tell him.

~

Where am I? Ben awoke to the realization that he was lying face down in a small, dark space with what felt like an axe in his head and his wrists trapped behind his back.

Is this a coffin? Wood surrounded him on all sides, but the space sloped down in the center, and something like a rope was coiled around his ankles.

The rocking motion of the box and the slosh of waves outside brought the memories rushing back at him. He'd been running from the Chatham County Police, who were shooting at him. A bullet had tagged his skull just above his ear. It must have just grazed him while also rendering him unconscious. He could smell and feel the blood drying under his cheek as he lifted his ear off the floor to assess his situation.

Oh, my head!

Maybe the police had taken him for dead. He could tell without even having to feel his pockets that the police had stripped him of his phone and wallet. Then, they'd handed him over to the fishermen who'd stuck him in this hold. And now, they were out at sea, which meant the nightmare wasn't over.

Given the feeble light filtering through the cracks in the wooden hatch overhead, Ben guessed it to be evening already. Hours had passed while he lay here. They were waiting for darkness to descend to dump him out at sea.

Adrenaline beat down the waves of pain that flared from his

temple. He gave himself a pep talk. *Could be worse. The bullet could have gone straight into your thick skull and killed you already.*

Rolling onto his right shoulder, he assessed his bound ankles. In the gloom, he made out the silhouette of an anchor—a big, thick, fifty-pound anchor tied to his ankles by the rope.

Gingerly, Ben laid his head back down and thought. So, the plan to dispose of his body was well underway. Evidently, he was being taken into deep waters, where he would be dumped with the anchor and left as fish food on the ocean floor—less chance of washing ashore that way.

His fast-beating heart made his headache flare again. *Oh, man, that hurts.* He suffered the urge to throw up.

Think peaceful thoughts. Diving into his happy place, he pictured the ten acres of farmland and the big, old farmhouse in Mount Vernon, Illinois, where he'd grown up with his siblings. Once the waves of agony subsided, he centered himself to pray like Emma did. What else could he do?

Lord, if I'm supposed to die this way, just make it quick. But You and I both know we have unfinished business. A vision of Emma in a simple wedding dress flashed into his thoughts. *So, please help me out here. You know I don't ask You all that often.*

Priority number one was to remove the handcuffs. He couldn't even feel his fingers anymore. Searching the small, dim space, he spied what looked like a spool of wire giving off a dull gleam. Ten minutes later, he had freed his right hand of the double-locked cuffs. His mouth tasted like a rusty crab pot, and his arms burned even worse than when he'd crawled over a mound of fire ants in Ramadi, but he had use of his arms now.

As he shook them to promote blood flow, nausea roiled up, forcing him to pause for a minute and just breathe. The bullet has probably concussed him. He might have lost a lot of blood. Or maybe he was just seasick from the boat bobbing up and down.

Once the nausea subsided, he got to work on his ankles, which he discovered were separately bound, secured by someone who tied knots for a living.

When the rope on his right ankle felt slack enough to wriggle his foot free, Ben transferred his attention to his left ankle. He shouldn't take his shoes off yet.

The sudden cessation of the boat's engines told him time had just run out.

Ben tugged and yanked more frantically until he heard voices directly over him. Sliding into the prone position from which he'd awakened, he hid the dangling manacle behind his shackled wrist to make it look like he was still restrained.

Hinges squealed, and cool, briny air washed over him as the hatch was lifted. Peeking through his lashes, Ben could tell night had fallen in earnest. Furthermore, all the lights on the boat had been extinguished, leaving just the starry dome of heaven for illumination.

"You get the anchor. I'll get him." The gruff voice summoned an image of a heavyset man with a beard.

Ben suffered bumps and bruises as he was lifted under the arms and dragged facedown from the enclosure. The man grunted at Ben's weight, but he was strong enough to drag him across the deck of the boat while his partner carried the anchor. All the while, Ben reconsidered Plan A, which was to take his captors by surprise before they could dump him overboard.

The man dragging him across the deck was impressively strong. Even if Ben could take him, he would still have to contend with the second man. Either one of them might be armed. One shot, and he would be as dead as they thought he was. Maybe he was better off with Plan B—getting tossed into the water and left for dead.

As he was heaved headfirst over the bow of the boat, his hips hinged over the railing, Ben made up his mind. Plan B it was. Let Jared Jones and the rest of the Centurions believe he was out of the picture. Given his precarious situation, he very nearly was.

"Ready?" His captor held him in place by his belt loop.

"Almost." The second man grunted as he set the anchor on the ledge next to him.

Seawater sprayed Ben's bald head as he craned his neck to find the shore. The beacon of a distant lighthouse told him he would have to swim a long, long way—provided he survived this next part.

Plan B was just as risky as Plan A.

"On the count of three," said the man holding him.

Ben drew a deep, stealthy breath, praying it wouldn't be his last.

"One, two, three."

As the anchor plunged into the water next to him, the man holding Ben's belt loop let go while simultaneously flinging Ben's knees into the air. Somersaulting into the cool water, black as ink, Ben toed off his shoes in the few seconds he remained near the surface. The rope went suddenly taut as the anchor yanked him *straight* down.

He managed to pull his right foot free. His headache intensified. Clawing instinctively toward the surface, he wasted valuable energy trying, in vain, to free his left foot.

Basic Underwater Demolition/SEAL training had nothing on this. Ben remembered a particular scenario when his diving instructor had disconnected his breathing tube and then tied it into a knot. Overhead, the hum of the propellers grew fainter as the fishing vessel moved away. But the pressure in Ben's ears was growing, and he'd made little headway on the knots.

The oxygen in his lungs dwindled, causing them to burn. Saltwater pressed in on him, heavy, crushing. Still, the rope held him fast. The anchor pulled him relentlessly deeper. Down, down into utter darkness. *Help me, God! I don't want to die this way.*

A sudden light speared the darkness. Warmth suffused Ben. He wasn't alone anymore. A familiar voice sounded in his head.

"Ben."

"*Shawn!*" Astonishment replaced his panic. "*Am I dead now?*"

"*Not yet.*"

Immediately, the shackle around his ankle went slack, and the rope vanished.

He felt himself being pushed toward the surface by an invisible force so quickly that he was forced to slow his ascent to keep from getting the bends. When his head broke the surface, he filled his lungs with glorious, beautiful air, then rolled limply onto his back.

I'm alive! Stunned by what had just happened to him, Ben floated on the buoyant water, reliving the experience. He had not imagined it. Shawn had spoken to him from *Beyond*, which meant his brother was still alive, just not in the flesh. All those prayers Ben and his family had poured out for Shawn hadn't been ignored. Shawn was healed and whole in spirit form. What's more, Ben would see him again one day.

But *not yet*, as Shawn had said. Ben still had work to do here, not the least of which was to look out for Emma and her boys.

As he stared at the sparkling expanse above him, the pounding in his head receded, leaving him quilted in a peace the likes of which he had never before experienced.

His brother lived.

Forgive me for doubting You, Father.

A beam flashed into Ben's eyes, rousing him to the present. He lifted his head to where the lighthouse beckoned him. *Hurry.* There was no time to waste. Emma's boys were still missing, and Emma herself had likely been told that Ben had vanished. Evil seemed to be winning.

Not on my watch.

With a deep breath of resolve, Ben peeled off his sodden socks, flipped onto his right side, and scissor-kicked toward shore, dragging the handcuffs through the water with every stroke.

～

Emma couldn't sleep with Ben gone. She lay on her bed in their hotel room, praying, thinking, and weeping. Was he still alive? If Reno was to be believed, then yes.

"If he escaped from the police, they're not going to find him," he'd assured Emma when she called him.

But what if he hadn't escaped? She spent agonizing hours imagining the horrible things that might have befallen him. He could be dead, even now.

The thought dismantled her heart and threatened to flatten her faith. Never in her life had she felt more alone, not even when she'd gone into foster care.

Remorse followed on the heels of despair. If Ben was dead, she would never get to thank him for all he'd done for her and her boys. She would never get to admit that she'd loved him from the day he'd rescued her on the side of the road—not that she'd wanted to make herself that vulnerable by admitting the truth, but she might never get the chance.

Without Ben, without her boys, how would she go on? Sure, she could drive his Mustang back to Virginia, but if there was even a chance Ben was alive or that her boys were here, she wasn't leaving.

"Oh, God." She was almost without words. "Take this burden from me. Please! I cast myself on Your mercy."

At two in the morning, she got up and opened Ben's backpack, taking out the yellow T-shirt he had worn the day before. Holding it to her nose, she breathed in his citrusy scent—the product of the soap he'd left in the bathtub—and lay down with it.

Pretending he was there with her, she finally fell asleep.

CHAPTER 15

*B*en roused to semi-consciousness. A crab scuttled across his field of vision, its claws making scrabbling sounds on the damp sand and informing him that he'd reached shore only to pass out from exhaustion. The roar of the ocean and the grit of tiny grains scraping every bit of his exposed skin made him think of Hell Week during BUD/S.

Only, this was worse. He couldn't get his chilled limbs to cooperate. And when he lifted his head to look around, pain knifed through his skull, dragging a groan out of him.

Through a haze of wind-blown sand, he spotted a lone figure jogging toward him and blinked to bring her into focus. Friend or foe?

In the pale-pink light, he decided he was looking at a woman, one whose dark ponytail swung as she jogged toward him in a purple hoodie, black yoga pants, and sneakers. He knew the exact moment she spotted him because her stride broke, and then she started sprinting. Ben rolled gingerly onto his side—the best he could do—to greet her.

"Are you okay?" She flew up to him, breathing heavily. Sinking onto her knees next to him, she exhaled warm, minty breath on his face. "You've got a nasty gash on your head." Ben noticed she was pretty but not especially young.

"Concussion," he grated. It hurt just to talk.

She examined the gash more closely. "You could use sutures." Her swift appraisal took in his bare feet, sandy shorts, green T-shirt, and then the handcuffs dangling from his left wrist. With an indrawn breath, she pulled away from him. "You're the man on the news! The Navy SEAL."

Ben grimaced. *Great.* The last thing he needed was to be turned over to the cops by some helpful citizen. "Trust me, I'm not the bad guy. Three boys are missing, and I still need to find them."

He watched her bite her lower lip. Thoughts ebbed and flowed in her brown eyes as she peered about, clearly hoping for some-body—anybody—to come along to help her. At last, she reconsidered him and sighed. "Well, lucky for you, I'm a doctor. I'm also a tenth-degree blackbelt, so don't try anything."

Ben chuckled at her bravado, only to whimper as his headache worsened.

"Do you think you can stand? You'll have to walk. It's illegal to drive on the beach here."

He'd survived death by drowning. After that, anything was possible. "Sure." Digging deep, he pushed to his knees, pausing to let the pain ebb.

The woman helped him straighten, then threw her arms around his waist as he weaved.

"We just have to make it to that house."

He knew better than to see how far away it was. One step at a time, and they'd get there eventually, just like in BUD/S when you fought to get through the next five minutes. Ringing the bell was not an option—not when that left Emma all alone, pitted against the Centurion Cohort.

~

In the maze of corridors beneath the Cathedral of St. John the Baptist, McKenzie located Father Jacob's office. The old priest had retired years ago, but he still volunteered his time as a counselor. She arrived at his open door and found him standing in front of his bookcase.

At her light knock, he turned around. "Good morning. Come on in." Eyeing her through his thick spectacles, she could tell he didn't immediately recognize her. But then, as she approached him, his face lit up with pleasure. "Why, McKenzie Jones, what a lovely surprise!"

They'd crossed paths from time to time at Savannah Hospice, but since the priest's retirement, she'd ceased to see him on the few times she attended mass. "It's been a while."

He caught her hand in his, clasping it warmly, his expression sympathetic. "How's your mother?"

"She had a lucid moment the other day." McKenzie forced a smile. "That's why I'm here, actually. There was something she said."

"Please, sit down." He urged her toward a collection of chairs while going to close the door to a mere crack. "How can I be of help, dear?" Returning, he sat across from her.

Where to start? McKenzie pulled her pendant out from beneath her blouse and showed it to him. "My mother said you know something about this key. I'm not sure if she was making it up or—" The recognition tightening his features cut her off. "It goes to something, doesn't it?"

A worried light entered the priest's rheumy eyes. "You've heard of Pandora's box, haven't you, McKenzie?"

"Of course." When it was opened, it released all the evils of mankind. She swallowed hard. "Why do you say that?"

Instead of answering, he got up, crossed back to his bookshelf, and slid open the cabinet at the bottom. Bending low, he pulled out a metal filing box and carried it toward her, placing it at her feet.

"When your mother gave me this, she called it Pandora's box. She said it was never to be opened by any hand but hers or yours."

McKenzie's scalp tingled with foreboding. She hesitated just a moment before reaching back to unclasp her necklace. With a tremor of discovery, she slipped the key with the chain still attached into the lock, almost surprised when it released with a *click*. Holding her breath, she lifted the lid, half expecting demons to come shrieking out. Instead, she found herself regarding half a dozen journals, not unlike her mother's gardening journal.

With a glance of surprise at the priest, McKenzie lifted out the journal on top and flipped through the pages, noting the date: 2014, just ten years ago. As she began to read, the priest resumed his seat beside her and waited.

Jared's guest tonight was a Russian arms smuggler by the name of Semion Mogilevich. I believe he's wanted by the FBI. He ate his dinner with a knife. Then he and Jared retreated to the study, where I overheard Jared offer the use of his shipping port at the harbor where, of course, no one dares to regulate the goods that come and go.

Amazed, McKenzie shut the journal and reached for another. The year was 2016. *Jared has been selling all our shares in Valeant Pharmaceuticals, tipped off by an insider in Wall Street.*

Growing more excited by the minute, McKenzie cracked open the third journal, the most recent one, opening to a page that read: *This morning, Jared was found not guilty in the money-laundering trial. Once again, the evidence was insufficient to convict him. I have heard him talking on the phone to the one he calls The Architect. From what I can gather, that man is a Centurion who works at the highest levels of the FBI.*

The humming in McKenzie's ears was the sound of her blood racing. It came as no surprise to read that her father was involved in smuggling, insider trading, and money laundering. She'd long suspected charities like the men's homeless shelter and the boarding school for boys were used to cloak more nefarious activities. And what she'd just read was the tip of the iceberg. There were literally 150 pages in each of the six notebooks, every page filled with her mother's recollections of her father's crimes.

As McKenzie lifted out the last journal, the meaning of Genevieve's words, *"It's the key to your future, darling,"* was suddenly clear. McKenzie drew a sharp breath. The pendant was her key to freedom! No wonder her mother had hidden these journals in a box and given them to the priest to protect. Her husband would have killed her if he knew…

That thought brought McKenzie to a sobering reality. She looked over at the priest, who'd sat with his interlaced hands resting between his knees, awaiting her reaction.

What her mother hoped she would do was clear: She would escape her father's expectations by turning over all this evidence… to whom?

"What will you do, McKenzie?"

The priest seemed to know exactly what was in the journals, yet he had chosen not to act. Why? Out of fear of retaliation?

"You know," he added, "both you and your mother's lives will be in danger if you give this box to the wrong person."

She'd realized that much. Searching herself, she discovered, beneath her fear, a steely determination to change her life. "Yes, the right person must be found." With trembling fingers, she returned the journals to the box and locked it. As she refastened the chain around her neck, she met the priest's expectant gaze.

"Would you keep this box a little longer for me?"

"Of course."

"Thank you." Rising with a renewed sense of purpose, she started for the door.

The priest followed her. "Is there anything I can do to make this easier, child?"

She hesitated and turned back. "Yes. Would you pray for me?"

"Of course, McKenzie. I will pray for you both."

"Thank you." With a nod, she strode from his office, feeling like a great weight had been lifted from her shoulders.

She didn't have to marry Ashton Ravenel! In fact, every decision she made from here on out could be her own.

As she climbed the stairs to exit the church, the last passage she'd read returned to her: *"I have heard him talking on the phone to the one he calls The Architect. From what I can gather, that man is a Centurion who works at the highest levels of the FBI."*

McKenzie's steps slowed, and her expectations dimmed.

With the FBI in her father's back pocket, who could she entrust with her mother's journals? And who would protect her and her mother when Jared Jones discovered the depth of McKenzie and Genevieve's betrayal?

A brisk knock on the hotel room door startled Emma from her sleep. She bolted to a sitting position, her heart thumping. Had the Centurions tracked her down? Were they here to get rid of her, the way they'd done to Ben?

Sunshine blazed through the crack in the curtains, telling her she'd slept well into the morning.

The knock came again. "Emma Stuart, are you in there?"

Emma didn't recognize the female voice. She remained in bed, too wary to answer.

"My name's Ruby. My fiancé is Ben's teammate Tony. Ben might have mentioned him?"

Tony. The memory of a SEAL who looked just like Joey from *Friends* came to mind. Emma had met him last Labor Day when he'd come to Amos and Grace's surprise wedding. The realization made her kick out of bed and fly to the door.

Setting the chain first, she opened it three inches. The woman outside jumped back.

"Oh, you're here!" She looked and sounded vastly relieved. "Hi, I'm Ruby." Her sympathetic gaze took in Emma's rumpled clothing—she hadn't bothered to put on her nightshirt—and her puffy eyes. "Poor thing. You must be so upset. I hope I can help you."

Ruby seemed about Emma's age. In sharp contrast to Emma's disheveled appearance, she wore form-fitting black slacks and a lightweight violet cropped jacket that hugged her perfect figure and complemented her long copper curls and porcelain complexion.

"Help me how?" Emma's voice sounded as scratchy as sandpaper.

The woman shrugged and smiled. "I'm a reporter." At the same time, she put her toe against the door in case Emma tried to shut it in her face. "Tony swears to me Ben would never hurt your children, so something else is clearly going on. If you can help me figure out what, I promise to convince the public of your innocence. All you have to do is share your story."

Emma rubbed the sleep out of her eyes. "Am I dreaming this?" Ruby's arrival seemed too good to be true—an answer to her agonized prayers.

"No. I'm real. Tell you what. While you get ready, I'm going to run down to the lobby to get you some coffee and something to eat. Sound good? I'll be right back."

She whirled on her smart pumps and strode away, followed by a young man Emma hadn't even noticed until then, toting a square case that clearly contained a camera.

Emma shut the door quietly and considered Ruby's offer. *My story.* She mulled over the offer, already knowing she would accept it. Ruby's timing was providential. Plus, Emma and Ben's side of the story needed to be told. And yet—a cold chill wafted through her—she would be pitting herself against the Centurions when she told it. There wasn't any way to avoid that, which meant the consequences might be lethal. If they could make Ben disappear... A fresh onslaught of worry gripped her.

She had to be brave like Ben was. God would protect her. With a shaky breath, Emma marched into the bathroom to shower. Flicking on the light, she groaned at her reflection.

Great day in the morning! If she was going to be on camera, she had better work on her appearance.

~

Miles's initial task as Jared Jones's gardener was to prune the trees and bushes Carl had let grow too large. It took all morning to trim back the spring growth and bag the clippings. Returning the garden shears to the garage in the carriage house, Miles ran into Carl holding open the Bentley's rear door for Mr. Jones, who was about to get in.

"Spenser's law office, please, Carl. It's just around the corner on Whitaker Street."

"Yes, sir." Carl's uniform hung askew. Closing the door behind his employer, he threw a superior smirk in Miles's direction as he headed for the driver's seat.

The garage door rumbled upward, opening onto the narrow street at the back of the house, and the Bentley pulled away, disappearing into a cloud-covered afternoon before the garage door lowered again.

Carl probably had no idea Lynwood Spenser was Jones's formidable attorney.

With Jones out of the house, Miles tugged off the gloves he'd worn, placed them alongside the shears, and shut the locker. Now was the perfect time to check in with his supervisor, even though the Undercover Unit should be well aware of Jones's movements, thanks to the tracking device secured to the Bentley's undercarriage.

Miles hurried into the big house. With a nod to the cook and the housekeeper, he swept through the kitchen, which smelled of fried green tomatoes, and headed for the servant's staircase.

His room on the third floor was wedged between the butler's and the cook's. The cleaning staff lived elsewhere and came just once a week. Only Carl was afforded total privacy in the apartment above the detached garage, which begged the question: Why the preferential treatment? Surely Jakes, the butler who'd been with Jones for twenty-two years, should get to stay in the carriage house.

As Miles reached the narrow staircase that zigzagged up the back of the house, the home's front door, visible down the length of the foyer, blew open. In stepped McKenzie, looking flushed and breathless. Perhaps hoping to avoid her father, she had parked out front. Her gaze went straight past the grand staircase to where Miles stood frozen in his tracks.

"Hey." Something was different about her, a wild light in her already vivid eyes. "Are you okay?" he added as she paused with her back to the door.

"I don't know."

The odd reply prompted him to approach her. For a second, she stood transfixed. Then, without warning, she pushed off the door and came rushing toward him. Throwing her arms around him, she crushed her soft lips to his.

Startled yet delighted, Miles hooked an arm around her waist, locking her against him and kissing her back. Her mouth was warm and luscious, her kiss full of emotion.

Something had changed. He didn't know what it was, but he tasted determination, excitement, and fear in her kiss. He was just about to detach himself gently when the phone in the purse hanging at her hip croaked like a frog, prompting her to release him.

"That's Ashton's ringtone."

Really? He burst into laughter that she'd chosen the croak of a frog to herald her fiancé's calls.

She laughed also, only to grow immediately serious. "I'm sorry. You must feel like I've used you. It's just…you're so easy to talk to, but that's no excuse. Forgive me."

Dying to tell her who he really was, Miles let her pull away. He watched her backtrack to the grand staircase and tear up it, even as the phone in her purse croaked and croaked without her answering it.

What on God's green earth had happened to McKenzie to make her act this way?

~

"Emma Stuart, thank you for sharing your story. I'm sure I'm not the only one who hopes your sons will be found soon."

Unable to look at the camera, Emma sent her a nod. "Thank you." Drained by the interview, she released a long, shaky breath as Ruby faced her cameraman.

"I am Ruby Bonheur, and this has been a WAVY 10 News special interview with Emma Stuart, Virginia Beach mother of the three missing boys." She sent the camera a long, earnest look while her cameraman ticked the seconds off his fingers, pushed a button, and lowered the box from his shoulders.

It was finally over.

"Well, I think that went well." Rising from the desk chair that they'd moved close to the armchair, Ruby smiled down at her. "You couldn't have sounded more sincere, Emma. The public will pull for you now, for sure. How do you feel?"

A blanket of calm quilted Emma's heart. "Better, thank you." The reporter's timely arrival had dispelled her frightening solitude and given her a means of fighting for her boys. "Sorry for crying like a baby." She'd been appalled when her tears had turned into full-blown sobbing as she relayed the painful details of the last moments of her sons' abduction and her feelings of horror and helplessness.

Ruby touched her shoulder. "Are you kidding? That was perfect. Believe me, you don't want to come off looking unemotional. You did great." Leaning over, she hugged Emma before rounding their chairs to reopen the curtains, which they'd closed to eliminate the sun's rays. "The only thing we have to prove now is why the Centurion Cohort would want to help Carl in the first place—apart from the fact that he's one of them."

Emma nodded. Ruby had embraced Ben's theory that Jared Jones had helped Carl kidnap his sons. She'd even used the handbook they'd found in Savannah Shelves to prove the existence of the Cohort to her viewers. "There has to be a reason why Jones would want to unite Carl with his sons in the first place."

"Right." Emma licked her dry lips. Why would a man that rich and powerful look out for a deadbeat like Carl? "According to—" Emma cut herself off as she remembered Miles's undercover investigation needed to remain a secret. "According to an insider, Jones treats Carl like he's someone special. The question is, why?"

Ruby pounced on her hesitation. "You know someone on the inside?"

Emma thought fast. "Well, not really." Far be it from her to blow Miles Ellis's cover. "I meant the leader's daughter, McKenzie. Ben and I met her at the Centurion Men's Shelter, where she volunteers. She's the one who arranged for me to meet Carl in her father's garden. She's lovely, really."

The journalist's jewel-like eyes narrowed. "Do you think she'd be willing to talk to me?"

"Oh, I don't know." Emma pictured young McKenzie Jones. She'd seemed truly sympathetic but understandably wary.

"We're obviously missing something." Ruby spun away to pace the length of the room, her coral-pink lips pursed in thought. An instant later, she threw herself down on Emma's bed next to the laptop where she'd looked up the Centurion Cohort, finding virtually nothing online about it.

Putting it back on her lap, she started typing. "Ah. Okay, here's some background on Jared Jones. He earned an MBA from MIT and a BS in finance before that from Rhodes College in Memphis. His income bracket puts him in the top 5 percent nationally. I'm searching for Mississippi in this document to see if there's a connection to Carl, but...there isn't. So, what's the connection?" She regarded Emma expectantly. "Tell me more about Carl."

Emma's gaze went to the box wedged between her bed and the wall. "Have a look for yourself." She picked it up, brought it to Ruby, and placed it on the bed next to her.

Carl's birth certificate was lying on top. Ruby studied it with a knit brow. "There's no father's name."

"Right. No, Carl never knew his daddy. His mama got pregnant in college and then lived with her parents. She never did marry."

Laying the certificate aside, Ruby selected one of Carl's photographs. "He played football?"

"Yes. He took our high school to the state championship and even got several scholarship offers, but he didn't go to college." He'd married her instead. Regret pinched Emma anew.

Ruby spared a glance for her cameraman, a light-skinned Black man, who was reviewing the recording they'd just made. "How is it, Reggie?"

He sent her a pleased smile. "Perfect."

"Good." Looking back at the photo in her hand, Ruby propped it against the screen of her laptop and typed another search.

Emma waited, not expecting much to come of it, but a minute later, Ruby gave a low whistle.

"What?"

"Check it out." The reporter stood, angling the laptop so Emma could see the screen. "I had this wild thought, and I think I hit the lottery. Here's a picture of Jared Jones playing football in college. Compare it with Carl's."

Emma divided her gaze between the grainy online image of Jones clasping a football and the photograph of Carl doing the same. Their pose was identical, but Carl's hair was lighter, his chin weaker.

"He looks just like Carl," Ruby insisted. "Reggie, what do you think?" She stepped toward Reggie to show him the two photos.

His eyebrows rose as he compared them. "I'd say they're related, maybe even father and son."

The thought of Jones being Carl's father pulled an incredulous laugh from Emma. She stepped toward Ruby for another look. This time, Jones's dark-brown gaze struck her as familiar. "Well, maybe."

Ruby's eyes sparkled with excitement. "Let's explore the possibility. Jones is exactly…" She crossed back to the bed to view the date on Carl's birth certificate, comparing it to the year of Jared's birth on her screen. "…he's twenty years older than Carl, which means he would have been at Rhodes College when Carl was born. Where did Carl's mother go to school?" She sat on the end of the bed again.

"I have no idea." Emma sank next to her and stole another look at Jones's young face. This time, his dark eyes sparked recognition, startling a gasp from her. She clapped a hand to her mouth. "Colton has his eyes, my second son. They're dark and sloped just like that." She looked up at Ruby. "Jared Jones is my sons' grandfather?"

Ruby shot a grin at her cameraman. "That would give Jones a *very* good motive for kidnapping the boys, wouldn't it?" She held up Carl's photo. "Can I keep this for now?"

"I don't want it back. Carl might."

"Well, Carl," Ruby said with confidence, "is going to jail. But first, I need to talk to your insider, Jones's daughter. What's her name again?"

"McKenzie." Emma pictured the sweet young woman, loath to drag her into this.

"You think she's volunteering at the shelter today?"

"I don't really know."

"Well, could you show us how to get there?"

"Sure, but—" Fear made Emma hesitate. "I'm afraid of these people."

Ruby studied her and frowned. "Yeah, I don't blame you. Not to worry." She slid a faintly critical eye over Emma's Target-store clothing. "No one's going to recognize you after I change your appearance. Also, you need to check out of this room. If I could find you without much digging, then anybody can. And if the Centurions made Ben disappear..." Her voice faded before she forced a bright smile. "Not that he's gone for good. In the meantime, you can stay with Reggie and me at the East Bay Inn. We have a double suite with a pullout couch." She queried her cameraman, who nodded his agreement.

"But how will Ben find me?" Emma eyed his duffel bag, which she'd carefully repacked after putting his T-shirt back.

"Don't worry about that." Ruby waved a negligent hand. "Ben will find Tony, and Tony will find me. There's really nothing those SEALs can't do when they put their minds to it."

Ruby's confidence kept Emma from despairing. "Thank you. You're the answer to a prayer."

Ruby's determined gaze softened. "Stick with me, Emma. We are going to expose these Centurions for what they really are, only I'll need to borrow this little red book for a while." She went to pick it up. As she dropped it into her oversized purse, she turned back to Emma and sighed. "I sure wish I could promise you that I'll find your boys, too. All I can promise is to try."

Emma managed a wan smile. "That's good enough for me." Her faith in a positive outcome had dwindled to a gasping flame. But thanks to Ruby's timely arrival, the flame was still flickering.

CHAPTER 16

*B*en woke up in a semi-dark and unfamiliar bedroom, his heart beating fast. A clock on the bedside table read 5:23—in the morning or evening?

The sky beyond the chiffon curtains was too bright for dawn, so it had to be evening. He tossed off his covers and slowly sat up, causing his head to thud dully. The unfamiliar boxers on his otherwise naked body had him taking a closer inventory of himself. The bandage wrapped around his head brought it all back.

Oh yes, he'd nearly drowned, but then Shawn's voice had told him it wasn't his time yet, and the rope around his ankle had vanished. If one miracle wasn't enough, he'd been rescued on the beach by a jogger who turned out to be a medical doctor. Ben closed his eyes. He would never again doubt God's abilities.

The doctor, who'd said, while cleansing his head wound, that her name was Molly, had kept him slumped on her couch for hours, where she'd annoyed him to no end by tapping his cheek, telling him to wake up and open his eyes.

Trained to obey orders, Ben had complied as best he could. He'd wanted more than anything to get on the phone and call his friends. But all he could do was ride the waves of his headache, unable to speak, let alone think coherently. After a couple of hours, Molly had escorted him to a guest bedroom on the second floor. He had no idea when she'd stripped off his sandy clothes and put him in these red boxers.

The handcuffs still dangled from his left wrist as he felt the bandage on his head. He remembered Molly stitching him up with supplies in a first-aid kit. She'd been so apologetic about not having any topical anesthesia, like he could feel her delicate needle over the cymbals of pain clashing in his head.

After swinging his feet to the carpeted floor, Ben rose slowly, experimentally. The smell of garlic sparked a gnawing hunger. The last time he'd eaten had been breakfast with Emma the morning before.

Emma! He had to get word to her that he was okay. Or had the Centurions already sought to dispose of her? He needed to make some phone calls ASAP.

The sound of a refrigerator closing drew him out of the bedroom onto a loft that overlooked a great room with a soaring ceiling and glass windows. As he descended a run of carpeted stairs, he could hear his rescuer in the kitchen. As he reached the ground floor, his gaze went from the peaceful view of the Atlantic Ocean to the woman hitherto out of sight. She was standing by the stove, her dark hair long and loose, stirring beef strips in a pan.

He announced himself to keep from frightening her. "Hi."

She was startled all the same. "Oh, you're up." Her wide-eyed gaze, now enhanced with mascara and eyeshadow, slid over him with interest. "How do you feel, Ben?"

How could she know his name? *Oh, that's right.* She'd heard about him on the news. Supposedly, there was a manhunt underway for him. Only a few Centurions, the ones who mattered, believed him dead.

"Better. Thanks for letting me crash in a bed. Whose, uh—?" he indicated his hips. "Whose boxers am I wearing?"

"My ex's. Your clothes are on top of the dryer, ready to wear again. Help yourself." She waved him toward the laundry room just off the kitchen.

"Thanks." Skirting past her, he found his clothes neatly folded on the dryer. He shut himself into the laundry room and dressed in his own clothes.

When he emerged still barefooted, she was pouring herself a glass of red wine.

"I'd like to take these handcuffs off. Do you have a small screwdriver? Paper clip works, too."

"Um. Sure." She retrieved a tool from a kitchen drawer. "These are for repairing eyeglasses."

"Perfect." Within seconds, he'd freed his left wrist. He put the screwdriver back where she'd got it and dumped the handcuffs into her trash can, all the while aware that Molly was watching him.

"I'd offer you some wine, but it's better if you hydrate. There's bottled water in the fridge. Help yourself."

"Thanks." He was as thirsty as he was famished.

As he drained the water bottle, she continued cooking. The oil in her wok hissed when she added vegetables to the sauteed beef. Ben's stomach growled, but his focus was on the phone in Molly's pocket. "Any chance I could use your phone to make some calls?"

She swung back around. "Oh, sure. I should have offered." Disabling her passcode first, she then handed him her cell, clearly still wary but willing to believe in him.

"Thanks." He went immediately to Google Maps to determine his location. "I'm on Tybee Island?"

"Yep." Opening another drawer, she pulled out a pen and a pad of lined paper. "You'll probably need this."

"Yeah, thanks." He was only eighteen miles from Savannah by car. Ben took the phone, pen, and paper to the living area and sat before the wall of windows.

Keeping Molly in his peripheral vision, he tapped out the

number to the Team building, glad that Amos made every SEAL on the Team memorize it. It was 6:00 P.M. on a Wednesday evening. The only person at Spec Ops would be the duty officer.

When Tony Caruso answered, Ben wanted to lunge through the phone and kiss him on both cheeks. "Yo, Bambino." He left it to Tony to guess who he was.

"Harm—holy crap! Is that you?" Tony sounded incredibly relieved.

"Yeah, it's me." In Ben's peripheral vision, Molly unplugged the rice cooker.

"What happened to you? We heard you were arrested in Savannah and that you eluded the police on the way to jail."

"Not exactly arrested. The police just did their best to kill me."

"Are you serious? Who wants you out of the picture that bad?"

Ben pitched his voice lower. "I'd rather not say over the phone. Can you come and get me? I'm going to need some help."

"Probably. Where are you?"

"A place called Tybee Island, twenty minutes east of Savannah."

"Yeah, let me talk to the CO. He was sweating bullets when Senior Chief told him you went missing."

"How'd Amos find out?"

"It was on the news."

Great, so the entire East Coast, from Virginia to Georgia, thought he'd abducted and killed Emma's boys and was now running from the law. "Listen, I need some phone numbers, like yours and the Senior Chief's. I can't remember either one right now—slight concussion."

"Sure, hold on a sec. I gotta dart outside to get my cell phone."

A minute later, Tony was back, relaying both his own and Amos's cell phone numbers, which Ben scribbled onto the lined paper, recognizing them immediately.

"Okay, I'm going to share my location with your iPhone. Listen, if the CO needs to reach me, have him call this number. Also, please text Lieutenant Strong and tell him I need to speak to Charlotte, ASAP."

"You got it, Harm. Anything else?"

"Yeah. I'm worried about Emma. Last time I saw her, she was being led into the Chatham County Sheriff's Office. Do you know if she's called Amos?"

"Not that I know of. But Ruby left for Savannah last night looking for her. Maybe she's found her."

Ben wasn't sure he liked that prospect. It was the journalist's fault that people considered them a couple in the first place. "Well, could you call her and find out?"

"Sure, but...she's not answering my calls or texts right now. We had a few words before she left."

Great. Worry clawed at Ben. "Just keep trying. I need to find out if Emma's okay."

"Sure, I hear you. If I get through to her, I'll let you know."

"Thanks. Make those calls for me. I'm going to reach out to Reno now. I think I remember his number."

"Call me back if you want me to look it up. Be careful."

Ending the call, Ben sat for a moment, picturing Reno's business card before tapping a number into Molly's phone. Hopefully, Emma had called him like he'd told her to.

"Hello?"

The familiar tenor of his lawyer's voice relaxed him. "Hey, it's Ben."

"Oh, thank You, sweet Jesus! Where are you?"

Reno had obviously heard of Ben's dire circumstances. "Did Emma call you?"

"Yes. Right before your story aired on the news. I'm so glad you're okay. I've been fearing the worst."

"Well, the worst is nearly what happened to me, but I managed to survive. How's Emma doing? What else did she tell you?"

"She told me Butler showed her some evidence, an email

exchange between you and her, making it look like you hatched a plan to kill off the kids."

"What!? Emma and I never exchanged emails!" Ben saw Molly glance sharply over at him and promptly lowered his voice. "Someone is manufacturing lies, Reno. Did you hear about the tire tracks and the Gerber blade with Colton's DNA on it?"

"Yes, Butler told me about both."

"You've spoken to *Butler*?"

"I tracked him down after Emma called me. I'm lucky he took my call."

"Don't believe a word he says, Reno. I think he's in on this."

"Oh, I doubt that. We spoke at length last night. He admitted the emails between you and Emma showed up in his mailbox in printed format, which suggests someone wanted him to see them. He told me Emma took a polygraph and appeared to pass it, but then the results showed up as inconclusive, like someone had gone into the system and made changes."

Ben pressed his fingers to his temple as it began to throb again. "You're telling me someone in the Bureau is protecting the Centurions."

"Sure sounds like it."

Ben blew out a flustered breath. "How's Emma doing? Did she say where she is?"

"She called me from your hotel room after Butler released her. She was worried about you, obviously."

"She's not safe there." Considering what had happened to him, she needed to relocate.

Reno hesitated. "Do you need me to come down there? I'm not sure I can get away until Friday."

"No worries. My teammates will probably come to collect me. I don't know what the plan is, honestly."

"Well, as your attorney, I urge you to turn yourself in to Butler. Would you like his number?"

Ben searched himself. "I'll take it, but I'm not going to call him yet."

Reno relayed the number, which Ben added to his list.

"Oh, and Butler told me something else."

Reno's tone told Ben it wasn't good news. "Go ahead."

"It's about your alibi, Tiffany Hughes. I'm afraid she's in a coma."

"What?" Ben's head began to throb in earnest.

"Yeah, supposedly, she had a brain aneurism or something, though I think it more likely someone tried to kill her, and she didn't die. She was found by a friend lying naked in her bedroom, no sign of a break-in."

Shock washed over Ben, keeping him speechless. He swallowed hard. "Is she going to make it?" God forbid Tiffany died because of him.

"I don't know."

The phone beeped in Ben's ear. He glanced at the incoming number and recognized it as Charlotte's. "Listen, I have to go. Lieutenant Strong's wife is calling. She's in the FBI."

"Stay in touch, Ben."

As Reno hung up, Ben took the incoming call. "Yes, ma'am. Thanks for calling."

"Bring me up to date."

Ben spent the next few minutes telling her what he'd just told Reno and what Reno had told him. "I don't know how Butler came by the evidence he has. He seems to be suspicious himself at this point, but I don't feel like I can trust him. He's answering to somebody who's protecting the Centurions. I'm sure of it."

Charlotte fell silent for a moment. "So I looked them up last time you mentioned them, and I have to agree, they've been on the Bureau's radar for decades, yet we haven't won a single case against their leader, Jared Jones. Let me talk to my boss. I think you met Fitz at Amos and Grace's wedding. He was there with Grace's twin sister."

An auburn-haired gentleman came to mind. "Yeah, sure, Fitz." Ben had heard only good things about the man. "Oh, there's one more thing you should know." Pitching his voice lower, he told her about the FBI undercover investigator, Miles Ellis. "I promised him I'd keep mum about his investigation, but maybe the Undercover Division knows something they can share with you."

"I'll look into it, Ben. Can I call you back at this number?"

"Yeah, for a while. I'll have to get a new phone." He glanced over at Molly, who was ladling food onto two plates.

"All right, Ben. Glad you're safe. Take care."

As he ended his call with Charlotte, Molly caught his eye. "You'll feel better if you get some food in you."

The smell of jasmine rice, beef, broccoli, and hoisin sauce made Ben's mouth water. Joining Molly at a large table in the dining area, he wolfed down his dinner, all the while aware that his hand still trembled from fatigue, and his mind reeled at the circumstances in which he found himself. Molly watched him with wary interest.

"This is really good. Thank you."

She sent him a tiny smile. "You don't have to thank me."

Avoiding her stare, Ben turned his attention to the wall of windows and the soaring ceiling. "This house is really nice."

Her mouth twisted with regret. "Too bad, I have to sell it. Divorce, as it turns out, is expensive."

Her comment explained the loneliness he sensed in her. "I'm sorry. That has to hurt." He glanced back outside. A line of dark clouds suggested it might rain that night.

"Yeah." Molly stabbed at a broccoli floret. "So, Emma's the mother of the missing boys you supposedly murdered?"

He lowered his fork with a clank. How could it have come to this—him being wanted for kidnapping? "I swear to you, I wouldn't harm Emma's boys. Chris, Colton, and Carter are like my own kids." His voice thickened with emotion. "I have a suspicion of who took them, and it's someone with a lot of power and influence down here."

Her dark eyes searched his face. "Who?"

"Have you heard of Jared Jones or the Centurion Cohort?"

She shook her head. "No, but then I'm from Atlanta."

He picked up his fork and started to eat again. "I'm going to reunite those boys with Emma if it's the last thing I do."

Molly picked up her glass, toasting his determination. "Do it, Mr. Fix-it. I'd hate to see the bad guys win."

The moniker startled him until he remembered that she'd seen his tattoo when she'd stripped off his clothing.

Her shrilling cell phone distracted him from his embarrassment. Ben recognized his commander's phone number. "I'm sorry. I need to take this." He pushed his chair back.

Disappointment flickered over Molly's face, but she gestured graciously for him to answer. "Go right ahead."

Caught up in her private musings, McKenzie didn't immediately notice the three people entering the courtyard as she left the shelter for the day. At this time of evening, residents usually trickled in for supper, and the dusky-skinned man leading the way might have been one of them. But the two behind him were women.

Rousing from her introspection, McKenzie slowed her steps. "Can I help you?" They clearly didn't belong here.

The woman dressed in a smart violet jacket sent her a dazzling smile. The setting sun turned her coppery locks to flame. "You must be McKenzie Jones."

"Yes." She glanced at the third woman, hiding behind a pair of dark sunglasses.

"I'm Ruby Bonheur, a field reporter with a Virginia-based news station."

McKenzie accepted the woman's handshake warily. "Hello."

"And this is my cameraman, Reggie. Could we trouble you to answer a few short questions about the Centurion's civic charities? I understand your father, Jared Jones, is responsible for the shelter's operation."

McKenzie heaved an inward sigh. She had neither the will nor the energy to tout her father's philanthropic endeavors, especially when she knew they were all just fronts.

The journalist persisted. "I understand the Cohort meets here every Wednesday and Sunday evening? Are they here right now?"

"Not until seven o'clock." McKenzie peeked at her cell phone. It was just past six, and she had no desire to run into her father, who could show up any minute.

"Have you heard the recent allegations against them?"

The unexpected question brought McKenzie's head up. The cameraman was filming her response. "Allegations?"

"That the Cohort helped one of its members, Carl Moulton, abduct his three sons almost a week ago. What is your response to that, Miss Jones?"

McKenzie digested the allegations while trying to recall the words she'd been taught to tell the media. "The Centurions Society teaches men how to improve their circumstances. Law-breaking isn't tolerated."

"I see. Do you know Carl Moulton, Miss Jones? I understand he's your father's chauffeur."

McKenzie sensed a trap. "Not personally."

"Um—" The pretty woman stepped closer, pitching her voice lower and adding, "This may come as a shock to you, Ms. Jones, but Carl Moulton may actually be your father's illegitimate son, conceived when your father was in college. Are you aware of that possibility?"

McKenzie stifled a gasp. Carl, her half-sibling? The thought appalled her.

Glancing at the woman hovering behind the reporter,

McKenzie recognized her suddenly. Her light-brown hair had been straightened. She wore different clothing and those dark sunglasses, but there was no mistaking the grief that hung around her like a shroud.

"Miss Jones?" prompted the reporter.

McKenzie looked back at her. What the reporter had suggested was entirely possible. In fact, it explained an awful lot. Betrayal started as a trickle and grew into a deluge. Was it not enough that her father was a crook? Now, he'd gone and chosen his illegitimate son over his perfectly capable daughter?

"Stop filming," McKenzie hissed at the cameraman. Putting her mouth to the reporter's ear, she whispered, "I will speak to you, but definitely not here." The stone griffins standing over the gate seemed to be watching her.

Ruby Bonheur's face glowed with excitement. "Just say where."

McKenzie considered the trio. "Do you have a car?"

"We're parked on the nearest square in a blue Chevy Caprice."

"I'll drive past you in a cream-colored Acura. Follow my car." With a nod and a final glance at Emma, McKenzie brushed past them, headed for her reserved parking spot.

A minute later, after giving the trio time to return to the square, she eased into rush-hour traffic, beeped her horn at the Caprice as she passed it, and then led the way toward the Islands Expressway to the same beach where she and Miles had walked and talked.

How she longed to talk to him now! The reporter's theory about Carl encased her heart in ice. In light of his recent words to her—*I will name a male heir*"—it rang horribly true. It also explained why Carl's three sons had been kidnapped. Her father wished to secure his legacy. *He* was the one responsible for Emma Stuart's devastation.

The truth dismantled McKenzie. For years, she'd clung to the belief that her father was a good man, a leader who helped other men find their way. Yet, nothing could be further from the truth.

Without recalling how she got there, McKenzie found herself standing on a lonely strip of beach, buffeted by a breeze that promised inclement weather. The threesome soon joined her, slogging through the thick sand to reach her.

In the fading sunlight, McKenzie was asked to compare a photo of Carl to a picture Ruby brought up on her cell phone of her father playing football for Rhodes. For the first time, she noted the resemblance between the two.

"You think my father's involved in the kidnapping of Emma's sons?" McKenzie got right to the point. Lightning sparked far out over the ocean, where dark clouds merged with the choppy water, reflecting the turmoil in her heart.

The reporter caught back the tendrils of her own streaming hair. "Yes. Maybe you could tell us something that would help us locate the boys. At least we can be confident he hasn't hurt them."

They both regarded Emma, who'd removed her dark glasses and stood there, hugging herself as if the warm air were cold. Meeting Emma's desperate gaze, McKenzie's stomach lurched. The poor woman's pain was unfathomable—first, her sons and now the Navy SEAL, who'd clearly been a friend of hers, was gone, and the man responsible, McKenzie's father, suffered not a drop of remorse.

"Tell you what I'll do." Fear made her voice waver. But she couldn't just turn a blind eye while her father ruined Emma Stuart's life, in addition to her own. "I'll look for proof to substantiate your theory. Tell me how to contact you."

Ruby handed her a business card. "Here's my cell phone number. You can text or call."

Thick raindrops pattered the sand at their feet, forcing them to break up their meeting. "I'll be in touch." Leaving them to find their own way back, McKenzie raced for her car.

As she dropped onto the cold leather seat and shut the door behind her, she watched the threesome jump into the Chevy Caprice and take off. In no state to drive, she remained in her quiet vehicle, listening to the rain drum on the rooftop in earnest.

It took a monster to rip three little boys from their mother's arms. If her father could do that, he could easily make a Navy SEAL disappear, just like years before, when he'd made his daughter's incident vanish like it had never happened.

This evening, her father was brainwashing his followers in the second-floor meeting room at the shelter. There was no better time than tonight to search his office.

With a shaky but determined breath, McKenzie started her vehicle and pointed it toward home.

As Reggie sped them through the downpour back to the downtown area, Ruby peered back at Emma, who sat in the back seat, utterly silent.

Imagine how she feels, having had her own flesh and blood literally ripped away from her. Longing to console her, Ruby acknowledged the only way to do it was to bring the Centurion Cohort to its knees. Step one was to learn everything about them. As the wipers beat a frantic tempo, she drew the little red book from her bag, set it on her lap, and accessed the flashlight on her phone to peruse its contents.

Imagine if she could topple a corrupt organization like the Centurion Cohort. There'd be no question Ruby was a *real* journalist if she accomplished such a feat. Tony would have to eat his words. She wanted him to grovel before deciding to forgive him—which was why she'd ignored all his texts. As of yet, there'd been no groveling.

Ruby cracked the cover and flipped to Chapter 1, titled *Hierarchy.* She skimmed the contents, making note of the various ranks within the Cohort and the time it took to achieve them.

Would you look at that? The rank of high consul was inherited.

At the time of this book's publication, Henry Jones had been the high consul. Now, it was his son, Jared Jones. Who was going to take over? Was it Carl, who was possibly his illegitimate son, or Emma's oldest boy, Christopher? Ruby bit her lower lip. Not if she could help it.

Chapter 2 described the behavioral expectations of Centurion men. Boring.

Ruby flipped to the next chapter: *History of the Centurion Cohort*. It had been founded within a year of the Civil War's end, and it was still around. Blah, blah, blah.

Symbolism in the Cohort, Chapter 4, broke each rank into stages, each represented by a different creature. Members were expected to wear signet rings to aid in recognizing one another's status. Now, *that* was interesting. She could use that fact to her advantage.

Chapter 5, *Charitable Works*, described the mandatory service hours required of all members. It scarcely held her attention. She was about to close the book when the name of a charity funded by the Cohort caught her eye. Ruby drew a sharp breath. A shiver of certainty raised goosebumps on her forearms.

Twisting in her seat, she startled Emma into looking up at her. "I think I know where the boys were taken! There's The Centurion Academy for Boys. It's one of their charities."

Emma's eyes became luminous. Ruby turned off her flashlight and accessed Safari on her cell phone, typing *Centurion Academy for Boys* into a Google search.

A website for the academy appeared. "Bingo." She clicked on the link and waited with a perspiring upper lip for the information to appear. "Okay, so it's a day school offering a fine classical education for boys K through eighth grade, but it's also a boarding school for underprivileged boys who get to attend for free." She looked back at Emma. "That has to be where your boys are!"

"What about Carter? He's only one."

The question stumped Ruby. "We'll figure that out later. I'm sure he's safe and being cared for." At least, she hoped so.

"How do we get them back without the police to help us?" Emma sounded completely overwhelmed.

"Don't you worry about that. That's my problem, not yours." Facing front, Ruby resisted the urge to call Tony for help. She wanted to do this without him.

As if summoned by the mere thought of him, her phone buzzed. She glanced at the caller ID, saw that Tony had given up on texting and was now calling her. Firming her lips, she silenced the call and stuck her cell phone in her bag next to the *Centurion Cohort Handbook*. She wasn't ready to forgive him just yet.

CHAPTER 17

*U*nder the light of the dimmed chandelier, McKenzie descended the grand staircase in her nightgown and bathrobe. Her father wasn't due back from his Society meeting for another hour yet. With Carl and Miles also at the meeting and with the servants enjoying the night off, McKenzie had the house to herself. Now was the time to find proof of Ruby Bonheur's theory.

Her bare feet gave rise to the subtlest of creaks as she crossed the centuries-old floorboards, past her father's bedroom to his study, and slipped inside. Putting her back to the door, she allowed her eyes to adjust to the dim lighting. The lit fountain in the garden out back put a glow on her father's cherrywood desk. Where in this lair of shelves and drawers might she find evidence of Carl's parentage? Probably the filing cabinet.

From her father's desk, she retrieved the key she knew was hidden at the back of the flat drawer. Crossing to the free-standing cabinet on the opposite wall, she then wriggled the key into the lock, releasing all four drawers with a *click*. She pulled the first drawer open and commenced her search under *C* for Carl.

Just enough light shone from the fountain for her to see there were only investment reports under *C* from a company called Citadel Financial.

She would try *M* for Carl's last name, Moulton. Opening the second drawer, she fingered the tabs until she came to *M*, where she discovered her parents' marriage certificate, a thick file labeled *Medical,* and another labeled *Mortgages.* Her father held the deed to multiple properties. The last file under M was named *Mercantile Vietnam.*

Disappointed, Emma felt behind it, not expecting to feel anything. Her fingers closed over an envelope. Pulling it out, she angled it to the light, noting the feminine script and a return address of Mantachie, Mississippi. *That's where Carl's from!* With a held breath, McKenzie pulled out the card inside it and carried it to the window to catch the fountain's light.

Dearest Jared,

I know you never expected to hear from me again, but life deals unexpected cards, as I've grown to realize. When you spurned me twenty-nine years ago, you never knew I was carrying your child, a son whom I named Carl, after my father. Since you'd chosen your path, I felt it my right to keep my secret. I also determined not to tell Carl who his father was, only that he was conceived in love, though in the end, you married another.

Now, as I find myself losing a battle with cancer, I wonder if I was wrong never to tell Carl what a great man you've become. He is a son I take little pride in acknowledging, a lazy and dissolute man who shirks his obligations—exactly the opposite of you. I think it ironic that you are, perhaps, the only soul on earth who can redeem him. That is why I've decided to inform you of his existence. Whether you choose to act on that knowledge or not is up to you. I've made peace with my past. It's only right to allow you to do the same, in your way.

Sincerely,

Darlene Moulton

Light-headed with her discovery, McKenzie read the letter a second time. Ruby's guess was right. Carl *was* her half-brother. And his sons were her father's grandsons.

With a tremor in her fingers, McKenzie returned the card into the envelope and slipped it into the pocket of her bathrobe. She had just closed the file cabinet and was turning toward the door when a shadow moved through the line of light beneath it. The doorhandle jiggled.

Alarmed, McKenzie dived onto her knees behind the nearest bit of furniture, a Victorian settee. Had her father come home early? Was she about to be caught?

The door opened and closed, quickly and quietly. The light remained extinguished. She knew she wasn't alone, but whoever had entered stood still and silent, perhaps sensing her presence.

A chill swept over her. With soft footfalls, the intruder crossed the Persian carpet to the file cabinet. Too late, she realized she'd left the key in the lock. A beam of light brightened the room and tracked across the floor toward her. McKenzie cringed, hoping to avoid discovery.

But then the beam moved away, freeing her to breathe again. There came the whisper of a drawer sliding open. At the sound of someone rifling through the files, she braved a peek over the arm of the settee, and her jaw dropped.

There stood Miles, holding a penlight between his teeth and a wand-like object in his right hand. It emitted a blue glow as he drew it over the contents of the file he held open.

Disbelief morphed into incredulity, followed by the realization that he wasn't a runaway teen—in hindsight, it was obvious. He had lied to her! Yet, she'd believed him, helping him get a job as their gardener.

Betrayal overcame fear. She shot to her feet, startling him into dropping the penlight. "What do you think you're doing?"

"McKenzie!" He jammed the file back into the cabinet. The blue light went out. "Why are you in here?"

"Why am *I* in here?" As he bent to retrieve the fallen light, she rounded the settee to approach him. "I don't think that's a valid question, do you, Miles? Or is that even your name?"

"Shh!" He snapped off the penlight, plunging them into shadow. "McKenzie, please keep your voice down. I can explain."

She whispered, "Explain what? That my father's a crook? That you used me to get to him—for what reason? Or do I even want to know?"

He took a sudden step toward her, causing her to flinch as his hand caught the back of her head. But all he did was press a reassuring kiss against her lips.

"That's an apology." His hand remained in her hair, cradling her head. "Believe me, I've wanted to tell you who I am for the longest time. I just didn't know how loyal you were to your father."

"Who *are* you?" His voice, his touch, and the taste of his kiss were all so familiar, yet he was now a stranger.

"I'm an FBI special agent. Your father's been under investigation for years."

His low confession made her eyes widen. "An FBI agent!" Had God answered her prayers for help already?

"I can prove it. My ID's upstairs, hidden in my backpack."

She didn't need him to prove it. She'd always sensed there was more to Miles than met the eye. "Miles." Surely, he could hear her heart pounding out a beat of freedom. "You don't need to search for evidence." She gripped his muscular arms as the floor beneath her seemed to tip. "My mother kept detailed journals describing all the bad things my father's done. If I give them to you, will you protect me and my mother both?"

He stiffened beneath her. "What kinds of bad things?"

"Smuggling, insider trading, and now kidnapping."

He didn't seem surprised to hear it. "Why would you give me evidence? Your father might go to prison for the rest of his life. And your life will *never* be the same."

His warning gave her pause. "I know. But it's better than living a lie and having to marry Ashton."

Miles heaved a sigh. His hand moved from the back of her head to stroke her cheek. "You realize you'll have to enter WITSEC—witness protection. You'll be taken somewhere else to start your life all over again. And I won't be able to see you, not for a long time."

The words weakened her resolve. Not see Miles? He'd become her closest confidant. "How long is a long time?"

"I don't know. Several years, at least."

Sorrow hollowed her heart. Still, she had to do it. A future as Ashton's bride was unthinkable. The time had come to open Pandora's box and to let the demons out. Nausea pitched in her stomach. *God give me the strength!*

Dipping her fingers into the pocket of her robe, she withdrew Darlene Moulton's letter and showed it to him. "Once I take a picture of this, you can have it."

"What is it?"

"It's a letter written by Carl's mother telling my father that she had his baby without telling him."

"Holy cow." The whites of Miles's eyes shone in the dark. "That explains everything."

"Yes. Emma Stuart's boys are my father's grandsons, and I'm sure he arranged to kidnap them. For that poor woman's sake, you have to help her get them back."

Amos stuck his head out of the passenger window of a black Ford Taurus, clearly rented from Hunter Army Base's motor pool. "How did you end up all the way out here?" he demanded of Ben, who stood with Molly on the elevated deck of her beach house, waiting for his ride.

"I swam."

Ben turned to bid his rescuer goodbye. It had been Molly's idea for him to wear the straw fedora, a tropical shirt, and tennis shoes, all belonging to her ex. Nobody would recognize him in his present guise.

"Thanks again, Molly. For everything. You saved my life, and you believed my story. God's going to bless you for that."

She mustered a brave smile. "I hope so."

"I know so." He hugged her briefly, ignoring the way she clung to him. Her loneliness roused his empathy, but he belonged to Emma—whose boys he still had to find if they were going to have a future together.

Leaving Molly gazing wistfully after him, Ben hurried down the long run of steps, pleased that his strength had returned and his head no longer ached. He marched up to the driver's door, stuck his head through the lowered window, and kissed Tony on both cheeks. "*Mwa. Mwa.* I love you, man." Funny thing was, he meant it.

"Ugh." Tony shoved him away good-naturedly. "Just get in."

As Ben slipped into the seat behind Tony, Amos reached over from the front to shake his hand. "Glad you're not dead, Harm. You gave us a scare there."

Ben gripped his hand hard. "Trust me, you weren't the only ones who were scared." Ben lowered his window and met Molly's gaze one last time, sending her a wave.

"Good luck," she called as Tony started backing up. "I'll be watching the news. Don't disappoint me!"

The prior night's rain had moved on, leaving the air crisp and cooler. The beach behind the houses looked as pristine as if it had been power-washed. Sunlight bounced off the hood of the car as it sped Ben back toward Savannah.

Tony angled his rearview mirror to study him. "Aside from those clothes, you look pretty good."

Ben lifted his hat to show off his bandage. "Bullet grazed me.

I've got no wallet and no phone, but at least I'm untraceable, which, I gotta say, feels pretty good. Hey, did Ruby find Emma?"

"Uh, I don't know yet. She hasn't texted me back."

Worry furrowed into Ben. "Mako, can I borrow your phone for a minute?"

"Sure." Amos unlocked his phone and passed it back to him. "Who're you going to call?"

"The Holiday Inn Express." The worry that the Centurions had targeted Emma also had grown with each passing hour, causing him to sleep poorly the night before.

Amos watched him look up the hotel's number. "Explain who these people are."

Delaying his phone call, Ben brought Amos and Tony up to speed on Savannah's secret society and its powerful leader. Then he put his call through.

"Holiday Inn Express, Savannah. Would you like to make a reservation?"

"Uh, no thanks. Just trying to find out if the couple in room 476 checked out yet. Last name's Harmony?"

"Uh, yes, sir. They checked out this morning."

Uneasiness tightened Ben's scalp. "Thanks." He hung up with a bad feeling. "Tony, can you try Ruby again?"

Tony heaved a long-suffering sigh as he accelerated onto the expressway. "I can try." He took out his own cell phone and put a call through. But Ruby didn't answer.

Ben listened to Tony leave a tense message. He found the little sheet of paper onto which he'd written important numbers and dialed Charlotte's number.

"Hello?"

"Hey, it's Ben Harmony using my senior chief's phone. Any news?"

"Oh, Ben!" Charlotte sounded excited to hear from him. "Actually, yes. I've got a ton of news. First, the bad news. Butler reports to the Criminal Investigative Division just like I do, but the Criminal, Cyber, Response and Services Branch, or CCRSB has over-sight, which means he answers to multiple supervisors, any one of whom might be protecting Jones. The easiest solution is for Butler to wrap up his case, with you as his primary suspect, thereby satis-fying whoever wants to frame you."

"Mmm." Ben wasn't thrilled by that solution.

"However, I reached out to the Undercover Division like you suggested and spoke at length with Special Agent in Charge Drake Ellis, whose son Miles is investigating Jones, just like you said. To save time and hopefully escape the notice of Jones's protector, Fitz and I are going to operate under the umbrella of the Undercover Division. We've learned that Jones has been visiting a boarding school, one of the Cohort's charities, called The Centurion Academy for Boys. Sounds like a plausible place for him to have stowed Emma's sons, don't you think?"

Ben's spirits soared. "They run a boarding school, too?"

"Yes, on the outskirts of town. Now, as far as recovering them goes, we're waiting on a warrant, but to save time, Fitz and I are flying to Savannah today to put together a hostage-recovery team."

Finally, law enforcement was doing something productive! "This is awesome." Ben couldn't wait to tell the others, especially Emma if he could find her. "Just, whatever you do, keep the police down here out of the loop. They're loyal to Jones."

"Oh, we'll keep it on the down-low," she promised him. "Is this a good number to reach you?"

"Yes."

"How's Emma doing?"

"I don't know." Worry overshadowed his contentment. "She checked out of our hotel yesterday. I just hope she's safe."

"I hope so, too. Keep in touch, Ben, and I'll do likewise."

Ending the call, Ben handed Amos's cell phone back to him. He stared at the back of Tony's head. "Why isn't Ruby talking to you?"

Tony brooded for a moment, then confessed, "I said something stupid the other night, which made her mad."

"Great." The pictures in Ben's head were starting to knot his stomach. "So, how're we going to find out whether she found Emma or not?"

Tony held up his cell phone and shot him a grin through the mirror. "I put Ruby on my phone plan a while back. I'm tracking her phone right now."

Ben glimpsed a map on Tony's phone with a pin marking her location. A portion of his worry eased. "Let's go find her." Maybe Emma was with Ruby. Surely, God had been watching over Emma until Ben could get there and do it for Him.

A knock at their door prompted Ruby, Reggie, and Emma to exchange startled glances. Room service at the East Bay Inn had already delivered their breakfast and had just wheeled away their leftovers, so who could this be?

Ruby, who was poring over the Centurion handbook, waved Emma wordlessly into the bedroom where they'd decided she would conceal herself in the closet behind the dozen chic outfits Ruby had brought with her, should undesired visitors come calling.

Pushing behind the plastic-lined clothing, Emma strained to hear over her fast-beating heart as she heard Ruby call, "Who is it?"

"Yo, Adrienne," came a muffled voice in perfect imitation of Rocky Balboa.

"It's Tony."

Emma heard the door click open. Relief left her feeling weak.

"How'd you find me?" Ruby's crisp voice betrayed both annoyance and satisfaction that he'd tracked her down.

Emma emerged from the bedroom in time to see Tony wave his phone under his fiancée's nose. "I used the Find My Device app."

"You put me on your phone plan so you could spy on me?"

"So I could protect you, *bella*." He scooped her up, ignoring her gasp of protest, and kissed her soundly.

Behind the kissing couple, two men squeezed through the door. Emma recognized the first one. "Amos!" The second man wore a colorful Hawaiian shirt and straw hat, but there was no mistaking Ben's blue eyes as they fastened on her. She gave an involuntary shriek. "Ben!"

As they rushed into each other's arms, Ben's hat tumbled to the floor. The strength in his arms assured her he was very much alive. Her prayers had been answered.

With her toes scarcely touching the floor, Emma hid her crumpling face against his neck. Ben was alive! She gripped him harder, battling for composure, taking comfort in the strength of his embrace. She loved this man to pieces. God help her.

The room got awfully quiet. Lifting her head, Emma caught everyone staring at them with smiles on their faces—everyone except Amos, who was glowering.

Ben eased his hold on her, then set her away from him to look her up and down. "Who are you?" he teased.

She wore Ruby's exercise clothing: black yoga pants and a zippered turquoise jacket over a black jog bra. With her hair straightened, she scarcely recognized herself.

"I could ask you the same thing." She lightly touched the bandage wrapped around his head. "What happened here?"

His expression darkened. "You wouldn't believe what those cops did to me."

"Tried to kill you, by the looks of it."

"Pretty much."

Ruby went to lock the door and set the chain. "Everyone, sit down. We have some catching up to do." She waved them into their little living area, which comprised the pullout couch where Emma had slept the night before, two armchairs, and a galley-style kitchen with a breakfast bar. Once they were all seated, Reggie brought bottled water from their mini-fridge and handed them out.

Ben pulled Emma down onto the couch next to him and threw an arm around her, which she had neither the will nor the inclination to remove. Reggie sat on the other side of Emma. Tony perched on the arm of Ruby's armchair, and Amos occupied the other one.

"Now." Ruby set her notebook atop the handbook and readied her pen. "Let's hear what happened to you." She stared pointedly at Ben.

For the next ten minutes, Ben described his attempted escape from the police and how two fishermen had tried to dump his body. As his harrowing tale progressed, Emma leaned into his sturdy frame, astonished that he'd survived, so grateful for his presence.

As he described his deep plunge into the ocean while being dragged down by a heavy anchor, he suddenly stopped and shook his head. "Well, you're not going to believe how I got free of the rope, so suffice it to say I was a long way down when the knots came undone, and I struck out for the surface."

Given the way Ben's voice went gruff, something incredible had happened to him. Emma searched his profile, wondering what it was.

"Once I reached the surface, I lay there floating until I had the strength to swim."

To think that Ben had been close to dead, floating out at sea, while she'd paced the floor of their hotel room, lost without him!

"Finally, I started swimming toward a lighthouse, which looked to be a couple of miles away. I couldn't tell you how I got there. Must've swum on autopilot. Next thing I knew, I woke up on a beach, and it was dawn. Some jogger found me—and not just any jogger but a medical doctor, of all people."

It was silly of her, but Emma pictured a man in a white lab coat jogging on the beach.

Ruby was so caught up in the story she had yet to write down a word. Amos and Tony looked a little envious that they'd missed all the action.

Ruby gestured for Ben to finish his story. "So, what happened next?"

"Well," Ben's expression turned inscrutable, "the doctor took me in and tended my head." He gestured at the bandage. "I slept for like twelve hours before I felt good enough to call Tony at the Team building. Thank you, Mako, for drilling that number into my head. It was the only one I could remember."

Amos inclined his head like a wise master. "You are welcome, grasshopper."

"Tony gave me some phone numbers, and I started calling people."

Ruby looked down at her notepad and belatedly scribbled down Ben's story.

"Everything that happened to me is because of the Centurion Cohort," Ben tacked on. "Jared Jones does whatever he wants down here, and the law dogs obey him."

Ruby glanced up at Emma. "Do you want to tell him, or do you want me to?"

"Tell me what?" Ben divided a frown between them.

"You go ahead."

Ruby sent Ben a knowing smile. "Emma's sons are Jared Jones's grandsons—hence his motive for abducting them."

He turned his head to gape at her. "Are you serious? Your ex is Jones's *son*?"

Emma nodded. "Illegitimate son."

"How do you know?"

"Well, Ruby was the first to consider the possibility. We went to the shelter to run it past McKenzie Jones, who promised to help us. Last night, she found a letter in her father's office, written by Carl's mother, who admitted to having Jones's baby. She took a picture of the letter and sent it to Ruby's phone."

Ben swiped a hand over his eyes, then looked at her. "I've got some big news myself."

When he caught up Emma's hand and squeezed it, she braced herself for bad news, though the gleam in Ben's eye suggested it was good. "You remember Charlotte."

"Yes." The last time Charlotte had called Ben was to warn him about the evidence piling up against him.

"She and her boss Fitz have joined the investigation already underway by the Undercover Division—you remember Miles, whom we met?"

"Yes."

"They think they know where the boys are."

"At The Centurion Academy for Boys?"

His eyebrows shot up. "How do *you* know about that?"

Ruby held up the Centurion handbook she was writing on. "It's mentioned in Chapter 5, *Charitable Works*. As soon as I read about it, I thought, 'Huh, I bet that's where Emma's boys are.' So, I looked it up online, and it's still in operation. It's just fifteen minutes out of town."

"That's the one," Ben agreed. "According to Charlotte, Jones has been driving out there every evening."

"To visit my sons." A possessive shudder ran through Emma. Had he been poisoning their hearts and minds against their mother?

"Question." Tony speared Ben and Amos with a hard look. "Are we just gonna wait for the FBI to get the boys back? 'Cause I'm feeling like this matter's gotten personal."

Emma sat forward, galvanized by his words. "I want to go get my boys."

"Now, slow down, sweetheart." Ben put a hand on her back. "We can't just march into this school and grab the boys. Only the FBI's hostage rescue team can do that. But I don't see why"—he looked from Tony to Amos—"the three of us couldn't recon the building tonight and pass on any intel to the HRT. Wouldn't that save them some time?"

Amos crossed his muscular arms and considered Ben's suggestion.

"I have a better idea," Ruby said before he could offer an opinion. "The academy is a charitable institution, right? So why don't I pop in and tell whoever's in charge that I'm a friend of Jones's and I want to donate to the boarding school? They'd have to give me a tour, right? I could wear my hatpin with the hidden camera—"

Tony cut her off. "We're not here to do a story, babe."

"Just listen! My hatpin will show the FBI what the building looks like on the inside. And if I manage to film one of the boys, that will seal Jones's involvement in the kidnapping. You can't tell me that wouldn't be helpful."

Tony sent Ben and Amos a grimace of apology for his fiancée's persistence.

Amos finally spoke up. "The idea has merit."

Ruby beamed at him, then raised an eyebrow at Tony.

"Well, you're not going in there alone," he insisted. "One of us should go with you. You'd have more clout with a husband."

She ignored what was obviously an offer to accompany her. "Reggie can be my husband. No, wait." She glanced at the handbook. "They're not fans of interracial marriages." She tapped her chin while considering her options. "They would recognize Ben. So..." Her lovely gaze traveled to Amos, skimming over him with mild distaste. "I guess that leaves you."

Amos sent her a stare so glacial Ruby had to look away. "I'm not playing anybody's husband."

"Amos." Emma sent him a pleading look. "If Simon was in there, wouldn't you want to see for yourself?"

His gaze seemed to thaw as he regarded her. "Fine." He looked back at Ruby, clearly no more thrilled to be paired with her than she was to be with him. "Wife for an hour and not a second longer."

CHAPTER 18

*E*mma gulped as The Centurion Academy for Boys came into view. They had decided they should all go look at it, traveling in two cars—Ruby and Amos in the Caprice to pay a call at the school, the other four, including Reggie, in the military-issue sedan.

"Wow." In the back seat of the latter, Ben squeezed Emma's hand by way of reassurance.

A Google search had informed them that the gray stone, three-story structure had served as a prison during the War of Northern Aggression—as the Civil War was referred to this far south. To Emma, the academy still resembled a prison despite the meticulously kept flower beds full of marigolds and geraniums and the cheerful sign at the head of the U-shaped driveway. It was the high wall enclosing the playground behind it that gave it such a grim air.

As Ruby guided the blue Caprice ahead of them into the long driveway, Tony hunted for a place to park their own car, out of sight of the building. "Betcha Jones owns all this land."

The adjacent acreage and even the land across the street were undeveloped and filled with trees draped in Spanish moss. Spotting a utility road, Tony turned down it, then stopped almost immediately so they could all gauge Ruby and Amos's success in being admitted into the school. The couple was parking the Caprice in the small VIP parking spot by the academy's front door.

"She does look like an heiress," Ben admitted as Amos opened Ruby's door.

Emma had to agree. Wearing a butter-yellow sheath dress with matching broad-brimmed hat and white gloves, Ruby looked like those wealthy women who attended the Kentucky Derby. Amos, in a white knit polo and black slacks, looked more like her bodyguard, however, than her husband.

Tony's dark eyes shone with admiration. "She'll get them in. Watch and see."

Sure enough, after a short wait on the broad front stoop, the academy's door opened, and the couple was invited inside.

Anticipation made Emma's pulse race as she imagined Ruby filming one of her boys using the tiny camera on her hatpin. This entire nightmare might be over within twenty-four hours!

With phase one of their reconnaissance successful, Tony pulled forward down the access road, taking their vehicle out of sight of the school before lowering all four windows and cutting the engine. "Ready, Harm?"

Ben planted a kiss on Emma's cheek as he unlatched his seat belt. "We won't be long. Reggie, keep her in the car."

Emma sighed. She'd asked to accompany them on phase two, only to have her offer gently declined. Reconnoitering by day required the ability to remain unseen and unheard, Ben had explained. Their objective was to acquaint themselves with the area, so it wasn't completely unfamiliar when they returned that night for phase three, a thorough reconnaissance of the building's exterior.

As the SEALs vanished into the dense foliage, Emma sat back, closed her eyes, and concentrated on sensing Christopher and

Colton's presence across the short distance between them. If they were in the school, and she believed they were, where was Carter? Longing swept through her, bringing tears to her eyes. Would she ever hold her youngest in her arms again?

Reggie angled himself against his door so he could look back at her. "So, I'm confused."

The confession roused Emma from her trance. "About what?"

"Tony told Ruby not to call you and Ben a *couple*, but from this perspective," he sent her a knowing grin, "y'all look like two lovebirds."

Emma's face heated self-consciously. Ben had been overtly affectionate since his return, making a point to touch her often and even in front of Amos, whose scowl did not deter him. "I'm just glad Ben's alive."

"Uh-uh." Clearly skeptical, Reggie was astute enough not to press his point. He produced his cell phone and was soon distracted.

Emma, who had no phone with which to amuse herself, dared to imagine what the future held. She could not deny that Ben's possessive touch thrilled her as much as it terrified her. In her current weakened state, she needed his optimism and his skillset too much to push him away.

Yet, Amos's silent disapproval gave her pause. If Ben wanted Emma solely as his girlfriend-of-the-moment, then she needed to set him in his place immediately, the way she'd done the night he'd come over to open the breaker box.

But what if he wanted something permanent?

Longing swamped her as she imagined Ben fathering her boys into adulthood. Was he seriously considering something like that? If so, would he be a good and faithful husband?

With his laughing eyes and easy smile, Ben Harmony could have any woman he wanted. Why would he choose a small-town Mississippi girl to be his one and only?

Mako had to admit Ruby was convincing. The figure-hugging yellow silk dress, paired with the elegant southern belle hat, complemented her copper ringlets so nicely that the white-haired matron who greeted them at the entrance seemed dazzled.

Ruby had introduced them as Mr. and Mrs. Bonheur, friends of Jared Jones, who'd told them they could just drop in whenever.

"We'd like to see for ourselves if this place is a worthwhile charity. You see, my father passed away, leaving me with more money than I know what to do with." To Amos's amazement, tears moistened Ruby's eyes as she added, "I would rather have my daddy still here with me than all the money in the world. But the least I can do is brighten the lives of others with his wealth, the way he brightened mine."

Miz Myrtle Banks, a matronly-looking woman with short gray hair and ample hips, visibly melted at Ruby's Oscar-worthy performance.

Ruby laid it on thicker, affecting a southern drawl she didn't normally have. "Would you help me make up my mind, Miz Banks?"

"Well, I'll certainly try. As you may already know, we are both a day school and a boarding school. We educate boys from well-to-do families alongside less fortunate boys, which we believe fosters tolerance and good character in all of them. While the tuition of the wealthier boys helps pay the bills, we are a nonprofit charity, relying wholly on monetary donations to care for our boarders so that boys from broken homes have a safe place to live and access to an excellent education."

"What a lovely mission! Isn't it, darling?" Ruby shot him a smitten look before peering expectantly around the foyer. "Do you think we could get a tour?"

Amos had observed that the marble-floored entryway was

spotless, though the scent of Lysol couldn't quite mask the musty scent of history.

Miz Banks glanced at her watch. "Well, I do have a few minutes before I'm needed in the cafeteria. The boys are all in class right now, so we'll need to be discreet and not disturb them."

"Oh, thank you! I promise we'll be quiet."

"This way, then." Miz Banks led them toward the wide marble staircase, its steps worn in the middle from the tramping of feet decade after decade.

As they chased the woman's swaying hips up the stairs, Ruby elbowed Amos and drew his attention to the oil-on-canvas portrait hanging on the landing where the stairs turned.

Jones, she mouthed.

"Ours is a classical curriculum," Miz Banks continued as she climbed the second run, "steeped in liberal arts and the great books. In addition, all boys are taught grammar, logic, rhetoric, arithmetic, geometry, music, astronomy, and, of course, Latin."

Amos couldn't help but like the sound of that.

As they reached the second floor, the murmur of children's voices became audible.

"Our upper elementary students, grades fourth through eighth, are on the east wing here," Miz Banks gestured to her right, "while the west wing houses K through third. Once our well-to-do boys finish the eighth grade, they usually transfer to the Habersham School. Our boarders are placed with foster families and usually attend public school, though they do very well thanks to the foundation offered here. Shall we peek into a Latin class?"

Ruby clasped her hands with delight. "Yes, please. I always wanted to become a teacher."

Miz Banks led them to an open door on the east wing.

Amos strained to see inside the classroom where approximately twelve young men, all of them in burgundy shirts and gray slacks, droned Latin declensions while their teacher, a man as old as Miz Banks, used a long pole to point to the suffixes written on the old-fashioned chalkboard. Amos searched for Christopher, only to realize these boys were at least a year older than he was.

"These are our sixth graders." Miz Banks gestured for the teacher to carry on. As several heads turned their way, she swept them away from the door and led them toward the west wing.

Out of the corner of his eye, Amos saw Ruby check that her hatpin hadn't shifted and was still pointed forward. All of the doors on the west wing were closed to contain the chatter of young voices.

"We'll just peek into the second grade." As the director cracked the first door on their right, a young female teacher straightened from bending over a student's desk. "Please continue, Miss Adams. Don't mind us."

The little boys, who were writing sums on individual slates, turned their heads to assess their visitors. As Ruby leaned into the room, Amos peered over her wide hat, hoping for a glimpse of Colton, as this would be his grade. A boy standing in the corner and facing the wall caught his eye. Wait, was that Colton?

Miz Banks, loath to interrupt, urged them back into the hall. Just as she closed the classroom door, the boy in question turned his head, intercepting Amos's stare.

"Hey!" His cry of recognition was unmistakable.

"Was that boy in trouble, the one in the corner?" Ruby's loud question muffled Colton's anxious cries.

"Oh, don't mind him, poor soul. He'll come around." Miz Banks ushered them swiftly toward the staircase.

"Is he from a broken home?"

"Worse than that, I'm afraid. He witnessed his mother being killed in a car accident."

"How awful." Ruby shot a wide-eyed look at Amos.

The shock of seeing Colton—not just alive but being disciplined—had set off a struggle in Amos. It was all he could do not to thrust his way back into the classroom and rescue Simon's cousin.

That's not why you're here, he reminded himself. The FBI would free both boys soon.

As they returned to the stairs, Ruby tipped her head way back in order to aim her secret camera at the upper level. "What's up there?"

"The third floor is where our boarders sleep, along with half our staff."

"Oh, could we possibly see their accommodations?"

Miz Banks was beginning to look like she regretted giving them a tour at all. "I assure you, the living conditions are excellent." She checked her watch and started doggedly down the steps, leaving them to follow her. "I'm afraid I am needed down in the cafeteria at this time."

Ruby grimaced at Amos and followed her. "Of course. You're a busy woman, Miz Banks. We apologize for the inconvenience."

As they neared the ground floor, the scent of cooked peas wafted from the end of the west wing. Miz Banks marched them straight to the door they had entered only ten minutes earlier.

"Forgive me for rushing you, Mr. and Mrs. Bonheur, but we run a tight ship here. If you come again, do call first and make an appointment."

"Yes, Miz Banks."

Sensing that the director might just call Mr. Jones to verify their connection to him, Amos took Ruby's arm as Miz Banks pulled the door open.

Ruby shot him a defiant look while taking a sheet of folded paper from her purse. "I can see your heart is in the right place, Miz Banks. That's why you need to see this."

As Miz Banks took the flier and unfolded it, Amos propelled Ruby out the door ahead of him.

"What did you just do?" he demanded as he escorted her off the stoop and across the driveway toward their car.

"Oh, hush." She tore her arm out of his grip and marched toward the passenger door, waiting for Amos to unlock it.

The only person in the world who got away with telling Amos to hush was Grace. Astonishment kept him mute until they were standing on opposite sides of the car. "What did you give her?"

"A printout from the FBI's Missing Children's page. That woman has no idea Colton's mother is still alive."

"Are you out of your mind?" Amos blasted her over the roof of the car. "You've just jeopardized the entire operation! She'll go straight to Jared Jones, and he'll relocate the boys before Charlotte's team even gets here!" He jabbed the button on her car fob, releasing all four locks.

Ruby's chin rose. "I don't think so. I think she'll call the FBI tip line." She ripped open her car door and dropped out of view.

Amos climbed in behind the wheel, as they'd decided earlier that he should drive. "And if she calls the *wrong* Feds, the ones who work for Jones? What then?"

He felt only moderately better as Ruby's lips firmed and her face paled. It was obvious she now regretted her impulsive gesture.

Twenty minutes later, they all rallied up at the East Bay Inn. As soon as Reggie let them in, Emma preceded Ben and Tony into the hotel suite, finding Ruby and Amos already there. Given the taut silence between them, they were at odds over something. Tony closed the door behind them all and locked it.

Emma divided an anxious gaze between them. "What did you see?"

Amos walked up to her and firmly clasped her shoulders as if worried she might faint. "We saw Colton," he said very gently.

Emma's knees nearly folded. "How...how did he look?" She was aware of Ben shifting closer.

Amos hesitated. "Physically, he looked fine. But the director said he was having trouble adjusting."

As Emma covered her mouth, Ben placed a hand on her back. "He'll be out of there soon, Emma, he and Chris both."

Bolstered between the two SEALs, she managed to retain her poise. "And Carter? Where is he?" They had yet to determine where her baby was.

Amos squeezed her shoulders. "He'll be found. If Colton and Chris are safe, then Carter is, too." He sent a dark look at Tony, who stood behind them. "That is, if Ruby hasn't jeopardized their rescue."

"Ruby?"

Five sets of eyes swung toward the woman connecting her laptop to the suite's television set.

"Mako's exaggerating. All I did was slip Miz Banks one of the flyers I printed off the FBI's Missing Children's page. She was told that Colton's mother died in a car accident. She deserves to know Jones has been lying to her."

The room went quiet.

Ben was the first to break the silence, his tone incredulous. "Are you kidding me? You tipped her off?"

"I'm sorry! I forgot that Jones has an FBI insider. I thought I was doing the right thing." Ruby jabbed the remote control while pointing it at the television. "Reggie, come help me with this technology. I can't figure out how to change the input."

As Reggie crossed the room to help Ruby, Tony joined him, going to stand beside Ruby in what was obviously a show of solidarity. Noting his loyalty, she sent him a small, grateful smile.

Reggie found the right input. "Here we go. Movie time."

"Finally." Ruby waved them all closer. "Why don't we look at the footage we got and stop thinking of worst-case scenarios."

Emma made a beeline for the television. She dropped to her knees on the chintz rug, eschewing the couch where Ben was tugging her. Undeterred, he went down on the floor beside her. Emma kept her eyes on the screen where the words **The Centurion Academy for Boys** hung above the double oak doors.

Once everyone was seated, Ruby tapped a key on her laptop, and the video started. Emma's mouth turned dry in anticipation of seeing Colton. Listening to Ruby's perfect southern drawl and her glib lies, her respect for the reporter rose.

"Ruby, you're so convincing."

"Thank you."

As the camera panned over a large, dim foyer and a ponderous set of stairs, Emma could only imagine that her sons felt trapped in a nightmare. Did they think for a minute that she wasn't looking for them? Tears blurred her vision as she sent them a silent message. *I'm right here, my babies. I'm coming for you.*

The director led Ruby and Amos to a Latin class filled with boys a year older than Christopher. Then, they backtracked and opened a classroom door in the K-to-three wing.

Amos spoke up. "This is where we saw Colton."

As the door swung inward, a dozen young boys looked up from their slates. Emma's gaze went straight to the boy standing with his back to the door. Colton's signature stance of mutiny was so familiar that she burst into tears.

"It's okay." Ben put a comforting arm around her. "They haven't broken him, Emma. Look how defiant he is."

All too soon, the camera moved away. The director made it clear she was needed elsewhere; their tour was over. When they returned to the foyer, Ruby said distinctly, "I can see that your heart is in the right place. That's why you need to see this." She handed the woman a flyer.

Five sets of eyes swiveled in Ruby's direction. With a firming of her lips, she leaned over and paused the video. "Okay, I admit I screwed up."

Fear closed like a noose around Emma's neck. What prevented the director from calling Jared Jones to demand answers? Or, worse still, she might call the FBI directly, thereby alerting Jones's insider that the jig was up.

Ben shared a grim look with Tony and Mako, then shrugged.

"Well, we were going to recon the building tonight anyway. Might as well stay there all night and make sure Jones doesn't move the boys before the FBI gets here."

Amos nodded his agreement, though the idea of staying up all night clearly held no appeal.

Ben requested to use Amos's phone. "I need to let Charlotte in on this."

Ruby watched the exchange with a pained expression. "You can throw me under the bus if you want to. It was my mistake." She met Emma's frightened gaze. "I'm sorry."

Admiration for Ruby's performance overshadowed Emma's concerns. "That's okay. You got inside. You proved that Colton's there, which means Chris has to be there, too. I'm grateful for that."

As the tension in the room eased, Emma told herself everything would work out fine. The FBI would arrive with their hostage rescue team, perhaps as soon as the next day, and recover her boys. By this time tomorrow, she might have two of them back in her care. Somebody at the academy would know where Carter was.

God willing, Emma's nightmare would soon be over. And the good that came from it might be something as simple as gratitude. She would never take her boys for granted again. That much was certain.

It was finally time for recess, close to the end of the day and the only time the lower and upper grades got to play together. Colton found Chris at his usual spot on the swing set. As he sprinted toward him, his heart felt like it would explode.

"Chris'pher!"

His brother glanced up only to look back at the dirt on his shoes. All he ever did was sit and stare. "What?"

Putting his voice to Chris's ear, Colton whispered, "Amos was here. I saw him this mornin'!"

His brother's expression didn't change. "No, you didn't."

"Yes, I did!" Anger made Colton's face burn. "Miz Banks brought him to my classroom, him and some woman."

"Miss Grace?"

"No, some other lady with curly hair."

"Then it wasn't Amos. He would never come here without Grace."

In his fury, Colton punched his brother right in the jaw. "I know what I saw!"

"Boys!" Mrs. Spellman, who always had recess duty, hurried toward them.

Regret for his actions kept Colton tongue-tied as Chris was looking at him with that same expression of disappointment that Mama got.

Mrs. Spellman stood over them with her hands on her hips. "Colton, you apologize to your brother this instant."

"Sorry."

"It's okay. He didn't hit me hard."

"We don't hit each other, period. Now, both of you go play nicely. I don't want to see any more hitting."

"Yes, ma'am." Christopher got up, grabbed Colton's hand, and towed him to the other side of the brightly colored fiberglass playground. "You're going to get us in trouble again. Stop making up stuff."

"I'm not! And I'm not gonna get in trouble neither, 'cause I won't be here after today."

Chris heaved a tired sigh. "What are you planning?"

Colton glanced toward the two little boys clinging to the climbing wall. He pulled Chris down so he could tell him without being overheard. "I'm gonna start a fire."

"How?"

"With your magnifier." Colton patted his right pocket where

he'd hidden the gift from Mr. Jones. "I already got a pile of kindlin' over there. See it?" He'd built it during the ten-minute break he got after lunch, stacking leaves and twigs and small bits of tinder that had blown over the wall. "Once the fire gets goin', all the teachers will be busy tryin' to put it out, and I'll be runnin' out the cafeteria doors, which they unlock every day at four for the delivery truck." He peered into Chris's worried eyes, desperate for his blessing. "And when I get out, I'm gonna find Amos, and we'll come back for you."

Chris just thinned his lips and looked away. "It won't work."

"It will!" Colton was tempted to shove him. "Just watch!" Without another word, he crossed to the pile of kindling he'd pointed out. He dropped to his knees on the mulch, took the magnifier from his pocket, angled it to catch the sun's full radiance, and then waited.

And waited.

It was good and hot today. Perspiration trickled from Colton's hairline as he held the lens perfectly still. Glancing over his shoulder, he was dismayed to see Christopher walking away.

"I *will* make a fire." Colton pursed his lips into a determined knot. His hand shook with the effort it took to hold the glass still. In the next second, a line of smoke rose from his kindling, rewarding his persistence.

With a spurt of excitement, Colton blew a gentle breath across the glowing edge of a leaf. A flame leaped up. *Yes!* And then, another.

He sat back on his heels, watching with satisfaction as the fire grew larger. He needed more kindling. Running to the corner of the yard, he scooped up some more debris, brought it back to the fire, and sprinkled it on top, careful not to snuff out the fire. Once the fire was big enough, he trotted across the yard to Mrs. Spellman, who hadn't noticed him behind the play palace.

"Can I go in and use the bathroom?"

"You can wait. Recess is almost over."

"Okay." Pretending to cooperate, he went and hovered by the door. The fire was blazing now. Seeing Christopher back on the swing, he whistled to catch his attention, then gestured toward the blaze. Chris looked over and stared, stupefied. Then he looked back at Colton, who nodded. *Tell somebody.*

Chris stood up slowly. "Mrs. Spellman?" he called hesitantly. "Is that a fire?"

The woman looked over and gasped. That was Colton's cue to push his way inside. He ran straight into Miz Banks, who was coming to call them all in. "There's a fire!" he relayed. "Mrs. Spellman needs help!"

"What?" As Miz Banks went to investigate, Colton took off running for the cafeteria. Sure enough, the chain at the double doors on the far side of the big room hung open. Colton tore straight for the doors, his heart about to jump from his chest, the taste of freedom on his tongue.

Just as he pushed through one of the doors, someone on the outside pulled it open, causing Colton to collide with a dark-skinned deliveryman.

"Whoa, there!" The man was surprised to see him but held on fast.

Powered by determination, Colton twisted out of his hands only to trip over the dolly the man was pulling along behind him. He toppled and crashed to his knees.

"Hold on, now." Before he could spring up again, the man caught him by the back of his burgundy school shirt. "Where do you think you're going?"

"Let go of me!" Colton fought the man with every ounce of strength at his disposal. He kicked and hit and flailed, to no avail. The deliveryman was way bigger and stronger.

He caught Colton around the waist and hoisted him under one arm. Leaving his dolly on the loading bay, he marched Colton, howling with frustration, back into the building.

CHAPTER 19

"*I*t's not like I'm going to sleep anyway," Emma protested as Ben led her to a room of her own, just down the hall from Ruby's suite, having used the credit card Emma had returned to him. "I want to go to the boarding school with you tonight. Please, Ben."

She waited with a held breath as he tossed his black bag onto the armchair, then took the Target sack from her hand and laid it on the only bed.

"You know you can't come, Emma."

Her pulse ticked upward as he caught up her hands in his. They were alone for the first time since his reappearance. As always, energy pulsed in him, and he seemed to have something to tell her. His thumbs swept over her knuckles, causing her stomach to somersault pleasantly.

"We're just checking the place out, making sure the variables don't change overnight. Your job is to get a good night's sleep. Hopefully, this will all be over tomorrow. You'll have your boys back, and our names will be cleared." His gaze slid down and to the left as if remembering something.

Emma studied him. "What? Something's still bothering you."

He looked back at her with a wry expression. "You know me better than anyone."

Her pulse skipped at the intimate statement. She drew her hands from his and folded her arms across her chest to keep him from taking them again. If she didn't start resisting him soon, he would assume she wanted to be his woman—but for how long? "So, let's hear it."

He cleared his throat as if the subject was difficult. "It's about Tiffany, the woman I was with when—"

"I know who you mean." Her terse reply betrayed jealousy, which was a ludicrous emotion, considering the woman's circumstances.

Ben grimaced. "Charlotte says she's in a coma."

"I know."

His eyebrows pulled together. "How did *you* find out?"

"Butler told me what happened to your alibi. Sounded to me like someone tried to kill her, only she survived…so far."

"Right." Ben clearly felt guilty about it. "Both the Virginia Beach police and the FBI knew about her, so it could have been Peyton who tried to kill her. Or Butler, or one of Butler's superiors. Ugh." Dragging his hands over his bald head, he stalked to the window to peek outside at the busy street below. "I can't believe the lengths these Centurions have gone to in order to frame us."

"I know. It's crazy." Emma sank on the end of the only bed in the room and toed off her Skechers. "Did you hear about the emails we supposedly wrote each other?"

He spun around. "Charlotte told me. But don't worry, those are printouts that showed up in Butler's mailbox one day. If the emails are fake, which they obviously are, then the digital versions won't hold up to scrutiny. And the other evidence—the tire tracks and Colton's DNA on my Gerber blade—it'll all be circumstantial now that Jones's motivation for wanting the boys has come to light."

Emma examined her palms, healing with a soft, new layer of skin on them. "I can't believe that man is my boys' grandfather."

"Don't think about that." Ben approached her again. "Think about Jones's astonishment when he finds out I'm alive."

Torn, she looked up at Ben. "Is it wrong to hope that man goes to prison for a very long time? I mean, he claims to help homeless men and children from broken homes, but he's a hypocrite. Just think of the lives he's ruined!"

Ben sat beside her, so close she could feel his heat through the yoga pants she was wearing. How she longed to feel his arms around her!

"Emma, I want you to know something."

Here it came. She wasn't sure she was ready for this, whatever this was.

Raising a hand, he tucked a strand of her straightened hair behind her ear so he could see her profile. "The only reason I went to see Tiffany was to try and forget about you."

She let the words run through her, aware that her eyes were rounding.

"I would never have called her up in the first place if Amos hadn't practically ordered me to leave you alone."

She licked her lips nervously. "Amos says you're a ladies' man."

Ben's wry grimace assured her he wasn't offended. "Well, Amos doesn't know the real me. Only God knows the real me." He laid a hand over her interlocked ones, his skin a peachier hue than hers. "Emma, you're all I thought about the whole time I was in Syria. After we find your boys—and we're going to find them—I want us to be a family. I want to be their father...and your husband."

To Emma's astonishment, he slid off the bed, going down on one knee to face her while still clasping her hands. "Please tell me you've reconsidered the whole not-needing-or-wanting-a-man-in-your-life thing. I want you to marry me."

Speechless, she could only stare at him. Was she imagining this? Dreaming that the vibrant and virile Mr. Fix-it actually wanted to marry *her?* The picture he painted of them being a family was so much more than she'd ever envisioned for herself that she didn't know how to react.

He cocked his head, worry creasing his smooth brow. "Did you hear me?"

"I heard." Panicked that she was letting him pull the wool over her eyes, she stood and stepped away from him, crossing to the window to gaze down on the rooftops of the historic buildings all around them. "I just...I just can't think about any of that right now, not without my boys here."

Ben remained silent for several seconds. "No, no, I get it." He surged to his feet, looking upset. "I'm sorry. I got caught up in the moment."

She watched him from the corner of her eye. "Don't be sorry," she said softly. "I'm not saying no."

He drew up short, a slow smile vanquishing the frown on his face, but then it faded. "You know I'd never treat you like Carl did, right?"

She slowly turned and faced him.

"You will never have to worry about me cheating on you or running off with some other woman. Got it? I'm not just your everyday, average Joe. I'm a Navy SEAL, and honor means everything to me."

The gruffness in his voice and the mistiness in his eyes were reassuring, but she wasn't ready for this discussion. "I hear you, but I want to know what happened to you under the water—that part you said no one would believe. How'd you get free of the anchor?"

"Oh, that." Ben gave a laugh as if the memory alone amazed him. "A miracle happened."

She waited breathlessly for details.

"My air was gone. And I mean *gone.* I was just about to inhale water and drown when I saw a bright light like God was coming for me. All at once, I sensed my brother with me, so I asked him in my head, "Am I dead?" And I heard Shawn say, "Not yet." Next thing I knew, the rope around my ankle just vanished, and I was being pushed to the surface."

"Oh, Ben." Emma raised her hands to her cheeks, marveling.

"You believe me?"

"Of course, I believe you."

He closed the distance between them. "All this time, I thought God had ignored my family's prayers for Shawn. I thought God was weak—weaker than disease, weaker than evil, and I had to fix what He couldn't. But that's not true. I wouldn't be standing in front of you if that were true. Shawn is alive! God *did* heal him, just not in this life. Emma, if God did that for me, I *know* He's going to reunite you with your boys—*our* boys, if you'll share them."

His faith and his optimism had her stepping straight into his arms, clasping him, and pressing her lips to his in what quickly became a toe-curling kiss. He broke it off with a groan.

"I love you, Em."

The gruff confession made her heart sing.

Maybe she was a fool for believing him. But the hope that everything might work out as Ben had described burned in her. She would be happy just to get her boys back. But for Ben to join her family, only God had the power to bring something that good out of this nightmarish experience. She swallowed hard, then whispered while her knees quaked, "I love you, too."

His slow grin made the risk of admitting it absolutely worthwhile.

"Mr. Jones?"

"Yes, Myrtle." Jared recognized Miz Bank's distinctive voice, even though it sounded more tentative than usual. He braced an elbow on his desk, his perusal of Citadel Financial's prospectus forgotten.

"We've had another incident with Colton Moulton, sir."

"Have you?" Jared tempered his annoyance. "What now?"

"He started a fire in the playground, then used the distraction to attempt an escape through the doors in the cafeteria."

"I see." Jared needed no more proof that Emma Stuart had left her genetic imprint on the second son. "I assume he was caught and is now being reprimanded?"

"Yes, sir. He's been locked in his room with bread and water for the remainder of the day."

Myrtle sounded truly shaken by the attempted escape.

Jared pinched the bridge of his nose. "Not to worry. Quite soon, his father will have the means to look after his own sons, and you won't have to do it for him."

"Yes, sir. About that…"

"Go on." What was she about to say?

"You told me he saw his mother die!" Affront and confusion laced her voice.

Jared's heart skipped a beat. "Who told you otherwise?" Only a handful of men knew the Moulton boys' true story, and none of them worked at The Centurion Academy for Boys.

"A woman," came the unexpected answer. "She dropped by this morning with her husband, claiming to have inherited money and looking for a charity worthy of her donation. She said they were friends of yours."

"Their names?"

"Bonheur, I believe."

He searched his memory. "I don't know any Bonheurs. What did they look like?"

"The woman had light-auburn ringlets. Her husband was an older man with a military bearing and a dark mustache."

The word *military* called to mind the Navy SEAL, who was supposedly dead. An uneasy feeling slithered through Jared's gut.

"In any event, the woman gave me a printout taken from the

FBI's website with the boys' pictures on it. It said they were kidnapped from their mother. You told me they saw her die!"

Jared countered the accusation in a harsh voice. "Should I have told you the truth, Myrtle?"

"I should think so."

Jared thought quickly. "Okay, here it is, then. The Moulton boys were being raised in filth by a drug-abusing floozy, who was well compensated for her loss. Their father wants better for them, as you can imagine. Parting those boys from their trashy mother was not an easy decision, but it was the right one."

"Yes, sir." Myrtle's agreement sounded only half-hearted.

Jared's thoughts raced. Whoever the meddling couple was, their suspicions were dangerous. He would have to remove the boys from boarding school immediately—tonight. And no one but his innermost circle was to know where he was taking them.

"Thank you for alerting me to this matter, Myrtle. You may expect my chauffeur and me to arrive for our visit, as usual. Kindly have both boys bathed and their possessions packed. I want the baby there, too. Tell the foster mother to drop him off by eight-thirty. She won't be needed anymore."

"Oh." Myrtle's exclamation betrayed surprise, but she was wise enough not to question him. "Shall I feed Colton a proper meal before you come?"

"No." Jared failed to conceal his disdain for the troublemaker. At some point, he would ship that boy off to Russia, where Semion Mogilevich could teach him the ins and outs of smuggling. "Let him go hungry."

"Yes, sir. I'll have all three boys ready for you, sir."

Jared hung up without a thank-you. After all, the woman had soured his mood with her call.

So. The proverbial cat was out of the bag, was it? Myrtle herself posed no immediate threat, but the faceless strangers who'd dropped in at the academy spelled trouble. Who were they?

Friends of Emma Stuart's? The Architect had been a fool for advising his minion to release her.

Jared would need a new chauffeur. He hadn't planned for Carl to move into his hunting lodge for another three weeks, but now the timeline was moved up. The lodge, situated on land inherited from Jared's distant ancestor, Noble Jones, was miles from the nearest neighbor, surrounded by marshland and forests.

The boys would be happy there. Jared would visit every weekend in lieu of every night. By the end of summer, all three of them would have forgotten their prior life. All was not lost.

In due time, Chris would be sent to a fine university to study finance like his grandfather. The Centurions had a saying that they had borrowed from the Bible: Train up a child in the way he should go; even when he is old he will not depart from it.

"God's will be done," Jared murmured.

The academy stood like a giant monolith with the last suggestion of daylight silvering its gray façade. Ben, Tony, and Amos hovered just inside the tree line, waiting for an approaching car to pass them so they could dart across the street and into the woods they had surveyed earlier that day.

The idea was to keep watch at the academy until the wee hours of dawn, just to make sure the boys weren't relocated. Ben envisioned Emma curled up in the king-sized bed in the room he'd secured for her. Longing tugged at him, but since nothing would progress between them without the boys in her life, it was best he stayed out here tonight.

The smooth, sleek outline of the vehicle passing them and then slowing as it prepared to turn into the academy finally caught his notice. Ben pitched his voice toward the next tree over where Tony, dressed in his night-ops attire, was indistinguishable from the tree trunk. "Hey, I think that might be Jones going to visit the school."

"I was gonna say it looks like a Jaguar or a Bentley."

"He visits them this late?" Ben had imagined when Charlotte mentioned Jones's visits that she meant 6:00 or 7:00 P.M., not nearly 9:00 at night.

Amos drifted out of the shadows next to him. "Looks like we're just in time for a reunion. Let's go see what we can see."

Carrying packs that included bug spray, meals-ready-to-eat, night-ops gear, camo face paint, and a grappling hook, all purchased at a Bass Pro Shop on their way to the academy, they hoofed it across the road and through the woods, making their way to the school's enclosed yard.

The plan was to make a thorough reconnaissance of the yard first, which already stood in darkness. Then, after midnight, reconnoiter the front of the building, making note of all ingress and egress points to share with the hostage rescue teams. After that, they would each take a two-hour shift keeping watch on the building while the other two slept in the car.

Within minutes, using the grapple and the rope attached, all three of them scaled the wall surrounding what they'd determined earlier that day was a playground. While Tony and Mako clambered down into the play area, Ben remained seated on the top to act as overwatch. In the absence of an inter-team radio, his imitation of a hoot owl would signal any trouble.

From his vantage atop the wall, Ben surveyed the academy's dark windows. Most of the lights were shining on the third floor, frosting the playground equipment below. Only a faint glow shone in the first-floor windows, which suggested the meeting between Jones and his grandsons was happening in some room at the front of the school. Ben was tempted to slide off the wall and nip around the building to look for himself when the reverse cones of two headlights brightened the sky on the west side of the building, accompanied by the sound of a motor. A second vehicle was visiting the academy tonight. Surely, this wasn't the hostage rescue team already.

Emitting one hoot to signal the potential for trouble, Ben pushed to his feet, then balanced his way along the twenty-inch-thick wall to investigate.

The wall ended at the corner of the building. Peering around it, Ben noted a parking area illuminated by the headlights of a van that was making a three-point turn as it backed toward a loading bay. This was probably where food was delivered to the school, but why would that be happening at this time of night?

The van's motor died. Its lights went out, and the front doors popped open. Ben pulled his head back before stealing a second peek. His gaze locked on the man hopping out of the driver's seat. He blinked and looked again. That couldn't be who he thought it was.

Charlie Chaplin rendezvoused at the back of the van with a stranger who resembled Emma's composite of the second kidnapper, the one with the beak nose and acne scars. That man pulled open one of the van's rear doors and out stepped Grimes. Ben nearly choked on their good luck. They'd hit the mother lode!

A brilliant light—motion sensing—blinked on by the bay doors, confirming Ben's identification of the newcomers. Why were they here? Was it to relocate the boys? Ben's blood flowed faster. No, no, no. If that happened, the boys wouldn't be here when the FBI showed up the next day.

As Charlie Chaplin pounded on the delivery doors, Ben dropped to a sitting position, twisted, and lowered himself down the inside of the walled enclosure, landing lightly on his feet. Amos, who'd been alerted by his hoot earlier, stood just feet away, waiting for the scoop.

Ben put his mouth near Mako's ear. "It's the kidnappers. They just rolled up in a van. I think they're about to move the boys."

Mako's clear gray eyes looked translucent in the darkness. A frog croaked in the corner of the yard. Without a word uttered, he signed for Ben to get back on the top of the wall and put eyes on the van. He was going to find Tony and send him down range to get their car, should they need to follow the van shortly.

Marveling that Amos could convey so much without talking, Ben nodded his agreement. Getting back onto the ten-foot wall required running to the rear of the playground to use the rope and grapple. He ran toward it, skirting a climbing wall and a tower with two different kinds of slides. God forbid Emma's boys vanished right under their noses!

She would never forgive him if he let that happen. His dreams of a wedding and a big, happy family would go up in smoke.

Emma answered the crisp knock on her hotel room door, knowing by the sound of it alone that it was Ruby. As she cracked it open, the journalist noted the nightshirt Emma was wearing. "Are you sleeping?"

"No." How was she supposed to sleep knowing her boys were only twelve miles away and mere yards away from Ben and his teammates?

"I've got some news." Ruby's gaze enjoined Emma to let her in.

"What is it?"

"Just remain calm, okay? Tony just texted me. He said the same men who kidnapped the boys are there at the academy right now, waiting outside. It looks like Jones might be moving them tonight."

A high-pitched ringing filled Emma's ears. "No." She would stop them herself if she had to. Turning her back on Ruby, she located her Skechers.

"Reggie and I are headed for the school right now. If we can film that van or the kidnappers, it'll validate your story. And if they're still at the school, that'll implicate Jones."

"I'm going with you." Emma was already wriggling her bare feet into her shoes.

Ruby stared at her outfit. "In that?"

Emma looked down at herself. "Yes." She grabbed her room key and her purse and headed out the door with Ruby chasing her. Reggie was waiting out in the hall. Seconds later, they were all in the elevator, taking it to the parking garage.

"I'll drive." A steely determination kept Emma's panic from kicking in. "That way, you can sit up front and narrate to the camera while Reggie's in back filming you. I'll drive," she repeated, holding out her hand until Ruby relinquished the key.

Within minutes, they had left the downtown traffic behind. Emma gripped the steering wheel like her life depended on it.

Ruby turned her head, her eyes glimmering in the dark. "Do you know where you're going?"

"Yes." Emma had memorized the route that morning. She knew *exactly* where her older boys were. The fear that they would be snatched from her again kept her heart pumping and her palms moist. But they wouldn't get away from her this time because she wasn't picking herself up off the road with her hands and knees burning. She had wheels to give her speed, and God's emboldening presence keeping her calm.

CHAPTER 20

*C*hris kept his eyes peeled. Something was different about tonight's meeting with the school's president. Mr. Jones had started bringing their father with him a few nights ago. On the first night Carl had shown up, Chris had gleaned by the uniform he wore that his job was to drive Mr. Jones's fancy car.

"Well, give your father a proper hug," the president had ordered the first night they'd been reunited with Carl. The small, cozy library on the first floor of the academy had seemed like a really strange place to run into him. Chris only ever pictured Carl in a bar, like the Steamboat Bar and Grille, which was the last place they'd seen him almost a year ago.

Out of fear of Mr. Jones, Chris and Colton had both embraced their father. But neither one of them was about to call him Dad.

The uniform didn't fool Chris for a second. Neither did the gold ring on his right hand. Chris could tell Carl was the same twitchy and aloof person who had lived with them in their blue trailer by the edge of a marsh in Mantachie. Furthermore, Chris could tell that Carl didn't want anything more to do with his boys now than he did then. After the first night, he'd hoped Carl wouldn't come back, but he had every night since.

During their previous visit, Mr. Jones had informed them their father would be taking them out of the boarding school to a house that Mr. Jones was giving them. They were going to love it there. There was a river and a marsh, lots of paths to ride bikes, and they wouldn't have to go to school because they would have a tutor.

Colton's answer, "I like school better," made Chris stifle a snort.

He'd imagined their move to the new house would happen in the distant future. But when Miz Banks came to their room that day with a zippered bag and told him to put all his gifts from Mr. Jones in it, plus his and Colton's toothbrushes and spare uniforms, anxiety cramped his stomach. They were leaving tonight.

Colton would have been asleep by the time Miz Banks fetched them, but he was too hungry to sleep. She brought them down to the library as usual, this time carrying the bag. Carl was the first adult to join them. Ignoring his sons, he paced from one side of the library to the other, tugging at his collar like it was suddenly too tight. He struck Chris as nervous. They could all hear Mr. Jones out in the hallway speaking to Miz Banks in a low, terse voice.

Colton cocked his ear to the conversation before meeting Chris's gaze. "Somethin's goin' on."

"I know."

The door yawned open, and Mr. Jones marched in, carrying a familiar baby.

"Carter!" Chris and Colton rushed toward their baby brother, who squealed at them in recognition.

"Kipu!"

Chris gasped and grinned at Colton. "He said my name!" His heart swelling with love, he held his hands up. "Can I hold him, please?"

Mr. Jones ignored the request and carried Carter straight toward Carl.

"You remember your youngest, don't you, Carl?" He thrust the baby at him.

"Um, sure." Carl took Carter into his arms, holding him awkwardly. He bounced him in his arms. "Hey there."

Chris could tell Carl would rather jump out the window than be put in charge of his children. Risking Mr. Jones's disapproval, Chris approached his father and held his hands out again. "I'll watch him for you."

"Thanks." Carl dumped the baby in his arms.

"Kipu!"

"Yeah, that's me." Loving the chubby, sticky sweetness of him, Chris hugged his brother while imagining how Mama felt without all of them. Longing for her put a lump in his throat.

He became aware of Mr. Jones studying him. "Did you pack for you and your brother?"

"Yes, sir." Christopher nodded toward the zippered bag on the armchair.

"Excellent. Well, don't be afraid. It's time for your father to take care of you. I trust you'll like your new home much better than this one. One day, it will belong to you."

Baffled as to why Mr. Jones would give them a house, Chris simply nodded.

The school president thrust a large hand at him, forcing Chris to free his right hand to accept the man's firm grip. He tried not to wince.

Releasing him at last, Mr. Jones sent Colton a dismissive glance, then patted the baby's head. "Well then. I guess it's time. Carl, grab the boys' bag and take this one." He handed Carl the diaper bag hanging from his shoulder, then swiveled on his fancy shoes and started for the door.

They all followed him, their father seemingly as confused as they were.

Miz Banks, who'd been in the hallway earlier, had apparently returned upstairs to her charges, turning out the lights behind her.

The corridor of the east wing stood in darkness, with the only light coming from the cafeteria. Mr. Jones herded them toward it, with Carl bringing up the rear.

The kitchen still smelled like Chris's dinner of tuna casserole, which had proven too messy to wrap up in a napkin for Colton.

When Mr. Jones pushed open the same doors Colton had tried escaping through earlier, a puff of fresh night air wafted in. A little man with a Charlie Chaplin mustache jerked to attention and tossed down a cigarette.

"Evening, Bates. Sorry about the last-minute notice." Mr. Jones looked past Bates at the two men standing by the van's back doors. "Really? You had to bring them both?"

Shock slid over Chris as he recognized the men who'd kidnapped them. Overhearing Colton's gasp, he hushed him and grabbed his arm.

"But it's the men who took us from Mama!"

"Just stay calm. They're not gonna hurt us."

The kidnappers swung open the van's rear doors.

"I don't wanna get in that van again!"

Mr. Jones spun toward Colton and stared down his nose at him. "Bates, put this boy in the back."

In the next instant, the man with the mustache leaped forward, grabbed Colton by the scruff, and toted him, kicking and fighting, to the van. With his heart in his throat and not wanting to be manhandled, Chris followed with Carter. Déjà vu washed over him as he joined Colton in sitting on the same folded blankets they had before. "They're not going to hurt us," he repeated.

"You don't know that!"

Their father stood aloof, clearly uncertain what to do.

"Give me the keys to my car, Carl," said Mr. Jones, "and join your sons. I suggest you bring that middle boy to heel."

Carl's Adam's apple bobbed as he fished the keys from his pocket. "But how will you get home, sir?"

Mr. Jones snatched the keys from his hand. "Believe it or not, I know how to drive. Go on. You knew this day was coming."

Carl regarded his three boys with dread. "Can't I sit up front?"

"No."

Obviously, no one ever crossed Mr. Jones as, in the next instant, Carl ducked his head and climbed into the back with them, sitting as far away from Chris as he could get. The whole van shook as the fat man who'd sat in the back with them before joined them.

As the second kidnapper closed one of the back doors, then the other, Chris met Mr. Jones's parting stare. The man who'd given him special gifts and told him exotic stories wasn't done with him yet. He still wanted something from Chris. But Chris had seen how Mr. Jones spoke to other people, how he treated his little brother. The man was evil. What had happened to their mother—what was happening to them still—was all because of him.

Ruby spotted the van pulling out of the driveway at the academy at the same time Emma did. "That's it. That's the kidnapper's van!" It was coming straight at them.

"Yep." Emma would have recognized the van anywhere. As it zipped past them, she deliberated how best to turn around.

"Do you think the boys are in the back?"

Emma wasn't going to take any chances. "Guess we'll find out." She zipped into the driveway before braking abruptly and jamming the gear into reverse. Rubber squealed on the smooth flagstone before she backed out into the street, tugged the shifter into Drive, and accelerated hard enough to fling them all against their seats.

Vignettes of the kidnapping flashed through Emma's mind. The abrasions burning her palms and knees, her abject helplessness as she watched the taillights of the van get smaller and smaller. *Not this time.*

Depressing the accelerator, she pursued the fleeing white van, determined to keep it in her sight while also hanging back so the driver wouldn't guess he was being followed.

"Where are the SEALs?" Ruby started texting Tony when the black carpool sedan pulled out of the utility road into the oncoming lane. "Oh, that's Tony. He's picking up the others, I think."

Emma spared a glance into her rearview mirror. Sure enough, Tony's brake lights flared, and he turned into the school's driveway just like they had done. Two dark shadows shot across the lawn to get in the car with him. "Yes, they're following the van also."

Emma relaxed her death grip on the steering wheel. Ben would be right behind them. While he wouldn't like her involvement in the chase, she wasn't about to fall back. None of them had the authority to stop the perpetrators from relocating her sons, but if that van got away, she might never see her boys again.

And that was not an option.

Help me, Lord. Help me get them back!

Ben kept one eye on the vehicles ahead of him while using Amos's cell phone to call Charlotte. Mako, who'd jumped into the back seat, leaving Ben to take the shotgun, had thrust his phone at him wordlessly. When Charlotte didn't answer, sweat breached the pores on Ben's forehead. Instead of leaving a message, he typed her a curt text: *Emergency update. Call back ASAP.*

Then he looked up. "Tony, just pass their car and force them to drop back. They're going to give us away."

"I'm trying to. Emma keeps cutting me off."

"*Emma's* driving?" Ben peered hard through the Capris's rear windows. "Why are the women even out here?" He shot a suspicious glance at Tony. "Did you tell Ruby about the white van?"

Tony glanced into the rearview mirror at the back seat. "Back me up, Senior Chief."

Mako sighed. "Think of it this way, Ben. Whatever goes down, we'll have the media right there filming. It would clear your name immediately to have footage of men fitting Emma's description."

That was true, but he couldn't shake his uneasiness. "Just as long as no one gets hurt."

As the van and then the Capris veered off Chatham Parkway, Tony followed it. Ben hunted for a road sign. Okay, now they were on Harry S. Truman Parkway, both cars speeding to keep up with the van. As the city limits fell behind them, the road grew relentlessly flat. Ben noted the exits as they passed them: One exit led to the Savannah Botanical Gardens, another to the Wormsloe Historic Site. According to the compass on the car's dash, they were heading southeast.

Tony grumbled as the van took yet another exit marked Skidaway Island. With a heavy foot on the accelerator, he managed to gain on the Capris, while remaining a healthy distance behind the van. Fortunately, the good number of cars on the road kept their pursuit from being obvious.

As they passed the Capris, Emma glanced over, and Ben gestured with big motions for her to fall back. He could have sworn she rolled her eyes, but to his relief, she lowered her speed and let their black sedan get in front of her.

Soon after, the phone Ben still clutched started buzzing. Thank God, Charlotte was calling him back. "Hello." He put the phone on speaker so his companions could hear.

"Hey, sorry. I was busy briefing the HRT. What's the emergency?"

"Change of plans. The boys aren't at the academy anymore."

"Then, it's true. Hey, Fitz!"

"Wait. What do you mean it's true?"

"We got a tip on our Kidnappings and Missing Persons Hotline earlier today stating that the Moulton boys had been at The Centurion Academy for Boys in Savannah but were being taken away tonight. It's a good thing we fielded the call. We're the only ones who know about it."

Ben shot an arched look into the back seat. As upset as Amos had been about it, Ruby's instincts about Miz Banks had been right on target. The director had done the proper thing and called the hotline. "Yeah, we saw them move out. In fact, we're behind the van right now, license plate BZN 2529, with the original three kidnappers in it, as well as Carl Moulton. We're all headed southeast on Diamond Causeway. I'll drop you a pin."

"That'd be great."

"Ma'am, please authorize us to neutralize this situation." Apart from the occupants of the Capris being in the way, the odds were good—just four to three.

Charlotte kept quiet for many long seconds.

"Ma'am?"

"Hold a minute."

He could tell she'd put him on mute while she asked Fitz for his input.

Ben noted that the road they traveled had narrowed to just two lanes. They zipped onto a bridge with nothing visible in any direction but glinting water fringed in marsh grass. This drive reminded him of his trip in the back of the squad car. Surely Jones wasn't having the boys taken somewhere and killed. His heart dropped at the thought. No, no. They were his grandsons, after all.

Charlotte's voice came back. "Ben, we are twenty minutes behind you with an eight-man HRT squad. Jones owns a house on Skidaway Island, so that's probably the van's destination. Just wait for us to get down there, and you won't be liable if something goes south."

Ben ground his teeth in disappointment. "Roger. I'll keep you apprised of our location. That van's not getting away from us."

"Don't let them know they're being followed. We're out the door now. Over."

Ben ended the call with a press of his thumb. He had to respect Charlotte's timely response, but twenty minutes could mean the difference between recovering the boys alive and trapping them in a shootout between the hostage rescue team and the perps. Emma's happiness—heck, Ben's and her future together—depended on them recovering those boys safely.

As he brooded, they crossed yet another bridge, this one higher than the last. Accessing the map on Amos's phone, he confirmed that they were approaching Skidaway Island. As the road widened again into double lanes, trees sprang up. Soon, they were passing bricked entrances to ostentatious neighborhoods. It couldn't be more obvious the island was a getaway for the rich. Jones probably thought he'd been doing the boys a favor, taking them away from their humble existence.

Twisting to see out the back window, Ben cast an anxious glance at the Capris. Emma was practically on their bumper. In the dark, her face looked ghostly pale behind the wheel. He could tell every one of her senses was trained on the van ahead of them. *Don't worry,* he wished he could tell her. *The FBI's on their way.*

"Woah, woah, woah. They're pulling into a gas station."

Tony's warning had him facing forward again.

"Go on past them, and we'll circle back. Right, Mako?" It would make their pursuit obvious if they all pulled in.

"Right."

Tony drove slowly past the BP station, his gaze swiveling toward the rearview mirror. When an Italian expletive came out of his mouth, Ben knew exactly what was happening. Emma had followed the van. Both he and Amos twisted in their seats to look back.

"Barnacles!" Amos thundered. "Turn this thing around."

Tony screeched into the first cross street they came to and pulled a U-turn, cutting off a Lamborghini that blared its horn at them. He laid the accelerator to the floor, pinning Ben and Amos against their seats. Ten nerve-wracking seconds later, they were back at the gas station, only to see the Capris parked on the far-right side of the mini-mart, nowhere near the van that had pulled up to the gas pumps out front.

The SEALs fell silent as Tony rolled into the adjacent pumping station. The pock-faced perp who was pumping gas didn't even glance their way.

Ben met Tony's gaze, then Amos's. Everything he needed and wanted was in the back of the van next to them. Theirs were the only three vehicles at the gas station. One attendant, scarcely an adult, sat inside the mini-mart watching television. Very few cars drove by. Imagine how Emma felt.

"We could take them right now." Ben held Amos's pale gaze, hoping for his agreement.

"Negative. We follow Charlotte's orders. Tony, hop out and get us some gas. We can't just sit here without drawing notice."

"I gotta pee," Colton repeated his statement in a louder voice. He didn't, really. He'd just figured he might be able to escape if they let him out of the van.

Sweaty Man glowered at Carl. "Make your kid shut up."

Carl, who stared off into space, barely even glanced in his direction. "He'll be fine."

"No, I won't!" Shaking off Christopher's grip, Colton rose to his knees and started unfastening his pants. "I'm gonna pee right here if you don't let me out."

Sweaty Man leaned forward and shoved him back onto the blanket, but Carl spoke up. "You know, I—I have to go, too. So I'll take him."

"Fine. Bates!" Sweaty Man yelled so the driver could hear him through the small metal door separating the back from the front.

"Tell Homer to open up the back. Mr. Carl's gonna take his son to the bathroom."

Chris tugged on Colton's wrist. "Please." He was the only one who'd guessed what Colton was planning. Colton shot him a look that promised, *I'm gonna get help.*

The man up front relayed the message out the window to the man pumping gas.

As one of the back doors swung open, Colton's heart began to thump. This would be his only chance.

"Hurry up," Ugly Man said as Carl scooted out, then motioned for Colton to join him. Colton's confidence grew. He knew he could escape from his father. As they started for the mini-mart, Ugly Man shut the van doors again.

Colton swept the station with all-seeing eyes. Mr. Ben had taught him how to see everything at once. There was a black car with some dark-haired guy pumping gas and two more guys inside. A big blue car was parked to the right of the store, also with people inside—that was weird. But Colton's attention flew to the dark trees behind the mini-mart, providing the perfect place for him to hide.

Carl grabbed him by the back of his school shirt and herded him toward the building. Colton was just about to kick him in the shin, wrench free, and bolt for the trees when he glanced at the blue car again. Why would people just sit in it, doing nothing? The face staring back at him through the driver's window made him stop and stare.

"That's Mama!"

"What?" Carl whipped around and gawked.

The door of the car swung open, and there was Mama holding her arms out to Colton. She flicked a burning glare at Carl.

"Let him go right now, Carl, or you're going to jail for kidnapping."

Carl let go and threw his hands up. "It wasn't my idea!"

"Mama!" Colton sprinted into his mother's arms.

~

"Go!"

Tony, who was pumping gas, had rapped on the windows, alerting Ben and Amos to what was happening. But Ben already knew. He knew the exact moment Colton had spotted his mother sitting in the Capris.

"Emma, don't," he'd prayed.

But she'd pushed open her door, anyway, demanding that her ex release the boy. Carl shoved Colton in her direction and ran into the store. The employee inside stood staring as Carl ran right past him. The SEALs had no time to work up a plan. As Tony put the gas nozzle back, Ben and Amos made eye contact and then ejected from the car.

The perp pumping gas glanced toward the building and finally noticed Emma hugging Colton. He immediately pounded on the side of the van. "It's the kid's mom!"

Tony swung around the island between them, his Beretta pointed at the perp. "Put the nozzle away. Now!" The pock-faced man stopped pounding. Instead, he tossed the spewing nozzle onto the ground. Backing up, he delved his hand into his pocket, maybe looking for a lighter.

With a roar, Tony ran straight at him, pushing him away from the spill.

Ben, armed with nothing but Amos's backup blade, flipped down the lever to stop the spill from getting out of hand. He wrenched open the closest of the van's rear doors while Amos tore past him to get to the driver.

A gunshot rang out as Charlie Chaplin came out of the van firing. Amos pulled back, joining Ben at the back of the van, where he'd quickly shut the door. His glimpse of Grimes holding Christopher in a headlock while Carter squirmed out of Chris's lap had made Ben's heart stop. Amos checked the magazine on his H&K.

This could get bad.

Tony was still grappling with the pock-faced man near the front-right fender.

The sound of running feet told Ben that Chaplin was making a run for it. Amos peeled away to pursue him, the crack of his Glock giving rise to a strangled scream. Ben would have given anything to have his sidearm right then.

"Secured!" Tony let Ben know that he'd won his hand-to-hand struggle.

Ben glanced toward the mini-mart and saw the young man inside with a phone pressed to his ear. Carl had vanished, probably out the rear exit. That left only Grimes in the back of the van, holding Chris hostage.

Ben clutched Amos's blade more securely. He readied himself to pull the door back open.

"Ben!" Emma called across the parking lot as she clutched Colton tight. "Be careful!"

The door practically popped off its hinges with the force that Ben pulled it open.

Carter, who was toddling around in the cab, pulled his thumb out of his mouth to grin at him. "Dada!" The word would have melted Ben if he weren't so distracted.

"Get back!" Grimes, with his arm around Chris's neck, was trying to squeeze both him and Christopher through the little cargo access door into the cab. Chris looked like he couldn't breathe.

Ben pictured the van's keys still swinging in the ignition.

"Get back, or I'll break his neck!"

Christopher's eyes, huge dark-blue pools just like Emma's, communicated desperation.

"Easy." Ben held Chris's gaze while putting one knee into the truck and scooping up Carter.

Grimes took advantage of Ben's full arms and thrust Chris into the cabin ahead of him. Then he, too, squeezed through the opening. A lock clicked on the cab doors. The engine turned over.

Ben hastily stepped back onto the concrete. Holding Carter, he couldn't do anything but watch the van pull away, one of its back doors swinging open.

CHAPTER 21

*A*mos and Tony fired simultaneously, unloading bullets into the fleeing van's tires. With loud pops and hisses, three out of four tires went flat, but Grimes didn't slow down. He steered straight toward Amos, who'd stepped into his path, pistol raised, then jumped aside at the last instant.

The van lurched onto the quiet street, its flat tires slapping the pavement.

Tony was kneeling on the back of the pock-faced perp, trying to hold him with one arm while still gripping his sidearm. He could've used a zip tie, but they didn't have any. Ben's arms were full, holding the chunky baby. Amos was chasing the swinging van door and about to jump into the cargo bay to affect a rescue when a dark, windowless SWAT vehicle came screaming up the road. In the nick of time, Amos veered away.

Crash! The FBI's vehicle rammed into the back of the van, sending it straight into the median, where it hit a tree, its radiator steaming. Eight dark figures sprang from the dark SWAT vehicle and swarmed the incapacitated van.

Alarmed for Chris, Ben held his breath. The FBI's HRT had

finally made an appearance. As they encircled the white van, one man smashed Grimes's window with the butt of his rifle. Another ripped the driver's door open.

Seeing Grimes being dragged to the ground bleeding from the bridge of his nose, Ben swiveled and ran the baby to Emma, who was now standing outside of the Capris in her sleep shirt, eyes locked on the van. Colton's face was pressed to the back window as he looked on. Ruby and Reggie stood on the far side of the Capris filming everything.

Placing Carter into Emma's arms was the best feeling in the world. Her expression of gratitude warmed Ben to the core, but her gaze went right back to the van.

"Please get Christopher," she implored as Carter hugged her joyfully.

Seeing Tony hand off his captive to an HRT member, Ben gestured for him to go after Carl while he sprinted back to the van for Christopher.

Grimes was being handcuffed on the median. Ben edged aside the HRT member who was trying to draw a rigid Christopher out of the front seat. "I got him. Hey, big guy."

Chris, who'd been staring straight ahead, seemingly catatonic, turned his head a scant centimeter to look at him. While unharmed, his face was as white as a sheet, his eyes enormous.

"It's all over, buddy." Ben ducked into the cab and caught Chris's cheeks in his hands. "You did it. You kept your brothers safe. Colton and Carter are with your mama right now. It's all over."

The lens of terror seemed to slip from Christopher's eyes. "She's here?" he asked in a thin voice. "And you are, too." It was taking him a while to come to terms with reality. "Was Colton right? He said he saw Amos at the school."

"Yes, he did. We came after you boys. You think we'd ever let you go?"

"Guess not."

"Come on out, then. I got you."

As Chris slipped bonelessly out of the passenger seat, Ben propped him against his side to escort him across the lot. Grimes, Charlie Chaplin, and the pock-faced perp were all getting their rights read to them. But Tony wasn't back with Carl yet.

Christopher, catching sight of his mother holding Carter, broke free of Ben and staggered toward her with a cry of, "Mama!"

As Christopher buried his face against her bosom and sobbed, Colton clambered out of the back seat and through Emma's open door to hug her from behind. Carter, who was still in her arms, beat Chris over the head while grinning at Ben.

"Dada!"

Through tears of bottomless relief, Emma met Ben's slow grin. He could have stood there all night just looking at them, hugging each other.

Emma responded to her youngest. "Yes, that's Dada."

As she met Ben's gaze again, joy blazed in him. *Message received, over.*

"So..." He stepped closer, sandwiching Chris and the baby between them as he put his arms around her. "Is that a 'yes' to my question earlier?"

With a loud sigh, Emma dropped her head onto his shoulder, the adrenaline no doubt flowing out of her. "How am I supposed to resist you?"

She'd been doing a good job of it so far. "Then don't."

In the distance, Ben heard Charlotte say, "Looks like Tony's got him."

Ben craned his neck, then smirked to see Tony propelling a sullen Carl out of the woods. One of Carl's arms was twisted painfully behind his back.

"I had nothing to do with it!" Carl shouted over and over, professing his innocence to anyone who would listen to him. "It was all Mr. Jones's idea. I swear, I never wanted those boys!"

Turning his head the other way, Ben made sure Ruby and

Reggie had caught Carl's condemnation of Jared Jones on camera. At the same time, he felt Christopher lift his face from his mother's shoulder and send his father a glower of disgust.

Ben put an arm around him. "Well, that's his loss and my gain, buddy, 'cause I want all three of you. You're the best, bravest boys on the planet, and your daddy doesn't deserve any of you."

At his declaration, four sets of eyes—even Carter's—focused on him expectantly. "I'll be your daddy from now on. Right, Emma?"

He watched her swallow. It was obvious she wasn't yet convinced she could trust him, but she was clearly willing to give him a chance because she nodded. "That's right."

Jared Jones hadn't slept well. At the sound of the kitchen door opening and closing, he snapped his eyes open. It was barely dawn, and the cook didn't come downstairs until seven in the morning. So, who was up and stirring at this hour?

Jared had waited all night for Bates's text assuring him of the boys' safe arrival at his hunting lodge. He'd even gotten up at three in the morning to call his henchman, but Bates hadn't answered.

The suspicion that something had gone amiss wouldn't leave him. Had Miz Banks turned traitor on him and called the FBI? Even if she had, nothing would come of it. The Architect had promised him he monitored all incoming calls.

As Jared lay there listening, the familiar purr of McKenzie's Acura had him kicking out of his covers to rush out of his room toward the parlor, where a peek through the windows showed her car disappearing down Jones Street. It was far too early to be visiting her mother.

Returning to his room for his robe, Jared hurried to his office, where he paced from one side to the other. McKenzie hadn't been herself since he'd told her she was marrying Ashton. Had he pushed her too far? Was she running away from him?

A thread of suspicion, based entirely on a look Jared had intercepted between his daughter and the young gardener, had him sucking a breath through his teeth. Surely not. Surely, she had more taste than to fall in love with a teenager, but that explained why she'd lobbied so hard to get the boy hired here.

Suspicion boiled in Jared as he tore up the servant's staircase to the third floor. Without knocking, he thrust his way into the room given to Miles Ellis and stared at the empty bed in disbelief.

They'd fled together—foolish, foolish children. McKenzie ought to know by now her father could nullify anything she chose to do.

With a sneer, he spun away, shooting a glower at the cook, who'd come out of her room and stood on the landing to stare at him.

This was an annoyance Jared surely did not need, not when his grandsons' current status was unknown. Had they arrived safely at their new home or not?

Unable to staunch his fears and furious with his daughter, Jared snatched up his landline and speed-dialed the sheriff's office.

"Spenser." He recognized the dispatcher, a former boarding school resident, by his voice. "This is Jared Jones. I want every patrol car in the city on the lookout for my daughter's cream-colored Acura convertible, with personalized plates, KENZIE 2."

"Uh, yes, sir. Do you want us to detain her or...?"

"I want you to arrest the boy with her. Plant some drugs on him. As for my daughter, drop her off here at my house."

"Yes, sir. We'll get right on it."

"One more thing. Were there any accidents reported on Diamond Causeway last night? Or on Skidaway Island?"

"I'll check for you, sir. Would you like me to call you back, or—"

"I'll hold."

Tamping down his impatience, Jared pulled open his desk drawer and frowned to see the key for his file cabinet lying, not at the very back of the drawer but three inches closer to the front. He had certainly not left it there.

Spenser spoke up suddenly in his ear. "Sir, there were no accidents on the Diamond Causeway. But the Whitefield Precinct responded to an incident at the BP gas station on Skidaway."

Jared broke into a cold sweat. "Tell me the details."

"Let's see. The officers arrived secondary to an FBI hostage rescue team. Apparently, some boys had been kidnapped, and the FBI recovered them."

Jared's mind went perfectly blank. He managed to find two words. "Any arrests?"

"Well, not by the police. Says here the FBI did take several men into custody."

His goose was cooked. Without a goodbye, Jared dropped the receiver back into its cradle. How could this have happened? The Architect had promised to protect him. Did his grandsons' white-trash mother have something to do with this? The mysterious couple who'd visited the academy?

Jared clapped a clammy hand on his forehead. What now?

Carl, Grimes, and Holmes would throw him under the bus in a heartbeat. Only Bates would lie for him, but the testimony of the others would be damaging. Even if The Architect managed to intervene, any probe would cause Jared to lose credibility with the Cohort's elite. They wouldn't thank him for undermining the brotherhood's reputation.

Gulping against his dry throat, Jared hurried for his bedroom to pack a bag.

$\sim$

"Morning, Tara."

"Ms. McKenzie! You're here awfully early." The attendant at the nurse's station eyed her and Miles with curiosity as they sailed past her, headed for her mother's bedroom.

"We're taking my mother out for breakfast. Can I get a wheel-chair, please?"

Expecting little resistance, McKenzie pushed into Genevieve's shadowed room with Miles on her heels. They found her mother awake but staring sightlessly at the curtained window, still under the influence of the pills they'd given her the night before.

Miles hovered at the foot of the bed. "Is she going to tolerate being moved?"

"I don't know. I've never done this." McKenzie pulled her mother's blankets down. "Come on, Mama. Let's go for a ride."

To her relief, her mother cooperated, swinging her feet over the edge of the bed. "Let's find you some clothes to wear." McKenzie rummaged in her mother's drawers. A minute later, she escorted her into the bathroom, where she swapped her mother's nightgown for a soft housedress. Out in the room, she heard Miles place a call.

By the time they emerged, Tara was delivering the wheelchair to their room. Genevieve sat in it without protest, and Tara backed away, perhaps sensing by their tension that she shouldn't ask questions.

Miles checked his watch. "The U.S. Marshals are going to meet us on the other side of the Talmage Memorial Bridge. We have half an hour to get there."

McKenzie drew a shaky breath. "Okay, let's go." Hopefully, her mother wouldn't pitch a fit at the last minute. She hadn't been away from the Savannah Hospice for over a year.

Miles stepped closer, lifting a hand to cup McKenzie's chin. "It's not too late to back out, you know."

She'd given him her pendant the night before, along with a note for Father Jacobs expressing her will for him to surrender the box to the FBI Undercover Division.

"I don't want to back out." Her life would never be the same. But she refused to be kept in a gilded cage, denied her freedom, not when there was a chance that one day, many years from now, she and Miles might have a future together. Any hardship she might have to endure in the meantime would be worth it.

"My brave girl." He dropped the tenderest of kisses on her lips before he stepped away. "Okay, then, let's do this."

Ten minutes later, the spires of the bridge that would take them out of Georgia and into South Carolina rose like ship masts in the pearly light. Genevieve sat placidly in the back seat of McKenzie's Acura while Miles drove. McKenzie had found the title for her car in her father's files and signed it over to Miles, saying, "I want it back one day." How many years from now might be dependent on the loyalty of her father's followers. All things Centurion were about to come to an ignominious end. The Cohort's elite would want revenge.

"Um. Okay."

Miles's uneasy tone broke into McKenzie's distracted thoughts. "What?"

"We're being followed."

McKenzie twisted in her seat to peer out the window. A Chatham County patrol car turned the corner behind them, its blue lights flashing.

"My father must have heard us leave." She studied her mother's vague expression. "What do we do? If they put on their siren, she'll probably go nuts."

"We keep going." Miles's calm voice betrayed his training. "The Marshals are waiting for us on the other side. We're going to outrun this guy." He laid a reassuring hand on her knee. "Hold tight."

With a sudden roar, McKenzie's Acura shot out from under the branches of the live oaks spanning Oglethorpe Avenue and sped up the curving road toward the double-suspension bridge.

Behind them, the cruiser's siren started to scream.

"Oh." Genevieve roused from her trance with a cry of alarm.

"It's okay, Mama." Putting her hand between the seats, McKenzie regretted not having sat in the back with her mother.

She'd wanted to be close to Miles in their final moments together.

Miles gunned them up the steep grade of the bridge toward the violet sky. The Savannah River swilled below them. Just when their breakaway seemed possible, a large Cadillac veered into their path, forcing Miles to slow down.

"Oh, come on," Miles grated.

The good citizen in the Cadillac figured it was his civic duty to block the speeder's escape and let the cruiser overtake them. McKenzie's view out the back window sent her heart into overdrive.

Keeping one hand on the wheel, Miles snatched his cell phone out of the cup holder and put a call through. "Are you in place? Over."

McKenzie overheard the faint response. "That's a roger, Ellis. We're parked on the breakdown lane fifty meters past the bridge. Wait, is that you being chased?"

"Yep, and I'm going to need your help. Get in a defensive position with your firearms drawn. Is there room for me between your vehicle and the guardrail?"

"Uh...yeah, plenty of room on the protected side. Come on in."

Miles tossed down his phone, broke into the right lane at the height of the bridge, and shot past the Cadillac. The patrol car, surging ever closer, did likewise.

The screaming of its sirens sent Genevieve into a sudden panic. "Stop the car!" Unfastening her seat belt, she launched herself at Miles, grabbing fistfuls of his hair.

"Mama, stop it! Miles is trying to help us."

With masterful concentration, Miles managed to keep control of the Acura as it flew down the far side of the bridge toward the South Carolina border.

While pinning her mother in her seat, McKenzie craned her neck and spotted the U.S. Marshals in the breakdown lane, just as they'd described. Crouching behind their black Chevy Tahoe, they pointed their guns at the oncoming traffic, prepared to fire if necessary.

"Hold on tight." Miles slowed abruptly, forcing McKenzie to protect her mother's head from lolling forward as Miles guided the Acura off the pavement onto the rough shoulder, threading it between the marshal's SUV and the guardrail.

The car wasn't parked for a second before he pushed out of it to open Genevieve's door.

"Go with him, Mama. I'm coming too." McKenzie started to crawl between the two front seats into the back. Mercifully, Genevieve had grown docile again.

As the Chatham County police car skidded to a stop behind them, Miles transferred her mother into the Tahoe's back seat. The two police officers popped out of their cruiser with their guns drawn.

"U.S. Marshal Service. Stand down!" warned one of the two agents as McKenzie climbed into the back seat after her mother.

"Get back into your vehicle," shouted the second U.S. Marshal. "You're outside your jurisdiction."

While buckling her mother into the center of the seat, McKenzie spared a wary glance out the back window. Her father's minions had lowered their guns and were looking at each other. With a shrug, they got back into their car and cut the siren. A moment later, they sped past them since there was no way to turn around.

"See, Mama? We're okay now." While keeping one eye on Miles, who'd walked to the front of the Tahoe to confer with the marshals, McKenzie soothed her mother's agitation by rubbing her arm. "Now, we'll be safe."

Regarding Miles through the SUV's tinted windshield, she memorized everything about him—his compact but athletic physique, the way his dark hair curled around his ears. With his mouth pressed into a firm line, nodding and then shaking hands with the marshals, she wondered how he'd ever fooled her into believing he was only eighteen.

At last, he walked toward her half-closed door. Pulling it open, he stuck his head and shoulders inside. As his regret-filled eyes met hers, she lurched toward him, throwing her arms around his neck, scarcely able to comprehend how this would be the last time she saw him for a *long* time.

He planted a fervent kiss on her lips. "Once I'm sure it's safe…" He paused to clear his throat. "I will find you again. I promise, McKenzie."

Tears stung her eyes. "I won't forget you, Miles. I'll be waiting."

With a wary glance at the marshals slipping into the front seat, Miles delved a hand into his pocket. In the next instant, he was pressing a business card into her hand. He put his mouth to her ear as if kissing her cheek this time. "Memorize my number, but don't call unless it's life or death."

The identically dressed marshals were hauling on their seat belts. "Let's go."

Relieved to have been thrown a lifeline, McKenzie slipped the card into her pocket. She forced a brave smile as Miles pulled back, closing the door softly between them. In the next instant, the Tahoe started forward, merging into the northbound lane and leaving Miles standing on the side of the road, watching her leave.

Emma realized she was wringing her hands in anticipation of seeing her home again. After days of despair, it was hard to believe the nightmare was over. Her boys were back in her care again.

"Almost there." Ben glanced over as he turned off the expressway and headed toward her neighborhood. A smile kicked up the corners of his mouth. "I can tell you're excited."

Colton piped up from the cramped back seat of Ben's Mustang. "I'm excited, too!"

"Dada!" Carter chimed in. He'd been shouting "Kipu" and "Dada" for the past nine hours. Every time he said the latter, Ben would smile smugly. Uncertainty kept Emma from relaxing fully. She'd told Ben at the height of emotion that he could be her boys' daddy, which meant she'd agreed to marry him. But had her attraction to him blinded her? Was he going to break her heart one day?

It had taken forever to get this far. For one thing, Charlotte had instructed them to remain in Savannah while she and Fitz worked to arrest Jared Jones and his followers, including Sergeant Peyton of the Virginia Beach police. The shakedown of the Centurion Cohort had begun in earnest, but it was by no means over, especially since Jared Jones had vanished on his private plane, and his mole in the FBI remained unidentified. Finding that man might require a complete shakedown of the Bureau.

Once they started the long trip back home, it took nine hours to get there since Colton's energy was off the chain, requiring stops at nearly every rest stop on I-95. Emma shot a worried glance at her oldest son. Chris was the opposite. Staring out the window with glazed eyes, he'd spoken scarcely a word except to say a short while ago, "So he was my grandfather."

Emma had shared a look of concern with Ben. Perhaps they'd made a mistake in explaining Jones's motivation for orchestrating the boys' kidnapping. She hadn't wanted them to think that the violence they'd witnessed was a completely random act that could happen any time, any place, anywhere. There'd been a reason for it—a crazy reason, but a reason, nonetheless.

Amos's offer to get her and the boys on a military hop that would have gotten them home hours ago had been politely declined. Emma hadn't wanted to leave Ben to drive back on his own—not after he'd nearly died to reunite her with her sons. And now, they were going to get married! The images in her head filled her with a breathless excitement that bordered on fear. Amos and

Grace had both warned her about Ben. Would she regret not listening to them?

If this day and every day before were anything to go by, she had nothing to fear. Not only had Ben put his life at risk for her, but he'd been the very picture of patience cooped up in this small car on a ride made endless by Colton's restlessness. When Emma's frustration got the better of her once, he'd pulled her closer and murmured in her ear, "He's got post-traumatic stress, Emma. Give him time."

They all had post-traumatic stress—except for Carter, who was all grins and "Dadas." The poor woman who'd looked after him had clearly treated him well. She had to be missing him.

"Here we go."

Emma's breath caught as Ben guided his Mustang into her quiet, tree-shaded neighborhood. The mid-May sun was still shining at eight in the evening, shooting burnished rays through the branches of the oaks and magnolias. Emma took what was probably her hundredth look at her boys all crammed into the back seat—Carter belted into a used car seat found at a thrift shop in Savannah.

"Y'all ready to go home?"

Colton was already casting off his seat belt and scrambling to his knees so he could see. "Yep!"

"Christopher, are you excited?" Ben prompted.

"Can Ben stay with us tonight?"

Chris's anxious response caused Ben to glance back at him, then over at Emma. "Sure. I'll sleep on the couch if that's okay with your mama."

"That's fine." Her pulse sped up to think that soon he would be sleeping in her bed as her husband. She wasn't one to go back on her word, but...

"Oh, look," Ben added on a casual note, "Amos and Grace are here with the boys."

Emma took note of the family spilling out of the black

Silverado in her driveway. She'd wondered whom Ben had been texting at their last rest stop. Now, she felt ashamed to think it might have been a woman friend.

As they pulled up alongside the truck, Colton bellowed, "Simon!" in a voice loud enough to shatter an eardrum.

"Calm down, Colton."

With a smile for Amos and Grace and their two boys, Emma pushed out of the Mustang and flipped the seat forward. Colton sprang out like a jack-in-the-box, running with a whoop toward his cousins. Ben let Chris out of his door, then reached in to unlatch the baby.

Grace greeted Emma with a damp gaze and a sisterly hug. "I have never prayed so hard in my life, Emma. Thank God you're all back safe!"

"Yeah." Emma clung to her. "God gets all the credit, plus Ben and his teammates."

Grace finally released her. "I hope y'all are hungry." She gestured at the cooler Amos was swinging out of the back of the truck. "Amos made food for everyone."

They'd snacked the whole way home to keep Colton entertained, but Emma wasn't about to mention that. "We're starving."

As a group, they made their way toward the front door. Emma noted that the blinds in the living room window were raised the way she liked them. The memory of Peyton and his sidekick turning over every container and dumping every drawer made her stomach hurt.

Grace caught the apprehensive look on her face. "Don't worry. Everything's been put back to rights. And after we eat, we'll leave y'all to settle in. We just didn't want you to have to go shopping for food tonight."

"You're so thoughtful." Emma counted herself blessed. She had friends who looked after her. She had three little boys who were *alive* and with her. And she had Ben.

Watching him moments later distribute fried chicken and

potato salad to the five boys gathered around her dinette table in the kitchen, she marveled at how easy he made it look.

The adults withdrew to the dining room, within earshot of the boys, to eat their own meal. As they spread out at the secondhand table that Emma had used as a desk, she gasped as a realization caught up to her. Grace, Ben, and Amos regarded her with worry.

"I never took my biology exam!" She set her plate on the table and sank into her seat.

Grace chose the chair across from hers. "I'm sure they'll let you make it up. It's not like you didn't have a valid excuse."

"But who would believe what happened?"

"It'll be on the news," Ben reminded her as he took his own seat. "Ruby's getting a lot of mileage out of what they caught on film."

Amos, who occupied the last chair, considered the two of them as he picked up his drumstick. "I thought Grace and I had quite a story to tell our grandkids. But I think yours might top it."

Emma held Amos's steady gaze. Was that his way of giving Ben and her his blessing? He sent her a nod as if to say yes. Then he said a quick prayer, and they all dug in.

Happiness spread through Emma, moving from her heart to every extremity. Glancing over at Ben, she pricked her ears to the sound of her boys in the next room. Because of the trial they'd all endured, she had discovered Ben was so much more than a breathless distraction. He'd been comforting her and championing her from the moment he'd heard about the kidnapping—even before that, when he'd stopped behind her broken-down car on the highway and helped her get it started.

God knew what He was doing when He put Ben in her life. She didn't have to be anxious, expecting the worst to happen. *All things work together for the good of those who love the Lord.* The verse flowed through her, easing Emma's concerns and bringing a tired smile to her face. How blessed she was to be able to lean into that promise!

EPILOGUE

$\mathcal{E}$mma knew an urge to pinch herself. She was Mrs. Benjamin Franklin Harmony, and she lived in this beautiful, contemporary home with a kitchen twice the size of the one in her rental house with plenty of room for her boys to run around in—if they would only stop using the floating staircase as a jungle gym!

Memories of Ben's and her wedding in the chapel on Dam Neck Naval Base made her feel like her feet weren't touching the floor as she puttered in the kitchen. Ben's closest teammates had all been in attendance—nearly the same group of people who had witnessed Amos and Grace's surprise wedding the summer before. Even though their honeymoon had been postponed—Ben had no more leave time available—Emma couldn't remember ever being so happy.

How could it possibly last?

On the other side of the sliding glass door, Ben manned the grill on the deck while all three boys clambered on the jungle gym he'd erected shortly after they'd moved in. Emma's job of warming up the baked beans and setting the table for their supper seemed so easy compared to overseeing both the burgers and her sons, but Ben did it with a smile.

Do I deserve all this? The fear that she'd overlooked some fatal flaw still nagged at her. Having been disappointed by her father and then by Carl, was it any wonder she expected her happiness to crumble?

Turning down the heat on the beans, Emma went to fetch the potato salad from the fridge when Ben's cell phone, sitting on the corner of the island, rang. She changed course to pick it up and read the name: Tiffany Hughes. With a tightening in her stomach, she carried Ben's phone to the door and cracked it open. "Phone call."

The warm August air was made hotter by the flames on the grill. Ben tore his watchful gaze off Carter, who was pulling himself up the ladder toward the top of the slide. "Who's calling?"

"It's Tiffany."

"Oh." He shot her a look of surprise, turned down the heat on the grill, and then held out a hand. "I should talk to her."

"Sure." After handing him his phone, she retreated to the kitchen to give him privacy. She trusted him with Tiffany. After all, he had abandoned the woman in Williamsburg because he'd wanted to be with Emma. More recently, he'd visited her in the hospital when she awoke from her coma, and he told Emma all about the visit. If anything, Emma pitied the woman who'd lost Ben's interest, not to mention whose golfing career was in jeopardy now that she required intensive PT to regain the use of her muscles and joints. She'd lain in a coma for ten days—just one of so many of Jared Jones's victims.

As Ben talked on the phone, Emma put the potato salad on the table and set out the condiments. The door opened and Ben stepped inside still talking.

"Thanks for calling, Tiff. I'm happy to hear the good news. Yep. Take care." He put the phone back on the island, then stepped around it to drop a kiss on Emma's lips. "She's doing great. Five more minutes till the burgers are ready."

"Okay." Ben's devotion made Emma's heart feel like a helium balloon. Would it pop or slowly deflate?

No sooner was he back on the deck, watching Colton perform some dare-devil maneuver on the jungle gym than his phone rang again. Emma heaved a sigh and walked toward it. There was just a number this time, no name, with the same area code as belonged to her ex-stepmother from Atlanta. Who was this? Another former girlfriend?

She decided to find out. "Hello?"

Surprised silence ensued on the other end. "Is this Emma?"

Emma didn't recognize the voice. "Yes, who's this?"

"I'm Molly."

Clearly, the caller thought that would mean something. "I'm sorry...I don't recognize the name." Emma shot a look outside at Ben, who was busy making Christopher laugh. He'd been doing that a lot lately, pulling her oldest out of his dark thoughts.

"He didn't mention the doctor who found him on the beach and sewed up his head?" Molly sounded incredulous.

"Oh, *you're* the doctor." She'd thought the doctor was a man. Ben hadn't talked much about his rescuer. Why not? Jealousy and suspicion banded her heart. "Yes, he...he did tell me. Thank you so much for helping him."

"Well, I was suspicious at first. I mean, the news painted him as this child killer on the loose, but once I got to know him better, I wasn't afraid."

Got to know him how much better? Envy tied Emma's tongue in a knot.

"Anyway, I got his number by calling a Mr. Silverman, whose number Ben had called using my phone. Mr. Silverman was kind enough to provide me with Ben's number. I hope that's okay."

"Sure."

"I just wanted to congratulate him for turning the tables on the

Centurion Cohort. It's all over the news—just incredible what's come to light down here. Did you hear yet that the FBI found Jared Jones?"

"They did?" Relief tempered Emma's jealousy.

"Yes, they just arrested him in Cancún."

"Oh, that's wonderful!" Emma had been tormented by nightmares that Jones would appear to whisk away her boys again.

"Is Ben around?"

"He's on the deck watching the boys and grilling our burgers."

"Aww. I bet he's great with them. No need to bother him. Just let him know that he surpassed my expectations."

"I will." Molly was okay with not talking to Ben?

"And just so you know, he's crazy about you, Emma. Totally devoted. I hope I find a man who loves me as much as he loves you."

The wistfulness in Molly's voice unlatched the envy cinching Emma's heart. Ben had told Molly all about her? Why hadn't he told Emma about Molly, then? The answer was obvious: He knew she would have jumped to the wrong conclusion. Shame on her.

"We just got married," she volunteered.

"Oh, my gosh! I'm so happy for you!"

The sincerity in Molly's voice was all it took to eradicate Emma's doubts.

"Well, tell him I called. And tell him about Jones. You two are an inspiration."

"I will. Thank you for believing in him." It was time she started to believe in Ben, too.

"My pleasure. Maybe I'll drop in one day. My work takes me up that way, and Mr. Silverman has offered to show me around."

"Well, then, please drop by. I'd love to meet you." She'd love it even more if Mr. Silverman and Molly ended up together.

"Same here. Take good care, Emma."

As the phone clicked in her ear, the back door opened, and in tumbled Colton, followed by Chris carrying Carter and, lastly, Ben bearing the platter with the steaming beef patties and toasted buns on top. He caught sight of her putting his phone down.

"Molly called." It was satisfying to see the worry that widened his eyes.

"Oh, what did she say?" He carried the platter to the table while directing the boys to go wash their hands in the half-bathroom off the kitchen.

"Jared Jones has been arrested."

Ben swung around with a look of relief. Christopher paused while herding Colton toward the sink. "Where was he?"

"Cancún."

They all looked at Chris to gauge his reaction.

Emma's oldest hitched Carter higher up in his arms. "I hope he goes to prison," he said in a hard voice.

"He will," Ben assured him.

But as Christopher turned away, Ben met Emma's worried gaze. Whoever had been protecting Jones from within the highest tiers of the FBI was lying low, as yet unidentified by Charlotte and Fitz. The Centurion Cohort had been crippled, but would it rise again one day, led by Jones's one-time protector?

Sensing her uneasiness, Ben stepped up to Emma, slipped his arms around her waist, and pulled her close. "Don't you worry. You're all safe with me. I won't let anything happen to any of you."

In the circle of Ben's arms, Emma's anxiety vanished. Molly's phone call and Jones's arrest had resolved it. Ben was nothing like her drunken father, even less like Carl. As he'd told her, he was a Navy SEAL, and honor meant everything to him.

She looked him dead in the eyes. "You should have told me Molly was a woman."

He sighed but didn't look away. "Nothing happened with her, Em. I'm all yours. I've been yours from the day we met."

She smiled a tad smugly. "I know that now. And I trust you, Ben. Just don't ever make me regret it."

He shook his head. "You will *never* regret it. And that's a promise."

"Good." She sealed their bargain with a lingering kiss.

"Ew!" Colton came out of the bathroom, shaking his hands dry. "Stop smoochin' so we can eat. I'm hungry!"

Ben nipped Emma's neck with a growl. "I'm hungry, too."

Chris emerged from the bathroom, still carrying Carter. "Me, three."

Carter chimed in. "Dada!"

Emma took in her four boys with profound appreciation. So, *this* was the good God had intended for her. Incredible. It surpassed everything she had ever imagined for herself.

FEAR NO EVIL

THE LOST ARE FOUND, BOOK 1

CASABLANCA, MOROCCO, PRESENT DAY

Am I dead? Pain seared Maggie's side as she tried to draw a breath. Lying flat on her back in a narrow, bricked alley just a few steps from her apartment in Casablanca, she assessed her injuries, took stock of her situation, and groaned.

The bit of violet sky visible between the overhanging roofs informed her it was nightfall. Raising her arm to check the time, Maggie launched a cloud of flies that had been crawling on her. According to her watch which glowed 8:37 P.M., she'd been lying there for at least an hour. Summer was peak tourist season in Casablanca. People must have skirted the comatose and bleeding woman, ignoring her plight. Even now, she could hear somebody edging around her—a woman with a baby. Maggie murmured reassurances and the young mother hurried past.

The jig was up. Her cover was blown. As Jake would have said in the Irish Gaelic of his paternal grandfather, *"Nách mór an diabhal thú,"* which loosely translated meant, *Well, aren't you the devil?*

The gut-lurching realization that her identity had been discovered had hit her on her walk home from work when Kamal's bodyguard materialized in front of her—no sign of Kamal anywhere. One look at the dark intent in Farid's dark eyes and she'd realized both he and Kamal knew exactly who she was. She'd been handily played, all the while thinking herself in control of the game.

But that was hours ago.

By some incredible stroke of luck, she still wore her watch, not yet stolen by one of Casablanca's many thieves and pickpockets. The watch contained a GPS chip, broadcasting her location. So long as she could get to her apartment to place the necessary call, an extraction team would be deployed to recover her. But what if Kamal and his bodyguard suspected as much and followed her? The whole extraction team could be targeted.

She stilled her ragged breaths to listen. Her neighbor's dog wasn't barking, which it always did when strangers were in the building. So maybe the path was clear.

Summoning her strength, Maggie rolled from her back to her front. A moan escaped her clenched teeth. Oh, man. Kemal's bodyguard had broken at least one of her ribs. Pushing to her hands and knees, she waited for the tsunami of agony to subside.

The CIA had assigned her here just fifteen months ago. Her objective was simple: verify the rumors that the weapons arriving in a warehouse on the waterfront were earmarked for the Russian Wagner Group, a circumstance with frightening implications for Morocco, not to mention Europe in general.

Born in Venezuela, Magdalena Montoya Ellis had been a shoo-in for the CIA. Not only was she fluent in Spanish and French but her father was a public corruption section chief for the FBI. The Ellises were patriots. She'd been assigned first to Bogotá, Colombia then to Caracas, Venezuela. Morocco was next. She pretended to be a French fashionista, selling clothing at a boutique not far from the warehouse in question. Befriending the warehouse's foreman, Kamal, had been laughably easy.

With very little coaxing on her part, Kamal had taken her out to dinner and for walks along the waterfront. To her relief, he hadn't pressured her for intimacies. In fact, he'd spilled everything there was to know about the shipments bound for Russia—their point of origin and how they would get there.

Now it was plainly apparent Kamal had been testing her. No doubt he had fed her a string of lies, and a mole in the CIA had reported them all back to him, proving Maggie was a spook, as he obviously suspected.

I'm sorry, Kamal. Despite his radical political convictions, she had genuinely liked the man, though he didn't hold a candle to Jake. And he must have liked her, too, because his bodyguard, Farid, whose fists were the size of hams, could have easily killed her. Instead, he'd roughed her up and walked away.

I have to get out of here.

With the help of the rough earthen wall next to her, she managed to get vertical. Blood slid from her split lip to her chin before dripping onto her Christian Dior blouse.

Gritting her teeth, she shuffled toward her apartment building, a two-story structure of dried clay, entirely whitewashed. Through her one good eye, she plumbed the shadows, terrified Farid would return to finish the job.

The neighbor's dog began to bark as she reached the building. She froze, looked, listened.

Was the dog just barking at her . . . or was Farid following her? The courtyard, with its burbling central fountain and decorative blue tiles, stood quiet. Everyone was having dinner, as evidenced by the aroma of roasting lamb and mint tea.

One step at a time, Maggie dragged herself up the stairs to her second-story flat. The fine hairs at her nape prickled as she spotted her door ajar. Someone had come this way before her—or were they still here?

She approached the door trying not to breathe, only to listen. The dog stopped barking, a circumstance that assured her whoever had been here was long gone. Thank goodness she lived alone, her brother Miles and his bride having returned to the States a few months earlier.

Shards of broken porcelain crackled under her soles as she waded inside. So much for her collection of ornamental plates, torn off the wall, shattered and scattered like confetti. They were supposed to be souvenirs of her Moroccan tour. She'd be lucky to have herself as a souvenir at this point.

In her semi-dark living room, Maggie could tell her furniture had been flipped over, cushions strewn across the Persian rug which she had haggled at the outset of her tour. She headed for her kitchen, where every dish had been pulled from the cupboards and smashed. Glass and ceramic crunched and squealed under her soles as she limped toward the counter. God forbid they'd found her Company phone.

The spray bottle of liquid cleaner was still beneath her sink. With a groan, she retrieved it, removed the false bottom, and breathed a sigh of relief. The phone was still here.

She cast a wary glance behind her before entering the passcode, followed by the letters E-X-I-T on the alphanumeric keypad. That would bring an extraction team to the escape-and-evasion point within one hour. Maggie swallowed hard and ended the call.

If she could make it there in time, she'd be whisked away. Not exactly a triumphant withdrawal, as had been the case in Venezuela two years earlier, when she'd been rescued with a thumb drive full of priceless intel. Not to mention the most astonishing thing of all: Jake Carrigan, her nerdy college boyfriend, had been the SEAL in charge of the extraction team.

What an exhilarating moment that was! He'd tucked her under his protective wing and delivered her to a U.S. aircraft carrier in the Gulf only to vanish on her, as suddenly as he'd vanished from Paris.

She'd made inquiries and discovered Jake was a Navy SEAL, additionally trained by the CIA's Special Operations Group to protect case officers like herself. Obviously, the bombing they'd survived in Paris had changed his mind about becoming an architect. But a SEAL and a SOG?

As Maggie bent to stow the phone in the secret pocket under her calf, searing pain made the room turn black. She caught herself on the counter to keep from passing out.

How am I going to make it to the exfil site?

With pure Ellis determination, that was how. She pushed slowly upright then limped out of the kitchen. As she crossed her living room, she took one last look at the apartment she'd called home. It had never occurred to her, not once, that she would be leaving with her tail tucked between her legs.

At least you're alive.

She stepped resolutely onto her balcony. Her Escape and Evasion plan involved going over the balcony, dropping to the flat rooftop of the building below, crossing the roof, then descending a fire-escape ladder to a different alley that zigzagged toward the coast. Easy, right?

In a nondescript mosque about a klick away, an asset would be waiting for her. Supposedly there was a tunnel under the mosque that led directly to the ocean, where the extraction team would pick her up.

If she made it that far.

Standing on her balcony, Maggie inhaled the warm Moroccan air, forever infused with the sweet and savory scents of couscous, *ras el hanout*, and fresh-baked *khubz* bread. Her thoughts flitted to the local baker, who always knew whose son fancied whose daughter and was always glad to see her. *I'll miss this place.* Probably because the French-influenced culture here reminded her of Paris and time spent with Jake.

A glance at her watch told her she had better get a move on. Only how was she supposed to climb when she could barely even stand?

Lifting her gaze to a dark sky obscured by a layer of dusty

desert haze, Maggie recollected the words Jake had spoken to her more than once. *One day, Lena, you're going to figure out that you can't save the world by yourself. If you ever need help, just reach up. God's right there, waiting for you.*

His faith had always inspired her. She gripped the railing on her balcony and swayed.

"So . . . I think I might need help right now."

She had some gall even talking to God. Not since she was a child and used to go to mass with her Venezuelan mother had she acknowledged her Creator's existence.

With no other choice, Maggie lifted a long leg over the railing, sat a moment, then heaved her other leg over. As she lowered herself to the outer ledge, she turned to face the building. Remarkably, only mild discomfort accompanied her movements.

One at a time, she moved her hands from the railing to the vertical balusters. Next, she shifted her weight to one foot and lowered the other to the flat roof of the bakery a meter beneath her. Her ribs barely protested. *Huh.* It was like God was helping her already, which wasn't likely.

Encouraged, Maggie crossed the roof to the fire escape on the other side. The last time she'd looked at the rickety ladder, some of the bars were starting to rust.

Climbing down the ladder backwards, she waited for the crushing pain to return, but it didn't. Maybe adrenaline was finally kicking in. She dropped down into a quiet alley, then made her way toward the mosque about a klick away.

The dark street kept her wary. She'd never ventured out at night without a *djellaba*, the hooded robe most local women wore, and for good reason.

Wait, what was that? The sound of furtive footfalls reached her ears as an old man walked up on her. He gasped in alarm at her disfigured face and gave her wide berth.

She had to look awful with one eye swollen shut, her lip oozing blood. Thank goodness the odds of Jake being the SOG to rescue her were low. She didn't want him seeing her like this.

In Venezuela, she'd been confident and still in one piece, just seven years older than the previous time she'd seen him in the hospital in Paris. His parents had come to collect him there, whisking him away before she got a chance to say good-bye. After snatching her from the Venezuelan warehouse, she'd expected to reconnect, but he'd vanished with his team just as suddenly as he had left Paris.

Dragging her thoughts to the present, Maggie glanced at her watch. Only thirty minutes remaining, and she was just now reaching the mosque.

Arriving at a door painted gold, she gave it three slow knocks followed by three swift ones. Her lower lip throbbed as she waited. At last, the door popped open, and a dark-skinned man dressed in the blinding white attire of an imam hauled her inside.

"I've been expecting you." He ran a worried gaze over her, his English perfect. "Can you walk?"

She swayed on her feet, clutching her side. "Sure."

"Good. The team is nearly here. We have to move quickly."

He pulled her into the mosque's dim antechamber, through a side door, and down a hall to an alcove. A push against the wall sent it rumbling backward, revealing the hidden tunnel. He ushered her inside, leaving it open as he clicked on a penlight. A curve in the tunnel beckoned them, its floor of hardpacked dirt angling downward, taking them beneath the adjacent buildings toward the pier where the team would be waiting.

They seemed to walk for forever, though Maggie knew it wasn't even one klick to the extraction point. Her pain was returning with a vengeance, shortening her steps.

"Just a little farther."

The man's confident encouragement was all that kept her going.

Moisture now hung in the air, dampening her cheeks. The tang of sea salt was unmistakable. When they came upon a door that marked the tunnel's end, she thought she might weep with relief. A glance at her watch showed her ten minutes late for the rendezvous. What if the team had left already? She'd be stuck here.

The door opened, and Maggie startled back, but the silhouette ducking through the opening was identical to the one that had come bursting into the office in Venezuela.

"Lena!"

When he tacked on a phrase in Gaelic, she knew she wasn't just imagining Jake. With a whimper of relief, she stumbled into him, letting him take her weight.

Just like the last time he'd appeared, she asked herself how this was even possible.

"What hurts?" He held her firmly but gently.

"Everything."

She felt him turn toward a teammate. "Decker, pass me an autoinjector of morphine."

His dense chest pillowed her head. She could hear his heart thumping sure, steady strokes that proved he was really with her. She closed her one good eye. She'd made it to the exfil site. Jake could take it from here.

A click and light sting sent morphine swirling into her bloodstream. It spread sweetly through her, smoothing the razor edge of agony, turning the world fuzzy.

She was only vaguely aware of Jake scooping her off her feet to carry her across his arms.

The *rat-tat-tat-tat* of a semiautomatic weapon shattered her relief.

Jake moved so fast, she didn't know what was happening, only that someone had fired at them from farther up the tunnel. *Oh no.* Had she led Farid to the extraction site?

She squirmed as the cacophony of the firefight spiked her adrenaline.

"Hold still!" He subdued her struggles while bounding up a run of steps. "We got this."

By the time they reached the top of the stairs, the burst of gunfire was over. Farid, or whoever had followed her, was probably dead. Jake was bearing her through an open door, out onto an unlit pier. Starlight winked through a thin layer of clouds. The warm breeze smelled of freedom.

Jake started passing her off to someone else. "Careful. She's injured."

"No." She clung to him, protesting the handoff.

"I'm just getting us in the boat."

Sure enough, she was lowered directly down to him, into a rigid-inflatable boat that rocked against the pier. He sat with her across his lap.

The boat pitched abruptly as several more SOGs jumped in. The stealth motor thrummed to life, practically silent over the slapping of water. Warm air streamed over her as they pulled away.

Up and over waves they went, kicking up sea spray that dampened every inch of her, though Jake did his best to shield her. The glow of Casablanca faded, leaving nothing but a star-studded sky above and waves below that had subsided into swells.

She was conscious of Jake asking his men to report in. One of them indicated he'd been nicked by a bullet, nothing too serious. Another stated that the target was dead.

Jake scowled down at her. "Did you know you were followed?"

She had trouble getting her tongue to cooperate. "Possibly."

"Who did this to you?"

There was no mistaking his fury. Regardless, she wasn't authorized to tell him. "My fault. I was played."

He adjusted his hold, cradling her like he never meant to let her go. The thighs she sat upon were as solid as tree trunks. The gangly young man she'd loved in Paris had morphed into something awesome.

She had so many questions to put to him. Like why had he vanished on her twice, first from the hospital in Paris, then again after plucking her from Venezuela? But she was too drugged to speak.

At last, their motor cut off, and a dark, massive shape appeared before them, scarcely visible against the night sky. They coasted silently into an enclosure—the port of a Navy vessel, given the smell of motor oil and steel and the sound of sloshing water. With a low hum, the jaws of the port closed behind them, and the lights blinked on.

Half a dozen sailors stood around what resembled an indoor swimming pool. They helped to moor and stabilize their boat.

Jake managed to clamber off the RIB without handing her off to anyone. Maggie's head lolled on his shoulder, too heavy to lift. Her clothing was damp. The urge to fall asleep nearly overwhelmed her. *Stay awake!* But the morphine he'd given her was dosed for a man half again her size.

His boots rang along a metal corridor before he ducked into a room that smelled of antiseptic. When he laid her gently on what had to be a gurney, she clung to the sleeve of his night ops uniform.

"Stay wi' me."

The words made him hold her gaze. He didn't wear glasses anymore. She wanted to ask if he'd had laser surgery.

"You need a doctor, Lena. And I can't stay."

The terse words betrayed a certain level of frustration. Was he mad at her? Sensing him about to leave, some desperate emotion pushed tears into her eyes. "Don't go."

With a firming of his lips that was all too familiar, he tugged her left hand from his sleeve, regarded her bare fingers for a split second, then ducked and brushed his lips across her knuckles.

The sweet gesture made the pressure in her chest expand. *Oh, Jake, I miss you!*

"Be well." Releasing her, he swiveled on his boots, ducked out the door, and disappeared.

Again? Her heart unraveled like she was a spool, and he was walking off with the end of the thread. How dare he blow in and out of her life like this without any explanation? This was crazy.

~

Available in Paperback and eBook from Your Favorite Bookstore or Online Retailer

ABOUT THE AUTHOR

Rebecca Hartt is the *nom de plume* for an award-winning, best-selling author who, in a different era of her life, wrote strictly romantic suspense. Now Rebecca chooses to showcase the role that faith plays in the lives of Navy SEALs, penning military romantic suspense that is both realistic and heartwarming.

As a child, Rebecca lived all over the world. She has been a military dependent for most of her life, first as a daughter, then as a wife, and knows first-hand the dedication and sacrifice required by those who serve. Living near the military community of Virginia Beach, Rebecca is constantly reminded of the peril and uncertainty faced by US Navy SEALs, many of whom testify to a personal and profound connection with their Creator. Their loved ones, too, rely on God for strength and comfort. These men of courage and women of faith are the subjects of Rebecca Hartt's enthusiastically received *Acts of Valor* series.

RebeccaHartt.com

Sign up for the Rebecca Hartt Newsletter Here

https://rebeccahartt.com/contact

www.ingramcontent.com/pod-product-compliance
Lightning Source LLC
Chambersburg PA
CBHW030644020726
47493CB00006B/1862